CW00972131

Bullied

Bullied, Volume 1

Vera Hollins

Published by Vera Hollins, 2019.

Edited by: Bethany Salminen

Cover Design by: Rasha Savic

Cover Girl Art photo by: annamile from Depositphotos

To Rasha, who has always believed in me and supported me through good and bad times. I love you.

And to my readers, who have encouraged me all these years to publish *Bullied*. Thank you for everything.

Prologue

TWO YEARS AGO

"That's a dumb movie for a dumb girl," Hayden taunted.

As usual, I couldn't respond to his mean remark. No matter how much I wanted to put him to his place, fear and hurt never let me.

"That's enough, Hayds," my best friend and his twin, Kayden, defended me, and I smiled at him in gratitude.

I was going to see a romance movie with my friend Christine, and Kayden wanted to escort me. I didn't need an escort since it was just 7 p.m. on Sunday and we were in a crowded part of our town, but Kayden had insisted. I had no idea why Hayden tagged along.

Maybe he wanted to see Christine, with whom he was in a constant on-off relationship. I'd told myself not to care about his love life, but it was difficult to shut down my feelings that always managed to drown the voices of reason. Hayden was my long-time, unrequited crush, despite being my biggest bully. The irony of it all was a bitter pill to swallow.

I glanced over my shoulder at Hayden, who walked behind us with his hands in his pockets and eyes on the shops we passed.

"Why is he here?" I whispered to Kayden.

"We're going to Blake's house to watch the game, but he wanted us to go together."

"That's strange, since you two don't get along at all."

"Maybe he wants to turn over a new leaf and hang out with me?"

That wasn't so likely. Hayden and Kay never had a good relationship. Also, Hayden had always been against my friendship with Kayden, which was all the more reason for him to torture me behind Kay's back.

I pulled my phone out of my bag, and my eyes bulged when I noticed the time.

"Oh gosh, I'm late!" I bolted, rushing to the theater.

Kayden's rich laugh followed me. "Hey, relax. We're nearby anyway."

"Yeah, but I was late the last few times. Christine is going to kill me!"

"I hope she will. There would be one less moron in the world." Hayden's voice was full of malice, and it made me even more impatient to get to the theater.

I moved my trembling fingers over my screen, writing a message for Christine to notify her I would be there in a couple of minutes. I glanced left and right and started crossing the street.

I was about to hit "send" when the sound of a horn blasted through the air.

I whipped my head to the side with my heart in my throat, squinting against two bright flashes of light as a car rushed toward me without slowing down. I grew paralyzed. The car swerved to the side, avoiding me, but it headed straight for Hayden on the sidewalk.

In a second that rolled in slow motion, Kay rushed between Hayden and the car as a living shield and wrapped his arms around him, right before they collided with the vehicle.

Screams erupted everywhere as they rolled from the hood to the ground, matching the maddening noise in my head that mixed with shock. The car didn't even stop, driving away in a cloud of smoke.

My gaze landed on Hayden, who was sitting up. "Hayden!"

I darted to him, able to move at last, but then I looked at Kay, and the world stopped moving. I halted.

No.

He was motionless on the pavement, his head and limbs positioned at strange angles.

No. No. No. No.

My wobbly legs took me to him, everything around me becoming a blur. I refused to believe what I saw. Kayden was okay. This was an illusion. *He's okay.*

I dropped to my knees and shook him, a puddle of blood beneath him spreading horribly fast.

"Kay, don't joke like this. Come on. You're all right," I said in a shaky voice. *He's okay. He'll stand up any moment...*

Hayden reached us on his knees and hands, the blood dripping from his left temple down his face. He didn't look good himself.

"Kayden." He grabbed his shoulder, his unfocused eyes becoming horror-struck. "Kayden!"

"Call an ambulance," someone shouted.

"Son, are you all right?" an older man asked Hayden, but he ignored him.

"Not you, too," Hayden said in a voice I could hardly recognize, and my heart splintered in pain. "Not again."

My vision grew blurry with tears, my gaze darting over Kay's unmoving body and the blood beneath him that looked surreal—like someone had splashed a can of red paint around him.

"Not again," Hayden whispered to him and looked at the blood. "So much blood. No. So much blood."

"The ambulance is coming," a woman said, crouching next to me, but I barely even heard her because I was looking at Kay's face, finally understanding what I was seeing.

His face was a mask of a sudden terror, and his *eyes*...

His glassy eyes were open, but they were devoid of life. There was nothing, and I felt something inside of me rip into a million pieces. The world turned into darkness—forever splashed with his blood.

My best friend was *dead*.

More people crowded around us. I could see their lips moving, but I couldn't hear them. All I heard was a static noise in my head. It didn't matter. Nothing mattered anymore.

Kayden Black died—leaving a crushing emptiness inside of me—and I felt like I died with him, too.

Chapter 1

PRESENT

A slight breeze cooled my heated face under the setting sun as my feet hit the pavement. The warm August evening was perfect for running. I'd started running only this summer, but I was already addicted to it. It helped me clear my head, root out the negative feelings, and prepare for what was yet to come.

I lived in Enfield, Connecticut's suburban area, which was a calm, beautiful neighborhood. The oak trees cast lovely shadows over the tree-lined streets during the day, and it was a breathtaking view worthy of a postcard.

The ubiquitous sounds of children playing in neighboring yards filled the streets, mixing with the sounds of Linkin Park's "Breaking the Habit," which blasted from my earbuds as I ran. I increased my speed, spurred on by satisfaction that I'd covered around six miles today. It was extraordinary compared to my first run, because back then, I could barely endure two whole minutes without a break.

These days, Enfield was more peaceful than usual since people were on their summer vacations. As a matter of fact, the whole summer had been perfect. I could do whatever I wanted, using my free time to work on my drawings and make some old ideas come true. I'd spent more time on my art accounts on Tumblr, YouTube, and Instagram, and I'd managed to gain more followers.

People actually liked my art, and they encouraged me to keep drawing. They were a huge support, which had felt rather strange in the beginning. At that time, I'd doubted their praise was honest, since I was called stupid, incompetent, and unworthy all the time. It took me a lot of time to get used to the fact that I really had some value and talent.

For the first time after many years, I could feel pure happiness and forget my misery. I'd started my first part-time job in the Raymond retirement home, there was no school—or *Hellhole* as I called it—and I didn't have to see any horrible people I saw each day in East Willow High.

The best of all: it was my first summer without Hayden.

4

Two years had passed since the night Kayden died. I missed my best friend so much it hurt, unable to get away from the dull pain that pervaded my chest each time I thought about him. Half of me had died with him that night, while the other half had been left to bleed, suffering Hayden's constant torment. He blamed me for Kayden's death, and he'd made my life a living hell.

Hayden had been my bully from the first day I saw him three years ago, coloring my grayish world into darker shades of pain with his hatred, but his constant bullying reached a whole new level after Kayden's death. He'd spiraled down a twisted path of destruction and insanity, dedicating his days to turning me into a helpless being with no hope or strength to keep going. I'd thought it would never end.

So, when I heard Hayden was going away to summer football camp for the whole summer, it felt like a dream. I'd literally spent the whole day crying from happiness.

It hadn't been a prank. Nobody had messed with me. Hayden went away, and I had the whole summer for myself, away from my bully who was—oh, the irony—my next-door neighbor. There wasn't even a fence between our yards, which proved yet again how cruel life was.

The only thing I didn't like about summer was that it had passed too quickly. There was only a week left until the beginning of my senior year, and I already felt anxious and terrified of going back.

I had one more week until I had to see Hayden again. I didn't know how he would react when he saw me, but whatever his reaction might be, I was done for, because I was sure he still remembered our last incident the last day of junior year.

I remembered it as if it were yesterday.

• • • •

THIS INCIDENT HAPPENED in the school cafeteria. He liked to embarrass me publicly, and the more witnesses, the better. We didn't have cameras installed, which was another fact in Hayden's favor, allowing him more freedom to do whatever he wanted.

I was more than happy to get out of that Hellhole, counting the minutes until the official start of summer break. The last day of school had begun peacefully, with no harassment or usual snide remarks from my classmates. I'd thought I would manage to end the day without having to go through the usual bullying. I should have known better.

My table, which I didn't share with others, was tucked away in the corner of the cafeteria, barely noticeable in the sea of tables occupying this large space. It was the best spot to pass unnoticed during lunch.

I regarded it as my safe place because it was located far away from the center of everyone's attention—the *popular* table, where Hayden sat with his friends Blake Jones, Masen Brown, and Josh Akers. They were the jocks of our school, our football stars. They were also the constant source of my unhappiness. Wherever I went, one of them was there, and they never missed the opportunity to humiliate me.

I was on the way to my table when Hayden appeared in front of me, making me stop. I tried to get around him, but he moved to the side, blocking me again.

"Please, don't do this now. I just want to eat." I hated that I was begging him.

His face didn't reveal a trace of emotion. It was expressionless most of the time when he spoke to me. The only emotions I could ever see on his face were rage, mockery, and coldness.

"Don't think you can get rid of me that easily," he sneered.

A heavy weight settled in the pit of my stomach, which I felt whenever Hayden confronted me like this. Fear, embarrassment, and pain were combined in one powerful ball, threatening to suffocate me.

He planned to do something to me in front of everyone, and I could guess what kind of thoughts were on his mind. He wanted to make a scene that would be talked about during the whole summer. It would be a hilarious story of how Hayden Black humiliated that bitch, Sarah Decker, *again*. It would be turned into a meme and get shared hundreds of times across all networks. I knew this for sure because it had already happened once before.

In that moment, I'd had enough of all of that. I wanted to spend my time peacefully away from Hayden and any horrible memes that could come out of his ultimate humiliation.

"Hayden, please don't start this now. I just want to eat my lunch in peace, and then I'll be out of your way."

"No. You'll never be able to eat or do anything in peace." He lowered his head until it was inches away from mine. "I won't let you have peace," he whispered. "Maybe you won't see me the next two months, but that doesn't mean you're free of me. You. Will. Never. Be. Free."

He emphasized each word with a poke of his middle finger into my forehead. The students closest to us erupted in chuckles. Some of them had already prepared their phones to take pictures or videos of what Hayden planned to do to me.

I felt the tears welling up in my eyes, and there was nothing that I wanted more than to disappear. I wanted to be erased magically from the Earth and from their minds.

If only hoping for a bomb to fall in that moment and wipe out East Willow High wasn't far-fetched.

"Now, move your ass to our table and twerk."

I gasped in horror. "Excuse me?"

"You heard me well, Sarah, or are you deaf, on top of your stupidity? You're going to get on our table and twerk for my guys and me."

"No."

"No?"

"Absolutely not."

He grabbed my wrist with enough pressure to hurt me. I barely managed to remain silent. There was nothing he liked more than to see me in pain. He was feeding on it. It fueled him and made him do even worse things.

He lowered his lips until they were touching my earlobe. I shivered. "If you don't obey me, you're going to be very sorry, and you know this isn't an empty threat. Now, do what I said."

I didn't know what came into me after his words. Maybe it was an all-consuming anger that he always got what he wanted, or courage because I would be safe from him for the next two months, but I let my emotions finally get the better of me. Without any hesitation, I thrust my pizza tray right onto his face.

I watched in shock and a bit of amusement as the slice of pizza slipped down his face, leaving a messy trail, and an unfamiliar wave of satisfaction washed over me. The students remained silent. Nobody dared to speak as we stared at each other.

"*No*. I won't let you torture me anymore. I'm done following your orders." My voice wasn't mine as I pretended to be brave. I was shaking, and I hoped my voice wouldn't betray me.

"I'm not your puppet, and I'm not afraid of you. You can go to hell." I didn't wait to see his reaction. I pulled my arm out of his loose grip and ran out of the cafeteria as fast as I could.

. . . .

ONE OF THE PERKS OF being popular and respected by everyone was that no one ever made an insulting meme about you. Nobody said a word about Hayden getting pizza in his face. There were no jokes on his account during the summer.

My moment of false bravery ended as soon as adrenaline left my body, and I felt queasy and terrified of what I'd done. I could have my summer away from Hayden, but summer didn't last forever.

I was wiped out when I stopped in front of my house, my loose workout clothes fully covered in sweat. I looked toward Blacks' place: a white three-story traditional house that looked similar to mine, except the size. It was enormous and well-maintained. Currently, there were no vehicles in front of their garage, which was clear evidence of Hayden's absence. He drove either his beloved black Kawasaki Ninja or black Chevrolet Camaro, and whenever he was home, one was in front of their garage.

It was odd that the house in which I'd made some of my best memories had turned into a place that terrified me. It wasn't Kayden's house anymore. It was Hayden's house now, and it was the home of a person I was afraid of the most. I despised him. He lived so close to me, making it impossible for me to escape from his abuse.

I entered my house, which was completely dark because my mother was currently working the night shift at her second job. Like usual, the feeling of loneliness crept in, but I tried to ignore it.

My mother had two jobs and the most erratic schedule. She worked as a shop clerk in a fast-food restaurant during the day and as a motel receptionist during the night. She rarely had days off, and when she had them, she preferred to spend her time in bars, satisfying her alcoholic urges and pursuing a new man to spend her time with.

I turned on the light in the hallway and pushed the wet bangs that had been stuck to my forehead to the side, taking my long hair out of my messy ponytail. I didn't need to look myself in the mirror to know that currently, I wasn't an attractive sight as the sweat slid down high cheekbones and sharp jawline onto my T-shirt. I could say I was average-looking, even when I wasn't a mess. I wasn't ugly, but at times, I wished I was prettier.

I remembered a compliment Kayden had given me once. He'd said I usually looked like a tomboy, but when I tried to relax and let the happiness show on my face, I transformed into a true beauty. He'd particularly liked my dimples and the way my eyes squinted whenever I laughed.

I had a pretty smile, but I smiled rarely. It became so unnatural for me to smile spontaneously. Usually, I used the smile to cover my real feelings and look tougher than I was, so the pretense ruined the real purpose of smiling for me.

I climbed the stairs and entered my room, ready to take a shower. I turned on the lights and started taking off my clothes. My room was small and had cheap furniture, but it was my sanctuary. It was the place where I could be myself without pretending I was someone I wasn't or thinking others might judge me.

My drawings and sketches were plastered all over my walls, injecting life to my space, while the piles of papers with the ideas for my next drawings were strewn across my desk. It was a complete chaos, but it was my chaos, and I was proud of it. It fueled my inspiration to keep drawing; it was a constant source of new ideas.

I started drawing toys at the age of five. At the age of eight I experimented with watercolor paints and depicted nature. When I was twelve, I gained interest in people, and I went all out to sketch all the details and add a sense of depth using various techniques. Last year, after I created my Instagram art account, I decided to challenge myself and start making digital paintings. I saved my allowances and bought a graphic tablet—my best investment and most precious thing.

I took off my sports bra and panties and threw them on a pile of dirty clothes on my floor, getting naked.

The continuous sounds of camera shutter tore through the silent air, sparking a sudden surge of panic in my chest.

I jerked my head up to look through my open window. What I saw before me chilled me to the bone.

Hayden was leaning against an open window of his room, which was directly across from mine with only twenty feet separating us. He'd raised his hand with an iPhone and aimed it at me. His eyes were as unreadable as ever as he continued to take shots of me naked.

I screamed, dashing toward the light switch, and turned it off. I bolted out of my room and shut the door behind me. I leaned against it, closing my eyes, hoping that the last few seconds had just been my crazy imagination. The warm tears spilled out onto my cheeks, followed by sickness that consumed me.

My heart felt like it was going to burst, my breathing becoming more irregular. How could I be so stupid, thinking I could finally raise those window blinds and do whatever I wanted without the risk of him seeing me?

I'd kept those blinds closed for years because our rooms were across from each other, having learned my lesson the hard way when Hayden got the idea to spy on me from his room the first time. I convinced my mother to get the blinds for my room and installed them the next day. They had been closed ever since.

I'd been so sure he wouldn't be here until our first day of school, so sure I would have my freedom for one more week, but it was a grave mistake. Hayden returned, and now he had nude pictures of me.

Oh God, what was he going to do now?

I wasn't aware of how much time had passed as I stood glued to my door, afraid to enter the room and sneak over to my closet so I could get my clothes. I decided it would be best to take a shower and use my bathrobe to cover myself. Then I could close those blinds and hide from him.

Showering didn't help me feel any less tense since the nausea-inducing thoughts of those photos were plaguing my mind. The reality of what had happened hit me eventually, and terror gripped my insides. He was sick for even thinking about taking them. What was he going to do with them? Post them online? Submit them to porn websites?

I stepped out of the shower, trying to suppress the anxiety attack. I had to calm down. There had to be some solution. He wouldn't share them just like that, would he?

Oh, come on Sarah! Of course he would! He was the guy who had promised me hell, hurting me in so many ways. He wouldn't stop. He would only step up his game.

I finally took some courage and entered my room, managing to win a fight against my anxiety and breathe evenly. I bolted to the wall next to my window and hid behind it, peeking through the window. I tried to see if he was still there, but I couldn't spot him. His room was completely dark.

Did I imagine that? Maybe I'd finally lost it and nothing actually happened? I stole another peek, but I couldn't see him anymore. I closed my blinds swiftly and turned on my desk lamp.

Why did he have to come back early? Why did he have to see that? If only I hadn't opened those stupid blinds. If only I hadn't undressed myself completely, the light in my room making me more visible. If only I hadn't switched that light on...

It had always been like this with Hayden. So many "whys" and "what ifs" whenever he hurt me. I'd always blamed myself. If I wasn't so weak and incapable of taking care of myself nothing would have happened to me, right? If only I weren't so detestable... If only I could change so people would finally start liking me...

If only Hayden didn't hate me...

No, don't go there, Sarah. That exact thought leads you along the most painful path and you don't want to go there.

I noticed the flashing notification on my age-old LG smartphone, signaling I'd received a message. Nobody sent me messages except my mother, and she rarely texted me during her night shift.

Imbued with sudden fear, I unlocked my phone. A bolt of ache hit my chest when I noticed a text from an unknown number.

I drew a deep breath that did nothing to assuage my increasing anxiety and opened it.

"I think you might want to reconsider following my orders. Remember what I told you. YOU WILL NEVER BE FREE. Either you'll be an obedient puppet, or I'll upload your nudes everywhere and ruin you completely."

Chapter 2

THREE YEARS AGO

For as long as I could remember, school was a living hell for me. My classmates started bullying me in elementary school and nothing changed in junior high. Whichever school I went to, people disliked me and found me an easy target. I was a child with a single mother, coming from a poor family, and I wore clothes from thrift stores. No matter how much I tried to make them like me, being friendly and helping them whenever they needed help, it wasn't enough. I was just being used.

It was like someone put a sign on me saying "Made to be Bullied."

Those few "friends" I'd had weren't good enough to stay and support me. Each one of them thought they were going to be bullied too or considered losers because they were hanging out with me.

It seemed that popularity meant more than true friendship.

I gave up on trying to make friends in junior high or get people to accept me. I became an outcast, and everyone began treating me like I was a disease—to be hated or avoided at all costs. The bullying had intensified ever since.

My mother's lifestyle wasn't any help to my reputation. In fact, it only made it much worse. The school kids called her *slut* and *alcoholic* and poked fun at me for not having a father. I didn't know anything about my father since I was a product of one of many one-night stands my mother had over the years, and even she didn't know who he was.

We kept moving from one place to another, changing towns. One year we changed our apartment three times. My mother often fought with our landlords over late rent or property damage, so we never stayed more than two years in one place.

Sometimes we moved in with her new boyfriends. Some of them were okay, but some were evil bastards who abused my mother. Occasionally, I was in the line of fire too. I would get hit if I was too bothersome, if I tried to protect my mother from being beaten, or if some of them were so drunk they got angry about every single thing.

The only thing that was worse than living with an alcoholic was living with the two of them. The first time I received a serious beating was when I was eight. Luckily, I didn't remember the beating or the pain. My mother didn't care because she was too drunk to notice. I never had bruises on places that clothes didn't cover, which I was thankful for, since I didn't have to worry about anyone seeing them. I was too ashamed and scared to talk about the abuse, and I felt like no one could help me, so the best thing I could do was try to be invisible.

Fast forward to my last year of junior high when the situation with her abusive boyfriends got worse. I never felt more miserable and trapped in my life. I hated going to school, and I hated returning home. Actually, there wasn't any place I could call home because I was sure the meaning of "home" didn't include the feeling of horror, pain, despair, and suffocation. People were supposed to feel safe in their home—a place where they belonged—but for me, that was nothing more than a castle in the air. For me, home was an embodiment of darkness and madness.

In the beginning of summer before ninth grade, my mother told me all too suddenly that we were moving from New Haven to her hometown. She mentioned she'd received my grandfather's will in which he left us their family house in Enfield. Saying I was shocked didn't even begin to describe my feelings.

First of all, I didn't even know that my grandfather Thomas had passed away. He died of cancer, alone in his home. My mother and he had never gotten along. She'd been the black sheep of the family because she was a rebel, constantly defying my grandparents, and didn't have college aspirations. When my grandmother passed away, before I was even born, Patricia Decker left Enfield for good in pursuit of a better life. Sad to say, Patricia Decker's version of a "better life" meant working in various bars and restaurants, expecting to find a "good catch" with loads of money—someone she could live off for the rest of her life.

Secondly, it felt surreal that we would finally live in a place that we could call *ours*. No rent, no landlords, no deadlines. We could stay in one place as long as we wanted. I could have a place I could call *home* at last.

And third, I could try one last time to make a fresh start and make some friends. I didn't have much hope since my past showed me that everything remained the same no matter which school I went to, but maybe—just *maybe*—high school would be different. Maybe moving to Enfield was a sign of a great change. A change for the better.

. . . .

IT WAS THE BEGINNING of July, but the morning in Enfield was a bit colder than I would've liked. I wore my sweatpants and a hoodie, which barely did their job of keeping me warm. It was too easy for me to feel cold, even in summer. My mother claimed this was because I was too skinny and there was no meat on my bones.

My body was nothing like my mother's because she was voluptuous and I was lanky, and that was just the beginning of our differences. She was a short blonde with green eyes. I was tall and I had brown eyes. I wasn't like her at all—looks or personality.

We'd been unloading the truck with our furniture the whole morning. When we arrived, I was astounded by how big our house was. It was two-story, much bigger than the small and cramped apartment we'd used until yesterday, and it was a major change for me.

Unfortunately, it was clear that nobody had bothered to maintain it for years, letting it fall prey to time. It looked old, decrepit, and its sky blue paint covering the facade had long faded away. The wooden railing on the porch was damaged, matching the crannied window casings, and some parts were missing white paint. The interior was nothing better since it was in desperate need of whitewashing and repairs. We planned to spend the next few days trying to improve it with our limited budget.

I took hold of a large box and picked it up before I looked around the truck, taking note of how many boxes were left to move into the house. I turned around and took a few tentative steps, struggling to get out of the vehicle with the huge, heavy box.

I tried my best to get down without dropping the box, but I put my left leg on the ground too fast and my knee gave out, making me stumble. The box fell down with a loud thump, while I barely managed to prevent falling flat on my face by outstretching my arms when I landed on the ground.

"Ouch!" That hurt.

I raised my head and froze. A boy stood on the sidewalk, watching me intently, and I felt my cheeks warming. I was looking at the most handsome boy I'd ever seen, and I wasn't exaggerating. I was drooling all over him and I never did that.

He was tall, slightly muscular, and had a striking face. His raven hair was cut very short, and it complemented his strong, angular jawline and narrow chin. His plump lips looked soft and kissable, inviting an unexpected thought of kissing him, which brought life to butterflies in my stomach.

What attracted me the most were his penetrating dark eyes that made me feel like they could see right through me—all my thoughts, fears, and desires—and it was unnerving and rousing at the same time. He kept looking at me, not moving at all.

I broke our eye contact, extremely embarrassed, and my blush increased. I stood up, trying to figure out what to do or say in order to appear less awkward.

Just as I opened my mouth to say something, I noticed a flicker of derision on his otherwise emotionless face. "You're stupid." His voice was flat. "You don't know how to carry even one simple card box."

I was so shocked to hear him insulting me out of the blue that it rendered me speechless. He sidestepped the box, which had landed on the sidewalk, and walked away without sparing me another glance.

He didn't even ask me if I was okay.

He was such a jerk.

• • • •

WE SPENT THE WHOLE day unloading the truck, so I was more than glad when we were finally finished. The next thing on our to-do list was to buy buckets of paint and painting supplies tomorrow morning so we could breathe life into this house.

There were two bedrooms upstairs. The master bedroom looked over the street, while the other, a much smaller one, looked right into our next-door neighbors' house. I chose the latter room because it was small and gave me a cozy feeling, and I already had some ideas on how to paint the walls and decorate them with my artworks.

I was starving, but there was no food in the house, so I had to go out and buy it. I stepped off the porch and stopped to enjoy the evening breeze. It was caressing my skin in soothing waves, giving me peace I hadn't felt for a long time, lulling me into thinking that everything was going to be all right. Summer was my most favorite season, and I couldn't wait to see what the summer in Enfield would bring me.

Someone caught my attention, and I faced a tall boy who pushed his bike on the sidewalk in front of my house. My heart skipped a beat when I recognized the jerk from today.

I was about to dash into the house when the boy stopped, finally noticing me, and cast me a huge smile.

"Hello!" He waved to me.

He *waved*? Was he serious?

I remained in my place, not sure if I should run away, ignore him, or insult him. Each option was tempting.

He propped up his bicycle on the kickstand and approached me. "I heard the new family was moving into Deckers' house, so I planned to come say hi. I'm Kayden Black."

He held his hand out to me, offering me a handshake. I just looked at it, becoming livid. I was sure he was making a fool of me.

We just stood awkwardly as he kept his hand extended, waiting for me to do something. He scratched his neck with his other hand. "Erm, now we shake hands?"

"I can't believe you. You want to shake hands after how you treated me today? Fat chance."

He dropped his hand and frowned, appearing confused. "I'm sorry, but I don't get you."

"Stop playing me for a fool!" I raised my voice, and the redness spread all over my face. I hated confrontations. My pulse was too fast, and I wished for nothing more than to go back to my house. "Today, you called me stupid and didn't even bother to ask if I was all right!"

His frown deepened. "No, seriously, what are you talking about?"

Was he demented? Did he develop sudden amnesia?

"I'm talking about how you insulted me when I fell carrying that huge box! You just stood there and called me stupid for not being able to carry boxes!" He looked as if he pondered over something, but I didn't plan to waste even a minute more on him. "No, you know what? Forget it."

I turned on my heel and headed back to the porch, but he caught my upper arm, making me stop. "Please, wait." I glanced at him over my shoulder, too uncomfortable because of his nearness and the physical contact. He smiled. "You must be talking about my twin, Hayden."

"Twin?"

He released my arm and widened his smile, revealing his perfect teeth. "Yep. Don't take it too personally. My brother can be rude, but I'm sure he didn't actually mean anything bad."

Was he pranking me? He'd humiliated me today and now he was pretending he had a twin? I watched him carefully, not sure what I should do. His eyes did seem sincere and somehow different. They weren't sharp and bleak, but beaming with light and cheerfulness.

"How about we do this properly now, okay?" He offered me his hand again. "I'm Kayden Black, your next-door neighbor. It's nice to meet you."

I let out a small sigh, embarrassed for attacking the wrong person. What was the possibility of meeting someone who had a twin? That wasn't so likely to happen, but this didn't make me feel any less ashamed. I managed to make a fool of myself in front of both brothers. Great.

I tucked my hair behind my ears, which was my nervous habit. "I'm Sarah Decker. It's nice to meet you too."

I let go of his hand as soon as we made contact, hoping he didn't notice how sweaty my palm was. Whenever I was nervous, I sweated a lot and blushed.

"As I already mentioned, I planned to come to your house and offer my help if you need it."

I didn't like receiving help from strangers. "Thank you, but I don't think we need it."

"Hey, don't feel nervous because I want to help. It's no biggie. I'd really like to help you."

"Okay, thanks," I answered brusquely, with no intention of accepting his help.

Maybe this was irrational of me, but the constant abuse made me wary of people. I didn't trust them, and I certainly couldn't believe anyone who offered their help so easily. It sounded more like a trick, but I couldn't tell Kayden that.

"All right, I won't waste your time anymore." He turned around, ready to leave.

"You aren't wasting my time," I was quick to clarify. I didn't want him to interpret my reaction as hostile and misunderstand me like everyone else. He seemed nice, but making friends at first sight was never my forte. "Thank you so much. I appreciate your offer."

"Hey, no worries. Everything's cool." He gave me the most radiant smile and returned to his bicycle. "See you around." He waved to me and walked to his house, pushing the bicycle by his side.

I grinned and waved back, basking in the feeling of pride that spread through me for managing to talk with some boy without getting into a complete disaster.

Chapter 3

PRESENT

How the hell did he get my number?

No, don't go there, Sarah. I'd known for a long time that Hayden was capable of anything. He was used to getting anything he wanted.

That night I couldn't sleep a wink. I kept imagining the worst scenarios, waiting for mom to appear and tell me my nude photos were all over the Internet. I might not be able to set foot in school ever again.

I didn't reply to his message, because even the slightest action could've provoked him. I'd checked a few accounts of East Willow High students, trying to catch any sign of those photos, but I couldn't find anything. As far as I could see, unless Hayden decided to publish them secretly on some foreign website, he didn't post them at all. He didn't send me any other message, and I didn't know if that was a good or bad sign.

I could never figure Hayden out. He was too unpredictable and impulsive, and his actions could be inconsistent. One moment he was cold, the next he was fuming with white-hot rage, and it was overwhelming. To top it all off, there was still that issue of our last encounter before summer. He had a score to settle, and to think he would let me off the hook would be a serious mistake.

The first day of school arrived all too soon, and I wasn't ready at all. I didn't want to go back to that Hellhole. I didn't want to face all those people.

I entered the kitchen and found my mother making breakfast. She wasn't a morning person, so she rarely spoke a word to me before her first cup of coffee. I looked at her exhausted face and saw dark circles under her eyes, clear proof that my ears hadn't deceived me—she'd indeed come home at three in the morning. She hadn't showered so she reeked of alcohol and cigarettes, and her hair was unkempt. Disappointment clouded my mind yet again.

How many times had I imagined her as a normal mother—cheerful and full of love? The first day of school was awful every time partly because of such depressing mornings. She was here, but it was like she wasn't. She didn't prepare me breakfast and didn't wish me good luck.

She wasn't one of those overprotective mothers who wouldn't let their children go outside unless they kissed them a hundred times, hugged them so tightly they could barely breathe, and checked twice if they took everything they needed.

These days she was terribly moody, whether she was sober or drunk, and I didn't know how to help her. I wasn't sure if she was annoyed because of me or if there was something else bothering her.

Since I wasn't hungry, I just took an apple from the kitchen counter, impatient to get out. "See you tonight?" I asked because she had an evening off.

"Yes." She didn't even glance in my direction. "Have fun in school."

And that was it. *Have fun in school.* She said it like she didn't know how horrible school was for me.

"I'm going now," I said, dejection coating my words as I snatched my keys out of the bowl in the hallway.

"Later," she replied.

I stopped, expecting her to say something more. There was a foolish part of me that still hoped she would show that she cared. Was she even aware that today was my first day as a senior?

She didn't say anything else, and I stepped outside, trying to suppress my tears. When did it become difficult to tell her "I love you"? When did our signs of affection stop? I wanted to hug her and kiss her, but it was so difficult—like there was some invisible barrier between us, and it was impossible to cross it.

As usual, the first thing I did when I got outside was to check if Hayden was in front of his house. It was my survival tactic I'd developed over time. I always tried to go to school before him in order to save myself from experiencing any potential embarrassment in the early morning. Luckily for me, he had a tendency to wake up late, and today was probably one of those mornings. Nevertheless, I couldn't let my guard down even for a second.

I sprinted to my old red Ford Escort, which was parked next to my mother's white 90s Nissan Sentra, hoping Hayden wouldn't go to school at all.

One could dream.

• • • •

THE ONLY HIGH SCHOOL in our small town, East Willow High, was a huge complex made of three wings, the athletic center, and a large parking lot. The modern building was a mixture of distinctive gray bricks and glass, its shape and structure standing out among maples that turned the most beautiful shade of red during fall. All windows were wide, providing a lot of light, and I loved the soothing brightness they gifted this otherwise gloomy place.

I parked my car at a remote part of the parking, which was as far as I could get from Hayden's parking lot. I took my time walking to the main entrance, the knot in my stomach getting tighter with each step closer to those glass doors.

A flock of students was packed inside, and it felt like it had been only yesterday that I saw everyone last. They were all the same, some of them displaying new hairstyles, combined with new fashion trends, and some wearing highly expensive fall pieces, which would strengthen their position among popular and rich kids. Sadly, people respected those who exuded money.

This was one of the things that made me different from them. I never followed trends, and even if I wanted to, poverty was like a cage that limited all my choices, laughing into my face at the possibility of buying anything pricey for myself.

So, I didn't know what the current fashion or the popular color was. My T-shirts and jeans were plain, baggy, neutrally colored, and paired with ordinary white sneakers. I didn't do hairstyles, preferring to wear my long wavy brown hair down or in a ponytail. My clothes might be drab and ugly to others, but they didn't attract any attention. They helped me feel invisible.

I tried to pass next to the seniors who had gathered close to the front doors, bumping into someone's shoulder in the process.

"Hey, watch it!" this person snarled at me, smacking my shoulder. It hurt, but I didn't even look at him. I just mumbled that I was sorry and dashed forward, attempting to be less noticeable.

School had always been like that—I tried to be out of the way and hoped no one would mess with me, but this was difficult when all they saw in me was a moving target.

They saw me as a creep, and they felt it was okay to insult me just because I was weaker than the rest. I never fought back, thinking—*hoping*—it would stop, and they would finally conclude that bullying me wasn't worth their time.

I came to my locker half expecting to find it covered in paint or graffiti and exhaled in relief because it was clean. However, this didn't mean that someone couldn't have put some trash or whatever else inside. I entered the combination on my lock, planning to open my locker carefully.

The first day last year taught me this particular caution when I opened my locker and was welcomed with open bottles of soda lying down, the liquid trickling from the upper shelf to the lower creating a large puddle. Not even a second later, they poured out and splashed all over the floor and my sneakers. I spent hours cleaning that mess after class.

This time, I stepped backward and then opened my locker. It was *empty*. A heavy sigh escaped my lips. Some students snickered behind me.

"Expecting something?" one guy mocked me.

"Maybe we can put a snake in her locker next time," the girl on his right side said to me and put her forefinger over her lips, as if she was mulling over something. "The more poisonous, the better."

They sniggered, and I turned to my locker so they wouldn't see how embarrassed they made me feel.

At all times, I put an indifferent mask on my face, pretending such hurtful words didn't affect me at all, but blush betrayed me each time.

I squeezed my eyes shut, my mood rapidly declining. Senior year hadn't even started, and I already felt defeated. At least nobody had messed with my locker, so that should comfort me a little. I placed all my books inside save for my notebook and the textbook I needed for calculus, which was my first period.

In a hurry, I almost bumped into Masen Brown, Hayden's friend. I cursed myself for not watching where I went, moving aside to walk away, but of course he didn't let me. He stepped in front of me and grinned with malice.

"Well, well, well. If it isn't Sars, my least favorite girl! How was your summer? Did you actually get out of your cave and have some real fun?"

I involuntarily cringed when I heard that horrible nickname again. Hayden and his close friends had been calling me Sars for years, referring to an illness that was contagious and could be fatal. They had used to say that East

Willow High should be afraid since I was a walking disease that could contaminate the whole school with her lousiness.

"Masen, let me through." My voice was barely louder than a whisper.

He didn't even pay attention to my words. "I guess you don't even understand the concept of fun. Are you still a virgin?"

Of all Hayden's friends, Masen was the biggest man whore. He was known as the "heartthrob" of East Willow High, and it was a common fact that he never dated. He preferred hookups with new girls each week. There was a long list of Masen's chicks that had the "honor" of sleeping with him only to be left heartbroken when he refused to be with them again.

He was around six feet tall, and his blonde hair and icy blue eyes were the "killer combination" for the female population around here. That was what they said, anyway, since I found him neither charming, nor beautiful. For me he was just a Casanova—a womanizer who knew how to charm others to get what he wanted. But inside, he was rotten.

"Of course you are. No one would fuck such trash." I winced at his choice of words.

He disliked me from the start and the feeling was mutual. He was keen on poking fun of me for being unattractive, wearing ugly clothes, and having zero sexual experience. Everyone knew I never had a boyfriend, which was something Masen liked to remind me all the time.

The students around us started paying attention, and I wanted to disappear into thin air. How many times had I wished to fight back and finally make them stop torturing me?

"What? Cat got your tongue? Now you aren't so brave like you were the last time, are you?" He hovered over me, his mean eyes boring into mine. "Why don't you tell me to go to hell too? Hm?" I took a step back, but he followed, and I felt intimidated.

I managed to find my voice. "We'll be late for class, Masen."

"We'll be late for class, Masen!" someone said in a mocking voice and sniggered. "Boo-hoo! Nerdy is afraid she'll be late for class!"

Masen laughed and winked at me. "We don't want you to be late for your class, Sars." He stepped aside, allowing me to leave at last, and I embraced my escape eagerly.

I moved, but I failed to notice Masen's extended leg, and I crashed to the floor. Masen and the group of students laughed as they walked away, adding to my humiliation.

My body hurt everywhere, but I pretended I was completely okay. Everywhere I looked, I saw prying eyes, and they made my skin prickle. They spoke in hushed whispers, waiting for me to finally lose it, but I refused to satisfy their twisted minds. I picked up my calculus textbook and the notebook from the floor and dashed to the classroom, not shedding a single tear.

• • • •

I WAS HOPING THERE would be some divine intervention which would enable me to have my classes without Hayden or any of his friends. According to yin and yang, everything was about balance. I endured three shitty years here, so my yang period was way overdue, right?

Unfortunately, as soon as I stepped into the calculus classroom my hope was extinguished because I found Christine Thompson and her best friend, Natalie Shelley, at the back. They noticed me and started talking in hushed whispers. Their evil eyes bore into me, allowing my anxiety to proliferate, and I could sense there was some confrontation ahead of me, but I didn't know what to do to elude it.

To say Christine and I weren't friends anymore was an understatement. Soon after Kay died, it became clear to me that she and I had never been friends for real.

It was convenient for her to hang out with me because I was Kay's best friend, and Kayden and Hayden were the most popular guys in school. This didn't mean I was a part of the popular students list. Hayden made sure I was excluded from it.

He and the rest of the school kept harassing me, and Kayden wasn't even aware of that, because I didn't want to admit to him how much of a loser I actually was or make the relationship between him and Hayden even worse. I pretended everything was okay, hiding the abuse his brother and others put me through every day.

Christine was one of the first people who had turned their backs on me after Kayden's death. She and Natalie were the most responsible for spreading the rumors about me being a murderer, and soon the whole school started blaming me for it, gung-ho about venting out their frustrations or bearing malice toward the easy prey.

Those months were a living nightmare for me. They hated me so much, bullying me at each corner, and there was even a period when I was so sick that I couldn't go to school. I was absent for weeks at the time, and I barely managed to end the year with high grades.

Natalie was Kay's girlfriend, and to this day, I couldn't understand what he'd seen in her.

Natalie was even meaner than Christine, and that was putting it mildly because I was certain she had no limits to hurting others, showing how truly mentally unstable she was. She went downhill after Kayden's death, becoming only a shell of the previously spoiled, frivolous girl who had eyes only for Kayden. I had firsthand experience of how far she could go to hurt others, remembering very well her words from the day of Kayden's funeral.

She made it clear to me that day, just like Hayden, that she would make me pay for Kayden's death, adamant on making my high school life even worse than it already was. I was terrified of her, and I never knew when to expect her next attack. Christine always made sure to join the abuse.

That was one of the reasons Natalie and Christine got along very well. They had same interests, which included gossip, boys, and torturing weak people like me.

Christine had short black hair and olive green eyes with skin so fair that she looked like a porcelain doll. Natalie was pretty, but Christine was mesmerizingly beautiful, so it came as no surprise that she'd caught Hayden's attention a long time ago.

From the beginning, it was clear to me that Christine and I were complete opposites, but I didn't question our friendship at that time because she was the first person who openly approached me and wished to be my friend. I didn't want to risk losing her, no matter how foul she was, deluding myself with naïve thinking that she was a real friend.

In the end, when everything came crashing down, I figured out that it was better to be alone than with the wrong people.

I wanted to keep my distance from her, but that wasn't possible when we shared the same class. I was late for calculus courtesy of Masen, which meant everyone had already taken their seats, and only three seats were unoccupied. I went for the one in the first row—far away from Natalie and Christine.

"Nope." The girl sitting to my right stood up and put her hand over the vacant desk. "I don't think so. My friend will come any moment, so you can't sit here." A few people around us erupted in giggles, which was followed by the mocking whispers around the classroom.

I tried not to think about my embarrassment and everyone's eyes on me as I scanned the room for another available seat. I continued to the desk in the third row, which was next to the window, but the same situation happened when another senior prevented me from taking that seat. Another round of laughter coursed through the room, reinforcing my mortification.

Were they going to prevent me from sitting in this classroom? What was the catch now? I'd have to stand during the lesson? There was no way Ms. Roberts would allow that.

There was only one seat left, and I plodded to it with great reluctance because the desk was next to Christine's. I could feel her watching me like a lion watching its prey.

"Look at her," Natalie said loudly, drawing my attention to her eye circles. Not even her makeup could hide how tuckered out she was, reminding me of the rumor that she was popping pills for insomnia. Another rumor was that she'd collapsed due to fatigue and anxiety during cheerleading practice last year, but somehow, I couldn't feel any sympathy for her.

"Look at those horrible clothes. She looks like she lives in a sewer," she added.

I arrived at my desk, doing my best to ignore the continuous laughter and nosy stares. Just a few more minutes and the class would start. Just a little more and their attention would be directed elsewhere.

I put my things down on the desk and sat.

A second later, I crashed down when the chair gave out beneath me and broke into several pieces. My head landed hard on the floor, which sent an explosion of pain through my skull, and my vision went black for a few moments.

I could hear the laughter through the haze in my head, and it bit at my mind, inducing more shame that intensified the pain. Natalie and a few others even picked up their phones and snapped the pictures of me sprawled out on the floor.

"She actually sat there!" someone said.

"She didn't even notice it was broken!" I heard another one. "She's so stupid."

"This was a great idea, Natalie! I'm posting this on Instagram!"

She was *heinous*. All of this to hurt and humiliate me, and they all reveled in it, seeking it like their next meal. It was like I wasn't a human being. It was like I didn't deserve to live.

Suddenly, breathing became difficult. My chest was constricting in pain, and everything was a blur. I felt like I was going to faint, and I truly hoped for that to happen.

I hoped I could faint and finally escape this nightmare.

Chapter 4

I DIDN'T FAINT. I DIDN'T escape. I had to put up with my classmates laughing at me and taking my photos like I was an animal in the zoo. I stood up, on the verge of leaving and skipping class, but then Ms. Roberts came, and I had to explain what had happened. Everyone waited for me to snitch on them so they could give me hell later. Been there, done that. I'd lost my faith in teachers and the school administration a long time ago.

"I wasn't careful, so I fell. It's nothing special. Faulty chairs happen."

"Are you sure you are okay?"

"Yep."

"Are you able to stay in my class?"

No matter how much I wanted to run away from this hole, I couldn't. "Yes, Ms. Roberts. It wasn't a big deal."

"Okay. I will call the school janitor and tell him to bring a new chair for you."

I couldn't wait for the period to finish.

After calculus, I went to my locker to get books for the next class and halted in horror when I saw Hayden leaning against it with his hands in his pockets and one leg crossed over the other.

He'd become even more muscular during the last two months. His arms were corded with muscle, which bulged through his tight black shirt. They were perfectly honed and standing out just like his abs. I followed the various designs, shapes, and words of the tattoos he'd put on his upper arms last year, thinking how good they looked on him. They were completing his "bad boy" look, along with his earrings.

The artist in me appreciated the fine contours of his face, the glint of his eyes that gave a mysterious depth to them, and the way the shadows accentuated his striking features that hid the inner ugliness. He was definitely the most beautiful boy at East Willow High and the cruelest guy I'd ever met.

I considered running away, hoping he didn't notice me, but I couldn't do that for two reasons.

1) I needed my art notebook and pencils.

2) He noticed me.

I was embarrassed and scared of him at the same time, my stomach feeling heavy as I approached my locker. The last time I spoke to him, I did something that was way out of my league—I defied him and made a fool of him in front of the whole school. The last time I saw him, he took my nude photos. He saw my naked body, and if that weren't enough, he threatened to post my photos online for everyone to see. It was nauseating.

I couldn't even look him in the eyes. I stopped several steps away from him, but he didn't move an inch, completely blocking my locker.

"Hayden, can you please move so I can open my locker?" I was looking at his black Nike sneakers, silently pleading for him to move.

He waved his hand in front of my eyes, trying to catch my attention. I dragged my gaze to his face and looked at the spot on his temple that had been scarred from the car accident. An inch-long scar was almost invisible now, perceivable only if someone knew about it, but it was quietly accusing me of my stupid mistake nevertheless.

"I'm up here." He pointed his thumb at himself. "Look at me when you're talking to me, do you understand?"

I blushed, and I cursed myself for not being able to prevent or control my chronic, excessive blushing at almost every single thing. I didn't want him to see that he intimidated me. I couldn't have an upper hand if he knew he could affect me that easily.

I stared at his eyes that seemed so black now as he glared at me. His jaw was set in a firm line, his full lips unyielding.

"Yes, Hayden." I wanted to avoid confrontation at all costs.

"Good. Now, hand me your phone."

My eyes bugged out, fear yielding cold in my limbs. "Why do you need my phone?"

"Your phone. *Now.*"

"I don't want to give you my phone."

Without any warning, he grabbed my phone out of my front jeans pocket. I yelped, jumping back, appalled by his audacity.

"What's the password?"

I crossed my arms on my chest and drew back a couple of steps. "No. Give me my phone back."

"Give me the password, or I'll break it."

He couldn't be serious. "I won't give you my password!"

I squawked when he let my phone slip out of his hand and fall. It hit the floor with a crash and careened off, ending a few feet away from us.

No. He couldn't be doing this! It was a cheap, used model I bought after Kay's death to replace the phone I had with me during the accident, but it was valuable to me because it contained some of my art ideas, notes, and art photos I took these last two years. It was like my diary. It was a container of my interests and dreams. Besides, I couldn't afford to buy a new one.

Several students passed, casting us curious glances, but I knew better than to expect anything from them other than morbid curiosity. Once more, I wished there were cameras, but then again, would they make any difference in this rotten place?

Hayden picked up my LG from the floor, and my heart sank upon seeing the broken screen. It was covered in a crack resembling the web, which now silently mocked me.

"Oh, look. It's still working." His piercing eyes bore into mine, and shivers ran down my spine. "Next time, it won't just slip. I'll fling it away. So you better give me that fucking password."

I exhaled a shaky breath. "Password is my birthday. It's 022—"

"I know your birthday," he interrupted me and entered four digits, unlocking my phone.

I tried to ignore the fluttery sensation in my belly caused by his words. *He knows my birthday... Why does he care to remember it?*

He kept swiping and tapping his thumbs over the screen, and each passing second brought more uneasiness.

"Please, give me my phone back. What are you even searching for?"

"I've been away for two months. That's a plenty of time for you to meet someone, and since you're stupid, I wouldn't be surprised if you thought you could hang out with them."

"For crying out loud, do you really think you can invade my privacy like that and decide who I can hang out with or not? You have no right to interfere in my life!"

Hayden lunged at me and backed me against the lockers. He slammed his left hand next to my face, making me flinch, and my breathing turned ragged. I was trapped, overcome with tension because our bodies were almost touching. I could smell the mossy scent of his cologne mixed with the smell of cigarettes, and it was distracting me.

His nearness was too much. I tried to look down, but he didn't let me, pushing my face up with his forefinger.

"You keep forgetting you have no freedom. You can't escape me or disobey me. Remember what will happen if you disobey me, and trust me, you don't want those photos to end up online. Besides, don't think I forgot about what you did in the cafeteria two months ago. You're going to pay for that."

I could hardly breathe, my pulse drumming. I hated him. How much longer did I have to suffer like this?

One more year, Sarah, and then you're off to college. You'll escape Hayden. Just a bit more...

"Now, as far as I can see, you have no male contacts here, and you better keep it that way. I don't want to waste my time on them too."

"If you think you waste your time on me then stop torturing me! I'll be completely out of your way. You won't even see me—"

"No," he cut me off. "Remember this?" He pointed at his temple, and my stomach dropped. "It's your fault that Kayden and I got into that accident. You deserve to suffer."

Our breaths mingled, mere inches separating our faces. I returned his heated gaze, unable to look away.

"Actually, maybe I shouldn't return this phone to you." He tilted his head to the side, looking at the device in his hand with narrowed eyes. "One can never know with you. Maybe you'll cause another car accident with it."

My throat closed up, my old scars bursting open, and it hurt more than anything. "Please, no more."

"No more? I barely even started. I won't stop until you completely lose your sanity. You'll be lost, hopeless, and broken, and every single breath will make you bleed. And that wouldn't even be a fragment of how I feel every single day." He tapped his scar. "That's justice."

We kept staring at each other, unaware of the people around us. I couldn't move.

A few long moments later, he pulled away from me, breaking the chain that had held us together. I could finally release my breath, and the fist that had been squeezing my heart hard loosened its grip.

He shoved my phone into my hand and strode away.

• • • •

I WENT TO ART CLASS and felt relieved to see there was no one I would have to keep my distance from. It was my most favorite class, and after the encounter with Hayden, I was more than glad to be able to have my full attention on studying instead of on my classmates or my depressing thoughts.

As much as I enjoyed this class, though, it was challenging for me since Mr. Xiong wanted us to experiment with various techniques. I liked sketching and drawing with watercolors and watercolor pencils, but I struggled with other materials. I was interested in drawing people, trying to portray them as realistically as I could in different settings, but Mr. Xiong made us draw still nature or animals most of the time.

The class passed too quickly for my taste. I dragged myself down the hallway that led to the cafeteria, wishing for a twist of fate that would send Hayden far away from this school.

The lunchroom was packed with students when I joined the lunch queue, some of them staring at me as if I had three heads. I was sure that by now my fall had become viral. It made me queasy, and I didn't actually have any appetite, but I had to eat something if I wanted to survive this day.

I placed my food on the tray, thankful that nobody tried to do anything to me in line. The students kept whispering and snickering, but I was used to that already. They always made the same reaction, which added to my social anxiety, making me more susceptible to my inner demons, self-deprecation, and extremely low self-confidence.

At least I could remain strong enough to go to my table and eat. Even though sitting alone plain sucked, it was better than skipping lunch.

As soon as I sat down, facing the rest of the cafeteria, Hayden arrived with Blake, Josh, and Masen. Like usual, they attracted the most attention, and I could already see some girls speeding to their table to join them for lunch. I lowered my head, hoping Hayden wouldn't remember to look my way.

When I finally got the courage to raise my head and search for him, I found him sitting at his table already surrounded by girls, looking directly at me.

Oh no. My stomach made a somersault, my face growing red and hot. He didn't even blink or move a single muscle, staring me down. What was he thinking about?

Several students around the cafeteria started whispering and pointing at something, and I turned my head to see what they were looking at. A short, chubby girl, dressed in jeans and a draped T-shirt, stood at the cafeteria entrance. I'd never seen her before. She had beautiful hair, which was long, straight, and sand-colored. She was so cute.

Blake stood up and strolled over to her, his ruthless eyes sizing her up. The whole cafeteria went silent.

"Well, you're something new." He grinned. "What's your name?"

She lowered her head and blushed, giving away her insecurity and shyness. Her timidity made her a perfect subject for torture, and I could see Blake sensing it like sharks could sense blood. I already knew he was going to do something, but what?

"J-Jessica," she said in a small voice. A couple of students laughed when she stammered.

Blake didn't even blink. "Jessica what?"

"Jessica Metts."

"What's that? I didn't hear you. Jessica what?"

"J-Jessica Metts."

"You mean Jessica Fats?"

The fits of vicious laughter coursed through the air, and I felt cold fear as if I were the one standing there. I'd been through this same torture so many times that it felt strange I wasn't the one who was experiencing it now.

Blake's crooked grin gave me the creeps. "Because you're so fat, Jessie."

Jessica looked like she was on the verge of tears. She shrunk, giving the impression that she would run away any moment. I glanced at Hayden and saw him looking at them with no expression on his face. Christine, who was sitting next to him, caressed his hair idly, but he didn't even pay attention to her. If he decided to join Blake, they were going to ruin Jessica and make her terrified of this place for the rest of her school life.

Jessica spun on her heel, ready to dart away, but Blake grabbed her forearm and pulled her back. "Where are you going, Jessie? Do you want to miss your welcome party?"

Oh God, no.

"My welcome party?" Her voice was so thin, and I was curious to know if that was her natural voice or she sounded this way because she was afraid.

"Yes." He looked at the students around them. "What do you say, guys? Do you want to throw a welcome party for Jessica?" Everyone was so keen on doing what Blake had said, and it was heart-breaking. I felt like I was going to cry, scared to even imagine what would transpire in a few seconds.

A "welcome party" was Hayden's invention. It was about "greeting" new students by throwing food at them in the cafeteria. Several students would participate, surrounding the person and throwing food at them. It was like some twisted rite of passage, which marked the beginning of student's abhorred existence in East Willow High.

The lunch monitors didn't care, and the cafeteria staff didn't intervene, because Hayden had some stupid power in this school and always got away with his bad deeds. His mother was one of the benefactors of this school, so going after one of East Willow High's most favored students wasn't considered smart.

He and his friends were highly protected, allowed to wreak havoc whenever they wanted and bully whomever they wanted. The school staff had never helped me and they wouldn't help Jessica now. Not when we didn't have any power or money.

Blake stepped aside and, as if on cue, everyone began throwing their lunches at her. The first food projectiles ended right on her face. She raised her hands to protect it, making the rest of her body exposed to various sauces, fruits, and vegetables. It kept going, with some students taking pictures of it, and it was horrible just watching.

Absolutely no one went to help her. She yelped whenever something hit her, and I wondered if she was hurt or not. I wanted to help her, but I couldn't. I couldn't go there. I couldn't do anything for her. If I did, I would become a target too, and I didn't need any more harassment today.

Fear and shame twirled inside me, and my whole body felt like it was set on fire. It was adrenaline, which put my body in survival mode for what was about to happen next.

I can't go there... Please, somebody help her.

I glanced at Hayden and winced when our eyes met. Surprisingly, he was staring at me, but there was no usual nothingness in them. Instead, there was fire. There was a challenge. A strange feeling I couldn't name stirred in my chest.

I returned my gaze to Jessica, who was now completely covered in liquids and food, hunched on the floor, crying. Blake still stood in the same spot, his lips twisted in a cruel smile as he filmed her with his phone. He probably planned to make it the next viral video of East Willow High.

The food throwing didn't stop. It always continued until the victim ran away, but Jessica looked so weak and small on that floor that I doubted she had any strength in her to get up and escape.

I can't go there...

My chest tightened, a scorching pain suffusing it.

I'm scared.

Breathing felt like suffocating.

Don't be like the rest of them, Sarah. Don't look the other way. Don't be a coward.

Somebody threw a carton of milk and it landed on Jessica's forehead. The carton burst open upon the contact and the milk splashed all over her face. A small trail of blood oozed from her forehead, mixing with milk on its way down.

No. This is so wrong. This is twisted. I don't want to be a part of this. I don't want to be a coward.

I need to help her.

I jumped out of my seat and stopped in front of her, extending my arms, shielding her from Blake and most of the students surrounding us.

I faced him. "Stop this!"

"What the hell are you doing?" Blake's face was a mask of surprise and fury.

"This is not okay! You're hurting her! Don't you see she's bleeding?!"

I looked over my shoulder to check if she was all right and met her terrified stare. Her face looked grotesque, covered in blood, milk, and food, and I hoped her wound wasn't deep. She needed to see the school nurse double-quick.

"Step aside, bitch."

"No." I was shaking in fear, expecting an attack from any side.

Blake marched to me and leveled his head with mine in a threatening way. His icy gray eyes and the vicious sneer terrified me, increasing my uncontrollable trembling. "You're going to regret this."

He grabbed a chunk of my hair and yanked it toward him, and I cried out in pain, my vision blurring with tears. Our bodies collided briefly before he pushed me to the ground, dropping my ripped out hairs from his hand. He gave a sign to others to throw food at Jessica and me, but everyone stopped in their tracks when the cafeteria doors opened.

"What is going on here?" Principal Anders rushed toward us, noticing Jessica and me on the floor. "Jesus Christ!" He crouched next to Jessica and touched her shoulder. She was so still. So fragile. "Are you okay?" he asked her, but she didn't respond. The only sound that came from her was her weeping.

"She needs to see the nurse. She's hurt," I told him, standing up.

He jumped to his feet when he noticed the wound on her forehead. "Who is responsible for this?" Nobody uttered a word. I glared at Blake, but he just returned my stare, daring me to snitch on him.

Luckily, I didn't need to say anything because it seemed that Anders connected the dots. "Jones, to my office."

If Blake's looks could kill, our principal would be a pile of ash on the floor already. "Why me?"

"Don't play innocent, Jones. This is not the first time something like this happened, and most of the time you are involved."

"That's not right, Mr. Anders. I just happened to be here trying to help the girls. Is that right?" he asked some guys next to him and they—to my complete disgust—nodded.

"Either way, to my office, Jones. Now." His voice left no room for argument, and I began gloating. "You too, Decker. I want you in my office now."

I let my frown show on my face. I didn't like the sound of it, but there was no escaping it. "Okay. May I take Jessica to the nurse first?"

"You may, but be quick about it." He cleared his throat before he addressed the rest of the lunchroom, "Why are you still standing there? I want this mess cleaned right away!"

I dared a glance at Hayden. He was leaning back in his chair with the arms crossed over his chest, not paying attention to anyone but me. His fierce eyes reflected anger and surprise. Surprise at what? I was sure he was mad at me for intervening and opposing Blake, which I was going to be sorry for later, but what else was in his mind?

With a faint blush blanketing my cheeks, I helped Jessica stand, sensing her shivers. She was shorter than me, and for some reason, I wanted to hug her and make her pain go away.

I placed my arm around her shoulder. "Can you walk?"

"Yes."

"Okay then. Let's see the nurse."

She just nodded, letting me walk her out of the cafeteria.

"Do you have any spare clothes?" I asked her when we reached the nurse's office. Her pants and shirt were completely ruined. She shook her head, the movement sending viscid droplets from her dripping wet hair to the floor.

"Nurse will give you some towels to clean yourself, and I think she will let you go home for the day." I looked away. I didn't know what to tell her to make her feel better since I was never good with pep talks.

I was never good with making friends, period.

"Thank you."

I returned her gaze. "Don't mention it."

"Seriously, thank you. What you did for me out there... I was so confused. So scared. I can't believe this happened to me."

"I'm sorry. They're the worst."

She shook her head again, outstretching her hand for a handshake. "I feel weird for meeting you like this but here... I'm Jessica Metts."

Smiling, I shook hands with her. "I'm Sarah Decker. Despite the circumstances, I'm glad to meet you."

"Does this... Does this happen a lot?"

No. It only happened to me and a few more people who had the misfortune to be declared losers. "Not really. It's their stupid prank. They call it a 'welcome party,' but as you can see, it's not welcoming at all." I frowned. I wasn't sure if I should tell her the whole truth.

She noticed my hesitation. "What?"

I averted my gaze. "Nothing."

"Please, tell me everything. It's okay."

"Did you notice them holding their phones and filming you?"

She tensed, visibly gulping. "Yes?"

"Well, there are several private Facebook groups and profiles on Snapchat and Instagram that post the bullying content from East Willow High. People share those posts, like, comment and..." I sighed. "Make memes."

Jessica looked shaken. She swayed, and I barely managed to grab a hold of her in time, afraid she might faint. Maybe I shouldn't have told her this. It was too much to take in.

"Look, I'm sorry to keep you here. You really need to see the nurse now, okay? Please, lie down in her office and get some rest, okay?"

"Okay."

"We'll talk again tomorrow."

"Okay. See you."

I waited for her to enter the nurse's office, disinclined to join Blake in the principal's office. A few deep breaths later, I willed my legs to move, giving myself a pep talk that did nothing to abate my soaring apprehension.

• • • •

ANDERS'S OFFICE WAS miniscule but thoroughly stuffed. It contained several cabinets, shelves full of books and papers, and his desk, which ate up all available space. This generated a fertile ground for claustrophobia. Two chairs were placed across from his, and they were so close to each other that I felt like my personal space was heavily invaded when I sat next to Blake.

Anders was a short, chubby man in his fifties with a bald spot in the middle of his head and prominent grays in his hair and eyebrows. His mustache was black, though, and I guessed he dyed it. His appearance didn't inspire

trust in me, but what I particularly disliked about him was the overconfidence that oozed from him. He acted like he owned this place, caring too little about the students and too much about his power and the "perfect" image
of our school.

"Did Metts go to the school's nurse?"

"Yes, she's there right now."

"Good. How is she holding up?"

Was he really asking me that? "She's probably been better," I said. Blake
snorted.

"As I said to Jones before you arrived, such incidents are unacceptable in
our school. I'm very sorry you had to go through that."

*No, you're not. You never cared. How many times was I here as a victim of
some vicious prank and you pretended like you weren't actually aware of what
was going on? All you care about is you and your school's reputation.*

"What are you going to do about it?" I asked him, fed up with authorities
turning a blind eye on the victims of bullying.

"Pipe down, Sars," Blake snarled, looking at me like he was going to
choke me.

Anders ignored Blake's jeer. "I'm going to make sure it won't happen
again."

"And how are you going to do that?"

"You really do have a big mouth." Blake's voice contained suppressed
fury. I glanced at his tightly-clenched hands on the arm rests, which were
sporting raw scrapes on his now-white knuckles.

Everything about him intimidated me. He was the captain of our football team, and he had a very muscular build since he trained really hard. He
rarely smiled; the ever-present ice in his eyes was outright menacing.

"Shut up, Jones. And you, Decker, watch your mouth. Don't disrespect
your principal."

"Are you going to punish anyone?"

"For now, no."

For now, no?

Oh my God. I was so furious.

I was so furious that, for once, I couldn't control myself. I knew I would
regret it later, but I needed to get it off my chest now.

"What do you mean 'For now, no'? People actually threw food at that girl and hurt her, and you won't do anything about it?"

"Jones mentioned already it was all just a misunderstanding—"

"A misunderstanding?" I yelled, standing up, and pointed at Blake. "He started all that mess! He told them to throw food at her, all the while filming it! You can't let him get away with this!"

Blake was so mad that his veins actually popped out on his temples, his eyes giving me a clear message: you're dead.

"Calm down, Decker! I will talk with Jessica Metts too and try to clear things up, but I won't push this matter further before that. If Jessica and certain witnesses can confirm it was Blake who started it, he will receive a proper punishment, of course."

This was unbelievable. I stared at Anders first, then at Blake. Blake's parents were rich—more than rich enough to buy Blake's way out of trouble—and his father was the mayor. On top of that, they donated to East Willow High, just like Hayden's mother. If Blake was punished, that could ruin the bright future of their heir, so of course they wouldn't let anything happen to him.

I felt defeated. Principal Anders was a corrupt snake, and he wouldn't move a finger to do what was right and protect his students. I was deeply affronted by this unfairness.

He dismissed us a while later, and we left his office in dour silence. As soon as we passed his secretary, turning around the corner, Blake grabbed me and pushed me against the wall in an empty hallway. Terror enveloped me when he pressed his forearm into my throat, making me unable to breathe properly.

"You just couldn't shut up, bitch! No, you had to tell on me." The pressure of his forearm increased, and it was becoming painful... "You're messing with the wrong guy. You'll be sorry for this." He dropped his arm and stormed away.

I gasped for air loudly, sliding down the wall. I felt beyond miserable.
When does it end?

Chapter 5

I REACHED THE PARKING lot and stopped in my tracks when I noticed a crowd of students gathered near my parking spot. They were all looking at something and taking pictures. I willed my legs to move, hoping the crowd wasn't there because of me.

As I got closer, I realized it was *my* parking spot they surrounded, and my pulse sped up. I'd thought I was finally free from hell after everything that happened today, but Yin—oh, that old fiend—was ever-present. I bypassed onlookers only to freeze when I saw my car.

No.

Someone had completely vandalized it. They had covered the doors, roof, and hood with various paints, but that wasn't the end of my humiliation. The word "snitch" had been sprayed in large white letters all over my windshield, taunting me with its derogatory nuance, and it was too much. My classmates pointed their phones at me to capture my reaction, and for a moment, I was too tired to move or react. The voices around me grew louder.

"She's so lame."

"Look at that reaction! She looks like she's going to shit herself!"

"Maybe she already did."

Tears filled my eyes, but I refused to cry. I wouldn't cry in front of them. I wouldn't give them the pleasure.

"Snitch!" one guy shouted.

"Snitch!" the student next to him repeated.

"Snitch!"

"Snitch! Snitch! Snitch!" Everyone started chanting, and it was more than I could handle. I needed to run away.

"Step aside!" I yelled at the students and pushed them out of my way, trying to ignore their goading shouts. I entered my car and slammed the door shut.

"Snitch!"

"Snitch-bitch!"

"You're a freak!"

"Go and die already!"

I ran the engine, sickened by their brutal chanting. Two seniors stopped in front of my car and kicked the bumper.

"Get out of my way!" I screamed at them, pressing the horn twice, but they didn't pay any attention to me.

I noticed Hayden and Blake watch this scene from afar, and I could clearly see the delight in Blake's eyes. This was Blake's retaliation. I was disconcerted by how easy it was for him to degrade me.

Tingles appeared in the back of my head and my heart rate accelerated as panic gripped me. I had to get out of here before I lost it. I pressed the gas pedal and released the clutch, making my car jerk.

"What the...?!" The guys in front of my car darted out of the way, afraid I would run them over, which was the whole point.

I started the engine again and sped up, finally getting out of here.

• • • •

THE CAR SERVICE JOHNS' Corner was one of the cheapest car services in Enfield. I used this service for two reasons. The first reason was the price. The second was that Mrs. Johns was one of the nicest ladies I'd ever met.

Mrs. Johns was in her fifties, always wearing flowery dresses that suited her plump body but were inappropriate for the car service. Her dyed black hair was usually collected in a ballet bun, and her russet brown face was covered with makeup at all times. Mr. Johns passed away many years ago, and they didn't have any children, which could be the reason why she'd always treated me as if I were her daughter.

Every time I came here with my vandalized car she got furious, urging me to report my bullies to the school's administration or the police. She had no clue.

I tried going to the police once. I went there when Josh Akers punched me in the face shortly after Kay died. They said they would investigate the case and called Josh and his parents, but in the end, they claimed I had no evidence that it was Josh who had done it. There were no witnesses, and it was my word against his. Josh's father was a judge, and he had good connections in the police, so I wasn't surprised at all that Josh was unscathed.

Needless to say, Josh doubled the torture he'd been inflicting on me ever since, so the moral of the story was that reporting my bullies to the police put me in even bigger danger.

This time, shame swallowed me whole when I got out of my car and took in Mrs. Johns' shocked expression.

"Who did this?" Her voice was brimming with anger.

"It's okay. Don't worry. It's just the paint."

"For Christ's sake, Sarah! This is a serious issue! This is a crime! Does your mother know about this?"

"No, but that's okay. It's pointless to make her worry. Besides, this can be solved quickly."

"Nonsense! You act like you have no mother!"

I never talked about my mother with Mrs. Johns. Somehow, that topic was too sensitive for me, and I wasn't ready to share my feelings about her to anyone. Whenever our conversation shifted to her, I would either skirt around the topic or give her a vague response.

I certainly couldn't tell her my mother wasn't giving me the money to fix my car. I was spending my own money.

I couldn't afford luxuries for myself for two reasons. Firstly, I didn't get much allowance from my mother. She had two wages, but those were barely enough to cover our bills, my school expenses, food, and her trips to bars. Secondly, my part-time job allowed me to save money for college and set aside a small amount I used for fixing things like a destroyed car, stolen or broken things, and so on.

Being bullied does take a toll on a person's wallet.

"It's really okay. That was just a stupid prank. You know how the school kids are these days..."

Mrs. Johns didn't buy it, but she knew there was nothing she could do if I didn't want to do anything about my bullies. She could only watch and fume with anger, but she couldn't help me.

Nobody could pull me out of my miserable life and give me the love, respect, and security I needed.

Eventually, she dropped the subject. My phone buzzed, and I opened a message from my mom.

"Sorry, but I changed my mind. I'm already out. I won't be home tonight, so you have to make something for dinner. See you tomorrow."

Her message was the cherry on top after a disastrous day. I felt so miserable that I just wanted to crawl into my bed and never wake up again. I turned my back to Mrs. Johns so she wouldn't see my teary eyes.

This wasn't something new. Mom was spending more time out during her free time, wandering from one bar to another. Then again, whenever she was home she was waspish, getting angry at every single thing, and it was draining my energy. So I didn't know what was the lesser of two evils.

I couldn't fall apart in front of Mrs. Johns. I sucked in my tears and put my best smile on before turning to her again. "So, what would be the price this time?"

We agreed on the fee, and she assured me it would be done by Thursday. I bid her goodbye and left the store, relieved that I managed to avoid my breakdown. For now.

$$\bullet \ \bullet \ \bullet \ \bullet$$

I WENT TO 7-ELEVEN to buy groceries for dinner, the thoughts of the empty house that awaited my return invading my mind. This was one of those moments when I wanted nothing more than to have a friend to talk with. Each time I fell, Kay was there to pick me up, doing all he could to make me cheerful and less miserable. It was easier to battle my depression when I had him.

Kayden was the first person who accepted me and genuinely cared for me, and I was happiest with him. Our friendship felt too good to be true—it felt unreal that someone could be friends with me. In the beginning, I walked on eggshells, so careful not to ruin our friendship and lose the only true friend I'd ever had. If only I knew that Kayden would be taken from me in the cruelest way possible... I was so careful, yet I destroyed us in the end.

No, I didn't want to go down that memory lane now.

I picked up two bags from the checkout counter and exited the store, ready to walk a few miles to my house. I was at the far end of the store's parking lot when I caught sight of Hayden and Christine together on his Kawasaki, and I stopped, cursing myself for looking at my feet instead of my surroundings. Hayden had parked several feet away from me, so there was no way for me to pass them unnoticed.

Christine stroked his abdomen from behind, and my stomach churned at the sight of the two of them close like this. She whispered something into his ear, to which he half-smiled.

I wasn't surprised they couldn't let go of each other even after so many breakups, because they were the same. They were both vicious jerks who were determined to make my life hell, and I couldn't stand the sight of them.

Christine noticed me first, and her lips curled into a derisive smile. She said something to Hayden, and he snapped his head to meet my gaze. The usual expressionless mask fell on his face in an instant, the traces of the previous smile already gone.

I scanned the parking area to see if there were any people and only noticed some teenagers, who couldn't be older than fifteen, passing close by. Since Hayden liked to humiliate me in public, without caring about the consequences, I was sure he was about to create some trouble.

I sped up in another direction, intent on putting as much distance between us as possible. "Please, don't come. Please, please, please," I whispered as I scurried.

I yelped when he caught my upper arm in a steely grip, killing all my hope of escaping him, and pulled me around to face him. I sucked in my breath, noticing how close our bodies were. His menacing 6' 2" frame daunted me.

"Where do you think you're going? You can't run away from me like that."

His firm grip was starting to hurt. "Hayden, let go of me. Why can't you just let me walk away? Why do you have to harass me every time you see me?"

"And why do you always have to make such dumb questions? What's in those bags?"

"Excuse me?"

He grabbed one of the bags out of my hand, completely surprising me. "Hey! You can't do that!"

"Why do you never learn? I ask nicely only once, but you always play dumb."

He released me and opened the bag to scan through its contents. "Food and even more food. What—mommy isn't home to make you dinner? You're alone again?" His voice was sardonic, his words slicing me all too easily.

He knew my mother was my weak spot. He always watched me and paid close attention to my interactions with others, checking if the relationships with them were good or not so he could exploit that information. Hayden certainly took great pleasure in knowing I didn't get along with her.

Christine stepped next to him and gave me a disapproving once-over. "You should've seen her this morning. Her fall was hilarious. She really is dumb."

I let my eyes slide down her body, studying her appearance. Her skinny jeans fit her long legs perfectly, accentuating how well-defined they were, and her low-cut neckline shirt revealed her huge breasts, which were, I was sure, an object of desire of many East Willow High boys.

My breasts were small. Usually, I didn't obsess over their size, but there were times when I wished they were bigger. I wanted to wear low-cut shirts or dresses, but since that was impossible, I covered myself with clothes that completely hid my shoulders and chest.

"I saw it on YouTube during break," he answered, not giving any further comment.

"She looked as if she were going to faint. She looked so disgusting, especially when her eyes crossed." She rolled her eyes and sniggered.

"You're sick," I hissed at her.

She raised her eyebrow. "Yeah? At least I'm not a creep and a murderer like you."

Murderer. It stung. It really did. Even after two years of hearing them call me a murderer, I felt pain whenever they said that. It reminded me of how stupid and careless I'd been. It reminded me that Kayden died because of me.

I couldn't escape the toxic guilt I'd carried with me since that night. It was eating away at me. It was unconquerable, shouting at me from the depths of my mind that I deserved all bad things that were happening to me.

"Screw you." My voice was unstable, giving out how shaken I felt.

"Oh, poor baby. Are you going to cry?" she taunted me. "Please, cry. I'd like nothing more than that."

Hayden took a package with tomatoes out of the bag and opened it. He bit into one piece, and before I even had time to react, he threw it at me. The tomato hit my shoulder, its juice splashing across my white T-shirt, and I jerked back. I lost my grip on the bag, and my groceries spilled over the pavement.

I gaped at Hayden. "What are you doing?!"

His face displayed nothing but cold indifference. "I'm finishing what Blake started today."

He took the second tomato out of the package, bit it, and hurled it at my leg, spitting the bite out. I yelped when a dull pain exploded in my thigh, followed by a sense of wetness when the messy contents covered my jeans. I wanted to run away, but just like Jessica today, I was too shocked to move. He turned the package upside down and the rest of the tomatoes dropped to the ground.

"Hayden, stop!"

The teenagers I saw earlier came closer to us, two of them taking out their phones, and dread settled in the pit of my stomach. I hoped they were using them to call the police and not to shoot this.

Hayden ignored my plea, switching his attention to the egg carton. "Would you do the honors?" he asked Christine and opened it, pointing at the eggs.

Her grin was full of malice. "Gladly."

She took one out of the carton and threw it with all her force at me. I cried out in pain when the egg hit my chest, splattering all over my T-shirt. I didn't even have time to check just how gruesome the yellowish-red combination looked on the previously white cotton, because she'd already picked another egg and aimed it at my head. I barely managed to cover myself before it landed on my face.

She didn't stop, hitting me repeatedly, and the pressure in my head got stronger. I fell to my knees, unable to see or hear anything as the laughter in my mind intensified.

All I heard was laughter—they were laughing at me. All I saw were evil faces—they were glaring at me, mocking me, haunting me... It was humiliating and degrading. I felt like I was less than a human being. I was all alone and there was no one who would listen. Nobody cared.

I wanted it to stop. Humiliation, pain, laughter... I didn't want to hide anymore. I wanted to live free, unashamed of who I was. Why didn't they let me live?

Why can't I fight back? Why?

Run away, Sarah. Just... Go.

I heard someone crying, and I needed time to comprehend it was me who was bawling, begging them to stop. I looked around in confusion, slowly becoming aware that there were no more blows. Nothing was coming at me anymore. I was curled up on the ground, but nobody offered me help. Nobody ever offered any help.

I looked up at Hayden, waiting for the next attack. He just stared at me with his hooded eyes.

"Pitiful," he said in disgust and turned his back to me, finally deciding to leave. He dropped my bag, and the food scattered behind him after the impact.

I glared at Christine, who was taking several shots of me with her phone.

"Thank you for being a good model, as always. Have fun cleaning those terrible clothes. Though, I wouldn't bother in your place. They're so hideous I would burn them anyway."

She joined Hayden on his bike, and he left the parking lot in a cloud of smoke.

The teenagers started dispersing and no one—absolutely no one—even asked me if I was okay. They had their fun, they got their pictures, and they left me on the ground with no remorse to wallow in self-pity.

Chapter 6

THE NEXT MORNING, I woke up contemplating how to explain to my mother why my car wasn't in our driveway. I planned to use a bicycle to go to school for the time being, but I didn't know which excuse I could come up with now. The school year had barely started and there was already something wrong with my car.

I didn't want to tell her my first day in school had been so awful that it could compete for the title of the "Worst First Day in High School Ever."

I could always say my tire had blown out, but there was a limit to how many times I could use that old excuse. I got out of my room, and I saw I didn't have to worry about creating the most convincing lie because mom hadn't even come home. I checked my phone for any messages from her; however, there were none.

I called her, but the call went to her voicemail. "Hey, mom. Where are you? I'm going to school now, but please text me so I know you're okay. Bye," I said and finished the call.

If today was the same as all those previous days, then she probably had spent the night at some man's place. Since it couldn't be helped, I had to be patient and wait for her message.

I was enervated, my body begging for anything that could boost its energy, so I decided to make coffee before I went to school. I'd been wakeful all night, unable to stop replaying yesterday's events.

Last night, I threw my stained clothes into the washing machine and took a long shower as soon as I got home. It was impossible for me to chase away all those frightening thoughts and forget about my day, so many images blending in my mind and amplifying my darkness. Everything nice I experienced during the summer didn't have value anymore. It was like they never happened.

I finished my shower feeling even worse. At that moment, I was masochistic enough to look for the social media accounts of East Willow High students, worried they had shared something related to me.

I usually didn't give in to the urge to look through their accounts, because whenever I did, I was extremely hurt. As long as I didn't look at those pictures and videos on the Internet, I could pretend they didn't exist. I could have an illusion of escape.

I'd seen them making fun of me, liking, and sharing my most embarrassing and dire moments. Natalie and Christine were the ones who always created a buzz about me and other poor souls who were bullied. They fed themselves with the hate they spread.

I could also pretend they didn't make fake accounts of me, posting all kinds of pictures and messages in my name. The more I reported those profiles, the more new ones popped up, so I'd given up on trying to get them removed a long time ago.

Sometimes, I wished the Internet hadn't been invented at all. "Out of sight, out of mind" completely lost its point in the 21st century. We could never be completely out of someone's sight, because we could easily have our photos and videos scattered all over the Internet.

I stumbled upon the cafeteria video right before I went to bed. The sight of Jessica hunched while getting hit with various foods set my insides on fire once more, each second of it filling me with more nausea. I reported it, but I doubted it would make any difference. If it got removed, who could guarantee it wouldn't be uploaded again?

Those individuals who filmed this and shared it online, spurring other people to leave horrible comments about the victim, were corrupt and twisted. It wasn't humane, yet so many classmates found a sense of achievement by competing to create the most clever put-downs.

Safety in numbers. It was so easy to join the bandwagon of hate when they were a part of the mass. I'd hardly seen any comments condemning the content. They were drowned out by hateful majority big time. I remembered reading that around nincty percent of teens who had witnessed social-media bullying ignored it, which explained why bullies could get away with it.

I got out of my house a bit earlier so I could get to school on time on my bicycle. The morning air was chilly, biting my cheeks and hands, and my jacket did nothing to shield me from the cold. I could hardly grip the handlebars with my icy hands.

The trip to school felt like forever, and when I finally arrived, my teeth were chattering from the cold. As I blew on my fingers to warm them, I found

Josh and Masen laughing together about something. Their faces instantly fell when they noticed me.

"Look. It's *Snitch*," Masen said.

Josh strode to me and blocked my way, and my blood ran cold, my senses on high alert. He was short for a guy, since I was 5' 9" and taller than him. Nevertheless, his frame was wide, filled with muscles, so he could overpower me easily. Among Hayden, Blake, and Masen, Josh was the biggest ruffian. I wasn't the only girl he'd hit. He had a horrible temper, and he liked hitting girls, resorting to cruelest acts provoked or unprovoked.

Josh hit me because I tried to fight him back. He kept calling me names, and I told him that at least I wasn't a midget like him. An instant later, he swung his fist at me, sending me flying over the school backyard. I didn't feel pain straight away, because I was in a daze after his unexpected blow and my brain needed time to process what the hell was going on. Only later I felt pain and tasted blood on my cracked lips, the horrible reality rendering me speechless.

He didn't regret it, of course. He only promised me a black eye next time if I rubbed him the wrong way again.

To my constant dread, there was more to his vicious personality, but I could never pinpoint what exactly. There were times when a crazy glint would appear in his eyes, which made me question his sanity, and the amount of hate in him terrified me.

He was similar to Natalie, so it was no wonder they were back together. They had been occasionally hooking up ever since Kay's death, though Natalie claimed she never stopped loving Kayden. I didn't know what she saw in Josh, but I guessed there was a lid for every pot.

Josh brought his hand to my shoulder and squeezed it so hard that I hunched in pain. I dug my nails into my palms, silently hoping he wouldn't raise his hand on me or else. "What you did in the cafeteria was incredibly stupid, dumb bitch."

"You got your revenge because my car is destroyed." My voice came out weakly. "Can't you just let it go?"

He applied more pressure, and I pressed my nails even harder into my palms, fighting not to make even a single cry of pain. We were in a hallway full of students, but I didn't doubt for a second he would hit me if irked.

"Do you think we play games, Snitch?" Masen appeared in my line of vision, leveling his face with mine. He flicked my forehead. "We hate you, and we won't let you have a single day away from us."

"You're a pile of shit." Josh's choice of words was, as always, full of expletives when he spoke to me. I hoped the bell would ring soon so I wouldn't have to endure this anymore. "You deserve to be beaten and taught a lesson."

He pushed me with all his force away from him, and I couldn't catch myself. I was falling, but somebody caught me from behind and yanked me up. Regaining my balance, I turned around and gasped when I met Hayden's eyes.

"You should've let her fall! Why did you do that?" Josh spat behind me, and I detected flickers of ire in Hayden's eyes at his words.

"She was in the way," he said through his teeth, glaring at him. "It was a natural reflex." Slowly, he brought his gaze back to me, which perturbed me. What was he planning to do now?

"Step aside," Hayden told me. "You're an ugly sight to see in the early morning." He moved me so he could pass down the hallway. Josh's features twisted with pure hatred as he watched him leave, but then he noticed me staring, and he flipped me off, storming after Hayden. With a sneer, Masen copied Josh's gesture and followed them.

I had trouble moving my legs since they felt like jelly. I couldn't believe them! I plodded to my locker, unusually relieved that Hayden had spoiled Josh's plans and let me go that easily. Whenever he popped out of nowhere I felt like there was some impending doom, and I was never ready for him.

I wished I could escape him. I wished there could be a day free from him. This summer had been like a beautiful dream, but unfortunately it couldn't last.

I learned one thing in my life. *Beautiful dreams never last.* I was always led back to my usual nightmare.

My phone buzzed, and I read the message from my mother saying she was okay and at work. I took a deep breath, closing my eyes. Just as I'd assumed. She had another "wild" night, huh?

I headed to English and entered the classroom, finding Jessica in the first row. She was sitting at the desk that was the nearest to the door, and it was easy to see the reason behind her seat choice. She wanted a quick exit if she needed one. The seat next to hers was empty, thankfully, so I decided to take it. The classroom was half full, but I didn't see Hayden or any of his friends here, which was a relief.

"Hey," I greeted her. She raised her head from the book she was reading. I lifted my eyebrows when I noticed it was written in French.

She blushed, glancing away shyly. "Hello," she answered in a tiny voice. So this *was* her real voice. It made her sound like a ten-year-old, but I thought it was cute.

"Sorry for interrupting you. May I sit next to you?"

"Yeah, sure." She didn't even look at me, her focus solely on her book.

I glanced at her, gauging whether she didn't want to talk or she was just extremely shy. I noticed that her eyes were staring at one spot, which meant she wasn't reading. I was making her nervous.

"I wanted to ask if you're okay." I pointed at her forehead. "I see you're wearing a Band-Aid."

"I'm okay, thank you. Though I probably look like a freak."

"No, don't worry. It's not a big deal."

She finally looked at me, and I spotted the insecurity on her face. "So. I wanted to thank you..." She glanced away. She took a deep breath and brought her gaze back to me. "I'm so grateful for what you did for me yesterday. Seriously, thank you. You were the only one who opposed them, and it was so brave of you—"

I shook my head and tucked a strand of hair behind my ear. "It's not like that. I'm not brave. I'm weak. I just couldn't stand seeing them hurt you like that—" I froze when Hayden walked leisurely into the classroom. The hair on my neck stood up, and I couldn't do anything but gape at him. He noticed me, and he didn't even blink as he walked to the back of the classroom.

The girls started whispering among themselves, which was a usual reaction wherever he appeared. Today he was dressed all in black—black jeans with a black T-shirt that hugged his rippled muscles, which fit him better than I wanted to admit. How could someone who looked so beautiful on the outside be so ugly on the inside?

I glanced at Jessica and noticed her observing me. "Do you like him?" she whispered.

My cheeks stained with my pervasive blush, my chest throbbing. "Of course not. Why do you ask?"

Her lips curled into a small smile. "I'm sorry. It's just... You didn't take your eyes off him when he came in."

Really? Did I look like I was attracted to him whenever I stared at him? "Hayden Black hates me. He... He makes my life hell, and that's not a secret in this school. It's a long story, but in short, no, I don't like him. I hate him."

"Oh. I didn't know that. I'm sorry."

Ms. Dawson entered the classroom, which did nothing to silence everyone's voices.

"Do you want to have lunch with me?" I asked, nervous for making the first move. She was new here, and she didn't know my story, so it was a little easier for me to talk with her. She seemed like a nice girl, and for once I didn't want to be unsociable. I needed a friend.

Kayden would be so happy with me for trying to make new friends.

Her radiant smile looked genuine, which eased my uneasiness. "I would love to. It's just that..." Her smile faded a little, her cheeks reddening. "I brought my own lunch. I don't want to go to the cafeteria after what happened yesterday..."

"That's okay. I brought my own lunch, too. So we can go somewhere else."

"That would be great!"

My classmates were becoming louder as the class progressed. There was no discipline in Ms. Dawson's class. The students always chatted, texted each other, or laughed, but she never scolded them. She was one of those teachers who was very quiet and afraid of her students. Nobody respected her—least of all me, because her classes were the ones where I was bullied the most.

I took my pencil to write down what Ms. Dawson was scribbling on the blackboard when something hit the back of my head. I turned around and found a crumpled paper next to my chair. I already saw where this was going, so I ignored it and focused on taking notes.

Soon after, a new crumpled paper hit Jessica's neck, and she picked it up from the floor. I tried to tell her not to bother reading it, but she already unfolded it. She read the words and yelped, growing pale. Her hands flew down to her bottom, checking if everything was all right, but there was nothing wrong.

I glanced behind to see who threw these papers at us. Nobody was even looking in my direction. It was like they were pretending nothing had happened.

"What does it say?" I asked her.

"It's horrible."

"Please, tell me. It can't be worse than what I've received so far."

She handed me the paper, and I read: *"Your ass is so fat it tore your jeans apart. Those are ugly panties."*

I crushed the paper, furious because they bullied her too. "Please, don't pay attention to them. Your jeans are fine."

She could barely look at me. Her face was crimson red, and she tried to hide behind her hair. "Are you sure?"

"Yes. They're just messing with us. Don't read those notes; they're just a prank. Ignore them."

I told her to ignore them, but I couldn't even ignore them myself as the papers continued hitting us. I heard people whispering about Jessica and me, and I hated not being able to have a normal class where I wouldn't be harassed in any way. I spun around, ready to glare at whomever was throwing these paper balls at us, and one landed directly on my face.

The classroom broke out in laughter, and the boy next to Hayden high fived him.

"You should've seen her face. It's too bad I couldn't take a photo of that grimace," a female classmate behind me told her friend.

Hayden's gaze didn't even waver when I scowled at him, and I felt ridiculous for trying to stare him down when it was clear he was the one who was in charge here. He never, *ever* got intimidated by me. To think I could put him in his place with just one glower was beyond absurd.

I spun around, but it was too late. He'd already seen me blushing, smirking in response.

Score one million for Hayden.

• • • •

I WAS WAITING FOR JESSICA next to my locker, just like we'd agreed, but she still wasn't here. I'd forgotten to take her number during English, so I couldn't text her and see what was taking her so long.

Maybe she changed her mind. Maybe she regretted accepting my invitation.

A usual feeling of disappointment settled in the pit of my stomach, dousing what little hope I'd had. I tried not to let hurt permeate me.

It's okay. It really is. If she didn't want to be friends with me, that was her choice. I wouldn't be disappointed. *I won't.*

I took my lunch bag out of my locker, determined not to let it get to me, and headed outside. I stopped at the nearest restroom to take a pee first and went for the stalls, but then I froze when I heard someone sobbing in one of them.

It would be best if I left because this wasn't my concern. I turned around, but this girl began crying so hard that it tore something inside of me. I couldn't leave her like this, could I?

Oh, screw it! I knocked on the stall door. "Hey. Umm, are you okay?" I managed to ask the stupidest question possible. *Of course, she isn't okay, you moron.* One point for my social awkwardness.

The girl stopped whining and sniffed several times. "Umm, yeah... Yeah, I'm okay."

I recognized the voice, and worry pervaded me. "Jessica? It's me, Sarah. Can you open the door, please?"

She didn't react at first, and it seemed to me she was thinking whether she should open the door or not. I expected her to refuse. Eventually, though, she unlocked the door, and I slipped inside.

A pang hit my chest when I met her bloodshot eyes. Her face was swollen from crying, covered by a few damp strands of her blonde hair, while tears streamed down her flushed cheeks.

"What happened?"

"I'm sorry, Sarah. I know we agreed to have lunch together, but..." She shook her head, her gaze trained on the floor. "It was Blake. I was on my way to meet you, but he stopped me and snatched my lunch bag. He threw the contents in the trash can and told me I was too fat and didn't need to eat since I had so much meat on me."

"Bastard."

She finally looked me in the eyes. "Why does he hate me so much? He doesn't even know me!"

I wanted to take her by the hand or hug her in comfort, but my reticence didn't allow me. I wasn't used to physical contact or initiating it.

"That's the way Blake is. He's the same as Hayden, Masen, and Josh. When they don't like someone, for whatever reason, they make them a target."

"I hate this place."

"I'm with you on that. Actually, I was bullied from my first day here."

She parted her lips, her eyes widening. "Really?"

It wasn't easy for me to speak about this so openly. I was too ashamed, and I still didn't want to admit that I wasn't accepted around here. I used to think that if I didn't speak about it, it meant it wasn't so serious. The moment I said out loud "I'm bullied by everyone" it would become more *real*, and I would have to accept the cruel reality.

Still, I wanted to help her and let her know she wasn't alone in this. "Really. In fact, students started bullying me in elementary school."

"The same happened to me. I was always overweight. I know I eat too much! I know I should lose weight, and I tried, but I—"

"Hey, it's okay. I don't mind how you look. If you like food, that's okay."

"But you're so skinny! How do you manage to stay slim?"

I shrugged. "I don't actually do anything. I was always like this. I did start running, but I started because I wanted to be healthy."

She sniffed. "I could start running too."

"Are you interested in running?"

She scrunched up her nose. "Nope. Not really."

A giggle erupted from my lips. "Then you don't have to run, but I won't mind if you join me sometimes. That is, if you're sure you want to give it a try."

She smiled to me, and for the first time after a long time, I felt happy because I could talk like this with someone. It was good to know I wasn't a complete loser or incapable of communicating with others.

"Thank you, Sarah. You're so good to me and you don't even know me."

"Don't mention it. You know, I would like us to know each other better. If you want to, of course."

"Of course, I want to. You're so nice, and you're actually the only person here who helped me." She fished her iPhone out of the front pocket of her jeans. "Let's exchange numbers."

I gave her my number and added hers to my extremely short list of contacts. She was actually the first friend contact I had now.

"I thought you ditched me," I told her.

"I'm so sorry. I wanted to send you a message, but I didn't have your number."

"Yeah."

"I hate Blake."

"I know."

"He is the worst."

"Wait until you get to know Hayden, Josh, and Masen."

"All the girls just swoon over them."

"That's because they only see their appearance. They see alluring, decorative paper wrapped around their rotten personalities."

"That's awful."

I sighed, tucking a loose strand of my hair behind my ear. "Yeah, it is."

I found it unbelievably easy to chit-chat with her, growing more relaxed with each passing second, and somehow, I didn't feel dejected anymore.

She wiped off the tears from her face. "What are we going to do now?"

Maybe it wasn't too late for me to have a friend. Maybe Jessica could become my best friend one day. I had to hope for the best, in spite of everything.

"We're going to stick together."

Chapter 7

MY LAST PERIOD WAS computer science, and the feeling in my gut told me Hayden would be there because we shared almost every Tech Ed class until now. Unlike Kayden, who had been interested in video games but not technology itself, Hayden's specialties were computers and programming. Being an amazing football player and a tech whiz were two of his several talents.

I hated programming, and I was terrible with computer languages, which was another thing Hayden liked to taunt me about. I entered the classroom, and it was like déjà vu. There were no free seats, just like yesterday in calculus.

Only one unoccupied seat remained and it was right next to Hayden.

Oh no.

I couldn't believe I'd have to spend the whole term with Hayden sitting right next to me! This had to be a cruel joke.

He sat in a reclined position, gazing through the window with his hands clasped behind his head and elbows spread out. I just stood and observed his profile—his straight nose, a clear line of his defined jaw, his delectably-curved lips...

I looked away, aware I was staring. My cheeks warmed instantly, and I cursed myself for being so dumb. I despised him, and I didn't need to ogle him, no matter how beautiful he looked.

I drew a long, shaky breath and moved to that empty seat, each step heavy. Knowing Hayden, I expected him to tell me I couldn't sit there. He turned his head in my direction, finally noticing me, and his eyes narrowed instantly. I swallowed with difficulty, my palms already becoming sweaty.

No. I couldn't do this. I couldn't sit next to him. I halted half-way, attracting everyone's attention. As if on cue, the hushed whispers broke out all around me, and I hated being in the spotlight again.

"I'm so lucky today. A fly just got caught in a spider's web," Hayden said in a loud voice.

I swiveled, ready to leave, but then I heard his derisive words, "Where are you going, wuss? Do you want to skip class?"

His words struck a chord. If I ran away now, I would skip this class, and that wasn't good. If I couldn't handle being next to him today, what was I going to do during the rest of this term?

Oh God, I felt sick. I strode to the seat, my teeth clenched hard.

His face showed nothing but contempt. "You look like you're going to puke."

I ignored him and took the seat, only two feet separating us. My skin tingled all over, hypersensitive to his nearness. I was too aware of him sitting so close to me, too uncomfortable. I focused on turning my computer on, noticing his incessant staring from the corner of my eye. My blush was glued to my cheeks, not going away anytime soon.

"I'm going to enjoy this year as I press your buttons and see you squirm." I flinched at his double entendre.

Ms. Clare walked into our classroom, saving me from thinking about the appropriate comeback or reaction. She started class with an explanation of the curriculum and announced she would assign us to work in pairs on a computer project. I tensed in terror because that meant I'd have to work with someone.

I dreaded projects I had to do in pairs. Since I had no friends, spending time with someone who didn't want to be paired with me could be frustrating. Besides, it seemed that everyone in this classroom was friends with someone, so they would have no problem finding their partner for this assignment. I'd prefer to work alone, but I knew Ms. Clare wouldn't allow it.

"Your pair is going to be the person sitting next to you. Since we have four students in each row, you know how it goes—AB AB," Ms. Clare said.

I gaped at her, not believing this was happening to me. She couldn't be pairing us according to the way we were sitting! She just couldn't!

On my left, two classmates, who were seemingly best friends, high fived each other. I reluctantly met Hayden's gaze.

"It seems destiny brought us together," he mocked me.

He found this amusing, enjoying seeing me like this. He knew I didn't want to be anywhere near him, so spending the next term working on a project with him was more than just a nightmare. It was absolutely impossible.

I debated with myself about whether I should object or not. I didn't want to attract unnecessary attention, but I also didn't want to work with Hayden.

In the end, the desire for freedom prevailed.

"Ms. Clare?" I raised my hand to catch her gaze.

"Yes, Sarah?"

"Can I change my partner?"

Everyone looked at me, eager to see what would happen next. Hayden snorted, but I maintained a neutral face, pretending I wasn't perturbed by his gloating.

"Why would you like to change your partner, Sarah? Hayden is great at this subject, and his grades are always among the best."

Yes, I was well aware of how good Hayden was. The funny thing was that he never studied. He was the type of person who needed to read something once to have it completely memorized. It took a genius to do that, and I always wondered if Hayden really was one.

That was another difference between Hayden and Kay. Kayden had been a good student too, but he'd always studied. He'd been passionate about broadening his knowledge and crazy about science, which I found admirable.

Hayden had great marks, but I never saw him studying. I asked Kayden about that once, and he told me Hayden was extremely smart. He was able to memorize incredibly fast and store a lot of information at the same time.

Unlike the rest of us mortals, Hayden didn't spend much time preparing for exams. Instead, he chose to waste his time drinking, smoking with his friends, street racing, and hooking up with girls.

"I don't get along with Hayden," I told her, though I was sure she already knew our history. Even our teachers were well aware we were enemies.

"All the more reason for you to be together, Sarah. It will be an opportunity for you to try and solve your issues."

Oh hell no. She couldn't be trying to solve the bullying problem by putting the bully and the victim together!

That approach never solved anything. In fact, it made things worse. Were teachers even aware of how traumatic it could be for victims to have to spend so much time next to their tormentors? They just couldn't be put together. It was like water and oil. They didn't mix.

"Please, Ms. Clare. Isn't there anyone else I can pair with?"

Her displeasure was evident on her middle-aged face. "As you can see, Sarah, everyone has their partner. You can't get a new partner."

"Can I work alone then?" I was clutching at straws now.

A couple of students snickered, and I could already imagine the gossip they would probably spread about me by tomorrow.

Ms. Clare's frown was a clear-enough message. She wouldn't let me work alone. "Sarah, you need a partner for this computer project. You will have to work with Hayden. If not"—she cast me a glare, which brought a prominent blush to my face—"Both Hayden and you will fail this class. It's up to you."

She stood up and collected some papers from her desk, abandoning the topic. Hayden's eyes dared me to give up. It was like he didn't care whether he would fail or not. I couldn't fail. If I failed, I might never have any chance of getting into Yale.

"The themes of your projects and the guidelines are on the papers I'm going to give you now. Your projects must be done until the end of this semester. I want you to think carefully about your themes and send me the outline of your project by the end of September."

No. The deadline for the outline was too soon. How in the world would I manage to get along with Hayden long enough to deliver that outline in time? He wouldn't cooperate, that was for sure.

She handed the papers to Hayden and me, and I read the words at the top of the page: "Theme: Building a Website (of your choice)."

"Please, don't make this difficult for me," I whispered to him. I despised imploring him, but what else could I do?

He leaned to me and brushed my hair aside, bringing his lips to my ear. I involuntarily shivered when they made a contact with my sensitive skin. "Actually, I plan to make this extremely difficult for you. I'll hurt you, and I'm going to enjoy every second of it."

Chapter 8

THREE YEARS AGO

Kayden kept coming to my house, and I had to hand it to him for being persistent and willing to help despite my reticence. After many years of bullying, I simply didn't know how to be sociable. If I showed my feelings, it felt unnatural. It made me feel naked, and I couldn't fend off shame or fear. So it was completely out of the question to truly open my heart to someone.

This was maybe the reason why I couldn't find any friends, on top of being unpopular.

Kay was ever so nice. He helped my mom and me a lot, moving our furniture, whitewashing our rooms, fixing some electronics, and cleaning with me. We got to know each other little by little and discovered we both liked anime and manga, playing video games, and studying.

We moved into our new house by the end of July, and in the beginning of August, Kay invited me to his house for the first time. I was on edge because I'd never been in a boy's room before, and the moment I entered, I felt like I'd stepped into a completely different world. I was excited and curious, trying to take in all the details.

I was blown away by two things. Firstly, I was surrounded by so many books, which were stacked on his shelf, nightstand, and desk. It completely debunked my belief that boys didn't read at all. Secondly, his room was quite neat. I'd thought boys were messy beings who left their clothes all over the floor, didn't make their bed, and couldn't care less about the piles of dust on their furniture. Either he'd cleaned it thoroughly before I came, or he was a clean freak.

He had a floor-to-ceiling bookshelf that was filled with a lot of manga volumes, video game and anime CDs, and astronomy books. He loved astronomy, and he wanted to work at NASA one day, which was a praiseworthy goal. It was extremely hard to become a NASA employee, but Kayden's strong will and determination made me feel like everything was possible.

An Xbox and a big flat screen TV stood in the corner next to his bed. We spent the time together in his room playing *Alan Wake*, and it was a memory

I would keep stored in a special place forever, sprinkled with the moments of shared laughter and mutual understanding.

Kayden never made fun of me for being reserved. He never said anything about my blushing, my nervousness around him, or my social awkwardness. He gave me time and space to get the courage to tell him about my problems on my own. The more I spent time with him, the more I saw how amazing he was, so it only felt natural to get closer to him.

His brother was his complete opposite. It was clear they were like Yin and Yang. They shared the same appearance, but everything else was utterly different. Yet together they made a whole. No matter how much they fought over different things or didn't get along, I could clearly see they loved each other. It was a kind of love I would never understand because only people who had been together in the womb could feel connected in that way.

Hayden was a mystery to me. He was difficult all right, but there was more to him than what he allowed everyone to see. He wasn't an open book like Kay. He was similar to me because he chose to be reticent, paying close attention to the rest of the world, but sometimes he couldn't control the intense, contradictory emotions brewing in him, lashing out on everyone around him.

He rarely spoke to me when I was in their house, but when he did, he threw insults at me. He liked rock music, just like me, and I actually enjoyed listening to Breaking Benjamin's songs coming from his room. I was in his room only once because Kay insisted to show me his brother's room while he was away.

I was surprised to see the black walls, which were an obvious contrast to Kayden's room, with lyrics and poems taped to some parts. There were many CDs scattered on the floor, out of their cases, creating a messy path to the stereo system in the corner. There was a unique fragrance in the air that was all Hayden, and it stirred my insides.

His Mac on his desk was surrounded by numerous sticky notes containing some programming language. A tall tower of books occupied the space next to his bed, which was across from his small shelf that contained several football helmets, trophies, and framed photos of him on various football fields.

I was intrigued by his room. On one hand, it had *something* that made me feel like I could relate to Hayden—like I belonged there. We both had darkness inside of us. Both of us were so much more than what we showed to others. On the other hand, his room was in complete disorder. It was like a combination of so many different styles and tastes, put in one tiny box. His room displayed inconsistency, and it didn't show who he was.

I tried getting him out of my head, repeating to myself that he was rude and cruel, but my attraction remained, stubbornly standing its ground in spite of my better judgment.

Kay and Hayden looked the same if I excluded a few details on their faces, like the mole above Kayden's lips and a slightly different shape of their chins. Someone else might look past these differences and confuse them for the other, but I felt completely different with each of them that there was no way for me to fall prey to that mistake.

As much as I fantasized about Hayden, wishing I could get to know him more, Kayden didn't attract me at all. He was comfortable to be with and easy to understand, and I hoped our friendship could last, but Kay was never able to reach that part of me that yearned to connect with someone on a much deeper level.

The only "wrong" thing about Kayden was that he was with one of the most awful girls I'd had the chance to meet. Natalie Shelley. She didn't hide how much she disliked me, dissatisfied that Kayden was spending so much time with me. She treated me like the dirt beneath her shoes, which was why I went out of my way to give her a wide berth whenever I could.

I could see this bothered Kay since they frequently argued about the way Natalie treated me, and I didn't like it one bit. I didn't want to affect their relationship, so I didn't talk about this issue with him, hoping that one day his feelings for her would change and he would see her for what she really was—mean, unstable, and sly.

• • • •

THE SUMMER PASSED SWIFTLY, its days filled with a myriad of potent feelings I'd never felt before, and it was hands down the best summer I'd ever had. By the first day of high school, Kayden and I became such good friends that I still couldn't believe how quickly and easily it happened. I would actually start my new school with one friend by my side.

Not everything was hunky-dory, though. My schedule contained an unpleasant surprise for me, since Kay and I shared only two classes together, while I had all my other classes with Hayden or Natalie. The irony of life at its finest.

I felt like a third wheel as I followed Kayden and Natalie to Natalie's locker, nervous about starting high school. I was ready to go to my class on my own, but Kayden wanted to accompany me, which meant I had to tag along with Natalie and him.

"Are you nervous?" Kayden asked me when we stopped next to Natalie's locker. Her face was blank as she placed her books inside, but I could see from a mile away that she wanted me to leave them alone.

"Definitely."

"It's going to be all right. Besides, you have your first class with Hayden, and it's a good time for you two to start getting along."

Natalie snorted, and I glanced at my notebook, uncomfortable talking about Hayden in front of her.

"How do you think that's going to happen?" she asked him, sweeping her long, light brown hair over one shoulder. "You know he hates her."

"He doesn't hate her." I couldn't understand how he'd concluded that when it was obvious Hayden couldn't stand the sight of me.

"I hate him," I piped in.

"You don't hate him, Sari."

"Yeah? Think again."

Natalie closed her locker door and wrapped her arms around Kayden, leaning her head against his shoulder. He kissed the top of her head and placed his hand on the small of her back with eyes full of affection as he gazed at her. I had to admit that they looked good together.

I never understood what Kay liked about her, other than her looks. Maybe it had to do with the fact that she always acted so sweet next to him and had eyes only for him. Then again, Kayden always saw the good in people, so it could be that he saw something in her too. He'd told me they met in seventh grade when he defended her from a girl who bullied her in the school yard, so I could understand her devotion to him.

"Seriously, Hayden and you are like a cat and a mouse," Kay told me. "I think there's something more going on between you two, but you won't admit it."

For an unknown reason, my heart started beating too fast with excitement, flutters kicking up in my stomach. I wished I could hide my red face, more than aware of Natalie's perceptive stare.

"Please, let's not go there, okay?" I said, not wanting to talk about Hayden.

I'd never admitted to Kay that I liked his brother. I couldn't. I knew this was really stupid of me. It was stupid to have a crush on the boy who did nothing but treat me like trash. I'd never done anything to him, yet he was always angry with me.

"Will you walk me to my first class, boo boo? Please, please, please?" Natalie asked him.

Kay groaned, clearly torn between his girlfriend and me as he glanced between the two of us. "I really want to, but Sari..."

"It's okay. I can go to my class by myself."

"See? She'll be fine." She gave him a sugary smile and planted a kiss on his lips. "Come on. Let's go before we're late."

"How about we walk Sari to her class first, and then we go to yours?"

I noticed a glint of hurt in her eyes, which contrasted the smile plastered on her face. "I guess you're right. We can do that."

Oh no. Not a chance. I already felt unneeded enough. "Don't worry about me. Go with Natalie," I said and moved to leave. "See you later."

"If you're sure. See you."

"Don't get lost on your way to your class!" Natalie chirped in and pulled Kayden away, and I cringed.

Kay looked at me over his shoulder and winked at me. "Good luck with your first class."

"You too."

He glanced at me again. "Remember, text me if you need anything. Okay?"

I chuckled, touched that he was so caring. "Of course," I replied and headed to my Algebra 1 classroom.

As I walked down the hallways, I noticed something different about this school—no one was turning in my direction or sneering at me, and it felt surreal, but mostly, it felt good. It felt good not knowing anyone and starting fresh. Besides, Kay was my friend now, so I wouldn't be alone here.

Please, don't let me be bullied again. I want to have a normal high school life. I don't want to have enemies or any more humiliations. Please, let me be accepted here.

I took a deep breath. Some girls passed by and cast their friendly smiles at me. Yes, everything was going to be all right. With a renewed optimism, I stepped into my classroom.

And I ended up falling flat on my face.

A crunching sound filled the air, and an excruciating pain spread from my nose. Horror veiled me when some people began laughing.

I needed a few moments to understand what the hell was going on. I could swear someone had tripped me with their leg, but it happened so quickly that I couldn't be sure... As I pushed myself to my knees, my mind still robbed of clarity, I sensed something wet on my lips. My eyes flickered to dark red blood on the floor, and I realized it was mine, coming right from my nose.

Oh God. I was bleeding!

Someone's legs entered my field of vision, and I raised my head to see who this person was.

Hayden's face was cold as he stared me down. There was no emotion in his eyes. *Nothing.* "You're so stupid. You should pay attention to your surroundings when you're walking."

There was so much blood on me now, and the pain didn't go away. It hurt terribly.

My legs felt numb, but I managed to stand up. "You tripped me!"

"As I said, you didn't pay enough attention. It's your fault for being such a moron."

His words drew a new wave of laughter from some of our classmates, which sliced deep through me. They found this amusing. They didn't care if I was hurt or not. They just stared and laughed at me, and I couldn't prevent the tears from flowing, well aware that I was making an even bigger fool of myself. They wanted my tears, and I kept letting them have them.

Once again, I was humiliated. Once again, I was the one who got hurt and nobody, absolutely nobody cared. I just stood frozen in fear, like a deer on the road in front of an incoming vehicle, and I had no inkling of what to do.

This was the first class of my high school life and I was already bullied. I was already a victim. I hated this.

I looked at Hayden, upset because it was him who did this. How foolish was it of me to like this person? Was I a masochist or just plain stupid? My chest ached as I stared at him through my tears.

Why? Why do you do this to me?

"Wipe off those fucking tears. Seeing you crying makes me so disgusted," Hayden said in a monotone voice. "Also, with all that blood and tears on your face you look really creepy." He walked over to his desk. I was still unable to move.

"By the way," he added, "You might want to go to the nurse. I think your nose is broken."

Chapter 9

PRESENT

On Friday, I had lunch with Jessica in the school's backyard, finally able to make some good memories in this school. It was a sunny, warm day, the sunrays creating a cheerful atmosphere for the best lunch break I'd had in years.

"We moved to Enfield because of my father. He owns a law firm, which has merged with Enfield's hotshot firm recently," Jessica told me and bit into her sandwich. I waited for her to swallow and continue. "I had a choice to stay with my uncle and aunt, but I was more than eager to come with my parents and transfer to a new school. I hoped I wouldn't be bullied and could make some friends."

It was as if I was listening to myself. Jessica and I were more similar than I'd thought.

"I hate being shy. Sure, my weight is my main problem, but if I knew how to speak to others..." She looked away from me, clearly embarrassed by her confession.

I was confounded that there was someone who was more introverted than me, although, there was a difference between shyness and social anxiety. I hadn't been so withdrawn before. It came gradually, after so many disappointments and betrayals, starting with my own mother. Beside Kayden, I never had anyone who would appreciate me for who I was. I could've been myself only with Kay.

"I was bullied all the time too," I said. "I'm from a poor single-parent family, which is one of the reasons the others made me their target. The more they tormented me, the more defensive I became, and soon I started thinking everyone was my enemy."

"My mom told me not to pay attention to other kids and to be who I am."

I smiled wistfully, wishing my mother could be like that. "You have a great mom."

"Yeah. I love her so much."

At least she isn't completely alone. She has someone, unlike me.

I pushed those negative thoughts aside, not letting them spoil these precious moments with Jessica.

After my art club, I went to the Raymond retirement home, thrilled that this school week was finally over. Since I had to balance school and my part-time job, I was only able to work on Friday evenings and weekend mornings, and it was going to be my welcome refuge. I loved coming here because it was the place where I could relax around people and forget about my problems.

My job was to help the recreation assistant organize activities for elderly people, but most of the time I was here just to talk with them when they needed it.

I learned soon enough that many people in this place felt lonely. They felt like they had been pushed aside and forgotten by their families. Some of them had difficulty getting used to their new lives and living with strangers. They enjoyed talking with me, and I was happy to be able to bring them joy.

It had always been easier for me to talk to older people than to people my own age. I was never nervous around elderly people, which was one of the reasons I wanted to work here. As I developed social anxiety, I knew it would be extremely hard for me to work and interact with people, and the lack of options was demoralizing. As luck would have it, one day I found an ad for a suitable part-time job in the local newspaper, and being desperate to finally start working, I applied without further ado.

"Hello, Mrs. Chakrabarti," I greeted the old receptionist, who rested her head on her hand as she stared at the computer screen. She clicked her computer mouse absentmindedly, and I knew she played Solitaire.

"Hello, Sarah. How was your day in school?"

"Peachy."

She grinned. "You like it that much, huh?"

"Let's just say I don't miss school at all."

"When I was your age, I couldn't stand to be in school. All I wanted was to be with the boy I loved..."

Once again, she began the same old story of how she'd met her husband in India, ran away with him to the U.S., got married, and gave birth to three kids. Mrs. Chakrabarti was a lovely lady, but she loved reminiscing about the same things over and over again, and it was tiring.

"I'm going to find Manny and see what the plans are for today," I said.

Manny was the recreation assistant. He'd helped me settle into my first job, introducing me to the residents, and showing me the ropes.

"A new part-timer arrived."

"Really?"

"Yes. She will assist Manny too. She is your age, but she is from Somers. She starts today."

"Okay." I hoped we would get along. I was the only part-timer who had assisted Manny so far.

"Oh, there is another thing. We got a new resident. Manny wants you to welcome him and make him relax a bit. You see, he seems a bit difficult and not so talkative."

A frown etched on my face. I didn't like the sound of this. People around here were always chatty and kind to me. I didn't know how to act around a person who was "difficult" and "not talkative." I was "difficult" and "not talkative," so how was I supposed to make him relax?

I hoped she didn't notice how tense I'd become. "All right. Which is his room?"

• • • •

MELISSA BROOKS, THE new part-timer, was tall and slender, with enough curves in the right places to make heads turn her way. Her shoulder length raven hair surrounded her heart-shaped face and blue eyes with a shade of white that made them striking and unique. She wore punk clothes, and her voice was rather loud when she spoke.

"How long have you been working here?" Melissa asked me.

"More than two months."

"Wow. You don't get bored?"

I raised my eyebrow. "Why would I get bored?"

"Don't get me wrong, but I can't stand being in one place for more than a month. I get bored easily."

"Why did you choose to come to this place?"

"It was this or flipping burgers at Burger King, and I'm a vegetarian, so you tell me."

"I always wanted to try being a vegetarian."

"It's not something you 'try,' duh. Either you're a vegetarian or not. This is not only about meat, as people think. Like, I'm not going to eat meat so it means I'm a vegetarian. No. It's much more than that."

"Do you like meat?"

"Do you think I don't?"

I never actually thought about whether vegetarians liked meat or not. It was a rather strange thing to talk about when we'd just met. "I guess so," I said and blushed.

"Hey, you don't have to be all shy around me. I like meat, but I haven't eaten it even once since I became a vegetarian."

Now that was a strong will. "Okay."

She was plain-spoken, and I wasn't sure I liked this because I wasn't like that. I didn't loosen my tongue when I met people for the first time. We reached the new resident's room and she was still talking.

"What's his name again?"

"Jonathan Lane. Seventy-eight years old."

"Righty. Jonathan. I have a classmate whose name is Jonathan Lockwood. We call him J Lo." She let out a hearty chuckle.

"Okay."

"He's a funny guy."

She looked like she was recalling something, but I didn't want her to start chattering about that boy now. "Let's see what this Jonathan is like, all right?" I interjected before she could say anything.

"Sure." She knocked on the door and, without any hesitation, entered his room.

"Melissa, wait!" She didn't even wait for his permission. No, she immediately strode into his room. I wanted to slap my forehead in frustration.

I entered Mr. Lane's room with hesitation, instantly unsettled by its miniscule size. Other rooms had wide windows and balcony doors, but this room had only one small window, and it didn't provide enough light. His bed and dresser on which a CRT TV was perched were set opposite each other, and there wasn't much space left between them. There were no usual decorations like flowers or pictures; the bare space was dismal.

This wasn't a room. This was a matchbox.

Mr. Lane sat in his wheelchair, staring absently out the window, his scrunched position speaking volumes about his current frame of mind. His gray hair matched the color of his thick mustache that was the prominent on his wrinkled face. His blue eyes were sad, but the moment he registered we'd barged into his room, hurt ebbed into anger.

"Who are you?"

I forgot to tell Melissa beforehand that Mr. Lane was difficult to handle. I had no idea if she had any experience working with elderly people and could recognize their responses, but she seemed unperturbed by his reaction to us.

"Hello, Mr. Lane! I'm Melissa Brooks. It's nice to meet you!" She offered him a handshake, but he just glanced at her extended hand, not moving a muscle. He sized her up and frowned deeply when he noticed the clothes she was wearing. I could almost hear his disapproval: *"These kids will wear anything these days."*

"I can't say the same," he retorted. "Do you know any rules of common decency? I don't want to see anyone right now."

Melissa obviously didn't get her cue from him. She didn't seem fazed in the least. "We came here to welcome you into the Raymond retirement home." And she kept talking. "We hope you'll have a pleasant stay here!"

For crying out loud! This was not a hotel!

"So far it isn't pleasant at all," he grunted, crossing his arms over his chest, and continued to glare at her. He clearly wanted to be alone, and I wished I could run away. I hated being where I wasn't welcome.

I stepped beside Melissa with an apologetic look. "We're very sorry, Mr. Lane. Please, forgive Melissa. She is new here." Out of the corner of my eye, I could see her shooting daggers at me, but I continued before she decided to argue, "We'll leave your room and let you have your rest. We'll see you tomorrow. Is that all right with you?"

He directed his gaze at me, raising his eyebrows. "And what might your name be?"

"Oh! I'm sorry for not introducing myself. My name is Sarah Decker. I work as a part-timer here." I outstretched my hand, hoping he wouldn't reject my offer for a handshake too. At first, he only studied me, but several moments later, he accepted my handshake, firmly grasping my hand.

"I'm Jonathan Lane, but you already know that."

"Yes, Mr. Lane."

"Call me Jonathan. I feel older when people call me Mr. Lane."

Melissa cast a glance at me which said "He's weird," but I ignored her. "All right, Jonathan. We're terribly sorry if we bothered you by coming here. As Melissa said, we just wanted to greet you."

I caught sight of a chess box on the table beside him. It seemed like it was custom-made, with beautiful floral carvings on the sides and the inscription and the tiny initials beside the handle.

"My wife gave it to me for our fiftieth anniversary," he said, noticing me observe it.

"Wow," Melissa said in a tone of awe. "Fifty years? That's true love, if you ask me. Today, some marriages don't last even five months!"

Jonathan was expressionless as he looked at her before he returned his gaze to me. "My wife knew how much I loved chess. She died last year."

"Shit!" Melissa blurted out and clasped her hands over her mouth. "Oops! Pardon my language."

I frowned at her. Seriously, what was her problem?

"I'm so sorry, Jonathan." What was the right thing to say to a person who had lost the one they loved? There wasn't anything appropriate I could say, so I remained silent.

"I miss her. Nothing was the same after I lost her. My daughter is too busy taking care of her family, so here I am—conveniently put into a box."

"No, Jonathan, don't say that. I'm sure your daughter wanted only the best for you."

"You find justifications for my daughter, yet you don't know her at all. Don't do that."

I blushed because he reprimanded me, and I wished I didn't try to make things better when I was clueless about his situation.

"I'm sorry."

"And stop saying sorry already! You said it hundred times since you entered this room."

"Oh... Yes. I'm sorry for doing that... Oh."

Melissa erupted into laughter, and Jonathan sliced her with his disapproving gaze. "Sorry!" she exclaimed, raising her hands in the air, and then burst into laughter again when she realized she'd apologized too.

"Do you play chess?" Jonathan asked me.

"Yes."

"Let's play it together tomorrow. Would you like that?"

"Yes, of course."

"Good. Now leave me alone. I don't want to talk anymore."

Melissa and I glanced at each other before we told him goodbye and left his room.

"He's sooo grumpy," Melissa commented in the hallway.

"He's lonely and he doesn't want to be here. You would be the same."

She sighed. "Too bad, but I don't know much about troubled seniors. Only about troubled brothers. I have one at home, and he's giving me headaches every day." Her grin was dazzling.

"Okay. Cool."

She couldn't stay quiet for too long. We went down the hallway, and she was already talking about some prank her brother pulled on her yesterday. Did this girl ever run out of steam?

Chapter 10

THE NEXT MORNING, I woke up at six and went for my early morning run, relief spreading through me when I noticed my mother's car in our driveway. She was always out somewhere on Friday nights, so she rarely spent Saturday mornings at home.

Maybe she'd finally decided to slow down and spend some more time at home? I could only hope.

I surveyed the Blacks' driveway and found only Mrs. Black's car. The absence of Hayden's bike and car comforted me, but I couldn't help but wonder whether he spent last night home or not.

As I sped down the sidewalk, I tried to convince myself that wasn't my business. As long as he was far away from me and couldn't hurt me, it didn't matter where he was. He could jump off a bridge if he wanted to, I didn't care.

Running gave me the positivity boost I needed, which was further enhanced with a hot shower that soothed my sore muscles. My mom was still sleeping when I dressed myself, so I decided to leave her a message that I was off to work.

When I found the job, I thought she would be proud of me. I hoped she would congratulate me and praise me for being responsible and diligent. I couldn't have been more wrong.

"That's good, Sarah. Now I don't have to worry about money as much as before, right? You can help me with bills," she said then, which led us to a huge fight.

I told her she wasn't fair since I never asked her for anything and my college saving fund was extremely poor. I wanted to work to save for college, not for bills or food.

I didn't actually mind paying for food and bills. The problem was that if I paid for them, I knew she would spend her money on alcohol, and that wasn't fair at all. In the end, I managed to convince her to let me save for college.

Saturday mornings in the Raymond retirement home were usually noisy and filled with activity. Most of the residents liked to gather in the sitting room to talk, play games, and listen to music or the radio. Since this was the visiting time, the place could become pretty crowded with all their relatives mingling around.

Jonathan wheeled himself into the room. Some of the residents turned their heads to look at him, but he didn't even acknowledge them, remaining aloof. He was like an isolated island in the sea, and I could only imagine how hard it was for him to come here and make an effort to interact with these unfamiliar people.

It could be convenient or wise to send seniors to a retirement home in some situations, but they were literally forced to live with strangers for the rest of their lives.

"He doesn't seem kind," a lady sitting next to me whispered. "I heard he shouted at the staff last night. Tsk. What is his problem?"

"I better go and greet him." I rushed to Jonathan before he decided he hated all these people and gave up on ever communicating with them. "Hello."

He just looked up and stared with lowered eyebrows. *Please, don't do something to humiliate me.*

"What took you so long?" he grunted. "I was waiting for you to come and play chess with me. Now I have to come here, among all these fossils. I would rather go back to sleep."

He was unsociable almost beyond repair. "I'm so sorry. I try to spend time with everyone as much as possible during Saturday mornings and—"

"You are apologizing *again*? Why are you apologizing when you didn't do anything wrong? That is your job, and there is nothing you should apologize about. Don't listen to this bad-tempered man."

"Hello, Mr. J!" Melissa hopped from behind me and waved at Jonathan. *Mr. J?* She was so merry in the morning, how come?

His frown went deeper. "I never let you call me that."

"Oh but it's cool! It makes you feel younger, right?"

"Not at all."

"Oh come on! Now, why don't you and Sarah play chess here? I'd like to see it. I've never played chess in my life."

He raised his eyebrow. "I can clearly see that. Do you do anything con-
structive for your brain, or do you just put those rags you call clothes on yourself and splash your face with heavy makeup?"

Melissa didn't seem offended in the least. In fact, she looked like she
found his disapproval funny. "Well, Abraham Maslow said 'What a man can
be, he must be,' and I fully intend to follow his advice." She winked at him.

"Why don't you bring the chess box from my room?" he asked her.

"Right on it, sir!" She saluted him and dashed away. I stared open-
mouthed at her, not sure if she was on drugs or if that was her usual behavior.

"She is an unusual girl," Jonathan said.

My eyes were still on her. Where was her energy coming from? "Very."

"So, where are we going to play?"

"There is a nice spot on the patio. It's one of my favorites here."

"Lead the way."

· · · ·

WE WERE IN THE MIDDLE of our second game, and Jonathan had the
advantage again. He beat me easily the first time. He was a great chess player,
so compared to him, I was a total beginner.

"I could never understand the fascination with chess," Melissa mused
loudly. "I mean, I get it. It's about strategy, thinking, and smart brains, but it's
so long!"

"That is exactly the problem with the society today," Jonathan grunted.
"Everyone rushes somewhere, not having time for anything. The only thing
they do is look at those small screens and waste their time on the Internet."

"But spending time on the Internet can also be educational!"

"Oh really? Then do tell me, what it is that you do on the Internet that is
educational?"

Melissa started her story about the great books she'd read last month,
and I must say I was a bit impressed since she'd read works of some impactful
and respected authors that not many people our age were interested in.

Completely focused on her story, I didn't pay attention to the game, and
Jonathan made a checkmate.

"You're very good!" I exclaimed in admiration.

"You're also good, but you need practice. With more practice, you can become a great player."

"I doubt anyone can become a better player than you, grandpa," a deep male voice said. "You always beat me, no matter how much I practice."

I glanced behind me, and someone's stomach came into my view. I raised my chin to look at him, a twinge assaulting my chest when our gazes met.

Oh boy.

I was staring into a pair of light brown eyes that looked directly at me. They twinkled with humor, accompanied with a flirty smile. His rectangle-shaped face was model-like, and I was impressed by how prominent and firm his jaw and chin were. His curly hair was a few shades darker than his bronze skin, reaching below his ears.

I whipped my gaze back to the table, my face burning from shame. Why did I have to be embarrassed every time I saw some nice looking guy? I couldn't even look them in the eyes without blushing!

"That's because you are thinking too much about things you young people like obsessing about," Jonathan answered him. "If you used your intelligence on more important things, you would've become a better man."

"Ouch, grandpa. Don't embarrass me in front of the girls!"

Melissa giggled. "You and embarrassment never go together, Mateo."

I gaped at Melissa. "Do you know each other?"

"Yep. He's my classmate at Rawenwood High."

"Yeah." He stopped in front of me, and I had no other choice but to return his gaze. "I'm Mateo Diaz."

I nodded and shook hands with him reluctantly, not failing to notice how strong his hand felt. He didn't break our connection immediately, holding my hand longer than needed, and this made me even more jittery.

I always overthought my actions or his reactions whenever I was next to some guy, and I hated it. I was too tense, taking extra care not to make some mistake and embarrass myself. I was inexperienced with boys, and I didn't know if they found me attractive, annoying, boring, or whatever, expecting the worst each time.

I felt his eyes on me as I pretended there was something extremely interesting on the chess board, and it made me think two things.

He must think there was something wrong with me.

He was probably plotting to humiliate me.

"You didn't tell me your name," he told me, and *dang*, my cheeks were like two tomatoes again!

"Sarah."

His megawatt smile almost blinded me. "It's nice to meet you, Sarah."

I looked at Jonathan who studied me carefully with his chin leaned against his hand. "I think you should play chess with Mateo."

"W-What?"

"What do you think, boy? Will you play a game of chess with this young lady?"

Mateo winked at me. "Gladly. I've never played chess with a girl."

"I doubt you play anything else with a girl beside those games among the sheets, Mateo. No offense, Mr. J." Melissa wiggled her eyebrows at Mateo, and I wanted to evaporate into thin air or become a fly and buzz away. Mateo snorted, and Jonathan erupted in laughter. I could only stare at them, dumbstruck.

"I agree with you, Melissa. I heard my grandson is a real lady-killer. I hope you were not one of his conquests."

She raised her hands in defense. "Of course not! Mateo is not my type at all!"

Mateo placed his hand over his heart. "You're making my heart bleed, Melissa. This is a huge blow to my ego."

"Your ego is oversized, so you'll be fine."

His laughter rang out. "Right. So, how about that game, Sarah?" he asked me, and since there was no way for me to get out of this, I had to accept it.

"Okay. Let's see what you got."

· · · ·

I WAS ON PINS AND NEEDLES, but playing chess with Mateo was fun nevertheless. He didn't make fun of me, acting friendly all the time, and I enjoyed talking with him. He reminded me so much of Kayden. He was also positive, funny, and didn't call me names because I was blushing or being socially awkward. He even laughed at some of my quips. It was too good to be true.

Afterward, Melissa told me Mateo's story, which was pretty typical considering his attitude and confidence. He was one of the popular guys in their school, and he was the captain of their football team. He rarely dated because he preferred casual hook-ups to serious relationships.

Melissa thought we looked cute playing chess together like we'd known each other for a long time.

"Besides, who plays chess these days? Playing it with a cute guy is so romantic!" Melissa remarked.

I didn't care. I actually hoped I wouldn't see him again. His gaze lingered on me too much for my taste, and every time he smiled at me I felt strange. My defense mechanism insisted that all beautiful people had some big flaws. Kayden was the only exception.

I reached my home around noon and breathed out a sigh of relief because mom's car was still in the driveway. I saw Hayden's mother, Carmen, moving some boxes that were too big to be carried by one person out of her house and to the porch. She looked dog-tired. I didn't see Hayden's bike anywhere, which meant he wasn't there.

No, I shouldn't go there. That house was a forbidden territory for me.

I headed to my porch and stopped, cursing myself. *Damn it.* She was fit to drop. Who knew for how long she'd been dragging those things around?

Maybe I could help her lickety-split before Hayden came back. Yes, I could do that.

"Hello, Mrs. Black!"

A radiant smile erased her previous frown. "Hi, Sarah! It's so good to see you! How are you today?"

"I'm good. I just came back from my job."

"That's great! I hope everything is well in school."

Everything is peachy, except your son and the rest of the school making my life a living hell.

"School is good. Anyhow, Mrs. Black, I saw you carrying those boxes, but they seem pretty heavy. Do you need my help? I'd be glad to lend you a hand."

She wiped the sweat off her forehead with her forearm. "Thank you for offering your help. Actually, I'll take you up on it because Hayden isn't here. I told him I'd be arranging the whole house today, but he went to his football practice and then to who knows where. I don't think he'll be back anytime soon."

She shook her head and sighed, her eyes glimmering with concern. "I don't know what to do with that boy anymore. Anyway, you know how busy it can be at the hospital, so I couldn't find any free time for rearranging during the whole summer. I'd really appreciate if you could help me with some things and furniture."

"Sure. What do you need me to do?"

"You can go to my office. There are some books that need to be packed in boxes. I set them aside already, so all you have to do is pack them."

"I'm on it."

. . . .

I JOINED MRS. BLACK in the living room and helped her out with the furniture. We spent the next hour moving her couch, armchairs, and coffee tables around, until she was satisfied with the order. Their living room was huge—twice the size of mine—luxuriously furnished, and bright, thanks to the spacious windows that provided a lot of light. It was almost two o'clock when she decided to wrap it up and invited me to her kitchen for snacks.

"I'm sorry, but I have to go home—"

"Oh please, you helped me a lot. At least take some cookies." She looked so sweet that I couldn't say no to her.

She and Hayden didn't look similar at all. Carmen was short and round because of the extra weight she'd put on over the years. She had an attractive oval face and beautiful turquoise eyes, but her tiredness clouded her pretty features most of the time since she worked a lot as a hospital doctor. Her honey colored hair was always placed in a bun, her face makeup-free.

I assumed Hayden and Kayden looked more like their father, but I couldn't say for sure since I'd never seen his picture. Kay had told me their father committed suicide when they were five, but the topic was too sensitive to ask Kayden more about.

Hayden certainly didn't have his mother's personality, because Carmen was kind, compassionate, and patient. Kayden had taken after her. Hayden was the complete opposite. He was like a ticking bomb ready to explode any second. He was gloomy, and his mood was volatile and unpredictable.

I sat at their kitchen table, feeling odd to be here after so much time. The last time I was in their house was on the day of Kay's funeral. That day marked the start of the worst period of my life.

I lost my best friend, and I lost myself. It seemed impossible to pull out of the depths of darkness, despair, guilt, rage, and hate. Everything was gray. No color. No sound. No taste. No love. No happiness. No reason for me to live.

I just breathed again and again, and each breath was more painful than the last. I desperately wanted to go back and change even a tiny fragment of that day... Of course, I couldn't. I was just one small, pitiful human being, unworthy of living.

Soon after Kayden's death, I touched bottom and started thinking about something that was seriously messing with my mind. *How about ending it all? How about giving up, giving them what they wanted all this time—my death?* These thoughts twirled incessantly, but luckily, I managed to break free from that dark circle.

The following months were painted black. The world continued moving, but I was still there, still in that same hour, still next to Kayden. And at the same time, I wasn't. I was running away from Hayden, Natalie, and their friends, desperate to save myself from their hatred and vengeance.

I'd thought I was dead inside when Kayden died. I'd been wrong. There was still a tiny living piece of me, breathing greedily, desperately wanting to live, but it was crushed day after day by my bullies.

In those days I lost my best friend, and I gained lifelong enemies. Nothing was the same after that.

"I've been thinking you haven't visited for so long. I remember how often Kayden and you were spending time in his room. You were usually playing games or watching Japanese animation. You were such good friends," she said with melancholy in her voice. "I hoped you would come sometimes—"

"I wanted to speak with you, Mrs. Black, I really did." I played with my cookie, unable to look at her. "You know, Hayden and I were never friends, but after Kayden died... It became worse. He became worse."

Her downcast eyes filled with sorrow. "Hayden was always a complex child. As much as I am ashamed to admit, I have to say I wasn't a good mother to him. He needed me more than Kayden, yet my attention was riveted on Kayden."

Worry embedded deeper into her worn out face, and I felt so ill at ease for having to witness her private moment. It was obviously something that troubled her a lot, and it surprised me that she was willing to share this with me. I didn't think I had the right to pry into her life this way.

"I guess it was easier for me to focus on Kayden, who was such a good child. He was obedient, never made any trouble, and his grades were always perfect. He had dreams and high ambitions. But Hayden... He was different from the beginning." Her gaze wandered into the distance, the glazed look in her eyes indicating she was recollecting something from the far past.

"Hayden is brilliant. He is highly intelligent—much more than Kayden—but he is extremely sensitive. Ever since he was a child, he's wanted some answers I couldn't give to him. I never could."

"What kind of answers?"

Her eyes met mine, her face displaying defeat, and my stomach sank. "He wanted to know his true identity. He wanted to know who he was."

I frowned, tongue-tied. I didn't understand why Hayden would ask his mother this.

"I'm so sorry for telling you this all of a sudden. Maybe I'm bothering you. It's just that I don't have anyone I can talk with about this, and Hayden and I are more distanced from each other than ever. I want to tell him all of this, but I... I don't know how."

"Why don't you just try? Even if you fail, at least you tried."

"I tried so many times! So, so many times, but it ends in disaster every time."

I remembered all those times I could hear shouting and crashing coming from their house. It was Hayden and his fits of anger, and it was horrible and brutish. I witnessed it once. Carmen wanted Hayden to sit with Kay, me, and her for dinner. He refused, and after she scolded him, he became so mad that I felt sick watching his ferocious outburst.

He was throwing kitchen utensils around, screaming at us, and calling us names. Kayden rushed to stop him and got injured when Hayden threw him against a wall. It was horrible. Kayden never talked to me about Hayden's dark side, and whenever I asked him about it, he just justified his brother's behavior somehow and changed the topic.

"I know how terrible he may be, but even if he doesn't show that, I think he needs you," I said. "Every child needs their mother. If you truly try and give your best to improve your relationship with Hayden, I'm sure that little by little you'll reach him."

I wasn't certain why I was telling her all of this, because, after all, their relationship wasn't my problem. Hayden was my enemy, so whether he could get along with his mother or not didn't concern me.

Then again, I understood what it was like not to have a mother when you needed her. I understood what it was like to have the need to tell her something—about life, dreams, fears—but you couldn't because the gap was too big, and you couldn't grow wings and cross it.

"Thank you, Sarah. You—" Her phone rang, and she picked it up from the table, frowning at the screen when she saw the caller ID. "Sorry, I have to answer this. Hello, Jack. What's going on?"

She listened intently to him, her frown getting deeper. "Jesus, can't they do anything without me for one day? Wait, I'll search for those documents in my office..." She looked at me. "Will you just wait, Sarah? They called me from work, so this might take a while..."

She got up, not even waiting for my answer. "Please, make yourself at home."

I wanted to tell her it was time for me to leave, but she was already gone, and I wasn't sure what to do. It wouldn't be okay to leave without saying goodbye to her. Maybe I could wait for her to finish her call. Maybe it wouldn't really take long.

I sat in silence for several minutes, relieved that Hayden still didn't arrive. I stayed here longer than I intended, and I wasn't ready to see him if my short-lived luck decided to turn its back on me now. I was never ready to see him.

Quite unexpectedly, a strange thought constructed a path into my mind, nearly stealing my breath.

I could quickly go upstairs and see Kay's room.

The pain came to life in my chest. No. I couldn't do that.

But then... I miss him.

I missed Kayden so much. There was nothing left of him anymore. In a moment of great anguish, I destroyed all the things he'd bought me as presents, which were mercilessly reminding me of him, and I deleted all photos, because I couldn't stand seeing his happy face. It was silently accusing me of killing him.

I could never get over blaming myself for his death. Maybe I didn't pull the trigger, but I brought the gun, and he died because I was so careless.

Now I needed anything that was his, just to remind myself that he'd been real. I needed to remember the happy times we'd spent together.

The more I thought about this crazy idea, the more I wanted to do it. I *needed* to go and see if his room was the same as it had been when he was alive.

I walked out of the kitchen, Carmen's distant voice reaching me from her office. I glanced at their front yard to check if Hayden arrived before I raced up their stairs.

Kayden's room was the second room on the right, directly across Hayden's. I took a deep breath as I studied Kay's door, assuring myself I would just take a quick peek.

I turned the knob and pushed his door open, thankful that they weren't keeping it locked. As I stepped inside his neat, bright room, Kay's lavender-vanilla scent hit my nostrils, and pain infused my chest. His smell was *still* present in here.

I looked around and noticed that everything was exactly the same. His bed was made, every single volume of his mangas occupied the bookshelf, and the video game CDs stood on a cube box shelf next to his Xbox. Even his controllers were there, left in the same place on the floor where he'd always kept them. It seemed like the room was regularly cleaned since there was no dust on the furniture.

Kay's telescope, which he'd bought several months before he died, stood next to his window, directed toward the sky. I clearly remembered his excitement when he showed it to me for the first time. He wanted me to look through it again and again, excited like a small child.

He kept talking about constellations, and I wasn't actually paying attention to his words because the topic was a bit boring for me at that time... Now

I wanted nothing more than to hear him talk about the stars and see his eyes shine with joy.

I stopped next to his telescope, looking through the window. The sky was clear, at contrast to the bleakness in me that confined me. What would Kay do at this moment if he were alive? He would probably put his shoulder to the wheel to complete his aerospace college applications. He would participate in many projects and seminars. He would have everything prepared in advance and he...

Tears appeared in my eyes, and I couldn't breathe. I wiped them off, but they kept coming. I knew this was neither the time nor the place to cry, but this room made me feel broken.

Coming to Kay's room was a mistake, after all.

It made everything worse. It was painful to look around his room and see that everything was the same, but Kayden would never appear in that doorway. No.

This was definitely a mistake.

This room suffocated me with its emptiness, and I needed to get out... I swiveled, ready to bolt, and stopped dead in my tracks.

Hayden stood at the threshold. He stared at me with murder in his eyes, looking like the devil himself.

Chapter 11

NO.

My eyes glued to his in fear. They were two pits of rage as he glared at me, his body shuddering. I stepped backward, and he immediately followed.

"What are you fucking doing here?!"

I flinched, hunching my shoulders. "I-I-I was—"

"WHAT ARE YOU FUCKING DOING HERE, BITCH?!" He pounced on me and pushed me into a wall.

"Why did you come here?" he spat out as he shook me by the shoulders. I was scared to utter a word because even a small mistake could set him off and he would hurt me.

His face was too close, so I had no other choice but to look him in the eyes. He reeked of alcohol and cigarettes, and I was appalled that he was completely drunk in the middle of the day.

"ANSWER ME!"

The blood pounded in my ears. I was so stupid for even setting foot in Hayden's house.

"I was... I was helping your mother... She needed help, so I came to your house—"

He grabbed my arm and yanked me, almost causing me to trip. Without stopping, he threw me out of the room, and I fell on my hands and knees. He loomed over me, but instead of hitting me like I feared, he pulled me up by the collar of my shirt and pressed me against the wall, fuming with rage.

"Did you already forget the last time we were here? Did you forget I told you never to come to this house again?"

How could I forget? On that day I finally realized Hayden was a monster with no compassion.

"You made a big mistake, bitch." Hayden squeezed my neck, cutting off my air supply. "Trash like you has no right to enter Kayden's room."

I couldn't believe this was happening! I couldn't breathe... It hurt. I put my hands against his shoulders, trying to push him away, but I couldn't... All I saw was his face that was distorted in fury.

A sinister voice came from the recesses of my dark, odious mind, telling me I deserved this. I caused the accident, and Kayden died because of me, so this was justice...

"Hayden! Stop!" Mrs. Black screamed at him, stopping a few feet away.

Hayden didn't release me yet, his eyes clouded by ferocious darkness I didn't recognize or understand, and it was beyond terrifying. It was like he wasn't even seeing me, lost somewhere far away...

"Please, Hayden!" she pleaded in tears, just as I hoped for blackness to finally consume me, so I wouldn't have to feel anything anymore. "Stop this madness! You are going to *kill* her!"

At this, his eyes flashed with horror and regret, and his darkness vanished. He released me with a whimper, staggering aside. My knees gave out, and I slid down the wall, coughing, but Carmen took a hold of my shoulders before I landed on the floor and supported me.

He just stood there as his shaking intensified, and I could see the distress on his face—like he couldn't believe what he was about to do. He looked at his open hands, his eyes widening, and he let out another whimper. I wondered if he really felt guilty or if that was just an act.

"Hayden, this has gone too far," Carmen said in a quivering voice.

Did his eyes become teary just now?

He closed his eyes and took a deep breath, his hands curled into fists. "I don't want to see her here again. Do you understand, mother?" His voice wavered, becoming hoarse. He still kept his eyes firmly closed.

I felt exhausted.

He tried to kill me. Feeling guilty or not, it didn't matter.

So much hate.

So much brutality.

No, I was sure he didn't care if I were dead.

He. Doesn't. Care.

Without even looking at me, he spun around and left the hallway.

• • • •

I STARED AT THE CHESS board, in the middle of the game with Jonathan, but I wasn't actually seeing anything. My mind had ventured back to the moment in Hayden's house when his darkness engulfed me and threatened to destroy me.

I couldn't come to terms that he choked me yesterday. Did he plan to go through it until the end?

You saw it yourself, Sarah. That is why it scared you so much. There was something twisted in his eyes that was bordering on unhinged, and I couldn't find any explanation for that...

I felt so empty and alone...

"Checkmate," Jonathan exclaimed, pulling me away from my gloomy thoughts. His rook and bishop were blocking my king, showing me that every single move I'd made was completely wrong. He defeated me too easily.

"You're good," I said, offering him a slight smile, and touched the scarf I used to hide the bruises on my neck to see if it was in place.

"And you are completely unfocused. What is happening inside your head?"

"Nothing."

"Don't lie to me, girl. At least be honest with this old man and say you don't want to talk about it."

"I don't want to talk about it."

"There you go. Was that so difficult to say? People should stop beating around the bush and speak directly. If you want to say no, say it."

"I find it very hard to say no."

"I can see that. Damn it, I need a cigarette." He slumped back in his wheelchair.

"You know you can't do that here," I warned him.

"Yes, yes, I know. Don't worry. I still didn't fall into temptation to buy a package."

"Smoking is completely unhealthy. It's good that you don't smoke. So many people die from lung ca—"

"Cancer," he interrupted me, quirking his brow. "Yes, I know. Smoking is killing us, blah, blah, blah. Everything can kill us, girl. You go outside and the next moment a car hits you. You are dead on spot."

I winced, remembering the night I kept trying to blank out. If Jonathan only knew how true his words were. *Too true.*

"How was your weekend so far? Is there any activity here that interests you?" I asked him, trying to change the subject.

"If you're asking me if I mingled with those coffin dodgers, no, I didn't. I can't stand them talking about their diseases and families. They are beyond stupid and boring."

I wanted to roll my eyes, but it wouldn't be polite of me to do that. He caught my sour expression and glared at me. "Come on. Say it."

"Say what?"

"I can clearly see you disapprove of my words. So if you disagree with me, say so."

Oh, he was really a difficult person!

I was about to answer him when Mateo showed up on the patio, and my heart contracted painfully in response, anxiety overtaking me. I didn't want to see him again and definitely not so soon. He was here only yesterday. Did he miss his grandfather that much that he wanted to visit him every day?

"Hello, grandpa." He slid his gaze from Jonathan to me. "Hi, Sarah." He flashed me a radiant smile, which was a little bit too dazzling for my taste.

One of the consequences of the years-long bullying was that I believed people had some hidden intentions behind their actions. I had extreme trust issues. If someone offered me help, they did that because they wanted to manipulate me and use me later. If they said my shirt was pretty, they were lying. If they offered me a smile, they were actually laughing at me, probably thinking I was an idiot or ugly. And so on. I dissected each of their actions and made negative conclusions. Bullying made me see enemies all around me. It made me become bitter and cynical. It made me doubt the sincerity of Mateo's smile.

"Hello," I replied, managing to curl my lips up.

"What are you doing here? Suddenly, you love your grandpa this much?" Jonathan asked him.

Mateo chuckled. "What? Can't I come to see you if I miss you?"

"I'm not sure if you miss me or someone else."

I looked between the two of them and decided it would be best to leave them alone. I got up.

"Where are you going?" Mateo asked me.

"This is your family moment, so I'll give you some privacy." Jonathan cracked up, and I glanced at him with raised eyebrows. "What?"

"I think that won't be necessary. How about we play another game, Sarah? Mateo can watch." He winked at him. This situation caused me huge discomfort, and I wished I was braver, so I could say "no" and give them the slip.

"Okay," I agreed with no small amount of reluctance.

Melissa joined us two games later, and I was more than happy to see her because I wouldn't have to be alone with Jonathan and Mateo anymore.

The time spent with the two of them felt like years, not minutes. Jonathan went on making cryptic jokes and laughing, while Mateo stared at me too often, asking me about my interests and hobbies. They made me blush every few seconds, and I couldn't hide beneath my hair or pretend I was cool.

"Hi, Mateo! What brings you here today?" Melissa chirped, sitting on the chair next to me.

"I missed my dear grandpa."

She rolled her eyes. "I'm surprised you're such a good grandson. Aren't you supposed to be somewhere smoking and chasing girls?"

"Hey, don't compare me to your brother. Not all of us are douchebags."

"Touché. My brother is really one of a kind."

"Why?" I asked her. She'd mentioned he was a bit of a rebel, but weren't all teenagers a kind of rebels?

She sighed dramatically. "He's rarely home. He usually spends his time with some shady people, smoking and doing drugs."

"Oh."

"Yeah. I suspect he's in some kind of gang, but that topic is forbidden in our house. My mom loves Steven very much, and even if we tell her he's the biggest junkie, she wouldn't have it."

"Your mother isn't doing your brother any favors," Jonathan remarked.

"I know. My folks argue about that all the time. She spoiled him too much. Actually, my dad and Steven aren't talking at the moment. Occasionally, they have that phase when they stop talking with each other because dad thinks he's ruining his life and Steven won't listen to him. Also, my brother isn't interested in college, which makes things worse." Her voice trailed off, and for the first time I noticed a trace of dejection in her.

"He should be careful of those guys he's hanging with," Mateo told her. "I heard some of them are from your school, Sarah."

"Really?"

"Yeah. They and some other guys from Somers are in some group. Maybe it's really a gang, I don't know."

"What do they do?"

"According to some rumors: illegal fights, steal, street race..." He shrugged. "Nothing good, anyway."

"Do you know their names?" I asked him.

"No. I don't hang around them, so I have no idea."

"I tried knocking some sense into Steven, but it's pointless." She shook her head, and we fell into silence.

"How about you give me your number, Sarah?" Mateo asked me straight out. *What?*

I was sure my confusion showed on my face, since he brought his hands up in the air in a defensive manner. "Hey, I don't mean anything bad. If you want to text me, or I can text you..." He scratched the back of his neck.

I watched in disbelief as he transformed from a confident guy into an embarrassed boy. Was he actually embarrassed because of me? Was he embarrassed because he asked me for my number and didn't know if I was going to reject him or not?

"Really smooth," Melissa muttered under her breath. "Asking for her number in front of his grandfather."

He was still waiting for my answer, but with each second I remained silent, he looked more disheartened. Ugh. I didn't want to give him my number, but how could I refuse him now? He actually looked cute with those puppy eyes he made. Was there really any harm in giving him my number?

"Okay," I replied. "I'll give you my number." I really hoped I wouldn't regret this.

He gave me his phone to type my number, and as soon as I did, he called me. My phone rang in my pocket. "Now you have my number too."

I took out my LG and froze when the crack on my screen reminded me of the way Hayden went through my phone on Tuesday. He'd warned me not to keep any male contacts.

It was better if I didn't save Mateo's number under his real name. After some thinking, I decided to save it as "Maria's Hair Salon." Hopefully, Hayden wouldn't doubt that. It was only natural for girls to go to salons.

"Hey, you and I didn't exchange numbers, right?" Melissa asked and looked at me expectantly, her phone already in her hand. Really? First Mateo and now Melissa too? What did I do to deserve this honor?

"Thanks," she said with a huge grin after we exchanged our numbers. "Be prepared to be pestered with my messages." She sounded vicious, and I almost grunted.

Once more, I strongly hoped I wouldn't regret this.

• • • •

IT WAS LATE IN THE evening when Mateo's first message arrived, which created a mess out of my heartbeat. My thumb hovered over my screen as I battled with my nervousness. Finally gathering the courage, I opened his text.

"Hi, are you sleeping? I'm with my friends, and we're drinking... Yeah. I just want to say you're cute when you blush. See you next weekend."

Chapter 12

EVERYONE HATED MONDAY, right?

There was nothing good about Monday. It marked the start of a new cycle of never-ending suffering in Hellhole, making the weekend seem eons away. Thanks to our A/B block scheduling, I was spared from attending the same classes as Hayden today, but that also meant I got to see Christine and Natalie in calculus first thing in the morning. That in itself was a good enough promise of another disastrous day.

I was about to enter the school when someone called me. I looked over my shoulder and saw Jessica rushing toward me, her smile illuminating her whole face. She seemed genuinely glad to see me.

I smiled back at her. "Hi."

"Hi to you too. I almost overslept, so I thought I was going to be late." She wiped a few beads of sweat off her forehead and fixed her loose gray shirt. "Phew!"

"How was your weekend?" she asked when we entered the overcrowded hallway.

It was rather out of the ordinary, taking the horrible episode with Hayden into account. "Eventful. How about yours?"

"Pretty boring, like usual. I stayed home and enjoyed lunch with my family. Actually, my parents make a big deal out of Sunday lunch. Since they work hard and we don't get to eat together during the week, Sunday lunch is rather special. We all gather, eat a lot of food, and maybe watch some family comedies."

I smiled at her, feeling envious. "That's awesome. I'd like to have something like that."

"Don't you have Sunday lunches with your mother?"

I thought about the sullen Saturday lunch we spent together. I was perturbed after I came back from Hayden's house, so I didn't even have an appetite, yet I sat there just so I could spend some time with her, wearing a turtleneck shirt to hide the bruises on my neck. There was so much I could've said to her, but I didn't want to. Not when she was already hugging her bottle of vodka. Not when we didn't have common topics. Not when I was reliving the moment of Hayden's hands on my neck over and over again…

We spent Sunday lunch in similar fashion. She complained about her work as the increasing amount of alcohol in her system made her snappier, and there was no chance we could converse normally. I just scarfed down the food and rushed back to my room to work on my art college applications and the new art video I planned to upload on YouTube.

I tucked a stray strand of hair behind my ear. "Occasionally, yes, but most of the times it isn't anything special or fun," I replied to Jessica.

We rounded the corner, and I spotted Hayden talking to a guy next to him in the distance. My pulse kicked up when his gaze locked with mine almost an instant later. He was impassive, and it astounded me to see there was *nothing* in his eyes—no rage, no coldness, no emotion. *Nothing.* This scared me more than seeing him mad at me.

Jessica was talking about something, her eyes set on the floor, but I tuned her out as we came nearer to Hayden, too aware of his nearness. Each inch of me was attacked with apprehension as I waited for him to do something, however, seconds ticked by without him doing a number on me. Not even a word.

I exhaled a long sigh when we moved past him and his friend and went around the next corner, arriving at Jessica's locker.

She yawned and opened her locker. "I can never get used to getting up so early for school. I'm so sleepy."

My pulse was still quick and erratic. I dared not look if Hayden followed us. "Me too. I didn't sleep much last night."

"Tell me about it."

"I better go so I won't be late for class."

"Sure. See you at lunch?"

I didn't get to answer her, because I heard Hayden's voice a short distance away, and my throat closed up. I could practically *feel* him watching me. I glanced in his direction and found his unrelenting stare directed at Jessica and me as he passed by with his friend. It was unnerving. I held my breath, expecting the attack, but it never came, and I didn't know what to make of it.

The frown lines appeared around Jessica's mouth. "Are you okay?" she asked me, staring at Hayden as he walked away from us.

"Yeah. As good as I can be when I'm near him, I guess. See you at lunch." I half-smiled at her and scurried in another direction, increasing the much-needed distance between Hayden and me.

• • • •

JESSICA AND I ENTERED the lunchroom discussing what to eat. She settled for spaghetti, while I decided to eat vegetables.

"How can greens keep you full? I get hungry right after I eat them!"

I chuckled, shrugging. "I don't know. They're enough for me."

"Well, if I don't eat one big slice of pizza I won't be—" She stopped abruptly, looking in front of her, her eyes growing large in fear.

I followed her stare and saw Hayden and Blake blocking the line. What now? I was stunned into stillness as Hayden strode toward me, awaiting my doom.

"Get away from her," he sneered at me, jerking his thumb over his shoulder.

"What? No!"

"You're not allowed to have friends. I see you two became too cozy and already inseparable. I won't let you have it."

"Why, Hayden? Why do you butt into my life? I have the right to have friends and—"

He grabbed me by my shoulders, and I recoiled, gasping. His pine tree scent was mixed with the smell of cigarettes and alcohol once again, but he wasn't drunk. *Yet.* Either way, drinking so early on a school day wasn't normal at all.

"Didn't we already have this conversation? You forgot what I told you then. *You have no freedom.* You'll stop being friends with Jessica, and only then you'll be able to eat here in peace."

I frowned when I looked at Jessica's ashen face. She didn't take her eyes off of Blake, who was now standing right in front of her with his arms folded across his chest. He looked like he got bent out of shape, his corded muscles shaking with accumulated tension. It was a disaster waiting to happen.

I moved my gaze back to Hayden, seeing red. *When does it end?*

He made my life miserable. I was so small—smaller than a pea—not able to speak for myself or defend myself when needed. I always ran away, and the more I ran, the less I could escape. I became a coward, trying to hide behind the shell I'd built for myself over the years so people wouldn't hurt me, but they did. Oh, they hurt me so much.

Hayden was above them all. He scared me so much that I couldn't get away from him even in my dreams. I dreamed of him embarrassing me, hurting me, *destroying* me. I would wake up disoriented, glad that it was just a dream, only to realize it wasn't. I would get up, dress, and go to school where the nightmare *was going* to happen.

I can't live freely.

He was taking everything away from me.

There were so many reasons to hate him, so many reasons to finally snap, despite being terrified of him. Out of the corner of my eye I noticed Blake grab Jessica by her upper arm to keep her in place and murmur something in her ear.

"You're sick," I hissed at Hayden.

His nostrils flared. "What did you say?"

"You're sick and twisted."

Something flared in his eyes, and he wasn't composed anymore, his blank face becoming a mask of fury. I was shocked at how fast his emotions changed, like from zero to hundred, as if someone had pressed his button. I stood frozen in fear, unable to do anything but wait for a disaster to happen.

Was he going to finish what he started on Saturday? Would he strangle me in front of all these people?

No, he couldn't do that. He couldn't be that deranged. He couldn't hurt me when all these people were watching us. There were many witnesses, so this was my chance to voice my thoughts.

I'd just met Jessica, and however unbelievable it felt, we were getting to know each other better every day. I didn't want to lose this chance. This might be my last chance to have a friend.

"And no. I won't stop being friends with Jessica. I'm fed up with you controlling my life. As I told you two months ago, I'm not your puppet. Screw you!" My heart beat too fast, blood pumping in my ears, but it felt good. It felt liberating.

I returned his gaze, feeling like I'd entered a completely different reality because we stared each other down and I didn't back out. His eyes ate me alive as he sized me up, his heated gaze creating a strange, tingling sensation inside of me, and I couldn't breathe.

I felt an unusual pull toward him, which was difficult to resist. There was no one else here but us. The time stopped. He was too close now...

What the hell is going on?

This isn't good.

I have to get out of here.

I finally snapped out of the enchantment, coming back to reality.

I was seriously dead now. I had to run away.

Still on my adrenaline wave, I gripped Jessica's hand and pulled her to the exit. We left the lunchroom, running like our life depended on it, looking over our shoulders to make sure no one was after us. I could almost feel Hayden dashing after us and catching me, my back and neck tingling in dreadful anticipation. He would grab me from behind any moment and make me pay for disobeying him...

Only, he didn't. Nobody chased after us as we ran through the deserted halls, trying to get far away from the cafeteria.

We stopped only when we reached the library, which was mostly empty, to my relief. I led Jessica to one of the tables in the far corner, and we sat down across each other. I jolted when I caught sight of her face at last. It was wet from tears, her eyes closed firmly.

"Jessica..." I paused with my hand in midair, wanting to touch hers, but I felt insecure. If I touched her, would I invade her personal space? Did she need my comfort? What if she recoiled and scooted away?

Stop it, Sarah. You're fretting over nothing. Just do what you think is right.

And I did it. I held her hand, and when I realized she wouldn't get upset, I hugged her because I could see this was what she needed. She needed someone to hold her and calm her down. It was weird hugging her like this, but it was also nice. I could finally be there for someone—I could finally be strong for somebody else—and that did make me feel stronger.

"I'm sorry for being such a mess." She sniffed.

"Don't worry. You're not a mess. Actually, I would rather cry myself, but I'm still in shock."

Her jaw dropped. "You're crazy! How on earth did you disobey him? You were so brave back there!"

My cheeks warmed half from embarrassment, half from pride. It felt great to stand up for myself, even if it meant I was dead the next time my bully caught me.

"I wasn't brave, and I'm still terrified. I don't know what's gotten into me."

She squeezed my hands in support. "For what it's worth, I think you were amazing."

My grin was huge. "Thank you."

"No, I should thank *you*. I was a coward because I thought about running away as soon as Blake said he was going to punish me for hanging out with you. I thought you were going to ditch me, and I was so scared of Blake that I almost left you..."

She started crying again, which attracted a few glances from others in the room, so I had to remind her that we had to be quiet.

"Hey, it's okay now."

"I'm so sorry, Sarah. You've been such a nice friend so far, and I've done nothing in return. Will you forgive me? I promise not to be a coward again, even if Blake and Hayden do something to separate us."

I winked at her. "Everything is forgotten."

We got out of the library after Jessica bucked up, ready to go to our next period.

"Just so you know, Hayden and you looked way different back there," she said. I halted, bemused.

"What do you mean?"

"I mean, it was kind of hot."

I blushed, looking away. "Hot?"

For some reason, my heart rate skyrocketed, and I hated my stupid reaction. I had to pull myself together.

"Yeah, but don't get me wrong. I know he is the incarnation of the devil, but the way you looked at each other there..."

"Yes?"

"Well, for a moment you didn't look like enemies."

"No?"

"No. You looked like lovers."

Chapter 13

TWO THINGS WERE CERTAIN in this world.

The first one was that Hayden Black hated me.

The second one was that Hayden Black hated me.

No one in their right mind would say he felt even a fragment of anything warm toward me. If he did feel this way, he wouldn't make me suffer each day of my life, and he wouldn't control me and do anything to prevent me from achieving happiness. He wouldn't destroy me as a person, making me completely unable to be who I am. He wouldn't destroy my social life, sentencing me to spending my time within the walls of my own room.

He wouldn't have tried to kill me.

I hated him.

Jessica didn't know our long and complicated history.

The writing club meeting after my classes lasted much longer than usual, so the parking lot was almost vacant when I finally got out of school. I was on my way to my car, planning to finish with my reading assignment and spend some time drawing, when Hayden stopped his bike directly in front of me, preventing me from moving forward. He was dressed in gray jeans and a black leather jacket, and I had to admit this combination suited him more than well because he looked sexy.

His hair was wet, as if he'd showered recently. He probably had his football practice until now, and I internally chided myself because I'd completely forgotten to pay attention to that. I could've avoided him if I knew he was still on the school grounds.

I scanned my surroundings and saw absolutely no one. We were all alone.

This was bad.

"Get on my bike."

As always, his order caught me completely off guard. "No way."

I tried to move past him, but he hit the gas and stopped in front of me again, almost running over my feet. Screaming, I jumped back. "Are you crazy?!"

"Your stupidity really gets on my nerves. Do you want me to hurt you that badly? You know what happens when you don't follow my orders. You. Get. Hurt."

"You hurt me anyway, whether I follow your orders or not."

"Yes, but playing dumb will only make things worse for you. What you did today was incredibly stupid, and I have a lack of patience since Saturday. Now, sit behind me, or I swear I'll upload those nudes online. You won't know what hit you when I finish with you."

I was trembling, seeing the truth in his eyes. He would do that, and he wouldn't even blink.

I sized up his Kawasaki and grimaced. How in the hell did he expect me to climb on that monstrosity? I was afraid of bikes, and I certainly never wanted to ride on one.

"Is it safe?" I asked, studying the back part of the seat. That wasn't even a seat. It was so tiny with barely any place left to sit. It wasn't safe at all, and I would have to sit right behind him...

I shuddered, cornered. I didn't want this. No.

Our gazes locked, and the contempt in his eyes was too much for me to handle.

"Nowhere is safe for you."

Oh God...

He put his helmet on, but I didn't see the one for me. "And the helmet for me?"

"I don't have one for you. You'll ride without it."

The nerve of him! I wanted to scream at him for such imprudence, but what was the use? It was futile to argue that if we ended up in an accident, I would be dead on the spot. I clenched my teeth, trying to prevent bile from rising up my throat. I felt like I'd sealed my destiny. I was going to die and there was nothing I could do.

You can run, Sarah.

And risk what? Another twisted retribution? Either way, I was doomed.

Grinding my teeth in all my hopelessness, I stopped next to his bike with no clue how to climb on it.

"I... Um, I don't know how..."

He rolled his eyes. "Step on a foot peg with your right leg." He pointed his hand at it. "Put your hands on my shoulders for support and bring your left leg to the other side."

I didn't want to touch him. I wanted to run away.

But I knew there was no escaping as I did what I'd been told. I grasped his shoulders for support and climbed up, sensing the hard muscles beneath his jacket. Against my will, I was amazed by the sheer strength that radiated from his body. I put my leg on the foot peg, sensing the hotness coming from the exhaust pipe, which almost burned me.

"Ouch!" I yelped, the pain biting into me when I thudded on his seat.

"Ooops. I forgot to tell you to be careful not to get burned. That pipe is extremely hot."

Jerk. I hated him.

Feeling utterly vulnerable on his bike, I wrapped my arms around his waist. I couldn't believe I was holding him like this.

To my surprise and embarrassment, Hayden pried my hands off him. "You don't get to put your hands on me like that. You'll hold the handles in front of me."

He placed my hands none too gently on said handles. With no warning, he started the bike and sped off, and I barely had time to grab the handles, screaming when inertial force pulled me backward.

"Slow down!" I shouted, but he did quite the opposite.

"Not on your life. Stop giving me orders."

He drove way above the speed limit as we went from one road to another, passing other cars one by one. I closed my eyes since I couldn't stand watching everything move in a blur, expecting us to crash any moment.

I made an effort not to touch any part of his body with mine, but it was barely possible with my chest almost touching his back. I was too uncomfortable on the hard seat, positioned at a strange angle. I could sense his scent, which was a mix of his cologne and cigarettes, but I refused to define it as alluring. I hoped the football practice had sobered him and he wasn't drunk anymore.

I flinched when some drivers honked their horns at us, my eyes flashing open. I was terrified, thinking we were seconds away from a horrible accident. He swerved to the left, and I couldn't stop my shriek of horror.

"Stop fucking screaming!"

"We're going to die!"

"The only person here who's going to die is you! I'm personally going to throw you off my bike if you don't shut up!"

"It was you who wanted me here! Why don't you stop the bike and let me go home?"

"And have you miss all the fun I have in store for you? No."

He entered I-91, and he almost doubled his speed. I continued whining as he zigzagged, switching lanes and passing vehicles dangerously close to them.

Like a bolt from the blue, a laugh barreled out of his mouth. It was dark, and it was feeding itself on my wretchedness, making me even more scared. The only reason Hayden ever laughed in front of me was to intimidate me, just like now.

"Don't you want to live on the edge?"

Was that what this horrible ride was for him? Living on the edge? Did he get off on the possibility to lose his head? It was like playing with death made him feel alive. How could he be so careless?

I didn't understand him at all.

"Where are we going?"

"You'll find out very soon."

"Why are you doing this to me?"

"You already know that."

"No, Hayden, I don't know. I want you to stop acting like a madman. I'm tired of not being able to make a single step without you tripping me and messing me up."

"You are tired?!" He started laughing like a maniac. "*I* am tired of seeing such a stupid, pathetic excuse for a human being that stole my brother away!"

It hurt. For some reason, every single word was like a shard, slicing my insides and leaving brutal scars.

You're not supposed to care, Sarah. You hate him, and you're not supposed to care about his words.

I attempted to shut it out, but it was impossible. It was suffocating, and I couldn't stop my tears, so I squeezed my eyes closed and cried in silence. I really was a pathetic excuse for a human being.

"Are you crying?"

I despised myself for showing him my weak side. I never wanted to cry in front of him, but I was scared to death as the merciless gusts of wind hit my face. He drove too recklessly. I counted seconds until the end of this drive, but it was so long, and it felt endless.

"It's none of your business."

"Everything yours, including your tears, is my business."

I found nothing to respond to that; not that any answer would make a difference.

It took us around half an hour to reach Hartford. Hayden exited the highway, but he didn't go deeper into the city. Instead, he entered route 44 and continued west.

I finally figured out our destination when Hayden proceeded along route 202. The sun was going down, which gradually painted the sky with darker shades, and the change in temperature was becoming noticeable, announcing a big degree drop.

The shivers ran down my spine. It was a physical proof of my unwillingness to be alone with Hayden in the dark.

He slowed down only to turn right at the Nepaug State Forest entrance. As he followed the forest path, I chewed over how he knew about this place, which had been one of Kayden's and my most favorite places. We'd visited it and camped at our special spot that offered a clear view of the sky a few times, always stargazing after hours of forest hiking, which was my unlimited source of inspiration for drawing.

Did Kayden tell him? Did he mention what we were doing here? And most importantly, did he tell him *that*?

"Why did you bring me here?" I doubted he wanted to have a picnic with me.

"Be patient, Sarah. You'll find out soon."

His secrecy only amplified my tension. The relief that I'd survived this crazy drive was short-lived, replaced by sheer uncertainty. Who knew what he would do? Besides, this forest was huge, so getting around it would prove to be a daunting challenge, even more so during the night. Kayden had been the one who led our way, and without him, I would've been completely lost.

"Are you sure you know your way around here?"

He let out another dark chuckle. "Awww. The poor little girl is afraid of getting lost. Imagine what would happen if I left you here."

I shivered, hoping against hope he was bluffing.

The depths of forest were dark and chilly, erasing almost all presence of light. I was wearing a thin jacket that did a poor job of keeping me warm, and I couldn't stop trembling.

"There is only one way for you to find that out. Wait and see."

He took a few turns, following a route I didn't recognize, reaching a path that was bumpier and hemmed in with much denser trees compared to the rest of the forest. I saw a clearing in the distance, which prompted alarms to activate in my head. It was *our* spot. No.

At last, Hayden stopped his bike and turned off the engine.

"Get off."

I was more than glad to obey him, this time taking care of the exhaust pipe. My body was stiff because of the uncomfortable sitting position, and my hands hurt from holding the handles too hard.

I glanced over the deserted clearing, which was encircled by tall trees that looked somewhat scary in night. Currently, they cast a shadow on the ground underneath the sunset sky that was colored in shades of purple, orange, and pink. However, this beautiful view didn't provide its usual solace. I was restless and perturbed by the sight and a rather piercing silence. Even with the sounds of leaves rustling in the wind, it was too silent.

I rubbed my arms to stop the chills, but it was useless, since fear wouldn't free me from its grip.

"Why did you bring me here?"

He took off his helmet. "You had such a nice time with Kayden here, right? Such love birds."

I gaped at him, my heart leaping into my throat. Kayden wouldn't have told him *that*. He'd promised me he wouldn't.

"What are you talking about?"

"I'm talking about the sweet, romantic meetings Kayden and you had here. Did you have fun watching the stars?" His voice was mocking me, as if stargazing was the stupidest thing one person could do. I still didn't get what he wanted to say.

"I never had romantic meetings with Kayden here. We were only friends."

"Friends?!"

He threw his helmet to the ground and stomped toward me. Frightened by his sudden move and the deadly look in his eyes, I bolted and tried to get as far away from him as possible, but he caught me easily. He veered me around and pressed me against his solid chest.

He was breathing fast, already furious, and I was taken aback by another one-eighty in his behavior. My instincts screamed at me to get the hell away from here.

"You were in fucking love!" He yanked my shoulders violently.

"What? That's not true!"

"Stop lying to me!" He pushed me with all his force to the ground, and I crashed on my side, scraping my arms and legs. My backpack fell off my shoulder and rolled away from me. "You loved each other! You were so close—the perfect love birds no one could separate!" He formed a cruel smile. "But death separated you."

I watched him, mesmerized, with tears in my eyes as the rage in his black eyes morphed into sadness and then violence as he approached me. I was terrified of him. His mood swings were happening so fast, and I didn't know what he was going to do the next moment. I didn't dare move from my spot on the ground.

He stopped right above me. "Forget about Jessica."

"What the...? Is this all about Jessica? What the hell is wrong with you?!"

"You'll forget about Jessica. If not, you're both going to suffer, and what you've survived until now would be a child's play."

I wrapped my arms around my waist to make myself warmer. "I doubt that," I said with a defiance I certainly didn't feel. "You already did all the monstrous things you could do."

A predatory grin tugged at his lips. "Now that's where you're wrong."

He pounced on me and pushed me down on the ground, covering me with his body, and I screamed. He held his face a few inches above me, and I could smell alcohol on his breath, which scared me witless. He was drunk all this time? Oh God, what was he going to do to me?

I tried to set myself free, but it was no use. He pulled my hands above my head and pinned them against the uneven soil, clasping them with one hand, while he put his other hand on my waist to keep me in place.

"You can't escape from me, Sarah. You always forget that."

"Please, please, please. Let me go. Please, Hayden, don't do this."

"Do what?" He smiled. "This?" He removed his hand from my waist and slid it upward, coming dangerously close to my breast over my jacket. A second later, he inched it down and over my stomach, reaching the waistband of my low-rise jeans. I felt so sick. No.

"You do realize now that I was actually really good to you so far. You see, I know you're a virgin. Kayden was a fool for not using his chance, but I won't make the same mistake. How about I take your virginity right now?"

He brought his lips to my neck, but there was nothing romantic in the way he kissed me because it was meant to punish me. I felt nauseated, my panic rising along with my pulse.

"Let me go!" I cried out. "Please, Hayden, I'll do whatever you tell me to do, just please... Let me... Let me go!" I burst into tears, shuddering. My kicks were useless. There was absolutely nothing I could do to get him off me. He was too strong.

He reached the edge of my jacket and slipped his hand inside, tracing my waist over my paper thin shirt. I flinched, feeling like there was no material to separate my skin from his hand. It was difficult to comprehend how such a gentle touch could make me so repulsed.

I gave up fighting and looked up at the darkening sky. The stars had already appeared, and I gazed at them... *They were mocking me.* They witnessed the downfall of one pitiful girl who had always been a coward but never herself.

I closed my eyes, expecting that atrocious moment to come any second...
I don't want to live this kind of life anymore. Enough.

A waft of cool air danced over my body, and I snapped my eyes open, finally realizing Hayden wasn't on me anymore. I sat back up, severely shaking, and found him on his knees several feet away from me. He was watching me silently.

"You really thought I was going to rape you?" I was not able to speak. "I never intended to do it, so stand up and stop crying already."

I couldn't move. I couldn't even breathe. *I can't believe this.*

"There is so much I could do to you tonight, but I won't. I find more pleasure in watching you squirm, expecting the worst from me. This was just to teach you not to disobey me."

"Why?" My voice was barely a whisper.

"Why what?"

"Why did you go to such great lengths to bring me here and do this?"

His smile was ferocious. "Because I wanted to stain your memory. From now on, whenever you remember this place, you'll remember this night. You'll see only me, not Kayden."

I looked at him, but I didn't see him anymore. Redness clouded my vision, and rage destroyed any presence of fear in me. I felt high on fury, and I wanted to kill him. I wanted his blood.

"I hate you!" I screamed at him from the top of my lungs, breathing heavily. "You're a crazy motherfucker! All these years you've been torturing me, destroying my life, playing with me like I'm a rag doll!"

I got up, too restless. "You're sick, obsessed with me, and living in illusions! I was never in love with Kayden, but I loved him! There is nothing you can do to take that feeling away from me! He was my best friend, and if I could turn back time, I would change everything! You can keep trying, but you can't ever ruin my memories with Kayden."

I stomped around, unable to slow my breathing down. It was getting quicker and shallower. He was looking at me like he couldn't believe my words.

"Why don't you just kill me already? Finish it! I don't want to live like this. I don't want to have to see you every day for the rest of my life. I would prefer to die, but you don't care. Everything I'm saying now doesn't matter because YOU DON'T CARE!"

I screamed, utterly broken, mad, and lost. I hit my head with my fists, hoping for physical pain to numb the inner one—hoping for anything that would end my suffering.

"I hate you!"

I punched my temples.

"I hate this!"

I punched them again.

"I hate myself!"

Two more punches.

"I HATE MYSELF!"

Another punch, and another, and another...

My vision started to blur, pain encompassing me, and I felt like I was going to faint any second...

Finally.

My body swayed and somehow, I ended up in Hayden's arms. I froze, staring at his chest beneath my cheek, feeling as if I'd entered some strange dream, because only in dreams Hayden would encircle his arms around me and hug me tightly like this.

What was this?

"Shhh. Slow down. Breathe."

Hayden's voice sounded tender and completely unknown to me, and my chest constricted at the softness in it. His hands on my back were soothing, making the cold go away, the warmth from his body engulfing me. I could feel his fast heartbeat underneath my cheek, which was even more bewildering.

"Don't do this to yourself..." He sighed. "Just don't."

He held me quietly as my shaking subsided. I couldn't believe I actually felt calmer with each second I spent in his arms. His thumb rubbed my neck slowly, sending an unusually pleasant shudder down my spine, and in a moment of weakness, I closed my eyes and let myself pretend this was real. I let myself pretend this was not Hayden, and I was not me. We didn't hate each other...

What the hell? Why are you allowing him to hug you, Sarah?

I opened my eyes, disgusted with myself. How much more was I going to be weak? How much more would I let him walk over me?

Stop being pathetic, Sarah. Stop being weak. You're the one who allows him to do this, so get a hold of yourself, and stop being a coward for once!

"No!" I shoved him away from me and took several steps back. "Stop touching me! Get away from me!" A surprisingly gentle expression on his face was gone in a second, replaced by sheer anger. "What are you doing now? Stop playing with me!"

"Playing with you?"

"Yes, playing with me. This is all just a game. Why did you hug me now? Another one of your manipulations?"

He opened his mouth to say something but then stopped himself. For a moment, he looked thoroughly confused. His jaw and fists clenched.

"Yes," he said slowly, as if carefully choosing his words. "This is all just a game."

"I can't believe you."

"You were supposed to get used to it already. After three years, I thought you knew me better. I live so I can watch you suffer. You're my fuel. Your suffering is what keeps me breathing."

His words sounded almost like a confession. A morbid and distorted confession.

"And I don't want you dead. You won't get rid of me that easily."

He was horrible. I still couldn't understand how one human being could say such hurtful things to another. It was worse than anything. It was cutting the person unfathomably deep with no chance of healing. They kept bleeding for the rest of their life.

"You're a despicable human being, Hayden. You're a *monster*."

His eyes flashed with something indescribable for the briefest of moments. "See if I care. I'm giving you one last chance. End your friendship with Jessica and there won't be any consequences."

"No."

"No? Fine. Your decision led you to this." He walked over to his motorcycle.

"Led me to what?" I couldn't prevent fright from showing in my voice.

He picked up his helmet from the ground and put it on, ignoring me.

"Led me to what, Hayden?!"

He sat on his bike and turned his head to look at me. "You'll have to find your own way home."

To my utter disbelief, he started his bike and drove away. Just like that.

Chapter 14

TWO YEARS AGO

Recently, Kayden and I started visiting the Nepaug State Forest, which was now our new favorite place. Each time I came here, I felt like a completely different person, truly lucky to be able to witness the true beauty and peace of this world. My dark past seemed insignificant in the moments I spent surrounded by stunning landscape. It seemed like it belonged to someone else.

Since Kay was obsessed with the sky, we had our special spot, which was a clearing located on a small hill deep in the forest, encircled with tall, dense trees of various sizes and kinds. The area provided a great view of the star-heavy sky, so we liked spending time lying on its ground and stargazing as the susurration of leaves created a calming melody in the background.

We arrived to the woods this Saturday morning so we could have a whole day for hiking and taking photos of the spots we hadn't visited before. By the time we reached the clearing, I was fried and ready to close my eyes and rest, but Kayden had another plans.

The evenings were chilly in the middle of June—especially inside the forest—so Kayden built a fire while I watched him. I admired his good technique, finding it too complicated for me to even try.

"You're a man of so many talents."

He chuckled. "I have to be when I have such a lazy friend."

"Hey! I'm not lazy. I'm just wisely avoiding the tough work."

"Yeah, right. You're always a slacker."

"I don't slack off when it comes to studying."

"I have better grades than you, so you *do* slack off."

"You have better grades than *everyone*. It's like you're some prodigy."

"Well, sweetheart, NASA won't accept me only because I'm pretty. I also must work hard."

I snorted. "Such overconfidence. Who told you that you're pretty?"

"The armies of chicks!" I burst into laughter, amused by his enthusiasm. "They did! Even you think I'm pretty."

I grinned from ear to ear. "And how would you know that?"

"Well, you're head-over-heels for Hayds, and Hayds and I look the same. So, basically, you like my face too."

I glanced sideways, the smile on my face eliminated and replaced with a frown. Whenever we touched upon this topic, my cheeks turned red, showing my absolute embarrassment and reluctance to approach it. I always wanted to avoid talking about Hayden, but he kept pushing me to talk about him for whatever reason.

I was ashamed to admit my infatuation with Hayden. Seriously, how could I even begin to explain what I liked about the boy who did nothing but torture me?

My feelings were based on a presumption that beneath all those black layers, Hayden had a pure heart. They began the day I witnessed his unexpected act of kindness and friendship toward Blake, who was going through some rough patches back then, which showed me a version of Hayden that was a far cry from the version I was seeing every day. It was a contrast like none other, sparking off the emotions and curiosity that remained in me ever since.

I clearly remembered the second time I entered Hayden's room and noticed so many things scattered around, none of them telling me who he really was. One impression remained, though—he was suffering. There was something that troubled him so much, and it seemed like he couldn't find a solution. It felt like he was held captive by his demons.

There were some lines written in red, hung on the wall:

> *"Feeling dead inside, breaking to pieces, but you don't mind.*
> *Forever lost, I turn to light, only to see it's useless to fight.*
> *I scream, suffer, and bleed inside; every single day is a tough ride.*
> *I love you today, but tomorrow hate will prevail.*
> *It's a roller coaster, and you'll never know*
> *What is like to be so high and then fall so low."*

I read them several times, trying to figure out the meaning.

"Hayds wrote them," Kay told me that day.

"What do they mean?"

He shrugged. "He never actually wanted to tell me."

"Weren't you supposed to share everything with each other as twins?"

"Contrary to popular belief, twins don't always know everything about each other. And you know we don't have a good relationship. Hayds doesn't let anyone break the walls he built around himself, despite being lost inside of them."

"Why is he lost?"

"I don't know. I tried to understand, but I'm not like him. I wish I could help him, but only he can help himself."

He was crippled inside, that much I could understand.

He was suffering so the reason he hated the whole world could be because he didn't know how to deal with his inner demons. If there could only be a way for him to snap out of whatever was holding him, he could be free. If we could both remove the shackles of darkness that were keeping us in the abyss, we could be who we truly were.

As I said, this was my presumption, and my reasoning wasn't convincing at all whenever Hayden bullied me. In those moments, nothing justified him being terribly mean.

Was I a masochist or maybe delusional thinking he would change? Did I actually think I would be in that "a problematic boy changed himself because of me" kind of situation? This was such a stupid way of thinking that it repulsed me.

"Hey." I was brought back to present when Kay touched my cheek and made me look at him. There was sorrow in his eyes I couldn't quite comprehend. "Don't be ashamed of your feelings for Hayds in front of me."

"You probably think I'm stupid for being infatuated with him and hoping he would change?"

"I never thought that. And I hope for Hayds to change one day too. No, not hope. I *believe* he'll change. Also, I really believe Hayden will come around when it comes to you. He won't treat you with contempt forever."

"Why do you think so?"

Kay looked into the distance, his eyes glazing as he ruminated on something. "Hayden was always so sensitive. You say one wrong thing and you become his enemy. It was always hard being around him, and only one wrong thing could trigger a whole bunch of ugly emotions in him. He would transform from a good person to an evil person, one moment treating you like an angel and the next treating you like you're the worst. That is why he and I could never have a good relationship."

"Do you know why he is like that?"

"I'm not entirely sure. Mom thinks he's like that because of our dad's suicide."

"Oh."

"Yeah. It seems it left a mark on him."

"How about you?"

"Honestly? I don't remember him at all. His death didn't leave such a big hole in me as it did in Hayden." I pursed my lips, dismayed by their difficult family situation.

"The point is that whenever one person becomes his enemy, they're on Hayden's black list for good. However, he keeps coming back only to those he truly, deeply cares about, despite everything."

"I don't understand what you want to say."

"I want to say that he can't actually push you away, Sari. In spite of what he says or how he acts, he's still keeping you close to him. He tries to push you away, but deep down, he needs you."

My chest tightened at his words, excitement impeding my breathing. This sounded too good to be true. I didn't want to get my hopes up only to get disappointed the next time Hayden hurt me. I wanted to believe in Kayden's words, but I was too afraid.

"That sounds nice, but you're forgetting one thing." I smiled, trying to turn this situation into a joke. "I might not want him then because after everything he's done, I should strangle him, not kiss him."

Kayden bit into his lip, looking insecure. "How about you kiss me?"

I tipped my chin down. "*What?*"

He sat next to me on the ground, coming so close that our bodies were almost touching. "You can kiss me and pretend I'm Hayden."

I just stared at him for several seconds, not sure if I'd heard him correctly. "Are you serious?"

He placed his warm hand on my cheek, offering me a tight-lipped smile. My heart began pumping tremendously fast. "I'll do it for you, if you want it."

I was barely breathing as I gaped at him, debating with myself whether I should accept his offer or not. It was too tempting. I'd never been kissed, and here was my best friend, offering it to me with no strings attached.

He wasn't Hayden, but he had a point. They *did* look the same, and I could pretend for a moment that in front of me was Hayden, giving me my first kiss—

Kay's soft lips landed on mine, not giving me the opportunity to answer, and I instinctively closed my eyes. The loud pounding in my ears made me deaf to everything else. He licked my lips slowly, parting them open, and he slid his tongue over mine. Hayden appeared before my eyes, and I got lost in the tingling sensation that was taking over me. I moaned and hugged him, losing myself in our kiss and forgetting about reality.

Hayden... All I saw was Hayden. All I felt was this warm feeling that was crushing me... It was spreading everywhere, painfully squeezing my heart in exhilaration and making me euphoric. This was all I ever wanted.

He moaned and my eyes flew open. Hayden's image in my mind dissipated immediately, and I saw this kiss for what it really was—a twisted illusion.

No, this is so wrong.

I pushed Kayden away and stood up, noticing hurt on his face. A heavy weight settled inside of me, crushing me more with each passing second. This was so wrong.

I was such a horrible person.

"Oh, Kay... I'm so sorry." I felt something wet on my cheeks, and I realized I'd started crying. Just great.

He got to his feet and frowned. "Please, don't cry. Was the kiss that bad?"

"Of course not, Kay. Your kiss was perfect. Too perfect."

"Then what's the problem?"

I couldn't even look him in the eyes. I was supposed to be excited about my first kiss, but I couldn't when this kiss wasn't what it should've been.

"It wasn't okay for me to use you like this. I feel so dirty... Imagining Hayden when you, my best friend, are kissing me is a complete mistake. And you're with Natalie... No. This is wrong on so many levels. This kiss shouldn't have happened."

He glanced away, frowning. "I know. It was a mistake. I'm sorry."

"Then why did you kiss me? Out of pity?"

"No, not out of pity." He ran his hand through his hair. "Look, I... I don't know what's happening to me."

"What do you mean?"

He licked his lips, still avoiding my gaze. I was surprised to see redness spreading across his features because he almost never blushed.

"Kay?"

He let out a long sigh. "These last few months... I feel different." He met my gaze. "I feel different toward you."

My throat turned dry. Now he looked really hurt, and I was actually scared of what he might say next. "Different? But... But what about Natalie?"

He let his breath out through his clenched teeth. "I love Natalie. I really do. But then I feel *this* when I'm with you and I don't know what to do."

I didn't say anything. I couldn't, fear stealing the air out of my lungs.

"I know you like Hayden. I know you see me only as a friend, and I didn't want to mention this..."

He smiled, but it depicted only his sadness. "But I like you, Sarah. And I'm afraid I can't fight it off."

Chapter 15

Hayden had always been a good manipulator. He was a master of his own mental game, evoking my fear and feeding on it. He'd always played the right moves, which were inducing my insecurity and terror, without even inflicting the physical pain.

He'd left me alone in that forest during the night with no means of coming back home, and it was another step too far. Too many steps too far. How could one human do such things without even caring about the consequences?

I'd been terrified when I couldn't hear the sound of Hayden's bike anymore, left high and dry in the middle of an eerie silence. The sky had become almost completely dark, making walking a hard row to hoe without a flashlight. Since there was no light or the presence of other people, I felt like I was being watched, which gave me the creeps, and I couldn't fight off that feeling.

Luckily enough, I'd had internet signal, so I did my best not to freak out, focusing on getting out of that forest using an online map. I'd taken an Uber ride to get back home, refusing to think about the dent that the Uber's fee put in my college fund.

To my immense relief, Hayden didn't show up for today's classes, so I didn't have to worry about seeing him after the last night's fiasco. I had a hard time coming to terms with it, pushing the memory aside because I was afraid I might fall apart if I reminisced about it any longer. I didn't want to remember the way he played with my mind and emotions by deceiving me with his false attempt of rape. It was downright ugly.

What did he want from me?

My phone beeped, pulling me out my gloomy thoughts, notifying me of Melissa's new message.

"Do you have Snapchat?"

I rolled my eyes. She was persistent. She'd started texting me about an hour ago and had been sending me texts ever since.

I'd been putting the finishing touches to my latest drawing when she sent me the first message.

"HEY! It is I, the Pesterer."

Really? Who used the word "pesterer" these days? Did this word even exist in the dictionary?

"Do you remember me?"

"Hey, I know you're rolling your eyes now. DON'T. You'll go blind."

She'd continued spamming me with her texts, making me more and more anxious. I'd been thinking so carefully about my answer as if I was trying to write a scientific research paper about the black holes, which produced a rather pitiful message.

"Hello! How are you?"

This situation was worthy of not one but two facepalms. Kudos to the antisocial me.

"I'm terrible and heartbroken."

I frowned. What happened?

"Why? What happened?"

"You didn't text me for 2 whole days!"

I could almost hear her whining voice. I'd breathed out, embarrassed for missing her joke in the first place. My inexperience led to awkward social interactions.

"So I waited patiently for you to come to your senses and admit that you miss me."

"But my pestering urge made me send you the message first."

"Hello? Anybody there?"

I'd smiled against my will. She really must be bored.

"Yep, I'm here. Reading your spam on my phone."

"Sarcastic, are we? That's good. I heard the scientists have proved that people who are sarcastic have 97% more chance to live longer than the rest of the world."

I'd burst out laughing. Somehow, I felt nice. I felt *warm* inside. No matter how nuts she was, Melissa was actually trying to befriend me.

I admired people who could easily make friends. Melissa was all that I wasn't. She was easy going, relaxed, and cheerful, which made me wonder why she bothered with me. After all, I was a reserved girl with no social skills.

I replied to her last message. *"No, I don't have Snapchat. It's boring."*

I couldn't admit to her that the reason for not having any personal social accounts was because I wanted to avoid being cyberbullied by my classmates.

My Instagram and YouTube art accounts didn't contain my photos or my real name, so no one knew who the person behind my accounts was.

"Really? Boring? You must be from another planet."

I barely had time to read her text before she sent another one. *"Do you have Instagram?"*

Why was she so insistent?

"Nope."

"Why?"

"Because."

"Do you have Facebook?"

Oh my God.

"Do you even know what the Internet is?"

I was just about to send her some excuse when I heard the front door slam. I jumped to my feet, leaving my phone on the bed, and sprinted downstairs. I was surprised that mom came home because she was supposed to be working her night shift.

Just as I climbed down the last step a loud crash came from the kitchen, and all my senses went into high alert. Scared of what I might see, I bolted to the kitchen and found my mother surrounded by broken plate shards. My blood ran cold.

"Mom?"

Her mascara ran down her face, her eyes bloodshot as she looked through me. She was swaying, standing at a rather strange angle, which conveyed just how drunk she was.

"What do you want?" she sneered at me.

I hated when she was like this. I hated when she became aggressive and despised everyone and everything.

"A-Are you okay?"

"Of course I'm not okay."

Something must have happened at her work. "Why aren't you working?"

She pivoted and opened the top cabinet stuffed with her liquor. She snatched a bottle of bourbon, opened it brusquely, and took a swig straight out of it. It sickened me to see my own mother doing this to herself. She didn't even care that her daughter was watching her go to rack and ruin all the while.

I'd thrown her alcohol away so many times before, but it made no difference. We always ended up fighting, but I could never get my point across, and despite all my pleas, she kept buying it without even trying to stop. That was what hurt me the most. She never tried to stop drinking. She didn't care that it pained me to see her like this. I needed a mother, not this angry, uncaring stranger.

"Is everything okay with your job?" She didn't answer or face me, taking another gulp from the bottle. "Mom, did something happen at work?"

She slammed the bottle down on the counter and swiveled toward me, her eyes filled with burning animosity.

"Will you just shut up?!" she screamed. "I can't stand your voice right now!"

"How can you expect me to shut up?! You just popped up here and you're drunk! Stop doing that to yourself!"

I marched over and reached for the bottle, but she grabbed it at the same time and yanked it. I pulled it back, trying to snatch it away from her, but she was strong. "Give me the bottle!"

"No! Get away from me!"

I lost my grip on the bottle, and she jerked it away, pushing me forcefully into the counter. "What I do is none of your business!"

"You're my mother!" I bellowed. "You're always getting wasted, and you don't even care about me! Stop doing this! Stop ruining us both!"

She slapped me, and the pain fogged my mind. I watched her with my hands curled into fists and bared teeth, my anger rising rapidly. I wanted to hit my own mother. I wanted to make her feel the same pain I felt next to her, both emotionally and physically.

"You will not speak to me like that!" She tried to push me again, but I grasped her wrist, defending myself.

"Don't touch me anymore, mom! Enough!" I let go of her and took a step back. "I'm sick and tired of you! I'm embarrassed to talk about you to anyone. I'm ashamed to have you as my mother—"

She slapped me twice, cutting me off. I met her raging eyes, horrified by the intensity of her hostility. She hadn't held back when she slapped me. She'd made my lip crack when it collided with my teeth, and I could taste the blood on my lips, feeling shattered. *This will never end. Never.*

"Get out!" I backed away, her shriek piercing my ears. "Get out of my sight!"

I darted out of the kitchen, rushing to escape her and this oppressive feeling. It spread inside of me—this blackness, this anxiety—and I couldn't be in the same house as her anymore. I needed to run away.

I grabbed my running shoes and jacket, but I didn't get far, because just as I scurried out to the porch, she came after me. "Where are you going? Come back here, cunt!"

I turned on my heel to face her and saw her charge at me with the bourbon in her hand. I staggered backward, terrified of her.

"You're not allowed to leave the house this late! You will go to your room and stay there. Do you hear me?!" She was yelling so loud that I was sure all the neighboring houses around us could hear her. This wasn't the first time she made a scene, but that fact didn't make this situation any less humiliating.

"No! I can't stand to be in the same place as you. I'm leaving!"

I turned around and took several steps, barely noticing Hayden and Blake watch us from his yard, when the bottle missed me by a few inches, crashing next to my feet on the ground. I jumped aside, yelping, and looked at her in horror. I couldn't believe my own mother threw a bottle at me. *No, no, no.*

"If you leave, you aren't my daughter anymore, Sarah!" she said these cruel words, certainly not for the first time.

This always hurt. Everything hurt so damn much when she had these aggressive-drunk episodes, and I couldn't bear it. I glanced at Hayden, who was watching me, and I felt even more humiliated because he got to witness this. He wanted this. He reveled in this. I couldn't stand that now he had even more ammunition to attack me.

My mother never meant this threat, but that didn't matter. Drunk or not, she had no right to attack me under the pretense of not being able to control herself. Nothing justified the hateful speech and violence.

"I don't care," I retorted and ran away as fast as I could.

• • • •

IT DIDN'T HELP. NO matter how fast I ran, trying to break free from the demons, it was useless. They were always next to me, clutching me, pressing their claws into me, making me bleed profusely. I didn't want to go back there. I didn't want to be stuck living this kind of life anymore.

I had no idea for how long I'd run when I heard the motorbike near me from behind. It slowed to a stop in front of me, and I halted when my gaze landed on Hayden, who removed his helmet and got off his Kawasaki. What was he doing here?

He advanced toward me, but I darted in the direction I'd come before he could come any closer. Unfortunately, my escape was short-lived because he easily caught me and spun me around to face him.

"Where do you think you are going?"

"Let me go!"

"Are you really planning to run away?"

"And so what if I am? That's none of your goddamn business." I writhed against him to set myself free, but his grip was as solid as ever.

"You really are incapable of getting some things into that stupid head of yours. Everything about you is my business. You don't get to make any move without me knowing about it."

I rolled my eyes. "You're not God."

"No, I just own you."

"You don't own me!"

"Do I have to remind you about last night?"

I tensed, instantly disgusted by the memory of his forced touches and kisses. "You don't have to remind me. I remember it very well. Especially the moment when you left me all alone with no way of getting back home."

His hands actually loosened their grip on me, and I used this chance to pull away from him. He just studied me, searching for something in my eyes. I wondered if that was regret I saw in his.

No, that can't be. You're delusional, Sarah. Why would he feel even a particle of remorse when he does everything with the intention to harm you? Besides, he crossed the line too many times.

Taking me by surprise, he outstretched his hand and touched my lower lip with his forefinger. I winced, watching him like a prey watching its predator, expecting the worst from him. His finger moved delicately across my lip, tickling me, and I stared back at him, astounded. I wanted to move, but I couldn't.

"What are you doing?" I whispered, not even blinking as I read the raw emotions in his eyes—insecurity and bewilderment.

I tried to read every sign so I would know where the attack would come from. This was a game for him, and he must be acting now. I knew I needed to get away from him, so why did I still stand in place?

"You have blood on your lip."

Without thinking, I darted my tongue out to lick that spot, which was my usual reaction whenever I hurt my lip, and caught his finger with it. We both tensed at the same time, our gazes locked on each other, and I went red.

What the hell, Sarah? How could you not think at all?

Could I disappear? Like, now?

His eyes were fixed on my mouth, non-blinking as he ran his finger over my lips. His touch was so intimate, and I wondered if I was imagining things. He had never touched me like this before. I didn't want to move, and that was what scared me the most.

"Why are you doing this now? What is your plan?" I asked suspiciously. My questions obviously flipped some switch in him because he dropped his hand at once and looked at me, perplexed.

"You'll turn around and go home."

I frowned. "What? No!"

"Yes. Right now."

"I don't have to listen to you. I have no idea why my whereabouts bother you, but I have no intention of going back to that house."

"Then I'll put you on my bike and bring you back home. Would you rather like that?"

He reached for me, but I dodged him and backed away. "Don't touch me!"

"Don't act like a spoiled kid and go home."

"Why do you do this?"

"Because."

"Because why?"

He raised his eyebrow. "Because I can. Just like everything else I do when it comes to you."

"You're lying."

I expected him to get ticked off or to yell at me, but his expression remained blank. "Consider it a payback."

Of course. He *did* promise last night that there would be consequences if I stayed friends with Jessica.

"What are you waiting for? Go home."

I gave up trying to reason with him. If I didn't obey, he would either put me on his motorcycle and drive me back against my will or follow me around, and I didn't intend to provoke him. I turned and started my sprint back home.

"Sarah!"

I stopped and looked at him over my shoulder.

"I don't want you anywhere near Kayden's grave tomorrow. You got this? You're prohibited from taking even a fucking step in that cemetery."

• • • •

I KNEW HE WOULD SAY something like that. I knew he would forbid me to visit Kay's grave, just like he did for his first death anniversary. However, back then I disobeyed him for the first time and went to visit Kay's grave anyway. The next day, Hayden smashed my locker, burned my belongings in the schoolyard in front of everyone, and started a rumor about me being a hooker, inviting all male students to use my "services" freely.

That particular rumor was not only humiliating but also ironic, considering the fact that everyone knew I was a virgin.

This year? Who knew what Hayden could do...

My mother was already passed out on the couch when I returned home last night. She was in such a deep sleep that she didn't even react when I shook her shoulder to wake her up so she would go to her bed. I covered her with a blanket, cleaned the mess she'd made in the kitchen, and picked up the bottle shards in our yard.

Back in my room, I found several messages from Melissa, but I wasn't in the mood for texting anymore. I sent her a message saying I'd been napping and was really tired so I would text her back tomorrow. Although, I doubted

I was going to do that, still not sure how I felt about Melissa and her overly friendly attitude.

It was already hard for me to get up today. Kayden's death anniversary reminded me of my life-altering mistake, and the guilt I'd suppressed reappeared. The need to talk to him was too strong, creating a pain that verged on physical. I missed his laughter. I missed listening to him talk about astronomy and stars. How could I lose someone so precious?

Why?

In school, students called me a murderer for months after Kayden died. There wasn't a day without their constant insults and hate, combined with Hayden's and Natalie's most vicious attacks. My mother turned into a heavy drinker at that time and became even more impossible to deal with. She would hit me every once in a while, failing to remember doing it when she was sober, and the rift between us soon converted into a chasm.

That had been the scariest and darkest period of my life, but I managed to keep going and focus on studying in hopes of becoming someone better, with a good future ahead of her. I promised myself I would escape everyone, even my own mother.

I also promised myself I would study hard and go to Yale art college. I wanted to show everyone, mostly myself, that I could become somebody one day, and my mother would see I wasn't just a nobody, as she used to call me. I could go to a prestigious college no matter the odds and make the most of my drawing talent.

Soon, I reaped the fruit of my determination. I didn't have social life, confined to my room, but that allowed me to become a straight-A student more easily, which became the only bright spot in my school life.

I entered the school, bracing myself for the worst. I didn't have any classes with Hayden today, but I wouldn't put it past him to go out of his way to exact his revenge in the most wicked ways. He could be extra difficult today, so I would have to work harder to stay under his radar.

I headed to calculus, growing redder under the inquisitive and condemning glances of a few students that passed, which heightened the guilt in me.

I ignored them and entered the classroom with my gaze set on the floor, concentrated on calming my breathing. I could only hope Natalie and Christine wouldn't give me a hard time during calculus.

"She's here," someone whispered and burst into a chuckle, which stopped me in my tracks.

Terror clutched me when I raised my eyes and caught a sight of the blackboard. There, all over it, was one denigrating word written countless times in many sizes with a white chalk.

Murderer.

It was flaring. It was omnipresent. It was stabbing me like a thousand needles all over my body, and I began panting, unaware of the sounds and movements around me as the world blurred. It was too much.

"How does it feel, murderer?" Natalie whispered into my ear, standing right behind me. Shivers ran down my spine, every muscle in my body tensing. I moved to get away from her, but she grabbed my wrists and pulled me back, pressing my hands against my back as she held me in place.

"Running away won't save you now." Her voice was chilling, inducing the worst kind of fear in me.

She dug her long nails into my forearms, and I bit into my lip so I wouldn't cry out in pain, refusing to let her know just how much she was hurting me. I jerked my arms to set myself free, but Christine appeared in front of me and clamped her hands on my shoulders, preventing me from moving. *No.*

"Where do you think you are going?" Christine asked with mocking face. I needed to get out of here.

"Let me go."

"You want to leave so soon? But we've just started having fun," Christine said, grasping my shoulders painfully, and fear took over me. I had to escape. Everyone was just standing there, letting Natalie and Christine get away with this, and it was horrifying. No one would help me. *No one.*

"Let me go! Our teacher will be here any moment—"

"And then what?" Natalie spoke into my ear. My heart pounded furiously, my shallow breaths failing to give me enough oxygen. "You think that would make any difference? You think we would get punished?" She twisted my wrist. A yelp tore from my lips.

"Please, let me go!" My heart... It was pumping too fast.

"If there was real justice in this world, you would have been punished a long time ago. How can you sleep soundly during night knowing someone died because of you?"

I was about to scream, but then they released me, pushing me to the floor before they stepped away. I was a broken mess, already losing it.

The last thing I remembered before I succumbed to my darkness was dashing away from the classroom, running into the unknown.

• • • •

I SAT ON A BENCH IN the schoolyard, staring at the scarlet red scrapes on my forearms that were a vicious reminder of Natalie's brutality. I'd lost track of time, having spent hours on this bench. I was too numb to even move let alone care about skipping classes. My tears had dried a long time ago, leaving only emptiness in their wake.

I knew something bad would happen today. I knew I shouldn't have even bothered to get out of my bed.

Wasn't I punished enough? How much more would I have to endure until justice was "served"? How much more until I could forgive myself and move on?

"I found you!"

I glanced to the side and saw Jessica walk in my direction. She was carrying two lunch bags and bottles of orange juice with a smile on her face. Was it lunch time already?

"When you texted me about this place, at first I wasn't sure where exactly—" She halted in front of me, frowning when she noticed my face. "Are you okay?"

I looked over the students that occupied other benches under the trees, their smiling faces as they chatted with their friends differing from the frown that tugged at my lips and eyebrows. It was such a nice, sunny day, but the sunrays bathing the backyard in warm tones didn't bring color to my inner gloom.

"Not really."

She frowned and sat down next to me, giving me a lunch bag and a bottle of juice. "You didn't say anything, but I brought you lunch."

"Thanks." I accepted it, but I had no intention of eating. I should just find some strength and go home.

"So, what happened?" She gasped and caught my wrists. "Sarah! You're injured!"

"It's nothing." I pulled my arms out of her grasp, unused to someone being concerned about me. "It's pricking a little, but it's not that bad."

"Who did this to you?"

"It was Natalie." I filled her in on what happened before calculus. "Don't worry, that was nothing. It could have been a lot worse, considering today's date."

She frowned. "What do you mean?"

I was about to respond her, but a gut feeling that something bad was going to happen cut into me.

I took in our surroundings, searching for any glimpse of Hayden and his friends. This place was far away from the lunchroom and it was quiet and peaceful, but for some reason, this didn't appease me.

You're being paranoid, Sarah.

I looked at the students on the benches again and spotted one guy glancing at me before he returned his attention to his phone. It looked like he was texting someone.

I shook my head to myself. I needed a distraction from these daunting thoughts, so I decided to tell Jessica the whole truth about Kayden.

"You know, I had a best friend here."

"Really?"

"Yes. He was the best. He was kind and so, so funny."

"Where is he now?"

My chest hurt with long-suppressed emotions. "He... He passed away."

"Oh." Her eyes were big as pools as she looked at me in sympathy. "I'm so sorry."

"Yeah. It's still difficult to accept that he is gone. Today is his death anniversary."

"Jesus."

She covered her mouth with her hand, her other hand clutching the lunch bag on her lap, and I realized that my timing wasn't so good. After all, speaking about a deceased friend and the tragedy behind his death wasn't a topic that should be talked about during lunch.

"I'm sorry for mentioning this now."

"It's okay. What happened?"

I sighed, finding it difficult to share this distressing story. Would she judge me like everyone else? "He was Hayden Black's twin."

She gaped at me. "What?"

"Yes. Here's the thing, Hayden and I are next-door neighbors. I met Kayden, his twin, the first day I came to Enfield. He was friendly from the very beginning, always so sweet and helpful... Soon, we became best friends."

"How about Hayden? Was he your friend too?"

"No." I laughed bitterly. "He was my enemy from day one. I have no idea why, but he always disliked me."

"I guess he wasn't happy about Kayden's and your friendship if he felt this way about you."

"Yeah, and that's an understatement. He did everything possible to hurt me. Anyway... Kayden died when he rushed in front of a car to save Hayden from being hit."

"*Oh gosh*," a sorrowful whisper slid over her lips.

At this point I felt a heavy lump in my throat, and tears began pricking my eyes. It felt worse when I talked about it. It hurt me to say that he died because I made a foolish mistake.

"I was with them that night. The accident happened because of me." I swallowed, hoping to clear my raspy voice.

"What? How?"

"I was crossing the road looking at my phone. I looked both ways before I started crossing, but since my attention was on my phone while I was on the road, I couldn't see that car on time..."

No. Don't lose yourself in pain. Not again. Take deep breaths.

"The driver was driving too fast. He swerved to the side to avoid me, but that led him directly to Hayden, who was on a sidewalk... Kayden jumped to save him a moment before the collision. They were both hit, but Kayden was the one who took most of the blow."

I took a deep breath, barely able to look her in the eyes, and wiped away a tear that had escaped down my cheek, recollecting the moment Kay and Hayden fell from the hood of the car to the unyielding asphalt.

"Kayden died on the spot."

Jessica took my hand in hers. "I'm so sorry, Sarah."

I searched her face for any trace of accusation, but I found none, and it took a moment for this to sink in. She wasn't blaming me for his death. She was genuinely compassionate, which touched deep parts of me that yearned for someone's understanding and sympathy.

"I keep thinking, if only I hadn't been so stupid—"

"It's not your fault." She squeezed my hands reassuringly. "You couldn't know."

"But he wouldn't have died if I'd been a little more careful. It haunts me. I put Hayden's life in danger, and as a result, Kayden was forced to save him."

"Still, he was the one who chose to save his brother." She said exactly what Mrs. Black told me after the accident.

"But he's his twin. Of course he'd save him."

"But there are other factors to consider. Like that driver. You said he was driving too fast? What happened to him?"

"He's in prison. Sentenced to six years."

"Only *six* years? That's—" She froze, and I followed her gaze. Blake, Masen, and Josh were coming toward us.

Oh no. No, no, no. Alarms went off in my head, followed by the urge to pull Jessica with me and run away.

They surrounded us in a threatening manner, which drew the attention of the students around us.

"You think you can hide from us, Sars?" Blake asked me with a scowl before he sneered at Jessica. "Playing friends with ugly Fats? Figures. Both of you are disgusting creeps."

He snatched Jessica's bottle of juice, opened it, and poured the juice over her. *Oh my God.* I tried to stand up, but Masen immediately pushed me back down, and my lunch bag slipped out of my hand to the ground.

"Sit down, bitch," Masen hissed at me.

Josh signaled to Blake, who took a shot of Jessica with his iPhone and sniggered, the sound of his laughter grating on my ears. "This goes online immediately."

"She looks so wet," Masen remarked, his words filled with sexual innuendo, and a few students who observed us from a short distance laughed. It was vicious.

Jessica was shaking, her tears welling up in her eyes. *No. No more.*

"Leave us alone," I said weakly. How could we get out of this? What could I do to make them stop?

"Not until you get what you deserve," Josh responded, his sinister eyes piercing me with hatred that was beyond comprehension. He grabbed my backpack.

I jumped to my feet and tried to take it away from him, but Masen shoved me down again. "Sit down," he sneered in my ear, making my insides crawl.

"Give it back."

My imploring voice did nothing to convince Josh to listen to me. In fact, it fueled him to do the opposite. He opened my backpack and turned it upside down, letting all its contents drop to the ground.

He reached for my sketching notebook, as if he knew that of all my notebooks it was the one that was the most precious to me since it contained some of my most important drawing notes and ideas for new drawings. I watched in horror as he began ripping the pages, shredding them into pieces.

"No!" I shouted at him and jerked upward, but Masen didn't let me move, keeping me glued to the bench.

Blake was filming Josh, who was throwing the pieces of my now-ruined notebook in the air like confetti, and tears escaped my eyes. All my ideas were gone. They were lost forever.

"This goes online too."

I felt like I was going to vomit any moment. I hoped to meet Jessica's eyes, but she was constantly staring at the ground, ashamed and terrified. I just wanted this to end.

A hushed whisper carried on between some students, their pale faces painting my grim reality. One blonde girl pointed at the school, glancing between us and the building as she argued with the girl next to her. She seemed torn.

"Please, no more," I implored. "You did enough."

"It's never enough," Blake said. "You know the date. You have to pay for what you've done."

Masen and Josh picked Jessica and me up and put us over their shoulders like we were two sacks of potatoes, further degrading us.

"Put me down," I screamed at Josh, wincing at the pain in my stomach when I hit his hard shoulder. Where were they taking us now?!

His response was to clamp his fingers around my calves, digging his fingers into them too hard. It would leave bruises.

"Keep talking and I'll break your jaw," he gritted through his teeth silently so only I could hear him.

I twisted to the side to see where they were taking us and cried out at the sight, my breathing turning erratic. We were heading to the nearby dumpsters.

This was *not* happening.

"Say cheese!" Blake took a shot of me.

I just wanted to die.

Blake started chanting, followed by a couple more students, engulfing me with misery and darkness. "Trash. Trash. Trash."

"Put this trash where it belongs!" one guy shouted.

"You hear this, bitch? A dumpster is where you belong," Josh said, a tone of something deranged eliciting the most intense fear in me. "How about we chop you into pieces first and then dump you?"

Masen threw Jessica into the dumpster first, evoking more chuckles from some of the onlookers, but this time I didn't quite hear it. The only thing I heard was the constant ringing in my ears, and it got louder and louder. I was beside myself with terror.

Before I could even brace myself for it, Josh threw me into the other dumpster, and I landed among the various litter, banging my head against the lid. My vision became blurry when I scrambled to my feet, managing to find my footing among the bags of junk that produced a terrible stench. I barely saw Blake take a photo of me while laughing with a couple of other students who pointed their phones at Jessica and me. I closed my eyes, feeling numb.

How could all of them be so cruel? Where was their humanity?

Everything hurt—breathing, thinking, seeing their thrill at our pain... I wished my body was weak so I could just faint and escape this humiliation.

"Stop this immediately!" Principal Anders rushed in our direction with two teachers and the blonde girl from before by his side, and everyone scampered to the side, tucking their phones away. "This is outrageous! Do you have any shame? Jones, Brown, and Akers! I want to see you in my office right now!"

Mr. Xiong and Mr. Smith, my biology teacher, approached to help us. Mr. Xiong picked me up from the dumpster and helped me out. "How are you feeling, Sarah? Can you walk?"

No, I feel weak, and I might faint any second. "I'm all right."

"Do you want to see the nurse?"

"No, I'm okay. Thank you."

"I'm sorry this happened to you," Principal Anders said, but despite everything, he didn't sound too concerned. He seemed like he wanted to solve this situation as quickly and covertly as possible. "I'll make sure the perpetrators are properly punished."

I wanted to snort at that, completely doubting it, but nothing I did or said would change the fact that some people around here were privileged and some were not.

"Are you able to go to your last period?" Anders asked Jessica and me, and I was relieved that he wasn't forcing us to go to his office too.

Jessica looked completely lost and unable to say a word. It was clear that she was in shock and couldn't understand what had just happened. I couldn't understand it myself, but I managed to find something in me that helped me stay sane through this.

I put my arm around her shoulders, surprised at how fragile she felt. Her shivers gave her inner struggle away, so I squeezed her hand to let her know she wasn't alone.

"If it's okay with you, I'd like to take Jessica to the counselor. She isn't okay."

"I see. All right, then you two are excused from your last period." He faced Blake. "Boys, to my office."

Masen and Blake followed Anders and the teachers to the school. I couldn't stop quivering, wanting nothing more than to be far away from here. I could only hope they would at least get detention.

Josh approached me, exuding deranged vibes that paralyzed me, and got into my face. He grabbed the wrist that Natalie had twisted this morning, cutting my circulation short. I whimpered in sheer pain, about to beg him to let me go.

"This isn't over yet," he snarled. "Not by a long shot."

Chapter 16

"I MISS YOU, KAY. IT feels like it's been forever since I last saw you. There are days when I wake up after a terrible nightmare... You would be in it and you would bleed again... There would be so much blood, and I would keep screaming."

"You would say such horrible things, things that somehow feel true. You'd say that *everything was my fault*. I was supposed to die then, not you or Hayden. You had such a bright future. You were a gem. You had such perfect dreams, and you wanted to help the world. Who am I? Nobody. I'm just some coward who desperately clings to her own dreams so she can escape her demons."

I knelt on the ground, holding onto Kay's headstone. I read the epitaph poem on the stone so many times, yet it managed to strike me to the core even now.

> *"Breaking into pieces, bleeding so deep,*
> *wishing I was the one who went into eternal sleep.*
> *You'll never be forgotten, you pure soul,*
> *you left a crushing emptiness, you left an immense hole.*
> *Rest in peace, my dear brother, and sleep tight,*
> *know that I'll always love you with all my might."*

Hayden wrote this soon after the funeral with a permanent marker.

"Even this year, there is nothing new I can tell you... I wish I could finally come here and say 'Hey Kay, I became stronger, I conquered my demons, and I fought against my tormentors.' I think you would be so proud of me because of that, right?"

"You, for some reason, always believed in me. You always thought I was strong and would find a way to save myself—not only from others, but from myself as well. I want to be strong. Not only for myself. I have a new friend, and I think you'd like her. Everything is pretty new since we've just met, but I have a feeling she's a really good person."

My tears kept flowing, and the pressure built in my chest. It was so difficult to breathe as I kept sobbing, curled into a ball. I pressed my head on my knees, trying to find some comfort.

The sky was becoming darker as the sun went lower, which painted it in various shades of purple, while the wind whispered softly in the distance.

"Today was an awful day. This isn't only about me anymore but about Jessica too. She has to suffer too, and she seems so fragile... I don't know what happened to her in her previous school, but I don't want her to become like me. Dark and lost. She still has that light inside of her, that innocence, that *faith* that the world is a bright place."

"Me? For me the world is a despicable place, filled with degenerate rats that live for nothing more than to make you bleed and watch you wither away slowly. People are corrupt. They want to witness your downfall because that is the only way they can bear their own hell."

"How can there be goodness when there is so much hate? How can you forgive a person and give them a second chance when all they ever do is crush you over and over again? How can you wish them happiness when they don't care about yours?"

I looked at the grazes on my forearms, unable to comprehend the venom that led Natalie to do this. Her love for Kayden had turned into something utterly frightful, her unhappiness seeping into me with each punishment she subjected me to.

"I'm afraid of Natalie. She's unstable, and it's frightening me because it feels so real. And I don't know what to do to avoid it. She wants me to pay for your death, but I'm already paying for it. I've been paying for it since the moment you died, and the pain never goes away. I go to sleep with it. I wake up with it. I smile with it. *It doesn't go away*."

The suffocating sobs kept coming, and I couldn't breathe anymore as anxiety drew me in its stifling cocoon. I felt the tingling in the back of my head and soon enough, it spread through my whole head.

"On top of everything, there is Hayden. Hayden hates me and there is nothing beyond that. You were wrong, Kay. You were so wrong."

The image from this Saturday came into my mind, along with that memory of the day of Kayden's funeral... So much pain...

"Can you imagine how it feels to get hurt again and again, and the bully simply doesn't care? Nothing. They make you bleed and there is no remorse, no pain, nothing. They don't care about you. You can die and there would be nothing. *Nothing.*"

I held my head on my lap, keeping my eyes squeezed shut, but saying these words out loud didn't relieve my pain like I thought it would. It made it stronger.

"I was so wrong about Hayden. I was giving him another chance and then another chance. I was always, somehow, justifying his cruelty. I thought he was suffering and lonely, just like me."

"I actually wanted to help him. Even after all those things he'd done to me, I wanted to be strong for him and wipe away our darkness. I wanted to forget everything and be there for him, without asking for anything in return. You would say I was selfless, but now I know it was foolish. You can't build castles out of thin air. Things get annihilated so easily, yet it can take centuries to build them again."

"Do you know what you can't build anymore? The lost trust."

I was still resting my head on my lap, trying to calm down my breathing. A dull pain in my chest refused to go away, but the tears had finally stopped. I raised my head and read the words again.

"*You left a crushing emptiness, you left an immense hole.*"

"I miss you, Kay. Thank you for giving my life some sense. You made me happy. I hope I made you happy too. Thank you for everything."

I finally stood up, but my wobbly legs disrupted my balance. Sensing someone behind me, I swiveled around.

A pale Hayden stood several feet away from me, watching me intensely. His eyes were red, like he'd been crying. I screamed and stumbled, barely catching myself before I fell. Had he heard my whole confession?

"I told you not to come here."

"He was my best friend. I need to be here because this is the closest I can get to him."

"You're responsible for his death. You're responsible for this." He tapped his scar.

I shuddered. Even though I blamed myself all the time, I always felt horrible when I heard this from him.

"That doesn't mean I don't love him. I want—"

"It doesn't fucking matter what you want," he interrupted me and closed the distance between us.

It was clear that he was drunk, and I was chilled to the marrow because he could become even more unpredictable when he was in this state. I wanted to bolt right this second, but my legs were glued to the ground, not allowing my much-needed escape.

"You don't deserve anything. *Nothing.*"

"Hayden, you've caused me enough pain. Stop this. Don't do this in front of Kay's grave. He wouldn't want it."

"Kay, Kay, Kay, Kay... It was always about what Kayden wanted!" he erupted, fuming in anger, and there was nothing I could do or say but stare at him. "Everybody always cared about him! He was the golden child! Everyone rooted for him and hoped he would achieve his dreams! Nobody ever paid attention to the black sheep!"

He stepped even closer. I couldn't breathe.

"I don't even know what my dreams are! Nobody ever helped me find them! Even you! You immediately ran over to Kayden and stuck to him. You were always by his side. Fuck, you even made him love you!"

A tear rolled over my cheek and fell. I couldn't move.

"I hated seeing you two together. Each time I wanted to rip Kayden's and your throats out."

"Don't say these things, Hayden. You don't mean this."

He grabbed my upper arms, yanking me against his body. I tried to move away from him, but he didn't let me.

"You don't fucking know me, Sarah! You never did! So stop telling me I don't mean it. I mean every single word! I hate you. I hate Kayden!"

"He was your brother! He saved your life!" I screamed from the top of my lungs, my voice piercing through the silent evening.

"He didn't care what I wanted!" His shout was even louder, forcing me to flinch violently.

"What do you want?!"

We stared at each other, frozen in time and place as the world turned silent.

Thump, thump, thump...

Our heartbeats became faster, working in unison.

"I don't know..."

Thump, thump, thump, thump, thump...

His furious expression cracked. I basked in every line of his face, memorizing the feelings I saw—sadness, regret, and *want*.

"I never knew... And when I see you... Everything is hot and cold. Light and dark... You confuse me even more."

I became bound to him by an invisible chain. Our breaths mixed and became one as he lowered his head and our lips almost touched.

"You have no idea how I feel," he whispered.

Don't go there, Sarah... Don't get involved...

"How do you feel?"

His eyes didn't leave mine, not even for a second.

"I feel like I'm thrown off a roller coaster. In one moment, it's maddeningly fun. I feel so high. In the next moment, I fall into an abyss, and I feel terrified. I'm lost. I can't breathe. I want to find a safe place... And then, there's you."

His breath on my lips tickled me. I felt tingles all over my body. He was so close...

"Me?"

"You crush me, so I want to crush you. You're so weak, and you terrify me. You don't know what love is, and I hate you."

And just like that, his lips were on mine. In a never-ending moment, he was pressing me against him, savoring me. I started resisting, trying to push him away, but he didn't move an inch. I opened my mouth to protest, but my voice came out muffled. Parting my lips was a mistake, since he immediately thrust his tongue inside. Our tongues met, and a hot pressure settled in my chest, spreading through my every single nerve. Hayden's taste was mixed with the flavor of cigarettes and beer, but this combination wasn't unpleasant.

Daze filled my mind, and warmth enveloped my whole body. His kiss deepened and became unrestrained, taking more of me. Despite everything, I felt feverish and thrilled. There were so many butterflies in my stomach now, and I let myself drown in them.

I stopped resisting, not thinking anymore. His hand grabbed a handful of my hair and yanked, tilting my head backward, which exposed my neck. He broke the kiss as he wrapped his other arm around my waist, keeping me flush against his body, and continued leaving hungry, wet kisses along my jaw to the sensitive hollow of my neck. These unknown, rousing sensations were too much...

Unintentionally, I let out a low moan. I flinched and opened my eyes in terror, feeling like someone had thrown a bucket of cold water on me. This was a serious mistake.

"No!" I pushed against him, and this time he let me go.

I gaped at him in horror, incapable of speaking, noticing the confusion on his face before the punishing smirk appeared. His eyes were mocking me now, and I felt disgusted with myself. I returned his kiss...

If only I could die now.

"Congratulations. You actually made an even bigger fool of yourself." He started chuckling, but it sounded so empty.

I wiped the tears off my face, refusing to cry in front of him, but they kept rolling down my cheeks. *Stupid, stupid, stupid.* How could I be such an idiot?

"Why?" My voice came out as a broken whisper.

"I wanted to stain another memory of Kayden. Now, his grave will remind you of your first kiss and me, who was stealing it from you."

It didn't matter that he got that "first kiss" thing wrong, because he was right when he said I would always remember it when I came here. No matter how corrupt it was, his kiss was affecting me like cancer, spreading through me extremely fast, and I couldn't control it. I hated him, yet the kiss didn't terrify me. It didn't make me feel anything negative, because it was surprisingly good. It was like I'd completely lost my brain, and with it, all my bad memories.

"You know what the funniest thing is?" he asked. "You actually enjoyed it."

His smile of satisfaction didn't last long. It fell, his gaze filling with nothingness, and it was scary. There was something about him—a glimpse of a broken soul—which chilled me to the bone. I had to get out of here.

My legs started moving before I was aware of it, running away from him.

Running away from myself.

· · · ·

*"HEY. DON'T CRY," KAY told me, holding my hand. "It's just a small scrape."
I couldn't believe he was comforting me when he was the one who had gotten injured.* Pull yourself together, Sarah.

*"It's not just a small scrap. Okay, your wound will heal, but what about
Hayden? This time he went too far. He attacked you!"*

"He didn't quite attack me—"

*"Don't defend him, Kay! You always defend him! Nothing justifies such
anger."*

*Hayden's violent outburst started unexpectedly, just like always. Mrs. Car-
men wanted me to stay for dinner and asked Hayden to eat with us. When he
saw Kayden and me together, he grimaced and refused, calling me ugly names.
Mrs. Carmen scolded him, and he started shouting at us. Kayden pleaded him
to calm down, but it only became worse.*

*He began throwing plates and utensils against the wall, smashing them vi-
olently. The shards flew all around the kitchen, and it was a disturbing sight.
Kayden tried to restrain Hayden, but Hayden was stronger, resisting Kayden
and pushing him against the wall. The force of the shove made Kayden lose his
balance and fall directly on the broken pieces spread on the floor.*

*It was in that moment that Hayden finally stopped. He was breathing heav-
ily, watching Kayden with regret. Our eyes met, and I thought he was going to
lose it again, but he just turned on his heel and left.*

"You don't understand Hayds—"

"And you do?"

"Maybe not, but he is suffering. I can understand that much."

"Suffering from what?"

"I don't know, Sari."

"It's like he is not human. It's terrible."

*"Believe me, he's more human than you think. He's actually feeling every-
thing much stronger than other people."*

"I can't understand him."

Kayden's expression was sad as he studied my face. "I know. He's not easy to read, but I believe that deep down he doesn't want to hurt anyone because he enjoys it, but because that's his defense mechanism."

"Well, that's a hell of a mechanism... Torturing others to the point of risking their lives."

"I think he isn't actually aware of the consequences of his behavior in that moment. The anger consumes him and he isn't able to think straight anymore... But, let me tell you this; Hayden rarely gives his heart to anyone, but when he does, that's forever."

He smiled mysteriously.

"What?" I asked him.

"He'll come around. Besides, he's jealous right now because I'm friends with you."

"Jealous? Why?"

I didn't get to hear his answer because my alarm woke me up. I jolted in my bed, clinging to that dream. It wasn't actually a dream. It was a memory of the conversation I had with Kayden a few months before he kissed me.

Even then I didn't hear his answer, because he changed the topic, as usual. I never understood their complicated relationship, and I feared I had a bad influence on it. I didn't want them to argue because of me, so I never told Kay how much Hayden actually hated me. He wasn't aware of how bad Hayden treated me, which could be why he thought Hayden wasn't much of an enemy to me.

I wanted to erase the previous day, especially the kiss. I couldn't even describe how mortified I felt because I'd made such a stupid mistake. It was one thing for him to kiss me, but for me to return his kiss? Ugh.

Wasn't everything he did to you before more than enough, Sarah? Are you brainless? You hate him. Usually, people don't kiss the person they hate.

Exactly; people didn't return a kiss of those they hated, and the same went for initiating it. So why did he kiss me?

To humiliate me? Check.

To make me more miserable? Check.

To confuse me? Check.

I didn't even want to think about when we saw each other again. He would probably tell the whole school about the kiss...

Oh no. He would tell the whole school…

My stomach was a mess as I dressed, and no deep breathing could calm down my erratic pulse. I didn't want to go to school. They would eat me alive there…

Calm down, Sarah. Maybe he won't tell them…

Who was I kidding?! Why wouldn't he tell? It was his latest and probably greatest victory! I didn't know if he was aware I'd liked him before, but now he would think that for sure. He would use that to toy with me!

No, *enough*. I always created these horrible scenarios in my head that may or may not happen, but if I continued like this, I would be late for school.

I brushed my teeth, pulled my hair back into a ponytail, and went down to grab some food. I wasn't hungry, but I couldn't let my anxiety over Hayden's potential future humiliation prevent me from eating. Mom sat at the table, munching a chocolate croissant and drinking her coffee. She offered me a close-mouthed smile.

"Hey," she told me.

"Hey."

As expected, she acted like nothing happened two nights ago. I was sure she didn't remember most of it.

"Are you going to visit Kayden's grave today? It's his death anniversary."

"His death anniversary was yesterday, mom."

"I see." I poured the milk into a glass and sipped it while eating the muffins left from yesterday. "How was it?"

I certainly didn't plan to tell her the truth. "Okay."

"Are you okay?"

She wasn't actually concerned about me. It was more like an automatic question. I turned around to look at her, but she wasn't even looking at me, focusing on some article she was reading in the newspaper. I wondered why she'd bothered to ask at all.

"I'm perfect. I'm off now."

"Have fun in school."

I couldn't prevent a sad smile from forming on my face. "Like always."

I took my backpack, more than ready to escape the sad reality of my own home. What made my life tragic was the fact that the moment I closed the door of my house, I stepped into another sad reality. I couldn't actually es-cape. Everywhere I went, I was imprisoned.

I made several steps down my driveway, double-checking if Hayden was outside. I exhaled a heavy breath when I didn't notice his car, which meant he'd already left. Good. I turned to my car, preparing my keys to unlock the door, and froze when I caught a frightening sight.

No. I couldn't believe this. My front tires were slashed.

Chapter 17

TWO YEARS AGO

Going to Kay's funeral was one of the hardest things I'd done in my entire life. It took me all the courage I had to stand in front of all these people knowing I was the one who had caused this. I'd spent the whole last night crying, and my mother had barely managed to make me come out of my room this morning.

Wherever I looked, I saw doleful faces, all of them dressed in black and standing in silence as we said our last goodbye to Kayden. Mrs. Black stood in the center, right across the patch of ground where Kay's resting place would be. She looked small and fragile, her silent tears pushing me further into desolation and shame. I couldn't even look her in the eyes.

She hadn't said even one bad word to me, and that hurt me the most. Instead of blaming me or yelling at me, she just hugged me that fateful night and told me it wasn't my fault. Just that. It wasn't my fault.

I broke down in tears in that moment, terribly ashamed to be in front of her, and she followed. We cried together for a long time, hugging each other and reminiscing about Kayden.

I glanced at Hayden, who stood motionlessly next to her with his stare fixed on the ground. He was dressed in a black suit and wore a bandage on his left temple, which covered an injury that was certainly going to leave a scar. My stomach turned at the thought. His dull eyes were red, but I didn't see him shed a tear after Kayden died.

Since that night, for the first time ever, he didn't speak to me at all. Completely ignoring me these last few days, he looked like a tormented soul that was lost in its own world.

There was more to their relationship than what they showed to the world. They weren't the best example of brotherly love, but no matter how different they were or how much they argued, I'd always known that deep down they loved each other.

Then I came into their lives and everything crashed down.

My whole life shattered the night I made such a stupid mistake. Carmen claimed that it wasn't my fault, and if that driver hadn't been driving too fast, nothing would've happened.

"He was the one who chose to save his brother. Nobody forced him to make that sacrifice."

Her words reverberated in my mind, bringing more pain because she couldn't be more wrong. He *was* forced to make that sacrifice, because Hayden was his brother. How could he not save him?

I tried to hold back my tears, but I couldn't. I wanted to be alone, so I could drown in my misery. I wanted to lock myself somewhere far away and stay there until I died a slow, painful death.

There was nothing more that I deserved now than *death*.

I tried not to pay attention to my classmates. There were some of them I didn't recognize, but it was obvious that they all knew exactly who I was, their accusing stares boring into me wherever I went. Christine and Natalie made sure to spread the news of the accident around the whole school, emphasizing the fact that it was my fault Kayden had died.

I felt betrayed because Christine had called me a murderer and slapped me, her attitude toward me making a U-turn after the accident, which marked the end of a friendship that had never even existed. I should've known better.

I looked at Natalie, who stood between Hayden and Josh. She was sobbing, her mascara running down her ashen face. Josh supported her frail frame with his arm around her waist, staring at her with tenderness I'd never seen before.

As if he sensed me looking, he glanced at me, and his eyes lost all warmth, conveying only hatred. Next to them stood Blake, Masen, and Christine, who all looked equally angry at me.

I couldn't stand looking at them and all these pale faces. It was twisted. This wasn't how it was supposed to be. It would've been better if I died. Nobody would care about me.

My heart squeezed with pain at this thought.

Nobody would come to my funeral...

My heart squeezed again.

Why did I have to be so stupid and make such a mistake?

My heart hurt so much now that it became difficult to breathe.

No. *Calm down, Sarah. You'll not break now. Save that breakdown for later, when there is no one to witness your downfall.*

Just a little bit more. They would bury him soon, and I would be able to leave and drown in hurt.

The loud crying intensified when they finally started lowering his casket into the ground. People threw a handful of dirt on his coffin, each taking their time to say their final farewell to him. I moved to the side because I didn't want to do something so personal in front of everyone.

My mother nudged me, and I looked at her, hoping she wasn't asking me to go throw the dirt. She inclined her head toward Kay's coffin, signaling that it was our turn to go pay him that respect. I couldn't argue with her and tell her I hadn't planned on doing it, because I didn't want to cause a scene. She was already hammered because she'd taken her time with her favorite bourbon before the funeral, and she could easily become aggressive and create a scene if I dared to oppose her.

My legs felt so numb, like they weren't mine, as I stood above his coffin. I bent to take some dirt into my hand, sensing everyone watching me. My face burned as I tried to ignore the anxiety under everyone's scrutiny. I felt like a fake. All my classmates glowered at me, and here I was, throwing the dirt for my best friend who was never supposed to die. All of this was my fault, and if I could go back in time, I would've never crossed that street so carelessly.

In a moment of despair, I looked at Hayden and found him staring right at me. The intensity of the feelings in his eyes twisted everything in me, and our regret, sorrow, and darkness mixed together.

I wanted to yell at him. I wanted to blame him for not avoiding that car. I wanted to hurt him, to scream at him, *anything*, but I knew that everything felt easier than facing the truth—one negligent moment was more than enough to change everyone's lives forever.

What if the driver weren't driving so fast? What if I weren't looking at my phone? What if Hayden or I avoided it? What if Kayden didn't receive a fatal blow to his head? What if, what if, what if. So many questions swirled in my mind, torturing me endlessly.

I threw the dirt onto the coffin, not even daring to look at it in fear of losing it in front of all these people, and stepped aside, counting the minutes until I could finally escape.

• • • •

I HADN'T INTENDED TO go to Kay's repast in their house, but I couldn't refuse Carmen when she begged me to be there. Hayden, who was standing next to her, tensed when I accepted her invitation, and I didn't even want to think about what he could do to me afterward. I expected him to make a scene right there, in the cemetery, but he said nothing, stomping away.

Attending Kay's repast with my drunk mother put me in a tight spot. She guzzled two glasses of wine as soon as we arrived, and I couldn't do anything to stop her. The longer we were here, the more improperly she acted, speaking too loudly and pestering people she'd never even seen before with her sad stories from the past. She was always doing this. Whenever something sad happened, she used it as an opportunity to get attention and complain about her own miserable life, acting as if everything revolved around her.

I couldn't stand her pitiful wails and babbling anymore, so I stood up, ignoring everyone's stares.

I didn't see Hayden or any of our classmates here, which was a relief since I didn't want to face any of them. I walked out of the living room, pretending I was going to the bathroom, and took the stairs instead.

I entered Kayden's room and closed the door behind me, enjoying the silence after so many distressed murmurs and sobs I'd had to listen to the whole morning.

Every piece of furniture my glance fell upon created a new surge of pain inside of me. I could still sense his smell. It was a vanilla mixed with lavender, and it increased my longing. I sat on his bed and closed my eyes.

Three months ago Kayden confessed to me. After giving me my first kiss, which was a big delusion I wanted to drown in as I shamelessly used him, he admitted he was falling for me. Now, more than ever, I felt guilty for using him that way and acting like he wasn't serious when he confessed to me.

I didn't stop even for a second to consider how he felt, scared and unprepared for his feelings, for how was I supposed to feel when I always considered him just a friend? I couldn't reciprocate his feelings. I couldn't give him what he wanted. And on top of that, he was with Natalie.

So I turned it into a joke, saying he was out of his mind, and switched the topic. I'd never seen Kayden so down as he was during the rest of that evening, but I pretended I didn't notice his hurt and behaved like nothing had happened.

And to think that I also pleaded him not to tell Hayden about the kiss, keeping it like a dirty secret, asking selfishly but not giving anything in return...

We never spoke about his feelings or the kiss after that night in the forest, and now I regretted every single second I'd spent ignoring him and disrespecting his feelings.

He had to sacrifice himself to save his brother, and it was all because of me. I was the worst being on the whole planet.

I wanted to die. It would be best if I died.

The door was thrown open, and I jerked my head up, spotting a completely drunk Hayden on the doorsill. The coldness in his eyes terrified me, sending my senses on high alert. I jumped to my feet.

"I-I'm sorry," I stammered. What was I apologizing for? "I'm sorry for coming here... I just wanted to..." I wanted to do what? I had no idea, but it didn't matter since he wasn't even listening to me.

"I knew right from the start you were a bitch. I knew you'd mess something up."

His eyes were as petrifying as ever when he approached me and grabbed me by my hair, pulling me until only inches separated our faces. His movement took me completely by surprise, messing with my already bad balance, and I grasped his hand, yelping in pain.

"Wha... What are you—"

"You had to text. You had to look at your fucking screen instead of paying attention to the road! And then you just froze there and did nothing. I could've died because of you! And now Kayden is dead. He's dead because of you, you stupid bitch!" He shoved me toward the door, making me stumble. "I don't want to see you in my house ever again!"

I backed away, wanting to separate myself from him as much as possible. There was such hatred in his eyes that chilled me to the bone and made me feel like I was completely worthless.

Exiting Kay's room, I took a few unsteady steps backward, my legs threatening to give out on me. He followed me, the lack of expression on his face even scarier. He didn't look human as he approached me, not letting me escape.

"You'll pay for his death. You'll pay for this." He pointed at his bandage. "I'll hurt you so much that you'll wish you were the one who got hit." I took another step back, and once more, he closed the distance between us. "I'm going to destroy you until you're only an empty shell, devoid of any happiness or hope."

I froze in place when I noticed the staircase several feet behind me, feeling cornered.

"And then I'm going to step on that shell and shatter you into dust."

We stared at each other, both breathing heavily, physically so close, but the distance between our worlds felt like a chasm. It was infinite and impossible to cross. Hayden hated me more than ever, and all my illusions about him growing to like me one day dissipated.

I couldn't stand his accusing stare, his hate... It hurt more than everything...

I couldn't take any of this anymore.

"I'm so sorry, Hayden," I said through tears. "I'm sorry for putting your life in danger. I'm sorry for your injury. I'm sorry for Kayden." There was nothing I could say that could make things right. Nothing could make this right. Kayden was gone.

"You will be sorry," Natalie interjected in a hoarse voice, and I turned around. She climbed up the last step and wiped the tears off her face. "You will be sorry for killing my Kayden."

Oh God. Her gaze was filled with venom and hatred, increasing the burning guilt that twisted my insides.

"I'm sorry. I'm so, so sorry." I was blind with tears, suffocating. I needed to get away from here.

I lurched toward the stairs, but I didn't even reach them before Natalie said, "Oh no, not so fast."

She grabbed my hair and upper arm and threw me into a wall with a strength I didn't know she possessed. A scorching pain exploded in my head upon the contact with the hard surface, leaving me slightly dazed.

Hayden didn't try to stop her or even move from his spot, observing our interaction with a blank face, and more tears flowed out of my eyes. This was too much. He was ripping my heart apart.

Natalie swung her hand and slapped me hard before I could dodge it, her eyes promising me more violence. She made a move to slap me again, but I found the strength to move before her hand could make a contact and I rushed to the stairs. I needed to escape from this house right this second.

I headed down the stairs, but I overstepped and lost my footing, which sent me falling down the rest of the stairs. I screamed and tried to grasp at something, but nothing came under my fingers. I tumbled down with my heart in my throat, completely losing my orientation as sharp pain burst in different parts of my body.

I sprawled at the bottom, breathing with difficulty. Everything hurt like hell. I didn't dare to move, wondering if I broke something.

I heard voices coming from all directions. "Jesus! Are you all right, Sarah?" Carmen Black asked and knelt next to me.

Several people appeared above me. I tried to move my legs and arms and sighed in relief because there was nothing broken.

"How did this happen? Can you stand up?"

I struggled to sit up, crying out when the sizzling shot of pain spread through my back. "Easy." She wrapped her arm around my waist to help me. "I'll call the ambulance."

"It's okay," I said to reassure her, but the truth was that I wasn't okay. I felt completely broken. Not on the outside, but on the inside.

I looked upward and noticed Hayden standing alone at the top of the stairway. He stared at me impassively with his vacant eyes, completely unperturbed by my fall. Without any emotion, he turned around and walked away, hammering the last nail into my coffin of misery and darkness.

I closed my eyes, my defensive barriers going down. I let myself cry in front of everyone, falling into the abyss of despair and burning pain. Of course he didn't care. No one cared.

Hayden Black and Natalie Shelley. They were the same.

I'd been so wrong. There was no goodness in Hayden. He wasn't that Hayden I always hoped for, *believed in*.

He was a creature with no compassion or care for others. He was a monster.

I felt my heart shut down, and all the warm feelings I'd once had for him began to disappear.

Chapter 18

A blend of anger and fear twirled in me as I left my bike on the parking lot, a few drops of sweat sliding down my temples. I'd had to pedal as fast as I could in order not to be late for my first class.

I darted through the groups of students in the halls, intending to confront Hayden because this was getting way out of hand. Why did he have to do that? Couldn't I spend at least one day in peace?

I hated him, and I hated myself for letting him me kiss me after everything he'd done to me. That kiss was indeed icing on the cake after yesterday's disastrous day in school. It was like someone had brainwashed me and made me enjoy that kiss. No, I didn't even want to think about it. I would erase it from my memory and act like it never happened.

I didn't even have time to explain to my mother what happened. I just told her I would deal with the issue after I came from school, but I couldn't keep having my car serviced. This had to stop.

Would it be better not to use my car anymore? I couldn't keep coming to school with my bicycle, but maybe I could use the school bus? No, the school bus wasn't a convenient solution since the bus stop was too far.

I hated my bullies for forcing me to change everything only so I could dodge them. I kept brainstorming how to avoid all the potential damage to me or my property.

So many ruined or stolen books, notebooks, my car... On top of everything, Josh had ripped to pieces my most important notebook yesterday, destroying my ideas and sketches. All those hours I spent planning and dreaming about making those plans come true... All of them extinguished.

My rage grew stronger just thinking about it, which was exactly what I needed so I could face Hayden. I was on my way to his locker, when Dan, one of my classmates, and his friend stopped me in the hall.

"Yo, Decker! Your car seriously needs some remodeling. Instead of buying new tires, how about you buy a new car? Something from this century?" Dan said. I gaped at him in distress, wondering how he knew about my car tires.

"And something that isn't cheap and ugly," his friend added.

Dan turned the screen of his Samsung to me and showed me the image of my Ford with the slashed tire taken in front of my house. It was on Twitter and retweeted 26 times already.

"I can't believe this," I muttered to myself, mortified because Hayden was subjecting me to more public humiliation. Seeing my reaction, Dan and his friend burst into laughter and walked away, calling me names loud enough for everyone around to hear them.

Choking back my resentment and shame, I proceeded to Hayden's locker. Just like I'd hoped for, he was there and he was alone.

"Why did you have to do that?" I bit out when I halted behind him, feeling the heat in my cheeks.

He turned around, his eyes narrowing at me. "Do what?"

"Don't act dumb. Now I have to buy new tires, and I was almost late for my first period because of you!"

He sneered at me in sudden anger. "What the fuck are you on? I have no clue what you're talking about."

I shook my head at him, doing my best to hold his furious gaze. "You know very well. You keep threatening me and messing with my life. How could you do that? Do you have any idea of what damage you have done?"

In a second, I was pressed against his locker and he was caging me in with his arms. "As I said, I have no clue what you're talking about. It beats me why you thought you could just come here and bitch about it."

He was lying. "I don't trust you."

He clenched his jaw. "See how much I don't fucking care." He gave me the middle finger and then kissed it, staring at me coldly.

Seconds passed as we just glared at each other, completely motionless, my body hyperaware of his nearness. He wasn't even admitting it, refusing to take responsibility for his appalling deed, and I hated feeling so powerless. It wasn't fair.

"And if I report you to the police?" It was an empty threat I used only to see his reaction.

He didn't miss a beat, his nostrils flaring. "Do it. And then let's see if you can prove it was me who did it."

The bell rang, giving fuel to his body to finally move, and he stepped back. Without even looking at him, I darted away before he could stop me, wishing I could make him and everyone else pay for everything they had done to me.

Jessica was already in the classroom when I arrived to English, her face pale and tired. The dark circles under her eyes told me she didn't sleep well last night.

"Hi," I told her, sitting down at my desk.

"Hi, Sarah. I was worried about you. I texted you last night, but you didn't answer."

After my encounter with Hayden at the cemetery, I was too shocked and upset to respond to her message. The only thing I could do was go to bed and try to fall asleep.

"I'm so sorry, Jessica, but I didn't feel well last night."

I didn't want to tell her about the kiss. I wasn't quite sure myself what that was all about, and it was also a long story, so it would be best if I didn't mention it at all.

"Why? Is it because of what happened in the yard yesterday?"

"Yes," I lied without blinking. I sensed Hayden enter the classroom, and my breath caught in my throat. *Don't look his way, Sarah.* "How are you feeling?"

"Horrible. I wanted to stay home today, but my parents didn't let me. I feel so bad, Sarah. How can they be so evil?"

Hayden passed my desk, and I released my breath when he walked over to his seat at the back.

"I've been asking that same question for years now," I replied to her morosely. "Hayden slashed my car tires this morning."

Jessica gasped. "What?"

"I got out of my house this morning and noticed that my front tires were slashed, and you know that my car insurance doesn't cover that."

"Jesus," she breathed out, paling. "That's horrible!" She glanced at him over her shoulder. "He's horrible," she whispered.

"He denied that he has anything to do with it, but it would be foolish of me to trust him. To make things worse, he took a photo of and put it on Twitter. Now the whole school will know about it!"

"You have to report him to the police."

I shook my head. "No. I don't believe they would do anything to punish him. Besides, I have no real proof that he was the one who did it. Hayden wouldn't be stupid to leave any fingerprints." I tucked my hair behind my ears. "Also, going to the police for such a thing... It's humiliating and tiring. It's never-ending."

"I get what you mean, Sarah, but it can't be that bad. I know that maybe they can't do much, but there must be something we, bullied people, can do? If we stay silent and don't report them, they'll keep doing it!"

I looked at her, feeling annoyed by her naivety. "They will always keep doing it, Jessica, no matter what. The police won't have my back always. Sure, they may solve the case and punish Hayden somehow, but there is always tomorrow, and tomorrow I'll be alone. There won't be anyone to protect me, and Hayden can punish me however he wants."

She was playing nervously with the edges of her French book. I felt sorry for both of us. "Then what can we do?"

I didn't reply, wishing I could finally break through the mud of fear that was keeping me in the dark and fight back.

· · · ·

I FELT MORE VULNERABLE than usual sitting next to Hayden during computer science. After yesterday's kiss and the slashed tires, my brain was in overdrive. I needed a way out. This school year had just begun, but too many things had already happened.

Much to my disbelief, nobody mentioned anything about my kiss with Hayden. It was impossible he didn't tell anyone about it, right? There must be some attack coming my way. It couldn't be that Hayden chose to keep it a secret, it just couldn't. Why would he?

"Do you even listen to me, Sarah?"

I flinched and looked at Ms. Clare, who was glaring at me. "Um, yes?"

Hayden snorted.

"I asked you about your project, Sarah. The deadline for the outline ends in two weeks, and I hope Hayden and you figured something out."

Oh. I completely forgot about working on a website project with Hayden.

I glanced at him, and my stomach sank when I noticed his cold smirk. He didn't care about the stupid project, and he couldn't care less about me worrying about it. No, scratch that. He *liked* me worrying, so he would probably make sure to stall so I would worry more.

"Yep, Ms. Clare," Hayden answered her, surprising both me and her. "We came up with something really good."

"Really, Hayden? What is it?"

"We're going to make a porn site." No. He did *not* just say that. "Sarah is going to be the main actress."

I desperately tried to ignore the chuckles and stares, hunching in my chair. I wished I could cover my blush with my hair, but it would look weird.

"Get serious, Hayden. If not, you're going to fail this subject."

He shrugged. "I'll live."

I didn't want to do this. I didn't want to beg him to get some sense into that head of his and work with me on this project. I despised him for humiliating me like this.

I already felt like a huge bundle of tangled nerves as I turned to face him. "Please, Hayden. If nothing else, just suggest the theme. Anything is okay. You don't even have to work on the outline. I'll do everything by myself."

"I told you. I want to make a porn site." He leaned toward me, his lips almost touching my ear. His nearness created shivers that traveled fast down my spine, and I fought to remain in my place so he wouldn't know how much he intimidated me. "I'll put your nude photos on that website," he whispered. "They would be a great addition. I'm sure guys would love them."

His words disgusted and terrified me at the same time. I didn't doubt for a second he would really do that, but despite my fear, there was some spark in me that made me speak my next words without thinking.

"Gee, thanks, Hayden. I didn't know you find me hot."

I held his stare, pretending I was brave and winning this round. As I took in the stunned expression on his face, my own surprise filled me since he didn't make any comeback. He looked as if he was dumbfounded by my words.

He broke our eye contact, not proving me wrong, and turned his head back.

I couldn't believe this.

I actually *won*.

Chapter 19

THE FIRST THING I DID when I got home from school yesterday was to call Johns' Corner to tow my Ford to their service. Then I talked to my mother, hoping to convince her that the tire slashing was just a stupid prank. She didn't seem persuaded, but she also didn't push the topic. She just wanted to make sure I was going to pay to fix it.

The sad truth was that I wouldn't have it any other way. Whenever some money issue was brought up, I felt uncomfortable and reluctant to ask for money because she was constantly reminding me that it was *her* money, not *ours*. At this rate, my college fund was going to disappear if I kept paying for everything.

After today's classes, I went to the retirement home on the bus. Melissa was already there when I arrived, standing next to her car. Her eyebrows formed a slight frown when she saw me getting off the bus.

"Where's your car?" she asked and fell in step with me on our way to the entrance.

How could I tell her the truth without sounding like a complete loser? "Um, I had some issues with it so I had to take it to the car service."

"Uh-huh. If you want, I can drive you back home."

"Um, I'm meeting with my classmate, Jessica, after work. We'll go out for coffee."

"Oh, okay."

Maybe I could invite Melissa to come with us because it could be a good opportunity to get to know her better. Hopefully, Jessica wouldn't mind this. "So how about you come with us?"

"Me? With that Jessica chick and you?"

"Yep."

She scratched her neck and looked away, insecure, which surprised me because I thought Melissa was self-confident 24/7. "Thanks, but I don't want to put you out—"

"Don't worry, you won't. Come on, it will be fun."

A radiant smile spread across her face. "Okay, if you're sure."

A surprise awaited me in the sitting room, for Jonathan was talking with Adelaine, a seventy-year-old widow who liked playing Angry Birds on her iPhone. She was truly amazing because her interests were the mix between old and new. She liked listening to classical music and watching black and white movies, but she was hooked on her iPhone games. Most of the time, she was sitting alone in a corner, staring intently at the screen of her phone as she tapped her fingers all over it.

Today, she was far away from that lonely corner, in the middle of a hushed conversation with Jonathan, and I couldn't help but stare at them in incredulity. She looked a bit embarrassed, but her dark ebony skin hid any potential blush. I didn't know what surprised me the most—her shyness next to him or the fact that Jonathan was *smiling*.

"So he can smile," Melissa whispered to me when she noticed them together. "I thought he didn't have the muscles required for smiling at all! He never smiles!"

"I'm glad he finally found a reason to smile. I was worried he wouldn't be able to get used to this place."

"They look cute somehow. That is, if we forget about the fact that they are old, heavily wrinkled, and decorated with a lot of age spots like Swiss cheese is filled with holes—"

"Melissa!" I whisper yelled at her. "That's not nice of you. Show them some respect."

"Hey, I'm showing them respect! I respectfully think they fit each other because they are both so old and ugl—"

"Oh, shut up," I interrupted her, walking away from her.

Her laughter trailed behind me. "Okay, okay! I know that was mean! I'm sorry!"

At noon, Melissa and I took a break and went to the patio. Several minutes into our conversation, Mateo arrived, and Melissa wiggled her eyebrows at me, a beaming smile forming on her face. I almost groaned.

I didn't forget about his message. There was no way I could when he'd said I looked cute. Ugh. He must have been joking. I was certain of it.

"Hey, girls," he greeted us and surprised me when he leaned in and actually kissed me on the cheek, the sudden contact leaving me baffled. He winked at me.

I glanced away, my cheeks heated. He was playing with me for sure. Besides, Melissa claimed he was a player, and as far as I could see, he didn't lack self-confidence or charm.

"How was your week?" he asked us. Melissa replied to him in her usual witty way, but my throat just constricted when it was my turn to answer.

Not good. Why couldn't I say anything in front of him? I surely looked dull or stupid to him.

"Um, everything was great. Fun." My voice sounded like I was a heavy smoker.

"Say," he started and pursed his lips together. "Did I offend you with my message or something?"

Oh no. I hoped he wouldn't mention that.

"Message? What message?" Melissa was ever so curious.

"You didn't reply to both of my messages that night, so I thought you might be angry with me."

Melissa raised her eyebrows at me. "Both?"

"Yes," I answered her, nettled.

Since I hadn't responded to his first text, Mateo sent another one asking me if I was okay. I was so surprised and nervous when I saw his texts that I chickened out and didn't text him back. I'd never received such a message from a boy before, so I had no idea how to act. Playing safe and ignoring him seemed like a best thing to do, especially because I wasn't sure if he really meant what he said.

"Mateo texted me last Sunday. I'm sorry, Mateo, but I was sleeping."

Melissa rolled her eyes. "Typical. She's been like that with me from the start. Not really responsive, are you?"

I shrugged. "I'm so sorry, guys."

"Then why didn't you text me the next day?" he asked, not buying it.

I blushed. Damn it. "Um, I forgot." The lamest excuse of all excuses. No, that couldn't even be called an excuse. It was more like a big fat lie. I really was incapable of communicating with my peers.

He crossed his arms across his chest. "Okay. I get it. I won't bother you if that's a big deal for you."

How could I tell him that texting guys wasn't my forte? Ever since elementary school, I was a pariah, a weird loner that boys didn't find attractive.

That seriously ate away at my self-confidence, but I couldn't divulge this to Mateo and Melissa. I didn't want them to pity me or dislike me because something was abnormal about me.

"That's okay. You can send me texts if you want, Mateo. I will... I will text you back."

The corner of his lips quirked up, but then he frowned. "Anyway, I looked for you on Facebook."

I flinched. "What?"

"I found your account, but I don't think it's actually yours." He stopped for a second, watching me carefully. "It looks like someone made you a fake account."

"Whoa! Really?" Melissa stared open-mouthed at him, then at me. "Is this true? Do you know anything about this?"

I took a deep breath, feeling the burning sensation in my cheeks. I had no idea if I felt more embarrassed or angry.

"What did you see?" My voice came out sharper than I'd intended.

"Nothing much—"

"What did you see?" I repeated more loudly. They both gaped at me. I was also surprised by my harsh reaction, but at this point I didn't care, getting angrier by the second.

"I saw some nasty photos and videos. I even found some photo with a slashed tire on Twitter..." He narrowed his eyes at me. "You don't look shocked."

I closed my eyes and took a deep breath. "That's because I'm not."

They stared at me, waiting for more details, but I didn't want to give them any. Besides, if I started talking about bullying I would start crying, and there was no way I would allow myself to cry in front of them.

"What's going on, Sarah? Why did they post those pictures and videos?"

"What do you think, Mateo?" I snapped at him. "Some people are very mean and like tormenting others. It's not difficult to figure that out."

"Did you report them?"

"Report what to who?"

"Report those accounts and the people behind them to the police."

"No. I didn't."

They didn't get it, did they? They had no idea how difficult it could be for a victim to say out loud they were bullied and make culprits known. For some people—especially those who hadn't experienced bullying—this might sound easy, but all I ever wanted was to live a normal life, not to complicate it more. Disclosing this was not only difficult, but it was also mortifying.

If I went to the police, what would happen? They would delete those profiles, punish the people behind them, and since they were minors, how serious would their penalty be? Also, it was so easy to make a new account if the old one was terminated. Cyberbullying can't be controlled, especially when everything is anonymous.

After all, reporting would only bring me more headaches. Who guaranteed me they wouldn't double their bullying if I reported them to the cops? I would have to live in fear of their retribution, and Hayden's retaliation was more than enough for me.

I didn't trust anyone, and I couldn't trust the police.

How messed up is my mind?

I got up, desperate to walk away. "You didn't have any right to search for me."

Mateo recoiled, his frown growing deeper. "What? Are you serious?" The way he looked at me made me realize I'd overreacted, but it was too late to take my words back.

"Why not, Sarah? The last time I checked, it was completely legal and normal to search for someone on Facebook. I wanted to talk with you. Is that a crime?"

"Why?"

"What do you mean 'why'?"

"Why do you want to talk more with me?"

Melissa smacked her forehead like I'd said something completely stupid. Mateo shifted his gaze to the side, looking uncomfortable.

"Hey, guys. If you want, I can go inside and—" Melissa started.

"No, it's okay. I can say this in front of you," he replied and faced me. "I like you. It's as simple as that."

Whoa. A pang of overwhelming surprise hit my chest, and for once, I was left without words. He said it was simple, but liking someone was never simple, and I had no idea how to react.

Was he serious? I studied his face for any indication that he was joking, but I found none.

What was I supposed to say? I hated feeling this self-conscious. Why would he like me? There were many prettier girls out there, and they were all more talkative and charming than me. All I ever did in front of Mateo was blush and act awkward. Unless he liked weird girls, I didn't understand why he would like me.

"I... I really don't know what to say, Mateo." This wasn't a good answer at all, I knew.

He shrugged and attempted to smile. "Well, that was a clear enough answer."

Oh no. I didn't want to hurt him. "No, really... Thank you, Mateo. I..." Oh God, I was making things worse.

"Hey, it's okay." He raised his arms as in surrender and smiled, but it was clear that the smile was fake. "I understand. You don't have to say anything. I think I should go now. See you tomorrow, maybe?"

"Mateo..." I didn't know what to say or do to make him stay, because I didn't want him to leave like this. I should've given him a more precise answer or been friendlier.

I felt like a villain.

"Don't sweat it," he said and left before I managed to say anything else.

Abashed, I returned Melissa's gaze. "What was I supposed to say?" I pushed my hands through my hair in exasperation.

"Don't be hard on yourself. It's okay."

"Is it?"

"Yeah, because as far as I can see, you don't like Mateo, right? So, don't force yourself to be with him."

"Well, he's cute."

She grinned. "Cute? How cute? Like mildly cute or super hot cute?"

I let out a chuckle, embarrassed all over again. "Cute cute."

"Hm. Isn't 'cute cute' enough to give him a chance?"

I sighed. "I don't know, Melissa. I... I'm not really good with guys."

"Really? I'm sure you're not that bad. You aren't a virgin, right?" I looked away, too ashamed to say anything. "You are. Okay, well, that's not bad. Not at all. Even though everyone has sex at an early age, it doesn't mean you have to. It's okay when you feel it's okay."

She was making me feel even worse. "Melissa, you're not good at pep talks."

"Hey! I really think that! It's better to be a virgin than to do it with a guy who doesn't deserve it at all."

"Oh. Did that happen to you?"

Sorrow flashed across her face, and I wanted to know what had happened to her. "Kinda. But that's a story for another time. Anyway, I'm sure Mateo doesn't care whether a girl is virgin or not. He's one of the good guys, and I think you can trust him. He won't trick you or something like that. Talking about tricks, what was that about your fake account?"

I'd been hoping she would drop that subject, but I had no such luck. "It's a long story. I'll tell you everything over a coffee later, okay?"

• • • •

JESSICA, MELISSA, AND I went to Starbucks at a recently opened shopping mall. Jessica was cool with me inviting Melissa, and I was glad they got off to a good start.

"So, the fake account?" Melissa probed.

With a sigh, I fidgeted with my hands. It wasn't easy to admit to someone who was so confident and easy-going that I was a bullying target. She'd probably never been bullied in her life.

"My classmates don't particularly like me. Some of them are very bad and like to bully, offline or online."

"That's awful. Why didn't you report this?"

I glanced sideways. "I went to the police once. It didn't end well." I told them about Josh's punch and the outcome. "As for those social accounts, I reported them several times, but it was pointless because new accounts keep popping up. Nobody can prevent those things from happening because even if you stop one person, there are always other people."

"That's true, but something should be done about that anyway. Although, I do witness the same things in my school, so I know it can be impossible to stop it. I'm trying, actually, to stop those bullies from hurting some of the victims, but I can't always be there to protect them."

"Wow," Jessica said, admiration clear in her tone. "You're amazing. To be so brave and able to defend those who need help... You're a great person."

Melissa made a face. "Not so much. My brother is one of those bullies, and since I can't talk him out of that, the least I can do is repair the damage."

"How come your brother and you are so different?"

She shrugged her shoulders. "I don't really know. As I told you, my mother spoiled him. He always gets what he wants, but it's never enough for him. A few years ago, he met some new people, and he started spending much more time out. At that time, he turned to drugs and got worse, becoming way more aggressive."

"Is it true that he's hanging with some people from our school?"

"Yes. I saw a few of them several times, but I don't know them that well."

"Believe it or not, I heard Blake, Hayden, Josh, and Masen are involved in some strange activities," Jessica said.

"Like a gang?" I asked her, and she nodded.

There was an old rumor that Hayden and his friends were in a gang, but I never paid much attention to it since it was never proven. I knew Hayden and Blake visited shady places, and sometimes I could even hear them talking about some matches and races in Hayden's yard, but I didn't know what that was all about. So, when Mateo mentioned that some of Enfield's students were a part of some gang-like group, he made me question whether that rumor was true after all.

"I heard some girls in the restroom talking about the fights between Hayden and some older guys," Jessica said. "It seems they're fighting somewhere and placing bets on those matches."

"Steven also fights in those matches, and I hate it. He comes home bruised almost every weekend."

"Have they ever been busted?" I asked.

"Not that I heard of." Melissa clasped her hands excitedly. "Anyway, Steven is throwing a party next Friday night, and you're more than welcome to come." She sounded sincerely excited.

"Are you sure it's okay to invite us? Your brother doesn't know us."

Melissa rolled her eyes. "That's not a problem at all. There are always so many people at Steven's parties, and many of them don't even know him. Besides, you're my friends. Come on, it will be fun. There will be booze, cute guys, and music."

"How about your parents?"

"They will be away for the weekend because they're going to our cabin in the mountains. They do that from time to time, and Steven never misses the opportunity to fill our empty house with loads of guests and alcohol."

I looked at Jessica, wondering what she was thinking. It sounded exciting and fun, and since Melissa was from Somers, I didn't have to worry about my classmates. It would be nice to be among people who didn't see me as a complete loser, for a change.

It already felt unreal.

"I'd like to come. How about you, Jessica?"

"I'd like that too."

"Great! Then, it's settled! Now all I have to do is invite Mateo."

My heart jumped at Melissa's words. Was she serious? "Wait, what?"

She giggled. "What? I have to invite him too! It will be a perfect chance for you two to get together."

What was she now? A matchmaker? No, I wasn't ready to hook up with Mateo. I didn't actually think I would be ready any time soon, not that I wanted it.

"Please, Melissa, don't do that. I don't think it's a good idea to—"

"Hush," she interrupted me. "You don't have to be with him if you don't want, silly, but if it happens, it happens. You two look cute together, I must say."

"No way."

"No, seriously. It was so sweet when he confessed to you."

Jessica's eyes widened. "Wait? Someone confessed to you? Why didn't you tell me?"

"It happened this morning. And it's not that important..."

"Not important?" Melissa squealed. "How is that not important when one of the popular guys in Rawenwood High says he likes you?"

"One of the popular guys?" Jessica inquired. "Who is he?"

I glanced back and forth between them, the headache knocking at my door. This wasn't going to be easy to explain...

Chapter 20

"MATEO SOUNDS LIKE A nice guy," Jessica said, driving me home.

It was incredible how fast time passed with Jessica and Melissa. I hadn't felt so relaxed and happy in quite a long time, and it was like I'd found one of the missing pieces of my life's puzzle. An overpowering joy had found its way to me, breathing life to a permanent smile.

I felt like I finally belonged somewhere, which was a long-lost feeling because only Kayden had helped me feel this good about myself.

"He's nice, but I don't know what to do about him."

"Why?"

Mateo was cute and all, but my deeply ingrained mistrust didn't allow me to believe he was attracted to me. Even if he was, I had no idea about guys. He was popular and experienced, and I was no one. He was way out of my league.

"Because I have no experience with boys." I was ashamed to say this. "What if I embarrass myself in front of him? What if he doesn't want anything serious with me?"

"I think you should give him a chance. You can't know it if you don't try. Besides, if you become his girlfriend, maybe Hayden won't bother you anymore. Mateo could protect you."

Oh no. I didn't even put Hayden into this equation. As controlling and obsessed as he was, it would be stupid of me not to expect him to ruin my chances with Mateo. He'd warned me not to keep any male contacts on my phone or he would make them pay, so what would his punishment be if I got a boyfriend?

Hayden's grasp on me was too tight, too suffocating. If I decided Mateo was worth a try, did I have to hide him from Hayden? Did I have to keep my relationship a secret?

"This is my house," I told Jessica and pointed at it.

She parked the car right across my house and gasped when she looked in the direction of Hayden's house. I turned my head to see what she was looking at and found Hayden and Blake tuning their cars in his driveway.

Blake was bent under the hood of his red Dodge Challenger, the outline of his brawny upper body clearly visible beneath his tight black T-shirt. Hayden stood in the same position under the hood of his Chevrolet Camaro, which was parked next to Blake's car.

"Blake Jones?" Jessica said in a small voice, growing pale. The intensity of her reaction reminded me of my own whenever I crossed paths with Hayden. Was she already that afraid of him? Maybe accepting her offer to drive me home hadn't been a good idea.

She shrunk in her seat. "Just my luck."

"I'm sorry. They often hang together at his house, so... Anyway, thank you for driving me home. I had a great time today."

"Me too. Melissa is super cool."

"Really? You don't find her too talkative?"

"I like talkative people. I don't need to think too hard what to talk about when I'm with them."

A giggle slipped over my lips. Really, it was impossible to get bored with Melissa.

Blake noticed us first and said something to Hayden. Instantly, Hayden spun around, and our eyes locked. He responded to Blake, not taking his eyes off of me.

"Will you be okay?" she asked me.

"I have to be. Don't worry, I got used to it."

That was a straight up lie. One could never get used to seeing their tormentors.

"See you in school," I said and got out of her car. Blake left his wrench and headed to us. Oh no. Not now.

"Please, go before he comes," I told her, but she wasn't paying attention to me at all. She stared at Blake, frozen.

He crossed the road and stopped in front of Jessica's Mini Cooper. He wasn't even looking at me, openly glaring at Jessica. He kicked the bumper.

"I'm surprised you managed to put your fat ass inside this can."

I flinched, angry at him for picking on Jessica. "Don't talk to her like that."

His head snapped toward me. "And what are you? Her lawyer? Since when is she mute so she can't speak for herself?"

"I'm her *friend*." I noticed Jessica shaking. Her face was white as a sheet.

"Aww how nice. You two losers absolutely suit each other." He walked over to her driver-side door and leaned on her open window with his elbow. "Why don't you come out? Are you that stuck in your seat that you can't actually move at all?"

Jessica remained silent, and I got madder at Blake for terrorizing her like this. I didn't want to just stand here and do nothing.

I went around her car, facing him directly. "Shut up. Stop harassing her."

His eyes turned into slits. "What the actual fuck?"

He yanked my arm and threw me against the rear door. Pain flashed through my spine, pulling me into a momentary daze. I couldn't move because Blake pressed me against the car, and my fear hit an all-time high.

"Don't speak to me like that," he hissed into my face, the venom in his words forcing me to shrink and close my eyes. "Look at me!" He pushed me against the car again, creating a new wave of pain, and I met his eyes, which spit fire.

I could already feel bruises forming on different parts of my body. His grip on my shoulder was too strong, and I couldn't escape it. My strength, or rather the lack of it, couldn't be compared to his sheer strength.

"You're trash. You're no one. I'll do whatever I want, and you don't get to say a word about it! Got it, bitch?!" I couldn't stop myself from whining, hating myself for showing him how much he terrified me.

Jessica rushed out of her car. "Please, stop hurting her!" I could see from the corner of my eye that she was crying.

"I don't want to. I enjoy hurting her."

"Please!" She touched his shoulder, as if pleading him to move away from me. He flinched like someone had burned him, fear flashing in his eyes, and he let go of me.

"Don't touch me," he roared at her, hovering over her. He started shaking furiously, his neck veins bulging, which scared the hell out of Jessica and me. A warning siren in my head went off.

Blake had these nasty episodes from time to time when the anger would consume him, and each time he looked like he was going to fly off the handle and hurt everyone around him. I saw Hayden and Blake having a fight several times, and it was terrifying just to witness it, let alone be involved. Mix Hayden's moodiness and Blake's anger issues, and you got an atomic bomb.

Luckily, Masen and Josh had always been there to intervene and separate them from each other before things took a turn for the worse, but now? What could I do against Blake now? He would hurt Jessica and me in the blink of an eye.

Just as Blake grabbed Jessica, Hayden stopped in between them and pushed Blake backward.

"Leave," Hayden told Jessica, and I looked at him in shock. He had no intention of bullying her? Was he seriously letting her go?

Blake glared at Hayden. "What are you doing, man?"

"Leave!" He raised his voice, which scared her enough to move from her spot.

She glanced at me with a guilt written all over her face. "I'm really sorry." She rushed into her car and was gone in seconds.

I was left all alone with the two devils. I gulped.

"Why did you butt in?" Blake scoffed at him.

"Because you know what happens when you let the anger get the best of you."

"Like you're one to talk! You deal with the same shit, but nobody is preaching to you about it!"

Hayden was becoming angrier with each second, visibly tensing. I didn't want to be a part of their fight, so I took a step back, hoping I could walk away without them noticing.

"You're preaching to me now."

"Somebody has to do it. I endured your shit all these years, but nobody cuts me any slack."

I took another step backward.

"Shut the fuck up."

"Why? Did I hit your sensitive spot, princess?"

I turned on my heel to dart away, but Hayden had good reflexes, grabbing my arm and pulling me back to him before I could escape.

"You need to chill," he told Blake, keeping me next to his side, his grip on my wrist made of steel.

"You did *not* just say that."

"Yes, Blake, I did. You can't race when you're like this. So go and fucking chill!"

Blake glared at Hayden like he was going to pounce on him any moment and take me down with him in the process. I was on tenterhooks about what would happen to me if Blake left us alone, feeling the dangerous heat that radiated from Hayden's body. In a painfully long moment, Blake's steely gaze was fixed on me, the promise of violence in them all too clear, and it took everything in me not to hunch in fear.

Surprisingly, Blake backed off, raising his hands as in surrender, and threw one last look at Hayden. "All right. As the princess wishes." He marched away, pissed off.

I thought Hayden was finally going to blow his top and attack Blake from behind, but he did nothing to prevent him from leaving. Instead, he directed his attention to me.

"Why did she drive you back home?"

"The last time I checked, you weren't my father. I don't have to give you a report."

I snatched my arm away from him, dashing toward my house, but as soon as I crossed the road, he grabbed me and trapped me against his body. He encircled one arm around my waist and placed his other hand below my neck, keeping me in place. I thrashed against him in hopes of setting myself free, but he was too strong for me, and fear greeted me. I braced myself for anything he might do.

"You became really bitchy these last few days." He started tapping his fingers on my belly, creating a pleasant, fluttery feeling in the pit of my stomach. My chest tightened, confusion triumphing over me.

No, I was sure that was not pleasure. That was fear.

"You get on my nerves more than ever. Do you want my attention that much?"

"Let me go."

His chuckle sounded punishing in my ear. He enjoyed this. His warm fingers moved to my neck and brushed my skin, creating shivers, and I didn't know what made me more sick—him playing me like this, or my own body that was sending me these confusing signals.

"I think you do. Your pulse sped up like crazy just now and you're breathing faster."

"That's because I'm afraid of you."

"I don't think so. Besides, I haven't done anything yet, babe."

Babe? What the hell was going on here? This wasn't the Hayden I knew. He never kept me this close to him or called me like that. What was his tactic now?

Not being able to recognize his intentions made me even more wary of him. One thing was certain. What looked like a lovers' embrace was actually Hayden's cruel game. A game in which I always lost.

"You didn't do anything? You were strangling me just one week ago, Hayden! Go to hell!"

I wriggled against him, trying to set myself free, but it was useless. He only increased his hold around my waist, pulling me into his body, and I could feel his heart pounding fast. His own breathing increased, and a new fear emerged in me. Not the fear of Hayden, but the fear of *this*—this sensation that filled me and enclosed me, making me want to stay right where I was. This... This wasn't *normal*.

I let my eyes close for a couple of seconds, my mind going blank as an unknown emotion twirled inside my chest. His lips touched my earlobe briefly, planting a feathery kiss, and I shuddered. "Hell is where you are, babe, and I'm glad to pay you unpleasant visits," he whispered and let me go.

I was brought back to harsh reality, the haze in my mind clearing immediately. I couldn't even look at him, feeling I could choke on my embarrassment.

Without looking back, I rushed into my house and closed the door behind me with a bang. I took two stairs at a time, rushing to shut myself in my room and stay there forever.

Stupid, stupid, stupid, stupid.

How could you relax? How could you let him know even for a second you enjoyed that?

Enjoy?

What the hell, Sarah? After everything he had done, you would fall that low to let him manipulate you that easily?

I reached my bed, and the hot tears had surged out, my breathing accelerating...

Take a deep breath, Sarah.

The tingling started in the back of my head.

Breathe slowly, Sarah. Calm down.

I couldn't! I was so stupid! I—

My phone beeped with a text message, and I flinched, taken by surprise.

I took my phone out of my backpack and entered the password. The hair stood up on the back of my neck when I unlocked it. Instead of seeing the caller ID, I saw two words. Hidden Number.

My thumb turned sweaty as it hovered above the message icon, waiting for me to gather the courage to open the message. I swallowed the lump in my throat and tapped on the icon.

The first thing I spotted through the crack on my screen was the photo of my slashed tire in my driveway, but it was different from the one circulating on Twitter because it was altered in Photoshop. This picture showed dark blood trickling down the tire and spreading on the pavement.

The scream lodged in my throat when I read the text beneath the picture, everything in me turning into ice.

"This is nothing compared to what I'll do to you. Get ready because I'll slash your face soon."

Chapter 21

"I FOLLOW YOU WHEREVER you go."

I deleted another message from the hidden number, just like I'd done with the previous two. The message I received last night was a dire picture of a dog that had been run over and lying in his own blood, with a text that said, *"I'll run you over too."*

I could barely sleep the last two nights. These threats scared the living hell out of me, and for the first time, I couldn't find the strength to go outside and work, panic holding me captive in my house. I called in sick and spent the whole day locked in my room, crying until all that was left was overpowering dejection. I didn't see the point in getting out of my room and continuing to live my life.

The only distractions Sunday provided were Melissa's and Jessica's messages. Jessica kept apologizing for leaving me alone with Hayden and Blake despite her earlier promise not to be a coward anymore. I *did* feel a bit hurt because of that, but I understood she couldn't just stay with me, right?

What would I do if I was in her place? Would I stay or leave?

You would stay, Sarah, because deep down you would do anything for the people you love.

Yeah, but it had been so long since I cared for someone that I'd forgotten how it felt to be there for others.

Soon after Jessica's first message, I received a text from Melissa. She mentioned that Mateo didn't come to the retirement home this morning, which wasn't surprising after how I treated him on Saturday. If his confession was real, I kind of blew my chances with him when I reacted the way I did, not that I was ready for dating when I had to deal with these disturbing messages.

I just knew it was Hayden who had sent them, and it was appalling. He wanted me to be terrified. He wanted me to be paranoid and too scared to get out of my shell. This was the first time he'd sent such an explicit warning, but the worst thing was that I was afraid he would really fulfill his threats.

Was it because I disobeyed him and stayed friends with Jessica, or was it because of Kayden's death?

I didn't have a clue what had gotten into him this time, but I knew Monday awfulness had just reached a whole new level. I didn't want to go to school, dragging myself around the house all small and hopeless. I got the guts to get outside eventually, but I was already too late for my first class.

I arrived at school and decided not to go to first period. Hayden was there, which was all the more reason for me to steer clear of the English classroom and head to the secluded part of the school that was deserted at most times. This way, I didn't risk getting seen by teachers.

I hated skipping classes. I felt guilty, like my chance of going to a good college would slip away. After I clung to my escape for so long, working hard and dreaming high, I couldn't let it go to waste. I'd started working on my college applications this summer, hoping that by some miracle Yale, which had great art programs, would accept me, and made it a mission to have good grades no matter what.

I was in the middle of hallway when I heard two familiar voices arguing, their angry words drifting from the outside through an open window nearby. I tip-toed and stopped next to the window, peeking around it.

Hayden, Masen, and Blake were smoking right in front of me, obviously skipping classes. I whipped my head back, my heart pounding violently in my chest. Unlike Hayden and Blake, Masen was facing the window, and I hoped he hadn't noticed me.

"Will you two stop it already?" Masen said in irritation. "First, you didn't want to talk to each other, and now, you can't stop arguing."

Blake snorted. "The princess here feels offended, as usual. I don't want to suck up to anyone, especially not to you, Hayden."

"Fuck you. I had enough of your crap."

"My crap?! What about your crap?!"

"What are you talking about?"

"I'm talking about that bullshit episode you had with Sarah Decker on Saturday."

"What?" Masen asked.

"That's right," Blake replied to him. "You should've seen them, Mace. He hugged her like she was his girlfriend or something. They looked like they were going to fuck each other right there, on the street!"

"Shut the fuck up, dipshit!" Hayden hissed, which was followed by the sounds of bodies colliding into each other.

"Hey! Hey! Stop it, you two! You aren't going to fight. I said, *stop it*!" Masen shouted. The sounds of their fight ceased, replaced by their heavy breathing.

"Is it true?" Masen asked. "You *hugged* her?"

"I didn't hug her. I just kept her restrained because she wanted to bail."

"Since when do you need to *hug* her to restrain her?" Blake remarked sarcastically. "And why didn't you just let her go?"

"That wasn't a hug, asshole; I just wanted to mess with her."

"Yeah, right. Let me tell you something, princess," Blake started. "I got used to your hot-cold episodes, and the shit you do can't scare the crap out of me anymore, but switching from one side to the other when it comes to that bitch? It's fucking crazy. I can't believe that."

Masen groaned. "Seriously, man. That chick is the reason Kayden and you got into that car accident. She's so irritating and whiny. We always hated her guts, but these last few days you're different. Actually, you're different ever since we got back from our summer camp, and if you keep on acting like this, I'll start thinking you missed her during summer or some shit like that."

"Oh come on. I'm playing with her."

"You're supposed to hurt her, not *play* with her," Blake spat.

"What's your problem, Blake? Sad because you couldn't *hurt* your toy on Saturday? You're strangely fixated on Jessica Metts."

"So now you're turning this back on me? And what if I am? What does that have to do with you?"

"I don't follow you two anymore," Masen chimed in.

"Blake almost peed his pants with excitement when he saw Jessica Metts on Saturday. She drove Sarah back home, and Blake was more than *glad* to see her. Now, I'm sad I separated the kids." Hayden's voice was dripping with sarcasm.

"I have the fucking right to do whatever I want to her. Besides, you're one to talk! You're fixated on that bitch since the day you met her, and after all this time, you're still playing that stupid cat-and-mouse game. I really wonder if you hate her for real, or that is just a bluff."

My heart thumped so loud that I feared they were going to hear it. I was incapable of moving from this spot. I should go. I should go right away, but my legs didn't listen.

"You have no idea," Hayden growled.

"You bet I don't have. When it comes to her, I don't know you, man."

"He hates me!" I wanted to scream to Blake. *"He tried to kill me, and he's sending me those awful messages now!"*

I looked around me, scared that someone would appear and expose me. I'd been eavesdropping long enough.

I stepped back from the window, intending to walk away silently, when Hayden said, "I don't know myself, man." He sounded defeated and lost. "I don't fucking know anything anymore."

* * * *

I PULLED MY WAVY BROWN hair into a ponytail, inspecting myself in the mirror. I was wearing all black, dressed in baggy workout pants and an equally baggy shirt with a Mickey Mouse logo. I was impatient to get outside and find some relief in running.

The current bundle of nerves had been piling up in my chest since I arrived home in my car thirty minutes ago. My mom was sober enough at last to realize it had been gone for days—I didn't know if I should laugh from the absurdity of it or cry because I was being neglected—and she didn't want to let it slide. It would be a lie if I said she treated me better when she wasn't tanked.

She stopped behind me and crossed her arms over her chest, glowering at me through the mirror. "How much money have you already spent repairing that old wreck?"

Why did she care about the money? It wasn't like she was paying for my repairs.

"I'm handling it, so you don't have to worry about it."

"How should I not worry when you're repairing it all the time?! Do you want us to be flat broke?! If you can't keep it in one piece, then you shouldn't drive."

"I'm sorry, okay? It won't happen again." I could only hope. "I'm going out. See you!"

I didn't wait for her answer or permission to leave. I darted out without even looking at her, needing to get this brewing unease out of my system.

Hayden's car was parked in his driveway, but he was nowhere in sight, which was a relief. I picked up my pace, checking the time on my phone. It was close to six. The sky was bright and clear blue at the moment, but it would be dark soon, which meant I had to return home real quick. Maybe I was becoming paranoid, but since I'd started receiving those dire texts, I didn't feel comfortable being outside during the evening anymore.

I gripped the phone in my hand, jogging along my usual route, my mind returning to the conversation I heard today. I couldn't help but feel that Hayden was setting a new trap for me, because how could he say he didn't know if he hated me when everything he did sent a message of hate? These text warnings were another clear sign of his feelings.

I mustn't be delusional again. Besides, even if he didn't hate me, which was impossible, that didn't change the fact that he'd done many horrible things to me. He still did. I couldn't just turn over a new leaf when it came to him. I couldn't be so foolish.

My leg muscles were aching, but it was exactly what I needed as I pushed myself to go faster. I had to force the thoughts of Hayden away. I was always thinking about him, and it started to feel like an obsession, which showed how much power he had over me.

I wondered if I would be ever capable of forgetting him. It was said that love and hate were similar, and I had to agree because I couldn't stop thinking about him, despite trying my hardest.

My phone beeped in my hand, and I stopped abruptly when I saw "Hidden Number" on my screen. I got the creeps, all the tension that dissipated as I ran coming back to me.

I didn't dare to open the message. How wise would it be to ignore and delete it?

I should go to the police immediately. I might not know for sure if Hayden was behind these texts or not, but this was serious. I didn't want to admit this to myself, but as far as I knew, this could be a real thing and not a cruel prank. I shouldn't treat it as something insignificant.

A hand of cold fear gripped me hard. I had *erased* previous messages.

Oh no. What was I thinking? What could I say if I went to the police? I deleted the first message on Saturday night, so I couldn't prove it existed.

Giving in to my curiosity, I opened the text.

"Aren't you too old to wear a Mickey Mouse shirt?"

Chills broke out all over my skin as I gaped at the message. In terror, I snapped my head up and twisted around, looking everywhere for this person.

It was only 6:30, but this residential street was almost empty save for a few passers by, who were either walking alone or with their partners, and no one held a cell phone or paid any attention to me.

I was horrified that I wasn't able to see the stalker when they could obviously see me. My heart thumped fast, the coldness paralyzing me. I could barely think straight.

I dashed as fast as I could, scared witless of what Hayden planned to do now, or was Hayden really behind all of this? Either way, I had to get home safely.

My phone beeped again. I didn't stop running as I opened the message.

"You can't run fast enough."

I threw my gaze over my shoulder, but there was no one. They were playing with me. They were somewhere, stalking me, enjoying my reaction... The horror was enveloping me more and more. I really couldn't run fast enough...

Another message arrived. *"That's right. Come closer to me."*

What? No!

And another. *"Getting closer."*

No! Where are they?!

This was bad. They would catch me... They would hurt me.

I reached the street corner, but before I could swivel around to go back, I slammed into something. I wasn't able to catch myself, falling down, but then someone grabbed me by the upper arms and kept me on my feet.

I brought my eyes up and screamed. It was Hayden!

"Stay back," I shrieked, shoving him, and pushed backward with my arms raised in front of me.

It was him! I was right! He was sending me these messages! Oh my God. He was sick, despicable, obsessed with me, horrible—

"What the fuck is your problem?" he growled, frowning. "Why don't you look where you're going?"

I backed away a few more steps, whimpering when he moved toward me. I noticed my phone on the ground at the same time as he did. My stomach churned with panic when he bent and picked it up.

He looked at the screen, and his frown deepened. *"Getting closer,"* he read the last message aloud and met my gaze. "What is this? Who sent you this text?"

I couldn't even speak. I had no idea what he was going to do now. He was unstable, clearly planning something... "Hidden number?" He moved his thumb over the screen, anger filling his eyes. "Will you tell me what the fuck this is?" He raised his voice, and I whimpered again, wrapping my arms tightly around my waist.

"You sent those messages, Hayden, so stop pretending like you have no idea what's going on."

"Messages? Which messages?" He returned his gaze to my phone, and his eyebrows furrowed even more. *"That's right. Come closer to me,"* he read the message before the last one. *"You can't run fast enough."* His face was a mask of pure rage now. *"Aren't you too old to wear a Mickey Mouse shirt?"* He raised his head and fixed his stare on my chest, studying the imprint on my shirt. His eyes widened, like he realized only now what I was wearing.

His body tensed, and he looked around us, scanning the area. It was frightening that he was acting innocent, just like when I accused him of slashing my tires.

"When did these texts start? Today?"

"Stop acting! I know you sent them! You're just playing with my mind now—"

"*I didn't send this shit,*" he shouted, and everything in me turned cold.

"You did! You sent the first message two days ago, warning me that you'll slash my face soon!"

"I'll slash your face soon?"

"Yes! And you sent me that horrible picture of my slashed tire covered with blood!"

He searched for something on my phone. "Where is that message?"

For a second there, I expected him to comment on Melissa's and Jessica's texts in my phone, feeling more than glad I'd erased Mateo's messages. I didn't even want to think about his reaction if he'd seen the messages from "Maria's Hair Salon" that had nothing to do with hairdressing.

Fortunately, it seemed that he didn't care about my social life at the moment. "I don't see any more messages from this sender."

"I deleted them."

He didn't answer. He just stared at me, or rather through me, deep in his thoughts. A couple of moments later, his eyes narrowed, focusing on me. "I have no idea why you think it was me who sent you those messages. I thought you already knew that when I warn people, I don't hide behind anonymity." He grasped my forearm and pulled me to him.

"Let me go," I screamed. I couldn't bear not knowing what would come from him next.

The middle-aged man and woman, who were passing by, looked at us. I pleaded them with my eyes to help me. Knowing Hayden, he was capable of abusing me even in front of them.

Hayden sneered at them. "Move along. There is nothing to see here."

"I think you are hurting her," the man said.

"I said, *move along*." The way Hayden looked at this man made him shrink in fear, and he scurried away with the woman, cursing Hayden and "these aggressive young generations nowadays."

I watched them rush away in disbelief. Hayden and I were alone again, which drew my attention to the dreadful fact that the sky had already become dark and the street lamps were lit. Hayden stood too close to me, and I could feel the warmth his body radiated. I could also feel him tremble in a barely controlled anger. Would he snap and hurt me?

"I have no idea what is going on with these messages, but if you're smart, you'll go home right now." My jaw dropped when I heard what he said.

He was speaking like he cared, like my safety concerned him, but I didn't trust him. It must be him who had sent those texts. It must be him.

"Unless you're stupid enough to wander the streets at night."

"If you didn't send me those messages, then what are you doing here?"

"That's none of your business." He released me and gave me my phone back. I didn't waste time to put some distance between us. "You can believe me or not, I don't give a fuck. Now, go home and stay there."

I wanted to tell him that he couldn't order me around, but the last few minutes left me too emotionally drained to do that. I just wanted to go home and curl up in my bed.

I scanned our surroundings once again, but I couldn't see anyone. Hayden's expression didn't give me any answers, like always, so there was no way for me to know if he was lying. If he was telling the truth, then this twisted situation had just become even more serious.

If this was someone else, hiding, playing mercilessly with my mind, who could hurt me in the most dreadful and unimaginable way... The terror rushed through my veins.

I dashed away from Hayden, the dire thoughts swarming my mind.

I reached my home, still contemplating whether Hayden was lying or not, when a new message from the hidden number arrived. I opened it, shaking and on the verge of a breakdown.

"It was fun seeing you accuse him. You really are stupid. You got off the hook this evening, but you won't be that lucky next time."

Chapter 22

THAT MESSAGE ON MONDAY night was the last straw that sent me to the police. I let my mother know about the messages, but she wasn't so optimistic that they would help me against this unknown sender.

I hated involving her. She was already drunk and lost in her thoughts when I returned home, so I couldn't count on her to go with me to the police. Once again, she failed me, and what pained me the most was that our conversation felt like we were discussing bad weather. Her reaction when she heard someone was threatening me was disappointing. It was as if I weren't her daughter.

"That kind of things happen, Sarah. That's life. You'll get to my age, and then guys will try to get into your panties," she said and downed the bourbon in her glass in two large gulps.

I watched her in disgust, wishing for the umpteenth time she weren't my mother. She was treating these messages like they were an ordinary part of life, which sickened me to the core.

"Just don't let it get to you. You'll have to endure much worse things in life than that teenage bullshit."

Seriously? She called it a "teenage bullshit"?

That was when I lost it and screamed at her, telling her she was living the kind of life she herself had chosen. We almost had another huge row, when I decided it would be best to just leave and go straight to the police. Alone.

I didn't have much to back up my claim, so reporting this case felt like another failure. The inspector agreed that those messages were worrisome, but they didn't exactly feel like a potential killer was after my head. He assured me they would try to find the sender, and that was it.

What if Hayden sent those messages after all? If he was pretending last night, he was even more unstable than I'd thought.

Today's computer science class didn't help matters, because it brought another moment that added to Hayden's resentment. Ms. Clare asked us about the outline of our project, but we hadn't started it. We didn't even have a theme of our website. I begged him to work with me on the project, but it fell on deaf ears.

Ms. Clare reminded us we had only one week left to send her the outline, but Hayden acted like he couldn't care less about it, and the fear of failing her class got the best of me. I decided on our theme alone and told her we were making an art blog, which caused Hayden to blow his top.

However, she left him no room to complain, accepting my theme. I could barely focus during the rest of the class, expecting him to retaliate any moment, but he didn't do anything.

Somehow, I found it hard to believe he was letting this slide, puzzling over it even after I arrived home.

It was close to seven when I finished a drawing I was going to send as a part of my college application portfolio. I didn't have time to admire the perspective and depth I nailed in this one, because the doorbell rang and I had to go down and open the door since my mother wasn't home.

I went downstairs, hoping this wasn't something about her. Was she all right? She had her episodes from time to time when she got too drunk and made a mess, so the police or her "friends" from bars had to intervene, coming to our house to notify me about her latest fiasco.

I was close to the door when the doorbell rang again. I approached it and looked through the peephole, expecting to see a police officer who had some news about my mother, but I could see only someone's shoulder.

They rang the doorbell once more. I sighed and cracked the door open, but then I was pushed backward when they shoved the door wide open. I stumbled, barely managing to catch my balance.

I shrieked when I saw Hayden step inside and lock the door behind him. I couldn't believe him!

"What are you doing in my house, Hayden?!"

This was bad. No matter how much he'd tormented me, he'd never *ever* set foot in my house. What was he going to do now?

"You wanted to work with me on that stupid computer project, so here I am."

Is he serious? I observed him carefully, looking for any trace of drunkenness or madness, but there was none.

"You entered my house without permission, and I absolutely don't want you here. Get out!"

His eyes hooded, his step forbidding as he advanced toward me. "I'm not going anywhere."

Damn it. I needed to get him out of here. He was intruding, and that was a crime. My quick inspection of the hallway told me there was no object I could use as a protection. "I'll call the police."

He curled the corner of his lip in disdain. "You won't call shit. It's up to you whether you'll play nice or not, but if you choose to make this difficult for me, you're going to regret it."

I didn't care. I darted to the living room to reach the phone and call the cops, but he easily outran me and grabbed me, snaking his arms around me. I started kicking, hoping to break his grip and escape him, but he was too strong.

"What do you think you're doing?" he growled in my ear, further reducing me to nothing but helplessness and anxiety.

He couldn't get away with this. He just couldn't. If I couldn't call the cops, then I had to save myself some other way. He couldn't terrorize me in my own home! This was too much!

"Let me go!"

"I won't."

"LET ME GO!"

I screamed and kicked wildly, my heart pounding a mile a minute. He clamped his hand over my mouth, muffling all sounds. "Enough, idiot. As I said, I'm not going anywhere. It's in your best interest to cooperate. That is, if you want us to complete this project successfully."

I didn't trust him. He couldn't expect me to let him stay in my house after everything. I couldn't let him.

Then again, we needed to finish our project. I didn't know if he really came here to work on it, but I couldn't be picky. I had to brace myself and go through this.

I went motionless, and he removed his hand from my mouth. "All right. We'll work together. Can you let me go now?"

He released me at last, and I scurried away from him, breathing more easily now that there was some distance between us. "Wait here. I'm just going to my room to get my laptop and notebook."

"No need," he said and rushed up the stairs, leaving me flabbergasted.

"Hey!" I shouted and went after him, fear seeping into my every pore. He couldn't be doing this!

By the time I reached him, he was already in my room. He was standing frozen, taking everything in. The lamp on my desk emitted a slight amount of light in the otherwise dark room, letting the shadows rise, and this alone made me feel extremely vulnerable.

He didn't pay attention to me as he studied the college portfolio drawing on my laptop screen and the papers scattered on my desk. His pensive expression didn't change a bit when he slid his gaze to the drawings on the walls, but then my pulse rapidly increased because he was seconds away from finding a drawing of Kayden, which was placed next to my window.

To make the humiliation more complete, I'd drawn Hayden as well and placed the drawing right above my bed, which happened a long time ago, when I was head over heels for him. Now, I deeply regretted not destroying it.

Kay's and his drawings were dissimilar, at least to me, because they depicted a different reflection in their eyes and showed those tiny differences on their faces. Also, I'd shadowed their facial lines differently, thus making Hayden's face darker and more mysterious.

It didn't take him long to notice Kay's drawing. He stepped closer to it, not taking his eyes off of it. "Of course you'd draw him," he muttered to himself.

What was that supposed to mean?

He didn't move for quite a while, looking at Kayden's drawing, while I racked my brain to think of a way to get him out of here.

"I figured out recently that I've never been in your room before, and that's a huge mistake, because this place means everything to you."

I felt sick. He knew. He knew that my room was my safe place; something that wasn't stained with his hate. Ironically, his room was just a few feet away, but despite that, this was the only place where I felt safe, where I felt far away from the world of pain—from Hayden's world.

As if he'd read my mind, he faced me and said, "I don't want you to feel safe anywhere. Not even in your own room. Besides, you went against me when you decided on that website theme alone, and I won't just let you get away with it."

Of course. He didn't come here because of our project. He wanted to re-taliate. He wanted to use this situation to hurt me on the most personal level.

Horror gripped my insides when I remembered that my Instagram and YouTube accounts were open in the separate tabs in my browser. If he decided to snoop through my laptop, he would easily see them.

Hell no. If he realized I had successful art accounts, he would most likely shut them down.

"Get out of my room. I don't want you here."

"Yeah? Well, I don't want you in my life, but there you are, always present and impossible to avoid."

"You can easily avoid me. Ignore me."

He swiveled around, his intense eyes fixed on me, creating a churning fire in the pit of my stomach. My small room felt much smaller, and I couldn't breathe evenly anymore. I willed myself to take a few deep breaths, watching Hayden move and stop right in front of me. What was he going to do to me?

"I could never ignore you, no matter how much I tried."

What?

My stomach did a somersault, and I actually felt weak. It was like my legs weren't mine. There was something about him that kept me in place, caus-ing me to forget about everything but us in this moment. I inhaled deeply, greedy for the air that could help me clear my thoughts, but that was a big mistake because the distinctive scent of his pine tree cologne met my nostrils. I liked it, which was befuddling.

"Please, get out," I whispered, battling to maintain the eye contact. He remained silent as he studied my face. It felt intimate having him here. It felt unusual.

I was afraid. I was excited.

"I make you nervous."

I swallowed with difficulty. "You already know that."

He came closer to me, and I couldn't move. After everything he'd done, after everything that was Hayden, I couldn't move. What was it in him that didn't scare me away? Where were my instincts that were always telling me to run?

I hate him, so why?

He raised his gaze above my head, focusing on something behind me, and grew still. "What?" he asked in surprise. I lowered my head in shame, knowing exactly what he was looking at. "You drew me."

He recognized it. He understood it was him in that picture, which I'd spent so many nights on, trying to make it perfect and working on every tiny detail until I was happy with my Hayden. I'd spent so much time staring at that drawing and dreaming of him, *hoping* he would grow to love me one day.

I'd been so naive.

"It was a long time ago."

He returned his attention to me, and the sudden fire in his eyes shocked me. "But you still kept it all this time."

Damn, why did he have to be so perceptive? Why couldn't he leave?

"You... Why did you do this?" he asked.

"Why do you care?"

I expected him to say he didn't care and include some mean remark. Instead, he tipped up my chin. I jerked when his skin came in contact with mine, but he didn't let me go. I tried to take a step backward, but he placed his other arm around my waist, keeping me in place, keeping me so close to him... Too close.

"Did you really mean what you said at Kayden's grave? You wanted to help me? You wanted to be there for me?"

His eyes... Oh God, his eyes were like nothing I'd seen before. They were burning into me, devouring me, and getting through to the farthest corners of my soul. There was no hate. Only... *Need.*

He was shaking my world.

And for the first time after a long time, I wanted to reach for him. I wanted to touch him.

I...

No. No.

This must be a trick.

This must be an illusion.

He didn't deserve this, and he didn't deserve me. I snapped out of it, becoming rigid under his hands.

"It didn't mean anything. I don't care about you, Hayden. And as far as I am concerned, you—"

Too suddenly, he grabbed my arms and pushed me down on my bed, pinning me to the mattress. He raised my hands above my head and captured my wrists in his hand, just like that evening in the forest, and fear clouded my mind. I screamed, expecting the worst. He silenced me by pressing his hand against my mouth, and I began kicking and writhing violently, trying to get him off me.

"Shhh," he whispered into my ear and kissed it softly. I closed my eyes, hating to be at his mercy like this. "I won't hurt you."

That... That is a lie. I don't trust you.

He pressed his lips against the sensitive skin bellow my ear, and I whimpered against my will. He licked that place, and to my complete confusion, it felt *good*. My heart throbbed.

He didn't stop, nibbling and leaving hot kisses all over my neck. Slowly, my fear turned into something else—something I didn't want to name.

Everywhere he kissed he left only pleasure, and my inner demon begged for more. That demon made me forget. It made me dazed and no logic or pride mattered. *What is Hayden doing to me?*

I had no idea when I stopped resisting. The way my body felt was too good to be true. It felt unreal, like a sweet nightmare.

His lips ended their journey on my jaw. He removed his hand from my mouth, searching for something in my eyes desperately as his breathing grew heavier. His eyes were liquid black, gleaming with desire. My throat constricted at his arousal, blood rushing through my veins in excitement.

"Why did you kiss me back at Kayden's grave?"

I just stared at him, totally baffled by his question. My mind was still enveloped in that sweet fog, intoxicated with his kisses, so I needed time to catch what he was talking about.

Finally, reason won over passion, and all the pleasant feelings Hayden had created in me disappeared, replaced by a potent wave of shame, anger, and regret.

"I didn't kiss you back. I just went along with you, hoping it would end soon so I wouldn't have to feel such disgust anymore," I lied without blinking, glaring at him spitefully. To my twisted satisfaction, he went stiff above me, the fire in his eyes turning into the ice.

"Bitch," he spat and gripped my wrists above my head even harder, punishing me. He was becoming aggressive in a hot minute, all rousing, ardent feelings forgotten. "You deserve everything I do to you. You deserve suffering and pain."

"Let me go!"

"No. I will never let you go. Never." His gaze slid over my trembling body under his, and a cold smirk formed on his face. "Maybe I should steal your virginity after all. Just like I stole your first kiss."

"You're horrible!"

"Just like you."

I stared daggers at him, wanting to hurt him like he'd hurt me. I wanted to shatter his control. I wanted to make him less powerful...

"You didn't steal my first kiss," I said spitefully, hoping this would throw him off guard.

Once again, he froze, letting me see the fleeting confusion on his face. "What's that supposed to mean?"

"It means that wasn't my first kiss."

"You're lying."

"I'm not."

He stood up with a deep frown, separating himself from me. An unexpected longing filled me because I didn't have his body against mine anymore, and I felt ashamed for it. I raised myself and sat on the edge of my bed, watching him pace around my room as he grew more restless. I wondered what was going on inside his head.

"Who kissed you?"

I averted my gaze. "That doesn't matter."

He grabbed my chin and made me look at him. "Who kissed you?!"

Why the hell did he care?

"Kayden!"

He opened his eyes wide and stepped away from me, looking at me like he couldn't believe what he'd heard. "So, you two *were* in love," he said, sounding like he was asking for confirmation from me. Why did it matter to him?

I certainly couldn't tell him the reason why we kissed. I would never tell Hayden that. "That's none of your business."

His face twisted in an ugly grimace of fury and madness, and for the first time since he entered my room, he looked like he was going to smash something.

"*You bitch*!" he screamed. "You'll pay for everything! I'm done sparing you!"

I jumped to my feet, beyond angry. "Sparing me?! Are you kidding me? You destroyed everything good in me! You made me a wreck! You hurt me in so many ways, and now you say you were sparing me? Are you out of your mind?"

"I still didn't destroy everything, but I will," he responded fiercely and marched over to my window. Startling me, he yanked my blinds violently, removing them from the upper part of the window and breaking them into pieces.

I screamed, frightened, not believing what I was seeing. He couldn't be doing this!

"What are you doing?!" I rushed toward him and grasped his arm to separate him from the blinds, but he snatched it out of my hold and pushed me away.

"I'm finishing something I should've done a long time ago."

I stared at the pile of broken blinds on the floor, feeling like my legs were going to betray me any moment. Tears formed in my eyes, so close to spilling out.

"Why did you do this?" I couldn't stop my voice from being whiny. Those blinds kept me hidden from him. They made me feel safe. Now, they were gone.

He moved to the door, ready to leave. He faced me one last time, shaking in rage. "You can never hide from me. Put up the blinds again, and I'll come back and completely fuck your shit up."

Chapter 23

"I'LL KILL YOU," HAYDEN said to me, hovering above me on my bed. My room was in total darkness, but I could see his fierce eyes staring into me, reaching my soul and trapping me.

"Hayden, don't do this."

"I will, and I will enjoy every single second..." He pressed his lips against mine, taking me by surprise. His tantalizing kiss made me hungry for more, unleashing my long-denied feelings. I stopped resisting and responded to him, melting inside when our tongues met. His hands moved all over me, drowning me in these addictive sensations that only made me want more. Much more.

I felt like I was going to burst from happiness... My Hayden...

I winced and tried focusing on Jonathan and Adelaine's game of chess, but I had a hard time paying attention because my thoughts kept rushing back to the dream I had this morning. My chest constricted at the thought of Hayden's lips and hands on me, which awoke something deep inside of me that had been suppressed for so long...

I felt ashamed for having such dream. I stopped dreaming about kissing him a long time ago, but something changed after Wednesday night, and I was unable to stop thinking about his kisses or his behavior. I hated that I was allowing him to affect me like this.

I could brush off his first kiss at the cemetery as a prank, but why did he kiss me in my room? Why was he kissing me like this, leaving nothing but the thirst for more?

After that fiasco, I decided to work on our project outline alone, hoping to be able to finish it on my own. It was above my head since I knew little about website building, but I was done begging Hayden to cooperate and use his programming skills to help. I had only six days left before the deadline for the outline, and I'd already wasted a lot of time.

I got a call from the police last night, and they told me they had found out that the number behind those messages was no longer in use. The burner phone was located in some trash can, so the investigation reached a dead-end. He advised me to report anything suspicious to them in the future and to take care.

I couldn't believe this person used a disposable phone to harass me. I was edgy because of this whole situation, and I couldn't know if this was something I should really worry about or if someone only went above and beyond to scare me.

"Do you even listen to me, young girl?" I flinched, meeting Jonathan's piercing stare.

"Oh, I'm sorry. I was just thinking about something."

"Look at her. She is always so cute when she blushes," Adelaine cooed. Ugh. Why did she have to point it out?

"You look distracted. What's wrong?" Jonathan furrowed his brows in worry, and something melted in me because he cared enough to ask.

I couldn't tell him about the threats or the weird behavior of my bully. "I'm thinking about tonight's party. I'm so nervous."

That wasn't exactly a lie, because I *was* nervous. Melissa and I had agreed to dress up in the retirement home after work, and I admitted I had no clothes suitable for parties. I never needed those, so there was no point in buying them. She assured me she had the right clothes for me and would bring them with her.

I tried to tell her I didn't think her style matched mine, not wanting to wear some patterned red skirt and black boots, but she told me not to worry about anything and that she would also do my makeup, which only increased my worry.

I didn't want her to dress me up or do my makeup. Melissa liked to wear lots of makeup, so I would probably look like a vamp queen. Either way, I didn't want to risk it, so I brought my most favorite pair of jeans and a plain, black shirt. That way I wouldn't attract any unnecessary attention.

"Is there anything special about this party?" Adelaine asked. "Maybe some boy?" She wiggled her eyebrows at Jonathan. I didn't need to respond to this, because a new wave of blush on my cheeks spoke more than enough.

Mateo was going to be there, and I *was* a bit nervous because of him. If he really liked me, and Melissa was one hundred percent sure he did, it could mean we could kiss tonight. Just the thought itself awoke flutters in my belly.

"This is my first party after a long time," I told them. "I don't go to parties."

She gasped. "Really? But why? You're such a gorgeous young girl and you should be living your life! You should enjoy your youth and have fun while you can, because when you grow up, you're going to regret not using your chances."

Grown ups always talked like this. *Live your life because you live it only once.* I got that, I really did, but it wasn't easy to live life to the fullest when you were poor, bullied, and had no way of getting people's affection.

"Yes, I'm aware of that, but I didn't have friends I could party with."

Her expression turned sympathetic. "That's just sad." *Yeah, tell me about it.* "But why?"

"I don't get along with people."

Jonathan was observing me silently, listening to Adelaine and me. He looked unsatisfied. I avoided his gaze, but then he said, "Every person can get along with people. You just didn't find the right people for you."

"T-That's not true!" I stammered in embarrassment. "Everyone hates me, and I'm sure there must be something wrong with me—"

"Stop making yourself a victim." Jonathan was as harsh as ever. "No one can be friends with everyone. That is impossible because we are all different, which is completely natural. What matters is that you find someone who is right for you. Someone you can be yourself with."

I gaped at him, incapable of forming words.

"Don't let yourself fall into despair. When the right time comes, you'll find people who will accept you for who you are. Just because you didn't find them in one tiny place on this planet, doesn't mean they don't exist at all."

My chest tightened with elation because he was right. It wasn't quite true that I couldn't get along with people. I had Jessica, and I had to believe that what we had was a real friendship. I had to believe she wouldn't run away from me or betray me.

I'd had Kayden. I had that sweet soul, who for some reason decided I was the right person to be his best friend. If I never had another friend for the rest of my life, at least I'd had Kayden who truly loved me.

Jonathan's words were on the mark. Making myself a victim was the worst thing I could do. That would never empower me. That would only make me weaker and throw me into a deeper ignorance.

"You're right," I told him with the full respect I felt for him right now.

"I know I'm right. Do you think I'm throwing my wisdom around here just to spend some words? I don't think so."

Adelaine giggled like a little girl at his impudence, but for the first time I wasn't offended by his blunt remark at all, because I finally understood who Jonathan was. Unlike those bad people who were wrapped in pretty packages that hid their true natures, Jonathan was crude and brusque, but he always told the truth. He wanted to help me in his own unconventional way, but it was a help nevertheless.

· · · ·

AFTER WORK, MELISSA took me to the restroom and put her makeup on my face, or "did her magic," as she called it. She worked quickly and let me take a look in the mirror only when she finished.

I couldn't look away from my reflection. My now-striking eyes were contoured with a black eye pencil and a bit of black eye shadow. The blush on my cheeks accentuated my cheeks and jaw, and I had a beige lipstick on my lips, which matched my fair complexion. I batted my eyelashes a few times, admiring what I saw. I looked very pretty.

Melissa took black jeans and a gray slim fit top out of her bag. The front part of the top was covered with gray lace, which looked cute, but it was something I wouldn't usually dare to wear. Once more, I tried to refuse her because I felt uncomfortable accepting her clothes, and I didn't feel confident enough to wear them, but she didn't change her mind in the slightest, convincing me to wear them eventually.

I put on my black ballerina pumps and followed Melissa out of the retirement home. She was wearing tight black pants that were ripped on the front and a shirt with a guitar imprint that hung loose on her hips. Her makeup was heavy, unlike mine, but it suited her well.

She drove us to Jessica's house to pick her up.

"I can't wait to see Mateo's reaction when he sees you! He'll totally fall for you even more," she said excitedly.

I gnawed at my lip, extremely keyed up. If everything went well, Mateo and I would kiss and maybe get together? I had a hard time imagining hooking up with someone this very evening. That would be my first time, and I was absolutely terrified.

What if I did something weird? What if I got so confused that I actually embarrassed myself in front of him? What if—

"Right. I forgot to tell you," Melissa interrupted my erratic thoughts. "There will be some students from your school too." I looked at her in horror, my heart picking up its pace rapidly.

"What?" I croaked.

"Yeah. Maybe you'll recognize some of them." *No.*

No, no, no.

She formed a gigantic smile. "Tonight will be so fun."

Chapter 24

I SPENT THE REST OF our trip twisting my hands and fighting my anxiety. I couldn't go to a party where I could see my classmates. All excitement had left me, and I felt like the tension would swallow me whole any moment. I had to take deep breaths in order not to have an anxiety attack.

What if Hayden was there? What were the possibilities of that happening?

Oh, who was I kidding? Melissa had already said her brother was friends with someone from our school. On top of that, Steven participated in fights just like Hayden.

No. Hayden mustn't be there tonight. He mustn't.

We picked Jessica up, who was wearing a gorgeous, flowery fit and flare dress that went to her knees and revealed her arms. She combined it with a red satin jacket and red ballerina pumps. Her long hair was curled and her face had a bit of makeup, but wearing makeup or not, she looked absolutely beautiful.

"You two are so going to make boys drool all over you," Melissa squealed.

"You think?" Jessica asked from the back seat.

"Absolutely."

I tried to relax, listening to Melissa chirp about many things, but I couldn't, especially when her house came into view. My jaw dropped because it was enormous. It had two garages and two long driveways that were filled with too many cars. I observed the parked vehicles to find any familiar ones, but it was dark and there were so many of them, so I couldn't find what I was looking for.

Melissa parked at the end of a long line of cars, and we got out, welcomed by the bass of the loud music coming from the house. Some people were sitting on the porch, already littering it with the plastic cups and cigarette butts. Jessica and Melissa looked equally excited, so I willed myself to relax and enjoy the night.

Come on. Her house is huge and there are a lot of people inside. You won't even see them, Sarah!

The blaring music assaulted my ears when Melissa opened the front door, eliminating any possibility of talking. We entered the dim hallway, which contained lots of smoke, and Melissa leaned to me to tell me something.

"What?!" I yelled, not hearing a word she'd said.

"I said I'll introduce you to my brother!"

"Ah! Okay!"

She took Jessica and me by the hand and guided us through the sea of sweaty bodies that moved to the rhythm of a popular pop song. I grinned at the sight of a gay couple kissing next to the staircase, who didn't take their hands off each other. Slowly, nervousness disappeared and thrill took its place, but then I realized I forgot my bag and my phone in Melissa's car. Just great.

I had to go and get my phone at some point later, but for now I would go with the flow.

Melissa led us to her gigantic living room, dimly lit like the hallway and furnished with expensive-looking pieces. It was crowded with people, many of them dancing or drinking, and this atmosphere gave me the feeling that everything was possible. At the moment, I wasn't that loner Sarah who couldn't hang out with other people and have some fun. Anything could happen tonight, and I loved the anticipation.

Melissa drew one tall guy away from the group of his friends. "Girls, meet my brother Steven. Steven, this is Sarah and Jessica."

I had to raise my head in order to meet his eyes. He was really tall, probably around 6'5". He gave off a bad vibe and a terrible smell; his face looked unhealthy because it was puffy and sallow, at odds with his too muscular physique. My skin crawled because of the way his blue eyes with dilated pupils looked at me.

"Nice to meet you," he slurred, not taking his eyes off of me.

It dawned on me why his gaze seemed strange. It was because he was stoned. I glanced at Melissa, and she shrugged her shoulders, uncomfortable about it. Somehow, I was glad that he didn't offer a handshake because I didn't want to come in contact with him.

"What would you like to drink?" he asked us, looming over me in a strange way. "We have everything, so you can pick anything you want."

I wasn't sure what I should say. I drank alcohol only a few times before, but I didn't know what I could drink now. Besides, I felt like I shouldn't take anything from Steven. He came across as one of those guys who could put anything in my drink, and I didn't want to take any risks at some stranger's party.

"I'll pour us the punch," Melissa said, pulling Jessica and me by the hands to the table with the punch. "Sorry. I didn't expect him to be so wasted already. That jerk. But don't worry about the punch. It's alcoholic, but it isn't laced with any drugs."

She handed us our drinks, and we tapped our cups together, saying cheers. The punch tasted unusually sweet, without the bite I expected. Just as she filled our cups again, I decided that this party was not so bad.

I wasn't used to alcohol, so several cups of punch later, I was already three sheets to the wind, all hyperactive and happy. When Melissa pulled us to dance, I didn't even hesitate, my body following the beat of the music. There were so many people around us, but I didn't care. I didn't care if they were going to find my dancing strange or think there was something wrong with me...

I don't care, and it's absolutely amazing.

We kept dancing, laughing at each other. I could unleash the wild energy that was locked inside of me all the time, and I felt free. I could do anything I wanted. *Anything is possible.*

Mateo. I couldn't wait for Mateo to come, and for the first time I didn't want to think about the consequences of my actions. Even if I got just one evening with Mateo, it was enough. It was more than I ever had.

As the tempo of the music sped up, Melissa grabbed Jessica's and my hand, and initiated some quirky, energetic dance, spinning us around. Everything became a blur, and I closed my eyes, enjoying the thrill coursing through my veins, laughing and laughing. I never wanted this to end.

However, the happy bubble that kept me high was broken when I hit someone's hard body behind me. I turned to face them, ready to apologize, but then I met Josh's harsh eyes. I frowned, taken aback, noticing his own surprise on his face.

"What are you doing here, cunt?"

I could ask you the same. "Enjoying the party, obviously," I replied sarcastically, failing to feel the fear I always felt near him. Somehow, after all that alcohol, it wasn't difficult for me to talk back to him at all.

"Talk back to me again, and I'll make sure you won't enjoy it at all," he threatened me with a sneer. Natalie and Christine appeared next to him, both of them glaring at me.

"What are you doing here?" Natalie fired her question at me.

Oh great. They were here too. Just my luck.

"I think Josh has already asked that unoriginal question." I cast her a mocking gaze, enjoying to press her buttons. Seriously, why wasn't I this brave when I was sober? Natalie fuming with anger was rather funny.

She dug her nails into my arm, looking at me like she was ready to chop off my head. "You're so dead."

She raised her hand, but Melissa intervened, seizing her arm. "Hey, hey, hey! Slow down! Take a chill pill!"

Natalie brushed Melissa's hand off her arm. "Don't touch me," she hissed at her. "I have no idea who let you in here, but you're leaving now!" Natalie told me, looking ready to throw me out right away.

This time it was Christine who moved to grab my arm, but Melissa blocked her, and Josh shoved her away.

"Hey! Lay off!" Melissa shouted, glaring at Josh. "I don't know what your problem is, pal, but you won't treat us like this, especially not in my house!" She scowled at Christine and Natalie. "The same goes for you, Devil's spawns! You're the ones who should leave!"

She stared them down, her tall frame hovering over Natalie and Christine. She looked like she could hit them any moment if provoked, and I felt a wave of admiration and gratitude toward her. She was ready to fight for us, not caring about the consequences.

I wanted to fight my battles like that. I wanted to be brave, strong, and confident. Encouraged by Melissa's strength and the amount of alcohol I consumed, I got into Natalie's face.

"I'm not going anywhere. You may live in an illusion that I'll always let you walk over me, but you're wrong. And if you don't like that, you can just go fuck yourself."

I watched her face fall in pure pleasure, finally able to let her feel some of her poison. Still high on adrenaline and power, I snatched Christine's drink out of her hand and poured it over Natalie, sending the liquid all over her face and chest. She shrieked and gaped at me.

Melissa went into a fit of laughter, and Jessica looked at me in awe. I felt so proud of myself, which was a long-forgotten feeling. I wished it could last.

"You ugly freak," Christine spat. "You're going to regret this."

The people around us turned to watch, finding amusement in Natalie's predicament. Josh's eyes were two menacing slits, staring at me with such hostility that a shiver rushed down my spine. In an instant, my instinct screamed at me to move away from him. He curled his hands into fists and took a step toward me.

He's going to hit me.

"Hey, hey, hey!" Melissa threw herself in between us, stopping him. "Hold on! Don't you fucking dare put a single finger on her! Do you hear me?!"

He looked like he was going to hit her, but then Natalie grabbed his arm and drew him away from us.

"Let's go," she bit out and laced her arm with Josh's. "I don't want to stay here even a second longer." She gave Melissa a dirty look. "I won't take a step into your trashy house ever again."

Melissa clapped her hands, grinning. "Wonderful! Now you really made my day. You know where the door is. Off you go!"

I shook my head when they walked away, finally able to breathe normally. *Phew.* I couldn't believe I poured a drink over Natalie. I fought, and I won.

I did this.

Oh, the victory felt so good!

"That was awesome!" Melissa high-fived me, sharing my joy. "You rock, girl!"

"Yeah," Jessica agreed, smiling from ear to ear.

"You turned into Super Wonder Woman Sarah and kicked their asses!"

I looked at Melissa in amusement. "Super Wonder Woman?"

"Yes! You were totally hot and dangerous, and your eyes were flashing with some power and—"

"Okay, okay. I get it. I was awesome."

"You really were," Jessica confirmed.

"You were awesome, too," I told Melissa. "Thank you for sticking up for me."

"No need to thank me. I would do it again if needed." She formed a deep frown. "They have some serious issues."

I shrugged my shoulders, too deep in my alcoholic daze to dwell on it.

"Anyway, girls, I think we should forget about those idiots and drink something else! Let's go to the kitchen."

I wasn't so sure about it anymore. Not after I saw Josh, Natalie, and Christine, which could mean that Hayden was here too. Melissa led us out of her living room before I could voice my doubts, and as we pushed through a large group of people blocking the way to the kitchen, I thought it would be better if I left. There was no way I could stay if Hayden was here.

We entered Melissa's spacious kitchen, and I stopped in my tracks. It felt as if someone was squeezing my heart so hard and blocking my airway when I saw Hayden sitting on the kitchen island countertop kissing *two* girls.

A blonde wearing a mini skirt and a golden top was in between his legs, moving her hands over his chest while kissing his neck. He was leaning into the redhead girl sitting next to him, kissing her passionately with his hand positioned low on her waist, and I had to look away, extremely embarrassed of what I saw. An unpleasant feeling spread through my chest, and I tried to convince myself that I wasn't bothered by it. I was just ashamed and disgusted.

Obviously, Hayden and Christine were in their breakup phase again.

"Those are Blake, Hayden, and Masen," Jessica exclaimed into my ear, and I looked around. Blake and Masen were necking with some girls in the corner of the kitchen.

Just why did all of them have to be here, of all places?

I must get out of here. If any of them saw me—especially Hayden—they would create mayhem.

"Do they have any shame? Kissing like that with those girls? Look at Blake! That girl is straddling his lap and grinding against him! Why don't they get a room or something?" Jessica continued, but I didn't bother to answer, plotting our escape tactic.

I tried to even my breathing, my heartbeat too fast. I was about to tell Melissa that Jessica and I needed to go to the bathroom, but it was too late because Melissa didn't even notice us stopping, on her way to the fridge on the other end of the kitchen.

There weren't many people here, so if Hayden decided to finally break that long kiss he was sharing with the redhead, he would spot me immediately. Opening the fridge, Melissa glanced at us over her shoulder. "Sarah? Why are you still standing there? Come here!"

As if someone used a spell on him, Hayden immediately broke his kiss and looked in my direction. The shock on his face was evident as he took me in. He gave me a slow once-over, and I grew unusually hot, extremely self-conscious. The urge to run away was overwhelming.

"Jessica, come with me." I swiveled around and caught her hand, hoping to hide us among all these people, but Hayden was always there to catch me whenever I tried to escape. We barely managed to get out of the kitchen, when Hayden took a hold of my arm, breaking my connection with Jessica, and dragged me after him. I glanced over my shoulder at Jessica, extending my hand toward her, but the crowd separated us and Hayden took me away.

Why couldn't he just let me go?

He forced me inside a small bathroom underneath the stairs before I could protest and slammed the door behind him. I couldn't believe him!

The panic rose in my chest when the darkness enveloped us, his body flush with mine. This room was too small for us two. His large frame was taking all available space with no way for me to break the contact between us. He turned the light switch on, and I blinked a couple of times to clear my blurred vision. He was staring at me in the way that paralyzed me, his eyes containing pure fire.

I was too aware of his body. I was too aware of how we touched and how warm and strong he was. His black jeans and shirt hugged his muscles all too tightly, revealing those perfect curves and lines of his body. He looked too handsome for his own good.

"What are you doing here? Who invited you?"

"I could ask you the same question," I jeered at him, surprising us both with my alcohol-induced boldness.

I was confounded because my response didn't further aggravate him. On the contrary, it slightly cooled down his anger. He looked at me with a new-found interest, and my gaze fell onto his separated lips. Had they always been so ample and kissable?

Kissable?

Oh hell no. That stupid thought didn't cross my mind. It didn't.

"You were always so weak and pathetic, and it was repulsive watching you crawl around and beg for mercy, but now all of a sudden, you think you can talk back to me like this?"

He placed his arms against the tiles, trapping me in between them. His smell mixed with his cologne, alcohol, and cigarettes did wonders to me. He wasn't completely drunk, but his glimmering eyes indicated he wasn't sober either.

"It's only fair because you were torturing me for quite a long time. You deserve much more than that."

His nostrils flared, his breaths coming out more quickly. "What did you just say?"

I was supposed to be scared. I should shut up, try to calm him down, or do anything that would help me get out of this place that reduced the whole world to only Hayden and me. Only we mattered.

No, I wasn't scared. I was excited. I loved being this daring and saying what I'd always wanted to say. I *loved* seeing him react like this. *What is wrong with me?*

"You heard me well, or are you deaf, on top of your stupidity?" I used the exact sentence he said three months ago when he wanted me to twerk in front of the whole cafeteria, catching him off guard.

He clasped the back of my neck. "You're playing a dangerous game now. I think you forgot who owns who here. You don't get to boss me around."

He wound his other arm around my waist, pulling me to him, and my pulse spiraled faster. I fisted my hands against his chest. As much as I pre-tended to seem unfazed by his nearness and actions, I was on edge. My eyes widened when I felt something hard press against my stomach.

He smirked, noticing my reaction to his erection. "Surprised? Don't think you're anything special." He ground against me, and I didn't know if I hated more that he did it or that I didn't dislike it. *I'm a contemptible person.* "It's just a natural reaction."

He was making out with those girls just a few minutes ago. "This only proves you're a manwhore."

"And you're a hypocrite. You're actually enjoying this."

His smirk was too punishing, and I realized he could see right through me. The longer I stayed here, the more dangerous of a game we played, and I didn't like not knowing the rules of the game. It was sick and twisted, and I willed myself to remember all the terrible things he'd done to me.

"Let me go."

I hated him for being able to make me forget everything, for making me lost in the present moment and in these confusing, overwhelming feelings. What was happening to me? I hated him. I wanted to be far away from him, yet here I was, not even trying to move away. *I'm so contemptible.*

"Hayden, let me go!"

"I won't until you say you'll leave the party. Did you already forget you aren't allowed to go to parties?"

"Enough. Just stop. You can't control my life and treat me like this. I have friends now. Friends who want me here."

Anger clouded his features, his grip on me increasing. "You became unpredictable these last few weeks, talking back and defying me, but I'm done playing around." His hand traveled down my back and to my bottom, squeezing it. "How about I take you right here and now?"

Oh God, he was crazy. He couldn't be thinking that seriously!

I didn't know this Hayden. Hayden never threatened me with sex, yet these last several days he crossed that line and made me feel things I couldn't even name.

I was in no way ready to deal with what was happening right now, and no amount of alcohol could give me enough courage for this.

Terrified that he could finally snap and break that boundary here, of all places—both figuratively and literally—I grabbed an air freshener spray from the sink next to me and sprayed it onto his face.

He jerked away from me and covered his eyes, hissing. "Bitch!"

I pushed him off me, not wasting time. I opened the door and dashed out of the bathroom, reaching the safety of the crowd in the other part of the house. Only then I allowed myself to stop.

What have I done?! Am I crazy?!

The bubbles of hysteria climbed up my throat, and I started laughing, unable to contain myself. I fought him back too! That felt so good.

I just hoped Hayden wouldn't get that air freshener out of his eyes any time soon.

Chapter 25

I INTENDED TO LISTEN to Hayden and leave the party. All the excitement and pleasure of this evening had evaporated into thin air, and as long as he was here, I couldn't relax even for a second.

I was afraid Blake and Masen would harass Jessica, and I hoped she'd managed to avoid them somehow. It would be best if she and I left immediately.

I searched for Melissa and Jessica around the house, determined to find them, but had no success. I went to the backyard as my last stop, but they weren't there. I halted next to a large pool illuminated by floor lights, enjoying the fresh air after being confined in a small space infused with Hayden's intoxicating scent. I gazed at the clear, star-spangled sky, wondering what was going on between Hayden and me.

How did it turn into the nearness, touches, smell, and the quickened heartbeat that blurred everything that happened before? What was it in his eyes that screamed his deepest thoughts at me? I saw inexplicable passion in his gaze that opposed everything we'd gone through so far, and I didn't know what to make of it. He hated me. He even tried to kill me. Still, his proximity and the way he kissed me confused me...

No, I was overthinking now. Hayden might be unpredictable and able to turn from fire into ice in a matter of seconds, but there was no doubt that he didn't feel anything for me.

He would make me pay the next time he saw me. I was certain of it.

I spun around, determined to leave right this second, but then I noticed Jessica and Melissa running in my direction.

"Hey, girl," Melissa said loudly. "We've been searching for you everywhere. Steven's pal just grabbed you and took you away... Are you okay?"

I nodded and glanced at Jessica. "And you? Are you okay? Did Blake and Masen see you?"

"Yes, but luckily, Melissa intervened before Blake could do anything."

"Seriously, those guys need a mental check up. They're like rabid dogs," Melissa said. "What do they have against you anyway?"

I didn't have a chance to answer her, because Mateo appeared in my line of sight, and my heart dropped. *Oh no, Mateo.*

I completely forgot about him.

I checked him out, noticing how attractive he looked in those dark jeans that hung low on his hips and a green button-down shirt. He spotted me and grinned, striding to us.

This wasn't fair. This wasn't how this night was supposed to be. I was supposed to be free to enjoy my time with Mateo and see if there could have been something more between us. Instead, I hoped to leave this party as soon as possible, ditching Mateo in the process, so I could run away from Hayden.

"I was looking for you," he said and halted in front of me. He didn't take his eyes off of me even once. He surprised me when he leaned in and left a lingering kiss on my cheek, his rather unpleasant cologne enveloping me, and I scrunched up my nose a bit.

I couldn't even be excited about this anymore. I couldn't enjoy my time with him, because my mind kept coming back to Hayden in that bathroom, who was probably planning my demise at the moment.

I took a slight step back. "Mateo, I..." I felt even worse because he was smiling so softly at me.

"Girls," he finally acknowledged Jessica and Melissa, nodding at them. I introduced Jessica, catching on the way Melissa was smiling at me. She looked like she was plotting something.

"I think Jessica and I should go get another drink," she said, clearly bent on giving Mateo and me some space. I wanted to stop her and say that wouldn't be necessary, but Jessica agreed all too quickly with her.

"But what about them?" I asked Jessica, referring to Blake, Hayden, and Masen. I was worried about her safety.

"Don't you worry about a thing," Melissa replied instead of her. "Everything will be fine. You two kids should enjoy now." I watched her take Jessica by the arm and scurry away with her, avoiding Mateo's gaze in embarrassment.

He cleared his throat, and I met his stare reluctantly. He was amused.

I giggled, all nervous. What now?

He grew serious. "There is something I need to tell you."

"Yes?"

"I thought a lot about our last conversation. I crossed a line then, but I was so confused and angry when I saw that fake profile."

I cast my eyes down. I didn't want to talk about my stupid reaction and that fake profile. "It's okay."

"It's not okay, Sarah. I know I don't have the right to interfere in your life, but I felt furious. I wanted to beat the assholes that were responsible for that."

A warm, joyous feeling spiraled through my chest, and I soaked in the feeling of someone really caring about me. I felt happy and ashamed at the same time because I didn't want to bother him with my problems.

"That isn't necessary—"

"It is, Sarah. We barely know each other, but I can't stop thinking about you." *Oh my God.* "I like you, as I already told you. I don't want to push these feelings on you, but know that I want to protect you from anyone who harasses you. I want you to give me a chance."

The doubt greeted me again because of what Melissa said about Mateo's love life.

"Um, Melissa told me you don't actually date..." *Great.* I said the worst thing I could say, probably totally ruining my chances with him.

"Actually..." He stepped closer to me and cupped my cheek. My breath hitched. "Melissa was right. *But.*" He flashed his cute smile at me. "I've never met a girl like you before. Other girls were always the same. Clingy and predictable. You were different from the start. You're so smart, and whenever you smile, your face glows." I couldn't believe this was happening to me. "And I love your blush." *Oh.*

He caught a strand of my hair and tucked it behind my ear. "You look so beautiful tonight."

My throat constricted. "Thank you," I answered timidly, desperately searching for something better to say. Somehow, everything was happening fast, and even though I'd been preparing myself for this, I felt unusually shy.

He glanced at my lips and lowered his head. *This is it...* My heart thumped faster. He was going to kiss me...

"Get away from her, piece of shit!" An instant later, Hayden shoved him away from me and punched him in the face.

Hayden's hit sent Mateo to the ground, and horror consumed me. Hayden looked animalistic, with bared teeth and veins popping out on his head. He was furiously shaking, his eyes two pools of fury and hate. He didn't give Mateo time to stand up, jumping on top of him and dealing him a punishing blow after a punishing blow.

"Hayden, stop!" He was going to kill him! "Stop hurting him!"

From the looks of it, Mateo didn't stand a chance against mad Hayden, who kept hitting his face, beating the crap out of him. There were a few people around us, and all of them seemed stunned to see them fighting, not doing anything but glancing hopelessly at each other.

What the hell, people?! Isn't anyone brave enough to stop this mess?!

I curled my hands into fists, adrenaline pumping through my body. I had to do something.

I knew it was foolish of me, but I couldn't waste more time. I jumped on Hayden's back and wrapped my arm around his neck, pulling him backward.

"Get away from him," I shouted into his ear.

"Get off me!"

Effortlessly, he threw me off his back, and I landed in the grass. My move was a much-needed distraction for Mateo to defend himself and punch Hayden back, which threw Hayden off Mateo. Soon, the tables were turned, and Mateo was on top of Hayden, giving him a taste of his own medicine.

I stood up with a racing pulse, watching them hit each other and drawing more blood. It was horrible, and with each crunching sound I became more distraught.

"Do something," I yelled at two guys who were the nearest to them. "Separate them before they kill each other!"

They glanced between me and them, looking as if they weren't sure if they should listen to me and risk their own heads. Just as they stepped forward, deciding to intervene, Hayden managed to get up.

He pulled Mateo up by the front of his shirt and punched him hard in his jaw, making him lose his balance and stumble backward. Unable to stop himself, Mateo fell right into the pool, hitting the surface with a loud splash.

"No," I screamed, afraid he might drown if Hayden's blow left him incapacitated.

"What the fuck is going on here?" Melissa yelled, running to us with Steven and Jessica. I was relieved to see her, hoping this madness would finally end.

"What do you think you are doing?" she shouted at Hayden and punched him in his already bruised cheek.

I let out a gasp, not believing my eyes. She actually hit him!

Feeling both awe and fear for her safety, I itched to do something to protect her from Hayden's possible violent outburst. Out of the corner of my eye, I saw Mateo swim to the pool ladder.

Hayden grabbed her arm and pulled her closer to him. "I'll kill you for this."

I could clearly see the fear in Melissa's eyes, but she didn't even flinch. "You can try, asshole, but you're going down with me."

"Hey, Hayden! Chill, bro!" Steven jumped in, separating Melissa from him. "That's my sister you're threatening!"

"Then keep her on a tight leash. She's barking too much for her own good," Hayden snarled at him.

"What did you just say?" Melissa shrieked, jumping at him, and clawed his face, which added to his bruises and wounds. Steven snaked his arms around her and barely managed to separate her from him.

"If you keep up with this bullshit, I'll forget you're Steven's sister and make you regret it."

"Oh, I'm so scared!"

Mateo was swaying, wincing after each step he took closer to us. Despite being injured, he looked like he would fight Hayden again, so I headed to him with the intention to stop him and protect him from further conflict.

Just as I passed Hayden, he yanked me to him. "You aren't going anywhere," he hissed into my ear.

"Leave me alone!" I jerked my arm away, but it was futile since his grip only increased.

"Didn't you hear her? Let go of her," Melissa shouted at him.

"And what makes you think I'll actually listen to you?" he jeered at her.

"Drop her arm, jerk!" Mateo spat out and rushed forward, set on hurting Hayden.

Hayden released me a moment before Mateo swung his fist at him, easily dodging his attack. They were about to continue fighting, but then Masen and Blake appeared and split them up.

"Hey, hey, man." Masen tried to hold Mateo still. "Calm the fuck down."

"What is going on here?" Blake glared at Mateo as if he was ready to fight him too.

Jessica approached me and placed her hand on my shoulder. "Are you okay?" she asked me, her voice giving away her trembling.

I half-smiled at her, feeling better with her next to me. "Yeah."

"Steven, get your hands off me!" Melissa broke their contact and stomped to Hayden. "This has escalated into a disaster. I don't know what your goddamn problem is, but if you don't leave my house immediately, I'll call the police."

Hayden's body tensed, his arm muscles flexing as he fought to keep his anger at bay. "Gladly; not that I actually believe you will call the police when your house is full of minors drinking."

She clenched her jaw, unable to find a response to that. He closed the distance between us, grabbed my upper arm, and tugged me after him toward the house.

"Wait, Hayden! Wait! What are you doing?" I yanked my arm and dug my heels into the pavement, trying to set myself free.

"Whoa!" Melissa came to a stop in front of us. "Where do you think you're going?"

"We're leaving."

"No, you're not! You're mental, dude! Leave my friend alone!"

"I own your *friend*!" A collective gasp sounded all around us.

"What did you just say?"

"You heard me. Sarah and I are leaving together."

"You aren't going anywhere with her," Melissa screamed at him, and Jessica joined her side, glaring at Hayden. "Leave her alone, or I'll call the police—a house full of underage drinkers or not."

"Be my guest," he told her with no sign of any emotion. He leaned down, his lips only inches away from my ear. "Right now, after your dick move in the bathroom and getting all mushy with this shitbag, I have zero patience," he whispered. "If you don't come willingly with me, I'll go back and kill the shit that put his hands on you. I don't care about the police cocksuckers or anyone here, so you better not test me."

He was definitely crazy! "Don't threaten him!"

"I'll do whatever I fucking want. Now do as I say, because I swear I'm two seconds away from snapping."

The way aggressiveness seeped out of him, twisting his injured, bloody face lines into ferocious hatred, made the dread flow through my veins, and I believed his every single word. There was that darkness in his eyes again, which gave him an inhuman appearance, like he truly didn't care about the consequences.

Besides, he had Blake and Masen on his side, who would support his craziness if needed. Mateo couldn't win against the three of them.

"Okay," I whispered in defeat, a wave of pure hate washing over every fiber of my being.

I hated him for putting me through all of this. He could use his brute force if he wanted, but what did I have? I wanted to finish what Mateo started and make him bleed. I hated him for making me feel this violent, but damn it, I was so mad!

"Fucking great. Now, move." He tugged my arm, moving forward.

"Stop," Mateo shouted and halted next to Melissa and Jessica, the three of them forming a sort of a barricade. I looked at them with my pleading eyes. I didn't want this to turn into an uglier mess. It was horrible already, and I felt miserable because I was the trigger for all of this.

Masen and Blake stopped in between us and them, prepared to pounce on Mateo.

"Please," I pleaded Mateo. I couldn't even look him in the eyes, ashamed and devastated.

There he was—a boy who wanted to give me a chance. He was the person who showed me nothing but kindness and the one I almost kissed this evening... And here I was, letting Hayden get away with his violence and hate. I didn't want Mateo to get hurt. I just didn't want to watch anyone get hurt because of me again.

"Let us pass," I said through gritted teeth. "Everything will be okay." They gaped at me, bowled over, and I forced myself to endure this humiliation.

"I'll be fine. Hayden and I live next to each other, so he'll take me home. Right, Hayden?" I had no idea what I was talking about, since there was no chance that would actually happen. I was burning with shame, awaiting his cruel response.

"Right," he replied, surprising me that he agreed this easily. Masen and Blake glanced between each other, their confused expressions telling me they had no idea what was going on with Hayden now.

That wasn't a good sign.

"There's no way I'd allow this—" Melissa started, but Hayden silenced her when he said, "Steven, either you make her shut up or I will, and we all know what happens when I lose my shit. Let's go." He pulled me after him.

Melissa and Mateo burst out yelling, attempting to stop us again, but Blake and Masen blocked them. Their screams and the sounds of commotion drifted after us, and I just wanted to tune them all out and forget about this complete chaos.

Hayden never took his hand off me as he led me around the house, following a garden path that was faintly illuminated by the street lights in the front of the property.

"You don't have to drag me around! I'll follow you!"

"No. I don't trust you."

We reached the driveway, but I still hoped someone would stop us. My hope was crushed when we reached his car.

He took the key fob out of his pocket and unlocked the car, bringing me to the passenger-side door. "Get in. And don't even think about running, because I'll easily catch you."

He released me at last, but he didn't move from his spot, waiting for me to obey him. Reluctantly, I opened the door and got inside, despising him for limiting my every single move.

I looked all around me, taking in the luxurious interior of the car filled with his pine tree scent and a faint cigarette smell. It radiated sheer power, just like Hayden, and I felt overwhelmed. I couldn't believe where this evening took me. Their fight had pretty much sobered me up, and I already missed the blissful alcoholic daze that made me feel like I had absolutely no worries in this world.

Hayden entered and started the car immediately. "You better buckle up."

I barely had time to do that because he sped up in the next moment, swerving around the parked cars, and reached the road at full speed.

He was driving too quickly for my taste, and I had to grab my seat to steady myself each time he made a sharp turn into a new street.

My stomach did a flip because I remembered I was in a car with a drunk person, and I glanced at him from the corner of my eye, as if that could bring me any reassurance that we wouldn't crash. The bruises on his cheek and the dried blood on his swollen lower lip were a grim reminder of how brutally he attacked Mateo.

"What you did to Mateo was horrible."

"So that dickhead has a name."

I glared at him. "Don't call him that!"

"I'll call that shit what I fucking like. Nobody touches you."

"Why the hell not?"

He glanced at me, his eyes searing into me. "Because I hate when other guys touch you."

My chest constricted at the undertone of his words, but I refused to give them any significance. "You hate everything. You hate me, you hate when other guys touch me... Enough."

"No, it's never enough. Don't even think about hooking up with him."

I couldn't believe him! "You're sick."

"Yes, you're right. I'm sick. You're making me sick."

"This has gone too far, Hayden. You can't control my life, and you certainly can't make my choices—"

"Of course I can. I already *am* making your choices."

I was fuming, digging my nails into my palms. "*Fine*. However, you can't control my heart. You'll never control my feelings. You can keep me away from other people, but you won't ever stop me from loving them."

He didn't answer, and for a fleeting moment, I felt good I said something that finally made him shut up, but then our eyes met and I noticed his distressed expression that took me completely by surprise. He was searching for something in my eyes, desperate for... What?

He tore his gaze away from me and brought his attention back to the dark, empty road. "This Mateo... Did you meet each other just now?"

What was up with that question? Did he actually expect me to spill the beans? First, he attacked him, and now he was acting like a police detective, so fixated on him.

"You sound jealous," I blurted out, even though this seemed implausible after all the monstrosities he committed.

His eyes found mine again, and all the air was sucked out of the cabin. I felt tingles all over my body as he gazed deeply into me. "Do you want me to be?"

Whoa. "What kind of question is that?"

"I kept thinking..." He focused on the road again, looking like he was lost in thought. "Once, Kayden said something to me that really made me curious. You two were in the Nepaug State Forest the evening before, almost three months before he died."

All the hairs stood up on my neck. I stared at the floor of his car, my heartbeat too fast.

Kay and I kissed that evening in the forest.

"Kayden looked like someone killed his puppy. I knew you two were together, so I assumed you argued. When I asked him what happened he said only one thing."

I held my breath, impatiently waiting for him to continue. He didn't.

"What did he say?" I hated that I was giving him the pleasure to see me curious.

"*You won.*"

I gaped at him. "What?"

He glanced at me. "Yes. He just said that and locked himself in his room for the rest of the day. I had no clue what he meant then."

Why did Kay say that? We kissed, but it only happened because he offered it. He even told me I could pretend he was Hayden...

A shot of pain coiled through my chest. I didn't want to remember that shameful moment. After our kiss, he confessed his feelings for me, and I reacted like a complete idiot, ignoring the way he felt.

I hurt him so bad, but he always knew how I felt about Hayden. Why would he go to Hayden and say that, especially when Hayden wasn't even involved?

What if he was involved? Hayden was jealous because I spent time with Kayden, but what if he wasn't jealous of me for taking his brother away from him?

What if he was jealous of Kayden?

"Why are you telling me this?"

"As I said, I didn't understand what he meant that day, because I was sure you two were in love. Then I heard what you said at Kayden's grave. You said you wanted to help me and be strong for me. I thought I was fucking delusional in that moment, convincing myself I probably heard everything wrong, but then you returned my kiss. And later, I saw your drawing of me. The drawing of a person who did nothing but hurt you."

Fear arose in me, sending my heart into overdrive. I finally understood what he was getting at.

"I put two and two together and got my answer."

I wanted to run away immediately. I wanted to be anywhere but here.

He cast me a glance, a cocky smirk plastered on his face. "Despite everything I did to you and having Kayden by your side, you actually *liked* me."

Chapter 26

NO, NO, NO.

This was terrible. I couldn't allow this to continue any further. If I confirmed I'd liked him, he would make my life even more difficult, and I already lived with a huge load of shame in me.

"That's where you're wrong."

He frowned, taken aback by my answer. "What?"

I snorted, faking my indifference. "I never liked you. How could I when I always loathed you? I could never stand the sight of you."

To my complete surprise, all his previous confidence evaporated into nothing and a hint of vulnerability appeared in his eyes. "You're lying."

"And you're delusional."

He clenched his jaw and the steering wheel. "Then why did you say those words in the cemetery?"

I winced, feeling like he had me cornered. "And why are you acting like you care?" I shook my head. "You're my biggest enemy. You swore to make my life living hell, yet you're concerned a lot about my feelings now. You even *kissed* me. What is wrong with you?"

He was gripping the steering wheel so hard that his hands started shaking, and as always, I was shocked at how fast his emotions changed. My instincts screamed at me to shut the hell up and stop provoking him.

"You didn't answer my question about Mateo."

I ignored my instinct and voiced my anger. "Oh, so we're dodging a question now?"

"Fucking answer me!"

"I *fucking* won't!" He crossed the line too many times, and I wouldn't let Mateo get involved in this.

He veered to the right and stopped on the side of the road, the screeching of tires grating on my ears.

"What are you doing?!"

Hayden killed the engine and unbuckled his seat belt. "Give me your phone. I want to make sure you didn't do something as stupid as taking that asshole's number."

"What?" My pulse was frantic as I attempted to come up with a way to avoid giving him my phone, but then I remembered one thing.

I left my phone and my bag in Melissa's car.

Damn it.

"I never ask twice," he growled and started searching for it himself, tapping his hands over the front and the back pockets of my jeans, reminding me of a cop frisking a criminal. I felt violated and vulnerable, and no matter how much I kicked and wiggled, trying to take his hands off me, it was pointless.

I closed my eyes, sensing like I could start crying any moment.

"Please, stop this," I whispered, defeated.

At that, his hand grazed the inside of my thigh, dangerously close my core, and we both froze, our eyes locking together. I was scared of his next move, but my body anticipated it, and I hated my reaction. I refused to acknowledge it as pleasure and hunger for that touch.

"Where is your phone?" he said so quietly, a note of insecurity shading his words.

For once, I was glad the truth worked in my favor. "I left it in Melissa's car."

He exhaled a heavy sigh and leaned back against his seat, breaking the contact between us. "What were you doing with that asshole?"

"That's none of your—"

"It *is* my fucking business," he shouted at me, making me flinch. "You won't see that guy again."

"What? You can't possibly be thinking that—"

"I won't repeat myself, Sarah. I'll fuck him up if I see him with you again."

I fisted my hands, feeling an unbearable urge to hurt him. "What the hell is wrong with you?!"

"You want to know what is wrong with me? YOU ARE WHAT IS WRONG WITH ME!" He hit my headrest with his fist, making the whole seat shake from the impact, and got in my face. Only inches separated our faces now, and my whole body buzzed with a dangerous mix of fear, excitement, and expectation.

"I was never able to control these destructive emotions inside of me, which were screaming at me to release them, no matter how much I tried to shut them down, but when it comes to you, I feel fucking turmoil."

Hayden's hot breath fanned my face, making my skin hypersensitive of his movements and his nearness. I could clearly see the painful shimmer of his dark eyes, which revealed his tortured side to me.

"It feels like something is pushing me to hurt you. More and more. Like an addict who feeds on their precious obsession, their lifeline. I feel great, but then the darkness arrives, and it feels like thousands of knives cut into my flesh, again and again, ripping me into pieces, and there is no one I hate more than myself." He looked like he was in pain, breathing with difficulty. "I hate myself for being this mess, for not being sure about anything. One day could bring me peace, but that same day could be my doom. I just want this fucking chatter to stop, so I won't have to live in this hollowness anymore."

Oh God. His unexpected words felt like a kick in the gut, revealing the great extent of his sadness and insecurity.

"What are you talking about, Hayden?"

"I'm talking about this everlasting hate. It spread toward Kayden. It spread toward you."

My lip wobbled, a warm tear finding its way down my cheek. I glanced at the spot where his scar was, but I couldn't see it in the darkness of the cabin. "Please," I whispered. "Don't say anything else."

"I hurt you, and everything has sense," he continued, ignoring my plea. "It's justice because you're a bad person, right? It makes me feel righteous."

"No more," I gritted through my teeth.

"But I'm like an addict, and you know what happens when the drug wears off. The reality hits you hard, and you feel like shit. And feeling horrible for hurting you becomes unbearable."

I closed my eyes, hoping the sorrow would vanish, but he took me by my chin and made me look at him. "Yes, I hate you, Sarah. And I don't hate you. I want to hurt you. And I want to keep you safe like that precious last drop of water in a dry desert." His devastating pain was eating me alive. Hayden was telling me so much, yet the more I learned, the less I knew. *Who is Hayden Black?*

"You, Sarah, are my last fucking drop of water, my last salvation, and despite everything—despite this never-ending fight against myself—I can't leave you alone."

Something hit my defensive barriers, threatening to break them completely. Warm tear after warm tear rolled down, and I despised myself for crying in front of him again, but then he did something that astounded me. He brought his cold fingers to my cheeks and gently wiped away my tears, touching me so slightly that I could well be imagining it. His eyes traced the places his fingers touched with a raw intensity that took my breath away.

For a moment, I felt like him—feeding on that precious, horrible drug I couldn't live without. Hayden was that drug, making me lose myself in the moment and marvelous sensations that permeated me and erased every trace of reason. I knew I had to move away from him, yet his fluttery touch snared me, and my heart crumbled.

This wasn't sane. I should get out of the car and distance myself from him. I hated him. Why was this happening to me when I hated him?

I hate him.

Why can't I move away from him? Why do I feel so warm inside when he looks at me like this?

Don't do this to yourself.

He tried to kill you.

I couldn't let him play me like this. I could never forget what he'd done to me.

Refusing to succumb to these confusing emotions, I pushed him away from me and unbuckled my seat belt.

"I'm out of here."

I knew we were in the middle of nowhere, and going out at this time and place was crazy, but I couldn't think normally next to Hayden. Everything was a blur next to him. Everything was confusing and twisted, and this everpresent sadness was crushing me.

"What? No. Don't go."

He caught my wrists, preventing me from opening the door, and my anger skyrocketed. "Let me go!"

I yanked against him, but he didn't release me, and I yanked again and again... I was burning with fury, tired of him controlling me. I was tired of this emotional roller coaster I was riding the whole evening. I was tired of everything. I couldn't take this anymore. The hot poison spread through my veins, and I wanted to hit something badly.

"Let me go, son of a bitch!" I tugged against him even harder, managing to break the contact, and pushed him away again. "Don't touch me! Don't you dare put a single finger on me!"

He recoiled. "Sarah—"

"I can't stand being here with you!" I hit my fist against the window, embracing the dull pain that came from the impact. "You're too much! After everything you've done, what more do you want from me?" Too restless to endure this a second longer, I reached for the door handle.

"Please, Sarah..." *Please?* Suddenly, Hayden hugged me from behind, as if trying to calm me down. He rested his head against my shoulder, holding me tightly, and the fierceness of his actions threw me completely off balance.

I stilled as I stared into the darkness outside, drinking in the warmth of his body behind mine.

He couldn't be holding me like this.

"Don't do this." His voice was pleading, opposite of everything that was Hayden, and that scared me more than anything. My blood rushed frantically through my veins as I waited for... What? "Don't go away. I... I... *I need you.*" Something clutched my heart, mercilessly crushing it.

And just like that, all my fury was gone, leaving disappointment in its wake.

I loved you, Hayden. Once upon a time, I wanted to wipe away your darkness. Now, after everything you've done... It's too late.

"Why are you telling me all of this?" I asked, my voice unusually hoarse. "For once, tell me the truth."

He flinched like he'd been burned, separating himself from me, and I turned to face him. The fear I found on his bruised face came like bolt from the blue. This was the first time ever that I saw Hayden looking insecure and lost.

I thought he would refuse to give me an answer or throw some insult at me, but he surprised me when he said, "Because I can't let you go. I tried, but I can't." He heaved a long sigh and looked away, unable to look me in the eyes. "I want you all for myself."

My defensive barriers finally cracked, and I couldn't stop that intoxicating warmth from filling me. I couldn't stop it from affecting my heart.

Despite everything, that warmth brought me back to life. It gave color to grayness, and it produced music for my ears. It was so wrong, yet I felt as if everything clicked. Every piece of this mess was in its place, and it didn't matter that he was so dark. I felt a strong pull to touch him and color his darkness into lighter shades, ending our loneliness.

I understood now that not all of my warm feelings died after the day of Kayden's funeral. There had always been a tiny flame, surviving all these tortuous days. There had always been a tiny part of me that was desperately hoping to hear these words from Hayden. It was like a dream come true or better yet—a nightmare—because he and I could never be together.

I wanted nothing more than to go somewhere alone, so that I could cry my stupid heart out.

He didn't deserve this. He didn't deserve me. However, I was still giving him a piece of me. What a foolish girl I was.

I might still feel something for him, but I wouldn't let him have it.

I let out a short chuckle. His eyes widened, as if someone slapped him. I chuckled again, this time longer, darker.

"You *want* me? You *need* me? You made my life hell. You hurt me in so many unimaginable ways. Tonight you beat Mateo and forced me to come with you and leave my friends, who are probably worrying about me right now. You're always punishing me, controlling my life, and making me live in fear and misery. Now you tell me not to go away? You tell me you *need* me? Screw you, Hayden."

I was shaking hard, but I felt good. It felt good to throw out this poison that circulated inside of me for so long. "I can't believe you're asking this from me after everything. You're insane."

My words sounded so horrible, so unlike me, yet they made me feel powerful. I was like him now—hurting others to patch myself up—but right now it didn't matter.

"I don't care how you feel, just like you never cared how I felt. I hate you. I feel horrible every time I see you, and I wish I'd never met you. You *need* me? Fuck you. You can go into some goddamn hole and die, I wouldn't care."

I was breathing heavily, seeing red. I didn't know if I was angrier at him or at myself for letting those old feelings return.

He didn't say a word, looking utterly broken. Anguish and loneliness veiled his eyes, which fully revealed his inner agony to me. His mask fell down, and I could finally see what he'd kept hidden all this time.

I didn't know this person. This Hayden was unknown to me, making me question everything I thought I knew about him. Right now, there wasn't even a trace of that powerful and confident Hayden, and I wondered if everything he'd shown to me before was fake—a facade.

He rested his head against the headrest and closed his eyes. Regret suffused me at the sight, followed by a nagging feeling that I'd gone too far. I was supposed to know better. Despite everything, I shouldn't have stooped to his level. I shouldn't have turned into my bully.

Maybe I should apologize to him and take my horrible words back. He didn't deserve me, but hurting him didn't make me feel any better.

I looked at him again, of two minds about what I should do, but then he opened his eyes and looked at the road ahead without any emotion, shutting down. The usual Hayden returned all too quickly, and my fear of him reappeared.

Remaining silent, he buckled his seat belt, started the car, and pressed the gas pedal harshly, which sent us racing down the road in three seconds flat.

"Hayden? A-Are you taking me home?"

He didn't answer me. I put my seat belt back on, noticing his tightened jaw and pursed lips. He was gripping the steering wheel too tightly, which was another sign for me not to provoke him anymore. I already said enough.

I just hoped he was really taking me home and not to some forest where he would dump me or do something even worse.

We spent the rest of our trip in uncomfortable silence. Relief washed over me when we entered Enfield and came closer to our neighborhood because he wasn't going to dump me anywhere, after all. He was taking us home, which increased my guilt for saying those harsh words.

I didn't have anything to do during our drive but reminisce about his words, my reaction, and the revelation that my feelings for him didn't die completely. I felt baffled and troubled with myself, and I needed some time alone to sort out my thoughts and figure the way out of this mess.

He stopped the car in his driveway, and even though I was more than ready to jump out and run away from him, there was still that uncertainty about whether I should apologize or not.

He turned off the engine, looking straight forward without blinking at all. "Get out," he said through clenched teeth.

"Hayden—"

"GET OUT!" He snapped his head to glare at me, shaking. I understood now that he was controlling himself during the entire drive back home, and I didn't want to play with fire. I hurriedly unbuckled my seat belt and scrambled out of the car, dashing to my house without looking back.

I fished my keys out of my pocket and entered the dark house that induced loneliness. My tears soaking my face, I closed the door and leaned against it. I finally remembered I was wearing a makeup, so it was probably all smeared and grotesque from crying by now. Strangely, I didn't care. I couldn't care when I was already sick with everything that happened in a span of just a few hours.

This evening was supposed to be completely different. It was supposed to be Hayden-free.

Instead, I was curled up in a ball on the floor, more miserable than ever.

After everything he had done, after all his monstrosities, I still loved Hayden.

Chapter 27

"I WANT YOU ALL FOR myself."

Ugh. I pressed my fingers against my temples, fighting to get his voice out of my head.

"I want to keep you safe like that precious last drop of water in a dry desert."

This was so wrong.

Stop thinking about him, Sarah.

It was easier said than done. It was late Saturday evening, and I had been trying to focus on my college applications for more than an hour now, but I kept coming back to the moment in his car when he said those words.

No. I should really stop this and concentrate on my future and college, which was my way out of here. I already decided I was going to ignore everything he said. It didn't matter. It also didn't matter that my heart worked against me, because I would crush these dumb feelings.

I couldn't sleep at all last night, and I was more than ready to stay in my bed and spend the whole Saturday away from the rest of the world, but I knew that wasn't the best or the healthiest thing to do. I was tired of wasting my days because of my bully.

So I got up early this morning, greeted by an empty house once again, and went downstairs to go on a much-needed jog. I was wondering how I could retrieve my phone from Melissa, but my quandary ended minutes later when my doorbell rang and I found one of the biggest surprises of my life: Melissa, Jessica, and Mateo were standing on my porch.

They had been so worried about me that they had decided to check up on me and come as soon as Melissa sobered up enough to drive. I almost fell into tears of joy right in front of them, touched and happy that I had people on my side at last. I wasn't alone anymore.

We sat in my living room, where I told them about the car ride with Hayden, deliberately skipping the sensitive parts of our conversation. It took some time to convince them Hayden didn't hurt me.

Mateo's and my gazes kept locking, which brought me back to the embarrassing moment when we were about to kiss but got interrupted by Hayden. I knew it wasn't my fault that Hayden attacked Mateo, but I couldn't get rid of the guilt. Mateo's swollen, half-closed right eye only enforced it.

"Can we talk somewhere private?" he asked me then, taking us all by surprise.

"Sure," I answered and led him to my kitchen, extremely nervous and embarrassed to talk with him.

His face was deadly serious when he faced me, standing so close that I had to force myself to stay in place instead of getting some personal space.

"What is the deal with this guy, Hayden? Is he one of those people from your school who bullies you?"

Sheesh. He didn't waste time, straight to the point. "Yes," I replied, glancing sideways.

I was fazed when his fingers caught my chin and pulled my face up to meet his. "Did you tell us the truth? He didn't hurt you last night?"

I couldn't stand his nearness anymore, so I took a few steps back, breaking our contact and putting some distance. "He didn't hurt me. He just brought me home, and that's it."

"Then why did he react the way he did last night? Why did he attack me?"

"I have no idea."

"Why did he say he owned you?"

"I don't know."

"Why did you let him take you away?" So many questions.

"Mateo—"

"No, seriously, Sarah," he snapped, and I gaped at him, recoiling. Where was this anger coming from? "What is his problem? Is there something between you two?"

"What? No!"

"Then what is his goddamn problem?"

"I know you're upset because he attacked you, and I'm so sorry for that, but—"

"My anger doesn't have anything to do with that!" he exploded. "I'm angry because some guy with serious issues is harassing you! I'm so angry that I wish I could smash his skull and teach him a lesson!"

I winced, taken aback by the intensity of his emotions. I'd never expected I would meet someone who would want to punish Hayden for what he'd done to me, which was strange and new for me.

Noticing my reaction, he scrunched his eyebrows together and took me by my hand in a reassuring gesture. "I'm sorry. I didn't want to scare you." He let out a long exhale, running his hand through his curly hair. "I'm just mad at that prick."

I offered him a smile, not quite sure how to react to this. I was happy that he cared about me, but I didn't want him involved in this. I didn't want him to cross paths with Hayden again, because if that happened, it wouldn't end well.

"Thank you for this. Seriously, I... I have no words to express how I feel right now. I understand you, but I don't want you involved—"

"I think it's too late for that now," he interrupted me, letting my hand go. "I'm already involved. I care about you, and I can't just stand by while that asshole is hurting you. I said I wanted to protect you, and I meant every single word."

Soon after our conversation, they left, and I spent the rest of my day in my room drawing and working on my college applications, but my mind was a traitor who wanted to keep thinking about Hayden and last night.

Maybe Mateo could protect me from the physical damage, but the damage to my heart had already been done. I was always thinking about Hayden, always calculating his every single move. I was never able to get him out of my head, but feeling even a flicker of warm emotions toward him was beyond dangerous and stupid. It would crush me sooner or later, so I couldn't let this go any further. My feelings for him didn't matter.

The art college would solve all my problems. I was so close. I had to endure just a bit more until I was safely away from him and all my bullies. I would be finally separated from the misery that was my life so far.

With a renewed resolve, I decided to hit the sack early. I turned off my laptop and slipped into my pajamas, positive that everything would be much clearer in the morning. Tomorrow was a new day.

• • • •

I WOKE UP IN THE DARKNESS of my room, wondering what made me jolt awake. The sky outside was pitch black, and I needed a couple of seconds to adjust my vision...

I froze when I saw someone standing at the foot of my bed. He was dressed in a black jacket and jeans, which enabled him to blend into the darkness, and my brain had difficulty processing what I was seeing.

I turned on my bedside lamp and met the intruder's eyes, confusion and fear rising in me when I recognized him.

It was *Josh*.

What the hell? Josh broke into my house?!

"Wha—What are you doing here?!" I barely had time to finish my sentence when I noticed the glint of metal. It took me a split second to realize he was holding a knife and was ready to pounce on me.

I screamed, horror coursing through my veins as he charged toward me with his raised weapon. I was going to die in a terrible, inexplicable way, and there wasn't much I could do—

Listening to my instincts, I grabbed the glass of water standing on my nightstand and swung it at his head, using all the strength I could muster.

The glass broke upon contact with the side of his head with a loud crash. He cried out, losing hold of his knife, and gripped his head, which was covered in small shards and blood that flowed out of the cuts.

I jumped out of my bed and dashed toward the door, relieved that I could buy myself some time. My mind went the extra mile to come up with a solution in the midst of countless questions.

Why was Josh trying to kill me? *Kill* me?! Was he getting back at me for what I did at Melissa's party?

I always knew Josh was unhinged, terrified of his violence that he unleashed on anyone who went against him, which I'd experienced first-hand, but this... This was something *else*.

I ran out of my room, glancing over my shoulder, and shrieked as he darted toward me with the knife that was already back in his hand. He looked like a monster with his bloody head and murderous face. I ran down the hallway, still unable to understand what was going on. I had to escape him and call the police.

"I'll catch you, stupid bitch!"

My heart threatened to burst when I reached the staircase. I was all alone in the dark house, desperately trying to scope out what I could use to defend myself...

I heard him right behind me...

No!

I was at the staircase, going down one step, when Josh reached for my leg and tripped me.

I screamed in terror, the world moving too fast, and I went flying down the stairs. The white-hot pain exploded in almost every part of my body, and there was nothing I could do except protect my head.

I hit the bottom with a thud. I willed myself to get up and run away, feeling more nauseated and weak with each step. If only I could get to the front door... I heard Josh too close behind me, and I looked around for any object I could use for self-defense, trying to ignore the rising panic that prevented me from thinking and breathing properly.

I couldn't hyperventilate now!

Enduring the pain, I grabbed the first fragile thing that came into my view, which was a lamp on a small table next to me. I was shaking like a leaf, sweat breaking out of me in fear, for he was in front of me, striking with his knife.

Hell no...

With a scream, I brought the lamp down on his shoulder. He stumbled and fell to the floor, losing hold of the knife again.

His face was contorted in rage. "*Bitch*! I'll kill you!"

I spun on my heel, relying on adrenaline to carry me as fast as possible out of the house despite my injuries, but I didn't escape even five feet when Josh tackled me and I crashed to the ground.

I hit my head hard enough to hear the ringing in my ears. I managed to turn on my back and knee him in the groin, relieved when he recoiled from the impact, but he recovered immediately. I tried kneeing him once more, but he dodged my knee and trapped me completely, punching me right in my face.

I was momentarily disabled when the severe pain surged in my head. I met Josh's glare filled with insanity, unshed tears pooling in my eyes. There was no trace of humanity in him, and this frightened me more than anything.

"P-Please—" He hit me again, and I had no strength left to try to push him off me, tears and pain blurring my vision.

"This is nothing compared to what I'll do to you, bitch. Remember the texts?" *What?* So that was him all along.

"Please, don't... Ah!" Another hit landed into my stomach, and I was blinded by pain. I was sure I was going to die because there was no way for me to defend myself or escape him...

"Your time is finally over."

No...

The front door burst open behind me, and a furious cry shot through the air. "*No!*"

Before I registered what was going on, someone shoved Josh off me, and the sound of cracking bones filled the hallway. I forced myself to my feet and cried out in dismay when I recognized Hayden's tall form on top of Josh. He was hitting him repeatedly, smashing his fist against his face in rage.

"What. Are. You. Doing. Here?" Hayden spoke after each punch.

I bolted to the phone in the living room and dialed 911, bewildered that Hayden had come to my rescue. I explained everything in a rush and gave my address, hoping the police would come before anything tragic happened.

By the time I finished the call, Josh managed to push Hayden off him, and they continued their fight on their feet. My insides churned with desperation as I tried to decide what to do.

Hayden received and dodged several blows before he got the upper hand. He pushed Josh against the wall and pressed his forearm against Josh's neck.

"I'll ask you one more time before I make a mash out of you. What are you doing here?"

Josh barked a laugh, wheezing and coughing blood. "What the fuck do you think, smartass? I came to finish her."

He looked at me over Hayden's shoulder with a sick grin, his face distorted from injuries. "This bitch was supposed to pay a long time ago, but instead of showing her her place, you decided you wanted a taste of her." He returned his gaze to Hayden, his eyes conveying the full extent of his hatred and lunacy.

"You can have any pussy you want, but you want this cunt that deserves—" Hayden cut him off by punching him in his stomach. Josh cried out in pain, but then he continued laughing, looking psychotic. "You were kissing her on your own brother's grave. You're a fucking disgrace."

"What are you talking about?" Hayden growled, pressing him harder against the wall. Josh looked like he didn't have any air left in his lungs, gasping for oxygen.

"Hayden!" I stopped behind him. "You'll kill him if you keep pressing his neck like that!"

"This shithead deserves to suffer," he bit out, staring Josh down.

"Hayden, please!"

Josh chuckled, or at least tried to, but it came out like a croak. "S-Shithead? And here I t-thought we were f-friends," he said with great difficulty, rasping.

"I'm not your *friend*. Now, answer my question!"

"You'll kill him if you continue like this! Please!" I tugged at his arm as forcefully as I could, hoping I could manage to pry his arm off Josh's neck. "The police will deal with him!"

I pulled his arm again and thankfully, Hayden moved it enough to allow Josh to breathe.

Josh let out another chuckle, which came out like sandpaper rubbing on dry wood. "You really fell hard for this cunt, huh? Listening to her like some lapdog. Was her pussy that good—" Hayden landed another punch on his stomach, and blood spurted out of Josh's mouth.

He sneered at Hayden. "I could never stand the sight of her. She was always so stupid, annoying, and whiny. I always told Natalie there was something going on between you two all along, but she didn't believe me. She had to see you two kiss at your brother's grave to finally get into her head what I was talking about." He stared at Hayden with such hate that it gave me shivers.

My thoughts returned to that day in the cemetery when I saw a drunken Hayden behind me. We ended up kissing, but I never saw anyone then, even after I ran away from Kay's grave.

"You started sending me those messages because Natalie saw us kiss?" I asked in astonishment.

"That kiss just sped up our plan because it confirmed you and Hayden weren't enemies. Natalie always wanted revenge, but she thought Hayden would finish you off sooner or later. So after she saw you kissing, she went to your place and slashed your tires, but then I thought it would be better to mess with you with those texts before we finished you off."

My legs were shaking, my mind racing to comprehend their cruelty. So, Hayden had told me the truth. He didn't slash my tires. It was Natalie.

"What do you have to do with anything?" Hayden asked him through gritted teeth. "Why are you helping Natalie?"

"Isn't it obvious? I love her," he said simply. "I always loved her. I was so jealous of Kayden, who couldn't even appreciate what he had. I would never betray Natalie the way he did. Never." He glared at me with accusation, as if it was my fault that Kayden fell for me while loving Natalie at the same time.

"Still, Natalie never stopped loving him, and my heart broke when I saw her after his death. She wasn't the same person anymore, and it was all your fault, bitch. You made her lose her mind. I would do anything to make her happy—anything to see her smile like before—even kill you."

The level of his obsession and lunacy sickened me. He was so attached to her that he would even kill me for causing her pain, and it was crazy. Both of them were deranged. No matter how much Natalie loved Kayden, nothing justified such hatred. She was plotting my *death*. That wasn't normal at all, and I couldn't wrap my mind around it.

"So you two plotted to *kill* me?"

His grin was sick. "Damn right, but because your *boyfriend* here decided to meddle into something that's none of his business, he'll pay too."

Josh drew *another* knife out from under his jacket and raised it quickly into the air with the intention to attack Hayden... "I'll kill you first!"

Hayden tried to dodge him, but unsuccessfully. The knife cut into him, and I screamed, watching him take several wobbly steps backward. With a growl, he clutched his left shoulder. His crimson blood soaked his T-shirt fast and trickled down his arm. My head spun. *Oh my God.*

He was hurt. There was so much blood already. Oh no.

No, no, no.

I reached with my hands to support him, a new-found fear for him gripping me, but he pushed me away with his right arm.

"Go away, idiot!" He glared at me, his bruised face twisted in pain. "You'll get hurt! Get out of the house!"

No. I couldn't do that. I had to stop being so useless and figure the way out of this craziness. Where were the police already? How much time had passed? Five minutes? Ten minutes?

I couldn't leave Hayden here alone! He got hurt, and if I didn't do something soon, he could...

Die.

NO.

Josh moved to the side, blocking the way to the front door, and directed his bloody knife at me. "You aren't going anywhere. I'm going to kill you before you get any closer to that door."

"No, you're not," Hayden grunted in response and lunged at him. He managed to dodge Josh's strike this time by a hair's breadth, receiving a kick in the stomach that almost made him fall. Josh didn't stop, swinging the knife once again.

In the last possible moment, Hayden grabbed Josh's arm with both hands and moved the knife away from him, despite the injury he suffered.

"Sarah, run away," he yelled, focused on the knife. Josh grabbed Hayden's neck with his other hand and squeezed it hard.

No, I wouldn't run away! I desperately looked around the hallway for any object that could help me defend him, but then I saw Hayden letting up, and the knife got dangerously close to his chest...

Josh kicked him again, and Hayden fell backward, hitting his head against a chest before he landed on his back on the floor. Josh raised his knife and aimed at stunned Hayden with a ferocity in his gaze that meant only one thing—*death.*

No, I couldn't let him do this! I couldn't let Hayden's life be in danger because of me, again!

I couldn't let him die...

I rushed in between them, facing Hayden as I stopped in the path of Josh's knife—

I flinched when Josh stabbed me, feeling the punch in my back, and looked right back into Hayden's shocked eyes. For a moment, I wasn't able to comprehend what had just happened. Random thoughts twirled in my mind.

I got stabbed.

There is no pain.

Hayden looks so horrified.

I saved him.

Several seconds passed as Hayden and I looked at each other, frozen and lost in our own eternity. His painful, dark eyes revealed the abyss of despair and tragedy, and all suppressed emotions came down on me. It felt like a dam had been opened. Love, relief, need, grief, and want... Everything imploded inside of me.

I saved him. He won't die because of me like Kayden did.

Something warm trickled down my back. At the same time, police sirens sounded in the distance.

In a quick movement, Josh pushed me and fled toward the back door. Hayden barely had any time to catch me before I crashed over him, and it was in that moment that the agonizing pain exploded inside of me, blinding me with its intensity.

I screamed and closed my eyes, becoming unaware of what was going on around me. I could feel Hayden's body against mine, but I couldn't process anything but the merciless pain.

So much pain.

"Sarah?" The voice sounded far away.

My eyes still closed, I inhaled and exhaled as a buzz filled my ears. Oh God, there was no way I would be able to withstand this pain...

"Sarah... Listen to me..."

There were some footsteps... Too many of them, actually.

"Open your eyes..." I felt too weak. When would this torture stop? "Open your eyes, dammit!" Too exhausted, I opened my eyes with immense difficulty and met Hayden's gaze. He was holding me upright against him, and I noticed he was shaking like crazy. "Stay with me, Sarah!"

"We have two injured people here," an unknown male voice said, but I couldn't care less. All I could see was a devastated Hayden through my fading vision. He was *crying*.

"H-How is your arm?" I managed to ask.

"You idiot." He closed his eyes for a moment. When he opened him, they burned with longing and adoration, and despite the confusion and surprise, it made me so warm inside.

"Why did you have to be so stupid?" His voice completely broke, sounding raspy and foreign to me. "Why did you jump in front of that knife to save me? You were supposed to run away..." I watched his tears slide down his cheeks, mesmerized. Suddenly, I felt another pair of arms around me.

"Miss? Stay with us! The EMTs are here..."

I was already falling into darkness as I looked at Hayden for the last time. Nothing mattered anymore.

I smiled sadly. *I'll miss you.* I tried to say something, but nothing came out of my mouth.

My eyes closed against my will.

And I finally drowned in the welcoming darkness.

Chapter 28

THE PAIN. THE DISTANT sounds. The utmost confusion. The pain...

Where was I? Everything was white. A blinding, endless whiteness... All I felt was pain.

I heard some distant murmurs, but where were they coming from?

• • • •

"HAYDEN, GO HOME."

I could hear remote voices. Why couldn't I see anything?

"She probably won't wake up in the next few hours, so you should go home already and get some rest."

Was that...? Ugh, I didn't remember her name. I didn't even remember her face...

"No. I'm not going anywhere."

Hayden? I looked around, but all I saw was the unlimited whiteness. It spread *everywhere*. I was sure this wasn't right. If Hayden were really here, there would be some blackness looming...

Ugh, this pain would never go away...

• • • •

I OPENED MY EYES TO a foreign sight. Everything was blurry and so light that my eyes hurt. I wanted to remove this fog, but blinking didn't help at all. I felt beyond weak and hurt.

I tried to keep my eyes open and focus on my surroundings. There was no strange whiteness, just the white walls and the hospital furniture. The hospital? I moved my head to look around, but it hurt so I closed my eyes, hissing.

"Sarah?" Hayden? I snapped my eyes open, flinching when the light hit me too hard. Why was the fog everywhere?

"Sarah, you woke up," I heard his relieved voice. "I thought I lost you too." An unfamiliar, gentle touch on my hand made me wonder if this was all a dream.

Everything was a daze, and I felt like I wasn't really here. Everything hurt.

I wanted to open my mouth and say something, but I couldn't. I couldn't voice my thoughts.

Where was I? Was this Hayden real? Why did he look like he hadn't slept in days? Why was his arm in a sling and his face covered in bruises?

The pain and sadness on his face turned into tenderness.

"I'm here. Nothing bad will happen to you anymore."

What did happen? Ugh, why couldn't I remember anything?

This fogginess was everywhere...

Seconds or hours had passed as I fought to stay in this world...

In the end, something dragged me away—away from this foreign room and this strange Hayden that looked tender and worried.

The last thing I felt was a numbing kiss on my lips... But then again, it could've been only my imagination...

• • • •

I WOKE UP FEELING LIKE someone had smashed me into pieces and then patched me up. Everything hurt, and I couldn't move without going through harsh waves of pain. Seriously, what was going on?

I blinked a few times to adjust my eyes to the bright morning light in the room and stilled when I saw I was in a hospital bed. The medical equipment, which produced regular beeping sounds, stood on my right side, and I was attached to an IV drip. I groaned. I hated those IV things.

"Sarah? You woke up." My mother got up from the couch on my left, looking exhausted. I was actually surprised to see her here.

"Ugh. I feel terrible. What happened?"

She clasped her hands together in front of her. She looked sober, but she was stand-offish as always. If I hoped for her to touch me or show me any sign of comfort, I was wrong.

"Wait for a sec. I will call Mrs. Black."

"Mrs. Black?"

"Yes. Carmen Black is in charge of you." She went out of the room and returned a few minutes later. "She will be here soon. How are you feeling?" she asked, stopping next to my bed.

"Groggy. My whole body hurts... So what happened?"

"You got stabbed in the back." My memories were a bit fuzzy, but I did remember Hayden...

Oh God, Hayden!

"What about Hayden?" I was sure my voice revealed my panic, but I didn't care. He'd actually come to my house and fought Josh, only to get stabbed in the end.

"He's all right, and he received treatment, so you don't have to worry about him at all. His shoulder wound wasn't serious because that knife didn't hit anything vital, so he wasn't required to stay in the hospital." She narrowed her eyes at me. "He was here with you all the time."

I gaped at her. "What?"

"Yes. It's weird, if you ask me, because I was never under the impression that you two were anything more than classmates." She had no idea. "Mrs. Black barely managed to convince him to go home and get some proper rest."

What was happening with Hayden? This didn't sound like him at all.

"You were lucky, too, because Mrs. Black said your vital signs were fine."

"How long was I unconscious?"

"More than a day. Today is Monday. You woke up a few times, but it was all temporary." She sighed loudly. "I still can't believe this has happened! The boy who attacked you is your classmate, for Christ's sake!"

I frowned, remembering Josh with reluctance. "What happened to him? To Josh?"

"The police caught him. He tried to escape, but he didn't go far."

"How did he get inside the house?"

"He claims he broke in through the back door. Ah, yes. The police detectives came earlier, and Hayden already gave them his statement. They want to talk with you too."

"Great," I mumbled, not too happy that I have to deal with this as well.

I wanted Josh behind the bars, but dealing with this issue along with my school problems, the part-time job, and college applications was too much to bear. Also, I was going to miss school, which meant I would have to study harder to keep up with the curriculum.

I didn't even want to think about the medical bills.

Carmen entered my room with the nurse, wearing a gleaming smile on her face. "Sarah! I'm so glad my favorite patient finally woke up. Do you plan on falling asleep on us again?" She winked at me.

"Hopefully not," I mumbled, anxious about being bedridden. I hated hospitals, and I hated lying in bed for a long period of time.

"Actually, you were really lucky, just like Hayden. Neither of you suffered any damage to vital organs or major blood vessels. We're observing you now to see if there will be any infection, but there is none so far, thank goodness."

Carmen checked my vital signs, asking me the usual questions, all the while scribbling something on her clipboard. "The detectives want to visit you and ask you some questions about the incident, so whenever you're ready to see them, I'll call them and let them know. Is that okay with you?"

"I guess."

"Also, a few reporters heard about the incident and came here to talk with you, but I didn't want to let them inside without your permission. Do you want to talk with them?"

I shook my head, mortified about having my story covered by the media. I didn't need extra attention. "No. Absolutely not."

She nodded. "I understand. You can rest assured we won't let them in."

"Thank you."

"I'm so sorry about what happened, Sarah. It's unbelievable." She placed her hand on my mom's shoulder. "Your daughter will be fine. The worst has passed."

My mother just nodded. I observed her, searching for any sign of worry or distress, but I didn't see anything. Her face was blank, like she was some stranger who was here for no reason, like this had nothing to do with her.

I clenched my teeth, ignoring the ache in my chest. I shouldn't be surprised. I couldn't feel sorry about something I never had, right?

"I'm sorry your son was involved in this mess," I told her politely. First Kayden, now Hayden...

"Please, don't even say such a thing. You don't have anything to apologize about. Now, I would like to talk more with you later, okay?"

"Okay."

"Great. I'll visit you when I finish my shift. I'd like to tell you something about Hayden, and it's very important."

• • • •

MY MOTHER AND I SPENT hours in uncomfortable silence, her presence only making me more nervous. She read health magazines that the hospital provided while I checked my art accounts and messages on my phone. I found a few texts from Jessica, Melissa, and even Mateo, who were worried because I wasn't answering them. They promised they would visit me in the hospital, which put a gigantic smile on my face.

It was hard to pretend that I didn't mind my mother's indifference. With each passing hour, she grew more restless, and I couldn't even talk to her, suspecting she needed some alcohol to keep her in check. I was actually relieved when she finally decided it was time for her to go and left my room.

Two detectives visited me during the afternoon, soon after my mother went home. They were completely focused on their task, writing everything I said down in their pocket notebooks, but I couldn't help but feel anxious under their unnerving stares. I told them about Josh's threatening messages and that Natalie, who had slashed my car tires, was his accomplice.

They seemed particularly interested about Hayden's role in this situation.

They asked me about the nature of my relationship with him, and I had no idea how to respond. What could I say about the person who had been my enemy from the first moment we saw each other? I knew it would sound suspicious if I said we hated each other, because enemies didn't rush to their enemy's house to help them.

Eventually, I said he was my neighbor and classmate, who probably heard my screams and saw what was happening in my room from his window. They wrote this down, wished me well, and went their way.

I still couldn't come to terms that Hayden actually tried to protect me. A deep longing washed over me, which was stupid because I couldn't expect anything from him, yet I couldn't stop thinking about the way he acted that night or the way he looked at me when I got stabbed.

No. I was a fool for letting those old feelings return, but I was smarter this time. No matter what he felt now, nothing changed. I was grateful to him for coming to my rescue, but he was still the guy who had made my life hell.

The knocks on the door pulled me out of my musing. "Come in," I said, and Carmen entered. She wasn't in her uniform anymore.

"I just finished my shift. How do you feel?"

"Everything still hurts."

"Yes, it will take a while. We gave you pain medication, but even that can't help sometimes. It's important that you rest as much as possible."

"When can I go home?"

She placed the chair next to my bed and sat on it, making an apologetic face. "Not before the end of this week."

That was too long! What was I going to do with the school stuff and everything else? "But that's too long."

"That knife didn't cause great damage, but your wound is still serious. We need to keep you here under observation and care. Now, I mentioned to you that I wanted to talk about Hayden."

I tensed. "Yes."

"First of all, I have to say I'm completely surprised by Hayden's reaction. I knew you two didn't get along, but despite that, Hayden decided to help you."

I shrugged. What could I say when I was also surprised?

"How is Hayden holding up?" I had to ask.

"His injury wasn't serious enough to be admitted into the hospital. He's okay, but I barely managed to send him home." She frowned slightly. "He didn't want to be separated from you. The rest of the staff and I tried to make him leave, but he didn't want to listen." She observed me too carefully. "Do you know why?"

I blushed, looking away. "I don't know. I'm completely surprised to hear this."

"He was terrified that you were going to die..." Her gaze lingered on her clenched hands on her lap. She raised her head and offered me a tiny smile. "I want to thank you for the day when you helped me with the furniture."

Why was she mentioning it now? "You don't have to thank me again. That was nothing—"

"No, you don't understand. I want to thank you for what you said to me in the kitchen. You reminded me that Hayden needed me despite everything, just like every other child needs their mother, no matter what they do or what they are like. I never did anything to improve our relationship and be there for him, and honestly, I already gave up..."

Regret clouded her features. "When I saw him strangle you..." Her eyes flickered away in shame. "That was a wake-up call for me. I realized the extent of my neglect and how terribly wrong I was. Hayden became the way he is because I didn't try to help him. What's worse is that I *suspected* why he is the way he is, yet I didn't move a single finger to do something about his serious condition."

My mouth went dry, my heart pounding fast against my chest. "Condition?"

She looked at me again. I was actually afraid of what might come out of her mouth next. "I sat down and had a long talk with Hayden. It was difficult for both of us, especially for him, but after Kayden's death anniversary two weeks ago, it seems like something changed in him. He finally understood he has serious issues and can't solve them on his own. He wanted to try to get better. He allowed me to help him, so we went together to see a psychiatrist and do a medical examination."

Her words made my hair stand on end. "I-Is he okay?"

Her face gave me the answer I already knew. He was far from okay. "He has BPD."

"BPD?"

"Borderline personality disorder."

"I've never heard of it."

"It is a serious mental disorder. People who have it are unable to manage emotions as we do." She sighed. "I'll try to explain it to you as simply as possible. In a nutshell, borderline personality disorder is marked by high emotional sensitivity, poor self image and self-esteem, and intense mood swings or displays of emotions.

"People with BPD have constant feelings of emptiness and a big fear of abandonment, and they need a lot of reassurance that things are going to be okay. They can also have a strong need for attention or start huge fights over something insignificant. Then there is splitting—seeing the world in black and white."

I tried to comprehend all at once, connecting these facts with my image of Hayden. "Black and white?"

"Yes. It's like considering someone good or evil with nothing in between."

"I don't understand what that means," I said, exasperated.

"Honey, it means there are no shades in between. Everything is either good or bad. So no matter how good a person actually is, if they do something negative—or maybe they didn't do anything negative, but a person with BPD perceives it as such—they can split and label that person as bad."

I remembered the moment I met Hayden. I fell down and dropped the box, and he reacted in a negative way, acting as if I'd done something bad. Maybe he labeled me as bad since that very moment. Maybe that was the reason for his hatred from day one. Then Kayden lost his life to save him because of me. I could only imagine the extent of his hate toward me in that moment.

"That is why one moment they can idolize you and consider you the best person in the world, but the next, if something goes wrong, comes devaluation," Mrs. Black added.

"How is that possible? I mean, people make mistakes, and that doesn't mean they want to harm us."

As soon as I said this, I realized how hypocritical I was. The truth was that I felt the same as Hayden about people. Most of the times, I saw the world in black and white. After almost ten years of school bullying and betrayals—especially from those I'd considered friends—I stopped believing in people and their "shades." Now, everyone could be my "enemy," and I always tried to gauge if what they did was with the intention to harm me or not.

"Their brains work differently, especially when it comes to controlling emotional responses, and it may be hard for them to have control over, for example, anger outbursts. When you have BPD, your emotions are too intense to think about other people's emotions or the reasons behind their actions. Everything is heightened. Each emotion—love, hate, happiness, sadness...

"Intensified love is amazing, because they can treat you like an angel. They can make you feel like you're the most special, most loved person in the world. Add their possible impulsiveness in the mix, and you're in for a pleasant surprise. On the other hand, if something goes bad, they can treat you like you're the worst person they have ever met."

Each moment with Hayden flew through my mind. Each horrible thing he did, each sudden change in his behavior, each amplified emotion... Then there were the moments of affection, the passionate kisses and touches, and the times when I was pulled toward him in an inexplicable way... He rushed into my house to save me from Josh. He stayed by my side in the hospital...

Through the fog, a fragment of my memory cleared. I could recall the moment I considered a dream, but it was real. He kissed me in this room. He was here, worried about me.

"*I thought I lost you too*," he'd said.

I could never decipher him. Even now, when I knew about his disorder, I still couldn't put the puzzle that was Hayden together.

How did he feel about me? What was happening inside his head or his heart?

"As I said, every emotion is heightened, and when I saw Hayden desperately wanting to be here with you and absolutely terrified to lose you... When I saw my boy's eyes..." She sucked in a deep breath. "He completely lost hope, and I couldn't reach him at all. Not until you stirred for the first time and woke up. Hayden looked like he was the happiest person alive. Such intensity of emotion was overwhelming."

What was she trying to say? It was so difficult to accept the fact that Hayden felt this way toward me.

"Why are you telling me all of this?"

"Do you have feelings for Hayden?"

I flinched, taken aback by this sudden question. "What?"

"I noticed it since the beginning, but at first, I wasn't sure if my impression was right or not. I saw the way you looked at my son back then." Her smile was tender, almost remorseful. "Mothers can easily see those things, just like I noticed the way Kayden looked at you."

I glanced the other way, ashamed and guilt-ridden.

"Please, look at me. I'm not saying this to embarrass you or criticize you. I want to help you. I heard you saved Hayden from getting killed, and I can't even express how grateful I am to you. I want to tell you that you don't have any debt toward my family. If you did that out of guilt, then stop doing this to yourself, Sarah. As I told you a long time ago, Kayden's death wasn't your fault at all."

"Mrs. Carmen—"

"No. Let me finish. As Kayden's mother, I feel I have to say this. I never blamed you for his death. Not even for a second. No matter what the circumstances that led to his death were, my son was the one who made the decision to save his brother. I told you before that nobody forced him to do that."

She took a hold of my hand and gave it a gentle squeeze. "I'm sure Kayden wouldn't want you to blame yourself your whole life or do things to repay that non-existent debt, such as saving Hayden at the cost of your life." I closed my eyes to stop the tears.

I wasn't able to breathe evenly from the pressure in my chest. It became larger and larger, and I just wanted to be alone and cry. I didn't want to talk about this. It was too raw and fresh...

"Please, Mrs. Black... I-I didn't do that because of guilt. I mean, feeling guilty was just one part of my decision to save Hayden, but most of all, I wanted to save him because—" I stopped, terrified to say those words. Somehow, saying them didn't feel right. Not after everything Hayden had done.

"I know." Her eyes glistened with tears, and I realized how difficult everything was for her too. "That is why I'm telling you about Hayden's condition. I know you love him, and I know *you*, Sarah. You aren't the person for Hayden."

"W-What do you mean?"

"Honey, you would never be able to be that person who would make him feel loved, secure, and strong, no matter how much you love him. He needs someone with control, mental strength, and stability. His condition isn't something temporary. Even with treatment, it can last his whole life. His partner needs to be strong and capable of bearing Hayden's hell."

Despite everything, her words angered me. Maybe I didn't want to be that strong person in Hayden's life anymore, but she didn't have the right to judge Hayden or me like this and declare us a failure before anything had even begun.

"You don't know that," I blurted out. "Yes, I'm weak and I have a lack of self-esteem. I have many issues and insecurities, but if I fight to become stronger and better—if we both do—we could conquer everything—"

"Sarah," she interrupted me. The broken look on her face killed everything in me. "Don't do this to yourself. There is no hope for you and Hayden. It would be too toxic for both of you. Get away from it while you still have a chance. Go away while you still have your sanity." She took a deep breath, shaking visibly.

"My whole life I was confident and mentally strong, and I did my hardest to be there for their father, but even that wasn't enough." She inhaled deeply once more, as if to calm herself down.

Why was she saying this to me?

"Their father and I loved each other profoundly. I was always his anchor and support. He had borderline personality disorder too, Sarah. And despite everything, despite all our struggles with his disorder, our love, understanding, and faith, he lost the most important battle. He lost to BPD. In the end, his darkness was stronger, and he killed himself."

Chapter 29

"BPD can be hereditary, but it can also be caused by some traumatic event. In Hayden's case, that event was probably his father's death. Then again, it can be my fault, because I neglected him, which could've worsened his condition."

I kept thinking about these words, even long after Carmen was gone and the evening came. I was all alone with my depressive thoughts.

I was appalled to hear that Hayden's father also had borderline personality disorder, and that he committed suicide in the end. He had Carmen and his sons, yet he couldn't cope with his pain, fear, and struggles anymore, lost and completely detached from happiness and love of the people around him.

Oh God, Hayden. He lived in the same world, facing the same demons... Did he ever think about suicide?

A searing ache claimed my chest. *No.* He couldn't kill himself... Not that.

What was going on in his mind?

"Fear of abandonment...," I muttered, remembering Carmen's words. "Need for attention..."

"I just want this fucking chatter to stop, so I won't have to live in this hollowness anymore," Hayden said to me last Friday night. *"I was never able to control these destructive emotions inside of me, which were screaming at me to release them, no matter how much I tried to shut them down."*

I closed my eyes tightly, desperately trying to connect all dots and imagine myself as him.

The intensified pain, nothingness, feeling lost and unable to see who you are, terrified to be alone, everybody is your enemy, your life has no purpose, you can't find any answer, hate... Hate, hate, hate...

Something crushed me on the inside, burning my chest, suffocating me, and I felt unable to breathe or move...

"One day could bring me peace, but that same day could be my doom," Hayden said that same night.

You feel great now, but how long will it last?

I remembered the poem on the wall of his room again:

"I scream, suffer, and bleed inside; every single day is a tough ride.

It's a roller coaster, and you'll never know
what is like to be so high and then fall so low."

You'll never know, Sarah, what it's like to be so high and then fall so low.
One moment you're feeling extremely happy—like you are on top of the world...
And then extremely sad—like you're thrown into an abyss... All alone... It's a
roller coaster, and you'll never know how it feels when you don't know when the
darkness is going to hit you.

The memory of Hayden's tormented eyes when he revealed his insecurity to me for the first time pained me. *"I hate myself for being this mess, for not being sure about anything."*

How could one person feel so lost? What made humans fall into such despair and feel there was no way out? How could our inner demons conquer us? Why was happiness too difficult to achieve? There were so many things that upset us. Why was there so much darkness, suffering, bleeding, hurt, and hate? Then, there were disorders, which chained people—labeling them—like they were born with some mistake, like they didn't have the right to live a normal life...

My tears soaked my face, my neck, and my hospital gown, everything in me hurting as the ceaseless darkness enveloped me.

I felt a touch on my cheek, and I flinched, snapping my eyes open. Hayden stood above me, staring at me silently as he brushed away my tears. I moved my face away from him, breaking the contact, astonished he'd touched me like this.

"Hayden? What are you doing here? I-It's late and the visits aren't allowed at this time..." I was rambling, but I couldn't stop, flustered because he was here.

"I don't care. I had to see you." My heart jumped in my chest, and I hated myself for reacting this way. A pang of guilt and sorrow hit me when I spotted a sling on his left arm. *He could have died... He came to help me.*

He was looking at me in a strange way, no usual coldness in his eyes, which now twinkled with soothing warmth. This confused me more than everything. He brought a chair next to my bed and sat down.

"How did you get in?"

"Does it matter?" He wasn't taking his eyes off of me, studying my face like he'd never seen it before.

"Why, Hayden? You didn't have to come here and—"

"Thank you."

I gaped at him. After three years of his hatred, something as simple as thanks came as a pure shock. "W-What?" My stupid blush made its appearance. "What for?"

He blinked, showing insecurity, but he quickly composed himself. "You saved my life. I always treated you in the worst way possible, yet you saved me."

I saw shame and regret on his face, but it was hard for me to believe this was real. All of a sudden, Hayden wasn't that Hayden I knew anymore, and I didn't know how to act.

My eyes were downcast. "You don't have to thank me. How are you feeling?"

"I'm okay. It wasn't serious. How about you?"

"I'm okay too."

"Look at me."

I closed my eyes. "No. Please, go away."

How could I look at him when my heart and thoughts were in a state of tumult? I didn't know what was right or wrong anymore. Mrs. Black gave me many answers, but I had more questions than ever. He had a mental disorder, and he needed to work on his issues, but where did I fit in? What was the reason for his hate?

"I won't go away." He touched my cheek again, but this time I brushed his hand away, opening my eyes to scowl at him.

"Hayden, I did what I did, but that doesn't change anything. We're still enemies."

He grimaced. "No. It changes everything."

"No, it doesn't." I frowned. "How can you say that?"

"You saved my fucking life. I was horrible to you all these years, but that didn't prevent you from stupidly taking that knife for me."

I blushed again. "It wasn't stupid."

"It was stupid, and you're an idiot."

I glared at him, irritated by his blank face. "So this is your way of thanking me? By insulting me?"

"I'm just saying the truth." He pinched the bridge of his nose. "Do you have any idea how I feel having someone risk their life for me *again*? Having someone *die* for me *again*?"

My heart lurched in my chest, and I glanced at his old scar. His voice was filled with self-reproach and self-blame, showing me his desperation.

"I didn't deserve that. I *don't* deserve it. And of all people, it had to be you, whom I always hated. From the first day I saw you, actually." I fought to keep my eyes on him, my pulse drumming in my ears.

"Please, I don't want to hear it—"

"You need to hear it. I want to give you the truth. The whole ugly truth. After everything I've done to you, you deserve my honesty at least. No more lies." He drew a shaky breath, nervous.

"You were so fucking clumsy the first time I saw you. Do you know what crossed my mind when you fell?" His cruel words froze me. I didn't want to hear him say another word, yet I stared at him, aching with anticipation. "I thought how pathetic and weak you were. You disgusted me with your weakness."

I blinked back my tears. "Stop this, Hayden."

"When Kayden told me he met you, calling you cute, I laughed at him. I told him he was stupid and had lame taste in girls."

"Stop."

"Then you two became friends, and it was making me crazy. I was mad at you for stealing my brother away. He was my twin, but he gave you more attention." The venom poured out of his words, slicing me deep. "I was mad at him for giving everything for such a stupid, weak girl. I observed you for months, trying to find out what was so special about you. I was revolted by how fragile you were. I was sick seeing you cry or whine."

"I know you've always hated me. You don't need to give me the horrible details."

"But you didn't get it then, did you? You were friends with Kayden, and no matter what I did, I couldn't separate you two. But then, one day, you infiltrated my mind and intoxicated me, and I couldn't get you out of my head.

I realized I'd misjudged you because you weren't as weak or empty-headed as I thought you were."

The way he looked at me made it difficult for me to breathe. "I saw a new side to you, and just like that, I became infatuated with you." Oh God. He was revealing everything to me, and it was too much. It was too intense.

"I actually wanted your attention, and then I couldn't stop. I had to see you snap and break because that way I got your eyes on me. It made me feel like I was something more in your life. Something much more than just the brother of your best friend."

Carmen's words about their strong need for attention popped in my mind, reminding me of Hayden's fear of abandonment and how strongly he felt all emotions.

I covered my face with my hands, crying silently, but he didn't let me hide. He moved my hands away from my face and covered them with his own on my lap, his eyes fixed on mine.

"But after the car accident, I hated you more than ever. I couldn't stand the sight of you. I thought you were the worst, and I blamed you for the accident and his death, so everything I did was in the name of justice. It was so twisted, but it felt right. It gave me the strength to continue living through the nightmare."

A loud cry escaped my lips. His truth was too ugly. It was more than I could handle...

"Hayden, don't. I-I can't handle all of that now... It's too painful."

"I know. It's too painful and too dark, but I want to tell you the truth. I was a horrible person." He shook his head. "I *am* a horrible person. There is still so much hate in me, and it's suffocates me. Sometimes, I'm sure it will never end. Sometimes, I fear I'll completely give up and give in to that inner monster."

He moved his thumb over my wrist in slow circles, creating a surprisingly pleasant feeling that distracted me.

"These last few weeks, whenever I hurt you, I felt even worse, and I couldn't cope with all those emotions. It was too much for me, and I was so confused. I'm still confused. You were my enemy, but a day ago you saved my fucking life."

He looked at my hands with tenderness that made my skin tingle, his keen eyes following every line. I wanted to pull my hands away from him, but for some reason I couldn't muster that strength.

"I'm a mess. Even now, I don't know what is happening to me, but when I saw you lose consciousness that night, I thought I lost you. I felt like I was going crazy... The pain was fucking ripping me from the inside."

He lowered his head onto my cold hands to hide his face from me, shaking terribly.

"I've been so horrible to you, yet you saved me. I didn't deserve that. Now, I don't know what to do. I feel so guilty, and it's unbearable. I need you, Sarah. I need you."

I looked around me, unsure of what to do. I should push him away or chase him out of the room, but I couldn't. Unable to stop myself, I brought my hand to his hair. He didn't even move as my trembling fingers threaded through his soft strands, looking too fragile.

"I was so jealous of Kayden," he murmured, keeping his head against my hand on my lap. "Actually, I still feel that disgusting jealousy. I hated him for always getting what he wanted—"

"Hayden—"

"As the older twin, I thought I deserved all privileges and attention, but I never had those. He was always the one who got everything. Our mother's love, everyone's attention and respect... Everybody only talked about him. They were always repeating how great he was and how amazing his future would be..."

I wanted to say anything to reassure him, but my throat constricted, the words failing me. For as long as I could remember, Kayden was the one everyone supported and looked up to. People were naturally drawn to him. Hayden was more the second choice than not.

Then again, it was Hayden who I loved. He was incredibly smart and talented in many things. He was loyal to his friends, no matter how much they argued. He was popular too because there was something about him that just drew people in, even though he didn't feel that way. I loved Hayden with all his imperfections, but I couldn't tell him this. I would never tell him I loved him. I couldn't.

"I'd always considered Kayden my rival in so many things. And when you two became friends, I wanted to knock some sense into him. I hated that my brother had eyes only for you when you were so wrong for him. I was his twin, but he cared more about you than me—"

"That's not true."

"I don't know. I don't fucking know. I thought he was blinded by you, and I hated him even more because of that. And then he saved my life and died, and my whole world was turned upside down. I didn't know anything anymore."

He took a sharp inhale, his hoarse voice and trembling revealing how upset he was. Suddenly, he raised his head, and my eyes widened when I noticed the tears on his cheeks. He quickly wiped them away.

"Did you ever love him? Tell me the truth."

I felt as if something hit me in the stomach. His eyes were full of pain, and I was shocked to see him so insecure and lost. He let all his barriers down, showing me how insecure and vulnerable he actually was, and it hurt me to see him like this. I had no idea what to do or how to feel, but I couldn't cause him pain now, despite everything he'd done to me.

"I've never loved him like that. I only saw him as a friend. I-I couldn't return his feelings..."

Hayden cupped my cheek, and I held my breath, wary of his touch at first. It was so gentle, and I was quickly losing myself in it.

"I never knew what made me so mad about you being in love with him. It made me sick." He removed his hand from my face, and for some reason, I missed his touch.

"This will sound ironic and unbelievable, but I feel guilty for everything I've done." I flinched, not believing my ears. Did he really say that now?

His lips curled into a bitter smile. "I feel guilty for not doing anything to protect you. I wanted to, but I didn't. When I read the texts you received, I didn't do anything. I thought someone was just messing with you. I should've known better. I should've done something, *anything*."

He fisted his hand. "I couldn't sleep that night, and when I heard you scream and saw what was happening in your room... I was terrified. I ran as fast as I could to reach you. *Fuck*." He hit his thigh with his fist. "I always knew Josh was mental. You and I were his least favorite people."

"Josh didn't like you?"

"Josh and I were never real friends. Sure, we hung out together and did each other favors, but we were always fighting. Since we moved in same circles, we acted like it wasn't a big deal, but he couldn't stand Kayden and me from the beginning. I get that he hated Kayden because of Natalie, but I guess he disliked me because I was his twin. I don't know. I always felt he held some serious shit against me."

Now I could understand why Josh didn't hesitate to attack Hayden first. It was surprising to hear they weren't friends because I always considered Hayden, Blake, Masen, and Josh as one solid rock—unbreakable. They all seemed completely loyal to each other.

I stared at my hands. He'd told me so much, but there was one question that burned at the back of my mind all this time, and I needed to know. Blushing, I asked, "What did you do with my nudes?"

He inhaled sharply and looked away, regret claiming his features. "Nothing. I didn't do anything but look at them."

"Really?"

He met my gaze. "Yes. I never meant to post them online or show them to anyone, Sarah. I just used them as leverage against you, but I hated myself for doing that to you. If it means anything to you, I erased them."

"You did? But why? I mean, don't get me wrong. That's a good thing. But... Why?"

He just looked at me for a long time, musing about something. "Because I'm ashamed for taking them like that. That was a dick move. There is no point in having them if you don't give them to me willingly."

I observed him quietly, trying to take all of this in. He sounded sincere, but I didn't know what to believe in anymore. What I thought I knew well turned out to be something different, and here was Hayden, who had come to my house to save me, confessing his feelings to me.

Confessing? I still couldn't believe this.

"Hayden?"

"Hm?"

"Where do I fit in now? After everything, how do you feel?" I glanced away, blushing furiously. "How do you feel about me?"

He lowered his head and closed his eyes, and I almost expected him to refuse to answer me or make a mean remark. Taking a deep breath, he looked at me.

"I thought a lot about our last encounter in the cafeteria when I was at summer camp. Before you hit me with that pizza, you had a fierce look in your eyes that was pure fire. You took my breath away."

What? He swallowed nervously, and I watched his Adam's apple bob.

"You were always on my mind during the summer. You finally fought me back, which made me furious, but at the same time, so damn attracted to you. I wanted to make you pay for that, but I also wanted you. It was totally confusing."

The passion in his eyes reached the deepest parts of me, and I had to look away, blushing again. However, this time my face wasn't the only place that felt hot. It felt unusual that he desired me.

I'd always thought he considered me ugly, but now his eyes didn't leave me as they grew more heated, and I felt embarrassed and exposed.

"Please, Hayden—"

"You're beautiful."

Whoa. "What?" I croaked. He smiled, and the sincerity of his beaming smile threw my heart into overdrive.

"Do you want me to spell it?" he mocked me, and I winced.

"Why do you always have to make me sound stupid?"

He chuckled. "You get offended so easily. I really enjoy playing with you." He was making things worse.

"Just like you. You always get angry by every single thing." His smile dropped.

Oh no. Did I go too far? Would he snap at me?

"You're right. For as far as I can remember, every single thing made me feel insecure. I would always analyze them, no matter how small those things were, and try to determine if they are good or bad. I would reach negative conclusions most of the times. Even now, I keep telling myself I was so wrong about you, but that monster inside me is trying to pull me back into that darkness and hate. Sarah, I want to fight against it. What you have done for me..."

He shook his head and sighed. "I want to change. I can't keep going on like this forever. I don't want to spend the rest of my life thinking every single thing would break me down. I don't want to hurt you anymore... I... I want to try. For me. For... For you."

I couldn't do anything but stare at him, battling all these emotions inside of me. It hurt. His words hurt so much. How long did I dream to hear these words? How long did I hope that Hayden wouldn't be my enemy anymore?

Now, after everything, it felt too late. I didn't want him to act like this out of guilt. I saved his life, but that didn't change anything. Now I knew how he felt, but I wasn't ready for this at all. He was too dark and difficult. How could I trust him? How?

Even after hearing his truth and learning that he wanted to change—no matter how inconceivable it was—I couldn't act like he didn't terrorize me from the moment we met. I couldn't forgive him for all the atrocities during last three years. He had a mental disorder, which was a fact that helped me understand our past a whole lot better, but his disorder didn't justify all those cruel acts.

I didn't know if I would ever be able to forget the abuse he put me through. He did come to my rescue, but everything was too fresh and I needed time and space. I needed to be away from him, because whenever he was near me, my emotions got the best of me, and I couldn't keep doing that to myself.

However, I itched to pull him to me and hug him, overwhelmed with want, love, and pain. I closed my eyes, wishing things were simpler. I loved him. Even now, I wanted to help him. I wanted to give him the reason to smile. I wanted to show him he wasn't alone anymore. I wanted his touch that made me feel wonderful and carefree.

I want him...

I opened my eyes and froze. He'd sat down on my bed, leaning so close to me now. His eyes burned into mine, creating chaos in my heart. My fast heartbeat was deafening in the anticipation of his next move.

He leaned even further and claimed my lips with an urgency that stole my breath and reason away. I left my hesitation behind and returned his kiss, losing myself when our tongues met. He slid his hand into my hair and cradled my head, holding me tightly as he played with my tongue, going deeper inside, and everything in me became tense and desperate for more. I clutched his waist, responding to his rough, passionate strokes with my own. There was no holding back as we took more from each other.

He moaned and pulled my lower lip into his mouth, sucking it greedily, and I opened my eyes. He was looking directly at me. *Damn.* His eyes glazed, he bit my lip and then licked that spot. We were both breathing heavily, not nearly satisfied and craving for much more.

He placed my head against his uninjured shoulder, snuggling up to me. "This was something I wanted for a long time," he whispered hoarsely. "I want to stay with you." I closed my eyes as the pleasure and bliss dispersed and the old sorrow returned.

I knew this was selfish of me. I wanted a taste of him, and I wanted him to make me forget everything just for a moment, but I didn't intend to forget. Or forgive. I wanted this last kiss—this last illusion—before I finally let him go.

A few tears flowed out of my eyes, a whimper escaping my lips. He pulled away from me and took my hand, frowning. "What's wrong?"

He told me so much tonight—much more than ever—but I still had a hard time believing him. I looked at the broken, *tender* Hayden in front of me. There wasn't even a trace of the cruel, cold Hayden, and I struggled to understand everything he'd just told me. It was a hard pill to swallow.

I wanted him happy, and I wanted his agony gone, but I couldn't be that person who would help him with his darkness. I had my own darkness, and it was too much to bear. I was afraid it would just expand if I tried to battle his. The reason why Carmen's words hurt was because I knew she was right. I wasn't the right person for him. He'd put me through so much because of the hate, revenge, insecurity, and pain, and I was too fragile and hungry for happiness that I couldn't be strong for us both.

I had to fight my own demons and try to find my happiness without him. On my own.

I pulled my hand out of his. "Please. Go away."

These words hurt more than anything. My chest constricted painfully, and I had to fight for air, ripping on the inside.

"What? *No.*"

I couldn't look him in the eyes. "It's too late. Please, go away."

"I know it's late, but I'll talk with the staff, and they'll have to let me stay—"

"No, Hayden, you don't get it. It's too late." I willed myself to return his gaze, giving my best to stay strong enough to do this. I had to do this. "It's too late for us. I can't forgive you. After everything you've done to me... I just can't."

His face fell, revealing utter sadness and insecurity. His eyes lost the light they had just a few moments ago. There was no tenderness now. Just raw suffering.

"No. It's not too late. I just told you the truth. I want to be with you—"

"You can't be serious, Hayden. You think all it takes is to finally spill the truth and decide you want me? After all these years of pain you caused me?" I couldn't breathe. I inhaled deeply, hoping the burning pain in my chest would go away.

"But you feel the same about me. You want me."

"So what?!" I yelled, the tethers of my self-control snapping one by one. I couldn't stand him hurting like me. He was shutting down with each passing second, going back to that old Hayden, and this made everything worse. My heart pumped so fast, the pressure in my head hitting all-time high.

We couldn't keep going on like this. He needed help, and he wouldn't be better next to me. I wouldn't be better next to him. He didn't deserve me.

"My feelings toward you don't mean anything. I can't forgive you, Hayden. Before anything, I have to love and respect myself. And even if you don't hate me anymore, you will always blame me for the accident and Kayden's death. You tried to kill me, and that is something I probably won't ever be able to forgive."

He got up and began pacing nervously. "Kill you? What the fuck? I never tried to kill you."

"You strangled me!"

"But I didn't do that to kill you," he shouted back, fear clouding his eyes. "His room was a fucking trigger, and you were right there! Everything was the same, like on the day of his funeral. That was the first time I entered his room since then, and when I saw you... I just felt so much rage. Too much! I couldn't control it." He clenched his hands. "You can't even begin to understand how I felt in that moment."

I looked at my shaky hands on my lap. It didn't matter. Even if he didn't really try to kill me, it didn't matter. I just needed him out of the room.

"Hayden—"

"Look, whatever I did or said, that was before. I don't hate you anymore. I want you—"

"It doesn't matter what you want, Hayden!" I was desperate to be alone.

He stopped pacing in the middle of the room, staring at me like I betrayed him. I needed him out of here. I pressed the nurse call button, hoping someone would arrive soon and get him out the room.

"It was always about you! Always about what you wanted or what you needed! You don't care what I want! I want you out of here. I don't want to see you. How can you be so selfish? How can't you understand that?!"

My outburst only left me weak. Panting, I stared at him in dread. He was visibly shaking. Would he hurt me? Would he lose it after I lashed out at him like this? I couldn't trust him. I always expected the worst of him, and despite these last few days and a few moments of tenderness, he was still that same unpredictable, dark Hayden.

He was completely still and silent for a few moments, his eyes glued to mine. "Don't do this." I barely heard his voice. One tear slid down his cheek, and I couldn't bear to look at him anymore.

"Go away."

"Please, Sarah. Please. Don't. Do. This."

"It's too late," I whispered. I would break any second. I didn't want to break in front of him. It was killing me. It was killing me being so close to him, yet so far away. We were never actually close. We would never be.

"Once upon a time, Hayden, I wanted to give my all for you. You lost your chance. Please, get out."

The door opened, and the nurse came in. She was about to say something to me, but she halted when she spotted Hayden, frowning in confusion.

"What are you doing here? You aren't allowed to be here after visitation hours." He didn't even acknowledge her, looking at me with red eyes, all muscles of his body tense. Everything hurt in me, and I was so close to losing it. So close...

"Do you hear me? You are not allowed here. If you don't leave the room right this second, I will call security and they will—"

"No need," he answered in a raspy voice. His teary eyes were still on me. "I'll leave." He spun around and stormed out of the room.

The nurse approached me. "I came as soon as I received your call. How are you feeling?"

I wasn't even paying attention to her, beginning to lose myself in all the pain. Everything exploded in me, and the tears, hurt, loneliness, and pain made me blind and deaf. It was suffocating, pulling me further into the depths of nothingness, and the anguish was quickly getting out of control, taking its reign over me.

I just wanted to forget everything and be free. I wanted to forget Hayden ever existed. I wanted him gone from my heart.

It was impossible, though.

He was in my core, and like a deadly disease, he was here to stay until the very end.

Chapter 30

I HAD A MAJOR BREAKDOWN last night, and the messages from Jessica, Melissa, and Mateo were the only bright spots and sources of strength this morning. The nurse had tried to calm me down, but I'd been far beyond gone, losing myself in the avalanche of pain after Hayden left.

How could losing someone I never had hurt so much? I wanted to be far away from him for so long, but now I was seriously losing my mind trying to accept the fact that no matter what, we couldn't be together.

My heart wouldn't listen, though. It ached whenever I replayed our kiss or his tender words in my head...

In the end, the nurse had to give me something to put me to sleep. My mother visited me after I woke up this morning, but she was tipsy, making everything worse.

Her daughter was in the hospital after she almost got killed, but that didn't have any effect on her. She was the same old Patricia Decker, who couldn't bring herself to care about her child. I didn't know why she even bothered visiting me.

Her indifference always pained me, and I could never make heads or tails of whether I was a good enough daughter for her or not. I tried to be as convenient for her as possible, but that didn't change anything.

As she stood next to my bed in this sterile white hospital room, barely speaking to me, I couldn't help but wonder if she'd ever really loved me. She left my room shortly after she arrived, which only reinforced the emptiness in me. It was too much.

I decided to focus on something else so I wouldn't sink deeper into this surrounding gloom. A glimmer of hope perfused me at the thought of my new-found friends who were going to visit today, and I couldn't wait to see them. At least I had them. Yes, it was fresh and fragile, but those fragments of joy could lead to better days. If I chose to be positive about this, I was off to a good start.

Suddenly, the door of my room flew open, yanking me out of my thoughts. My breathing halted when I spotted Natalie, who looked like she'd

268

had a rough night. Her long hair was greasy and unkempt, her wan face free from any makeup. What was she doing here?

She closed the door and approached me without taking her dead eyes off of me, and everything in me tensed with the need to get away from her. She didn't look sane.

"What are you doing here?"

She'd wanted to kill me, and now that Josh was in jail, did she come here to do it herself?

"Don't think you'll get away with everything you've done."

Excuse me? "I think I'm the one who's supposed to say that. Josh and you wanted to kill me!"

She stopped too close to my bed, her hand clutching the strap of her purse too tightly, and the hairs on my neck stood up. "You deserve to die, murderer."

Despite my fear, I was livid. It was like everything she'd done to me wasn't enough. She actually had no shame, appearing here and saying these horrible words to me. "You're the murderer. You accuse me of something you were planning to do to me."

"With a reason! I loved him!" she screamed, and I flinched, terrified by the amount of hate she held in her. "You have no idea how devastating his death was for me. He meant everything to me! He saved me when I needed saving in more ways than you can ever imagine. If I hadn't had him, I would've killed myself a long time ago."

I shivered, shocked by her words. Only now, I noticed how terribly skinny she was, her T-shirt and jeans too baggy on her small frame. She was wasting away.

"Natalie, I understand that he meant everything to you and that—"

"No, you don't understand! How could you ever understand? You weren't the one who had to see the love of her life look at another girl as if she was his everything. You weren't the one who lost that love because of some stupid girl!"

A fresh wave of guilt hit me, but I refused to let it rule over me. She was a victim here too, but this didn't justify her lunacy.

"You can't possibly understand how it feels to lose the only person you will ever love. And I won't be satisfied until you pay."

"But we're in the hospital," I tried to reason with her. "If you do anything, you won't be able to get away with it. There are cameras and—"

"I don't care about the stupid cameras or if I'm going to get caught."

She was now maliciously hovering over me, and I had to figure out how to defend myself. I still felt a dull pain everywhere, and since I'd been lying for days, my legs were sluggish. I reached for the nurse call button and was about to press it, but she snatched it away from me.

"You won't get away this time, Sarah. That stupid Josh failed, but I won't. I'll kill you."

"You aren't a killer, Natalie. It won't bring Kayden back."

"It won't bring him back, but justice will finally be served. For three years, I've been watching you get away with everything. I'm sick of you playing innocent, twisting everyone around your little finger. First Kayden and now Hayden. I thought he was smarter. I thought he would avenge Kayden, but after I saw you two kissing at Kayden's grave, I understood you managed to trick him too. You managed to make him fall in love with you too, you disgusting bitch!"

Before I could react, she grabbed my neck with her hands and squeezed hard, cutting off my air supply. At the same time, the door opened, and Mateo appeared on the threshold with Melissa and Jessica behind him. Noticing Natalie, he dropped a bouquet of flowers he'd been carrying and bolted toward us. He restrained her all too easily and pulled her away from me, too strong for her, but she was still putting up a fight.

"Are you crazy?" he yelled at her.

She didn't stop kicking, trying to set herself free. "Let go of me!"

Melissa and Jessica stepped out into the hallway and called the nurses, screaming about a lunatic who had choked me. I just hoped the security would come soon and take Natalie away, who completely lost it, screaming obscenities at all of us.

"You're all so wrong! She doesn't deserve to live!"

The nurses rushed in as Mateo fought to keep Natalie in place, followed by the security guys. They grabbed a hold of her, mentioning that the police were already on their way, and dragged her out of the room.

I gripped the edge of my bed and placed my hand over my sore neck, my adrenaline fading and giving space to intense pain in all parts of my body. The nurse leaned toward me and inspected my neck.

"The doctor will come to check for injuries any minute. Do you have difficulty breathing?"

I drew a deep breath and exhaled it. "No. But my neck feels sore."

She nodded. "Make sure you mention that to the doctor. You should rest now and try to move as little as possible." She placed her hands on her hips, shaking her head. "It's unbelievable that this went down in a hospital—of all places! Anyway, the police officers should arrive soon." She looked at my friends. "I think they will need your statements too."

"That's not a problem," Mateo said.

I sighed when the nurse left my room, done in. "Thank you," I said to Mateo, unbelievably grateful to him and also ashamed because he had to witness this craziness.

"When I saw her choking you, I thought it was too late." He placed his hand on my shoulder with a gentle smile. "But you're okay now, and that's all that matters."

Jessica moved to the other side of my bed and hugged me, careful not to hurt me. "I'm so glad you're okay."

Melissa stopped next to Jessica and took my hand. "How are you holding up?"

"I'm okay. All thanks to you guys."

"I couldn't even imagine Natalie would be this crazy," Jessica said. "I knew she was bad, but this? Trying to kill you? That's sick. She's as crazy as Josh!"

"Why did she do this?" Melissa asked me.

I told them what happened with Josh and mentioned it was Natalie who had conspired with him to kill me as a part of her revenge. I had to tell Melissa and Mateo about Kayden and my role in the car accident, so they could understand the whole story. They were shocked, to say the least.

I still couldn't come to terms that Josh had tried to kill me and Hayden, but to see Natalie come here, of all places, was even more difficult to grasp. It was outrageous.

Jessica was particularly surprised by Hayden's role on Saturday evening, wondering what had made him come to my rescue. I couldn't tell her the real reason, though; not when Mateo was here.

And Mateo... Oh, I felt awful that he had to witness and hear all of that. We hadn't even had our first kiss, but here he was—staying by my side despite all the mess that was my life.

What was he thinking about me now? Did he regret coming here?

I wouldn't blame him. My difficult past wasn't something I should've bothered him with.

It didn't take long for the doctor to arrive. He assured me the injury to my neck wouldn't leave long-term consequences and left us to talk with the police officers, who had come in the meantime and took our statements. I hated that I had to go through this ordeal again and involve my friends, but at least Natalie would get punished for all the things she'd done.

The officers went on their way, and the atmosphere in the room became somewhat lighter. Jessica had already picked up Mateo's bouquet from the floor and put the flowers in the vase the nurse had brought her.

"I hope you like it," Mateo said, and tears welled in my eyes. The bouquet was huge, filled with various beautiful flowers of different colors, small wooden decorations, and glittery dust sprinkled all over it. It was one of the prettiest flower arrangements I'd ever seen.

This was the first time I'd ever received flowers, and even if they had been the simplest flowers put together without any arrangement at all, I would've loved it. I was touched.

I looked at my new friends, and my heart inflated with happiness. I'd gained so much in such a short time. Just one month ago, I didn't have anyone, but now I had Jessica, Melissa, and Mateo. They were here, and they cared about me.

That was some progress, right? No matter how long this would last or wherever we were going to be tomorrow, all that mattered was here and now, and having them here was more than enough for me.

"I'm sorry for worrying you," I told them.

"Come on, girl! What are friends for?" Melissa said. "I promise we'll throw a party when you get out of the hospital. Just you wait. Things will be amazing when I organize them, just like me." She winked at me, and I laughed, wondering how I could've misjudged her so much in the beginning. She was one of the best people I'd ever met.

The morning flew by with them. At noon, Melissa had to go to work, and Jessica decided to leave with her.

"How about you?" Melissa asked Mateo, who didn't stand up from his chair next to my bed.

"I'll stay here for a little while." He smirked at me. "If that's okay with you." We all grew quiet, and I could feel my cheeks heating. I would stay all alone with Mateo...

"Of course. I..." I swallowed, willing myself to say how I really felt. "I'd like that."

Melissa exchanged a knowing look with Jessica, and I already knew they would press me for details later. They waved at us and scurried out of the room, leaving us in sudden silence. I cleared my throat.

"Once again, thank you for helping me. You were always nice to me, and that means a lot."

"You don't have to thank me. I would do it again, but let's hope it doesn't come to that, okay?" He winked at me. "How do you feel?"

"I'm okay. I'm still a bit shocked, I think. I experienced first-hand how twisted Natalie is a long time ago, but I never thought she would come here and actually attempt to kill me... It feels weird saying someone tried to *kill* me... Anyway, I'm fine now."

To my surprise, he took my hand and cradled it between his own, and my eyes fell on his hands. I followed the lines of his fingers, strong knuckles, and prominent veins that went up and under the sleeves of his shirt, and I couldn't help but compare them to Hayden's. Hayden had long and straight fingers, while Mateo had short fingers with small bulges in the mid section. Hayden's palm was long, while Mateo's resembled a square.

I continued to compare, and then I realized I should stop doing that. Hayden should stay in the past, but I was still letting him come into my present. I had to live in this moment. Mateo deserved more than this.

"Sarah, you're definitely something else. You survived two murder attempts, and you're still positive. You're amazing." I didn't know how to respond to that, embarrassment coloring my cheeks. "From the first moment I saw you, something pulled me to you. You were so shy and quiet, which was refreshing."

I bit into my lip, unsure if I liked what he'd just said. "Refreshing?"

"Yes. There are so many girls who hit on me when they see me, but not you. You were reserved, which only made me more curious about you."

"So you want me because I'm a challenge?" There I went with my bitterness and mistrust. *Sarah, he doesn't deserve this.*

"I'm sorry. It did sound like that. No, you aren't a challenge. I mean, I always wanted to get closer to you, but I never wanted to pressure you." He brought my hand to his mouth and kissed it, leaving me open-mouthed.

"The way you looked at me when I was about to kiss you at Melissa's party... So cute." His light brown eyes hardened. "But then that asshole turned up and ruined everything."

"I'm really sorry for what Hayden did. I still feel awful about it."

"You don't have to apologize. It wasn't your fault."

"But you got involved into all this mess and—"

"And I don't regret a single thing." He kissed my hand again, his seductive eyes locked on mine. I was excited but also afraid of the unknown.

"You're vulnerable now, and I don't want to use this situation to get closer to you. I want to be with you, but I'll be patient and wait until you recover."

Was he for real? Did such nice, understanding guys really exist? He was such a sweetheart.

"There's just one thing I need to know," he said with a guarded expression on his face. "Are you sure there is nothing between this guy, Hayden, and you?"

Oh. I looked at my lap, reflecting on what happened with Hayden these last few days. I'd already made my decision. It was painful, and it scared the hell out of me, but it was the right one because I couldn't handle Hayden now.

I had the right to be happy, and no matter how good and happy I felt during those unexpected, precious moments with Hayden, it wasn't enough. The tiny fragments of utter happiness weren't enough to annul the years of sorrow and grief.

He wanted to change, but I couldn't know how long his decision would last. One day, one week, or forever? Mrs. Black said his condition could last for the rest of his life, which meant he would always have to fight it, just like his father. *Oh God. His father.*

His issues couldn't be solved overnight. He needed to change, but was that possible?

I loved him, and I wanted him happy, even if it meant we were separated. Maybe that was for the best. We needed space, and he needed to treat his condition, so being with him wouldn't be good for him.

Right?

Oh, I could only hope I was right. I had to give Mateo a chance. I couldn't keep coming back to that old darkness that was Hayden.

I met his gaze. "There is nothing between Hayden and me. He doesn't matter." *Wrong.* I ignored that silent, terrifying voice. "I-I can't wait to get better so we could... You know..." I smiled, not sure what to call us.

He got up from the chair and sat next to me on the bed. He took my face in his hands, flashing me his pearly smile. He even had dimples in his cheeks. I had to give whatever was going on between us a chance. I had to.

"Remember, I don't want to push you. Okay?" He inched closer to me, and I stopped breathing. "If there is anything you don't want or like, tell me."

His lips were so close to mine, and I was sure he could hear the loud thumping of my heart. I wanted him to kiss me. No, I needed him to kiss me so I could be certain that this was the right thing. I needed to forget. I needed that happiness, and Mateo was so nice...

His soft lips grazed mine and pressed against them softly. He took his time playing with my lips, and I couldn't help but remember Hayden's urgency when he kissed me. *The way his searing kiss made me incapable of thinking, leaving me breathless.* Mateo reached inside my mouth gently, and I recalled Hayden's fierceness and possessiveness. There was nothing possessive in the way Mateo kissed. Mateo's kiss was too sweet.

I had to stop comparing them. I was kissing Mateo, and the way Hayden kissed me didn't matter. Hayden didn't matter.

He leaned away, looking at me like I was the most beautiful girl he'd ever seen. "This was amazing. Can I have more?" I couldn't help but smile. I was completely inexperienced, and I didn't know if I could kiss well or not, but it was nice knowing he wanted more.

I initiated the kiss this time. The way our lips moved seemed like a slow dance, and it felt soothing. I laced my fingers through his curly hair, and the image of my fingers roaming through Hayden's short hair flashed through my mind. Mateo placed his hands on my waist, which brought me back to this moment. I had to forget Hayden... Mateo was here, and he was touching me like he really cared about me—

A loud thud ripped through the air, and I jerked away from Mateo at the unexpected sound. I was rooted to the spot when I found Hayden at the door, who was staring at us like he couldn't believe his eyes.

I noticed a paper bag dropped in front of him, along with the notebook and the pencils that had slid out of it. My eyes fell on an envelope laying next to the notebook. What was he doing with these things?

Hayden stomped inside and crossed the room in three big strides. He grabbed Mateo by his shirt collar using his right hand.

"What the fuck do you think you are doing?"

"Hayden!" I attempted to get up, but the sharp pain in my back prevented me from moving. "Leave him alone!"

Since Hayden was injured and couldn't use his left arm that was in a sling, Mateo could easily remove his hand from his collar and push him away. "Get off me, asshole."

Hayden glared at me. "You! You're such a slut, kissing this dickhead and—" Mateo punched him in his face, causing him to stumble.

"Mateo! Stop! Don't fight!" I had to get up. I gave my best to ignore the pain as I pushed my legs off the bed, but I was drained. I clung to the medical equipment standing next to my bed, my legs unsteady.

"Sarah, don't get up! You're hurt." Mateo caught me before I lost my balance.

I could barely look at Hayden, hurt by the betrayed look on his face. Why did he come back?

"So you're with this dick now? Kissing him just like that?"

I had to do this. I didn't know what this thing between Mateo and me was, but I couldn't let Hayden destroy it. Not that too. Enough. "And so what if I am? I have the right to do whatever I want or be with whomever I want."

Hayden stepped closer to me, but Mateo immediately shielded me. "Make one more step, and I'll beat you to a pulp," he hissed. It seemed that Mateo's warning was effective, because Hayden drew back, looking at us like we were his worst enemies.

"So after everything, you're going to be with this shit who just wants to get into your pants?"

Mateo launched at him, but I managed to keep him in place, gripping his upper arm. "Please, Mateo. Don't let him provoke you." I looked at Hayden through my teary eyes. His eyes... Oh God, his eyes were filled with such hatred and sorrow.

A heavy weight settled in my stomach, everything in me screaming not to say my next words.

"What I do with Mateo is none of your concern. I already told you. I can't forgive you. I could never forgive you. I want to be far away from you, Hayden." I tried my best to feign my feelings. I couldn't let Hayden see just how much these words hurt me—just how much I wanted things to be different. I wanted to cry, but I didn't shed a tear as I pushed these cruel words out of me, masking the indifference. "I don't care about you. So go away and don't come near me again."

I willed myself to return his burning stare and withstand the pain that was crushing me on the inside, a deep voice inside of me claiming this was all wrong. I couldn't stand the way he looked at me, like I'd destroyed everything in him. I had to remind myself that he was my bully, my enemy, my unreasonable love... However, life was everything but black and white. It would be perfect to have a switch that could turn off our emotions and make our brains rule over every situation, but that was what human beings were—imperfect.

Right now, my heart wanted to bleed out, begging me to go to him and tell him everything was going to be all right. It begged me to do something to make the fear that was evident in his eyes go away. It begged me to remember there could be much more between us only if I let it happen... Despite knowing Hayden could bring me a huge amount of pain, there was always the slightest possibility that he could make me the happiest person alive.

I closed my eyes, refusing to listen to my stupid heart. Maybe Hayden deserved a chance at redemption, but it was too late for us.

Taking a deep breath, I met Hayden's gaze. I had to pull myself together. I would be okay. I was falling apart now, but I would be better. I had to be.

Hayden's face was completely blank now, and his eyes didn't show anything anymore. He'd shut himself off, returning into his old shell that made me feel like we were so far away from each other. He looked at Mateo, noticing his arm placed around my waist, and slowly returned his eyes to mine.

"I was right about you, after all. You're a heartless, cold bitch. I was so stupid thinking you were different. I was stupid for coming here today." He took a step backward, separating himself more from me. "You don't deserve anything but pain. You can forget about everything I said to you last night. You can forget about *that* Hayden because you'll never see him again. You want to be with this dickhead? Fucking suit yourself, bitch. From this day on, you don't exist for me anymore."

And just like that, he rushed out of the room and slammed the door shut.

My legs failed me, but Mateo managed to catch me before I fell on the floor. "Sarah! Easy."

He helped me lie back down and tucked me in. I closed my eyes, pressing my forearm against my face, and finally burst into tears. Being free of Hayden was all I ever wanted... So why did I feel this searing pain?

"Don't cry. That jerk doesn't deserve your tears." He narrowed his eyes. "I can't believe him. Seriously, you shouldn't have stopped me. I should've smashed his face for all the disgusting things he said to you—"

"Mateo," I interrupted him weakly. I couldn't even listen to him. All I felt was sorrow, which drowned me more and more, and I felt so lost. I hurt Hayden. I hurt both of us.

I made the right choice, but why did it hurt so much?

"I'm sorry, but can you go now? I need to be alone."

"Sarah—"

"Mateo, please. I want to be alone. Please, leave me alone." I couldn't stand having anyone by my side at the moment, least of all Mateo. I desperately wanted to be alone. I couldn't think straight at the moment...

"But, you aren't all right. That asshole was—"

"Please!" I cast him a pleading gaze. Right now, I needed a lot of space. I needed to forget. "I want to be alone now." I looked away, feeling ashamed, but my shame was nothing compared to the devastation in me after my separation from Hayden. As if last night wasn't enough, I had to go through this pain again.

Hayden returned even though I told him it was too late for us.

I swallowed my hot tears. It didn't matter anymore. It didn't.

Mateo put the contents of Hayden's bag back inside and placed the bag on the nightstand next to my bed. "I'll just leave this here, okay?" he said. "I'll go now."

He covered my hand once again, but I didn't react. We kissed just a few minutes ago, but I couldn't feel happy about it anymore. I knew I had to pull myself together before this thing with Mateo went any further, but right now I couldn't battle this darkness. I wasn't strong enough, and I didn't want Mateo to witness that.

I just nodded at him and watched him walk away. He opened the door and glanced at me, offering me a smile of comfort, but I couldn't return it. He left the room, and a searing pain clutched me, leaving me more miserable than ever.

I was shaking and sobbing, cursing my life and all this blackness that surrounded me. I felt like one tiny step I made forward was destroyed with a dozen steps backward, and all I could feel was the poison that was killing me fast.

I took the bag from the nightstand and looked at its contents, shuddering. My heart contracted painfully when I realized that he'd brought me a sketch pad, which had a special type of paper that allowed for better sketching. I opened the cover and found Hayden's message on the first page.

"I suck when it comes to gifts, but it can get boring in hospitals, so I thought you would want to draw something while you're here.

Hayden."

Oh my God. I cried out in pain. My hands were cold as I picked up the graphite and watercolor pencils from the bottom of the bag. He knew. He knew exactly how I drew, and he knew what I would need.

He brought this for me. He never gave me anything, but now he'd given me this, and it was so precious. It was small, but it meant everything.

The pressure built in my chest and head, and I couldn't fight off the nausea. It was too much.

The last thing in the bag was the letter I saw on the floor earlier. I took a deep breath, terrified to open it. Somehow, I felt it would be my undoing.

Gathering my last particle of strength, I took the envelope in my quivering hands and opened it. I unfolded the long sheet of paper and stared at the written words through my tears.

"It's difficult for me to explain how the devastating darkness feels, so I wrote this poem for you. I'm not asking for forgiveness. You already said you won't ever be able to forgive me. I just wanted to give you a glimpse into my deranged world.

I'm sorry.

Everlasting Black and White

A long time ago, my dearest brother was only mine,
But then you arrived, brought turmoil, and became his greatest shine.
One regretful day he died and left havoc, darkness, and pain,
All of a sudden, I lost my twin; I lost my everything.
You were there, the light on my terrifying road, the sweet toxin in my veins,
But you got lost, too, in the darkness that took me away.

Without you I'm lost, but with you I'm crushed,
You're my everlasting sorrow and my sweetest rush.
I hurt you, and my heart and bones break,
But it doesn't matter because I'm taking my easy way out of the pain.

The limitless hole in my heart threw me into a suffocating despair,
I drowned, and there was no more peace, only an eternal nightmare.
There was no more fight, sanity or hope; just hatred, vengeance and death,
How could I believe there was light when he had taken his last breath?

You were the darkness that ripped my heart out,
And it came to destroying you or destroying me.

Without you I'm lost, but with you I'm crushed,
You're my everlasting sorrow and my sweetest rush.
I hurt you, and my heart and bones break,
But it doesn't matter because I'm taking my easy way out of the pain.

On the day of his funeral I couldn't feel anything.
But two years later, the pain became excruciating.
I realized your death would be the death of me,
But it didn't matter anymore that you were my key.
I was in the middle of nothingness; saying sorry was far too late,
I guess being together with you after everything wasn't my fate.

Without you I'm lost, but with you I'm crushed,
You're my everlasting sorrow and my sweetest rush.
I hurt you, and my heart and bones break,
But it doesn't matter that I love you, because after everything I've done...

...It does sound fake."

Afterword

IMPORTANT BPD DISCLAIMER:

Hayden isn't a representation of all people with borderline personality disorder, and this author's intention wasn't to portray this disorder or people with BPD in a negative way. Each person with BPD is different and may react differently in the same or similar situations. Hayden is just one person with this disorder whose own life circumstances played a role in some of his actions.

. . . .

BEING BULLIED MAKES you feel alone. You're trapped inside a cage with no way out. You bleed from hurt, and you feel like the whole world is covered in darkness. You want to escape—to find some way toward the end of the tunnel—but you don't know how. You hope someday that the torture will pass. You truly hope.

You feel weak and you want to fight, but you just can't. You are so afraid—afraid that fighting back might make things worse, afraid that the next step will lead you into a trap, afraid of insults and pain. You fear people, and you hate yourself. You want to fit in badly, and you need friends. You try so hard to be who you are not, just to be with people you can call friends... And you lose yourself.

Ignoring it won't help. Pretending to be someone you aren't won't help. Hoping for others to save you is not a solution.

Be who you are. Accept who you are. Fight for who you are. There is no greater misery than when we can't be true to ourselves. Don't spread hate, violence, and negativity. Hate creates more hate. Violence creates more violence. Negativity ruins everything.

You're the only one who can save yourself. There is the light at the end of the tunnel; you just have to keep walking no matter what.

You're strong. No matter what others say—you're beautiful. You are you.

. . . .

WHEN I STARTED WRITING *Bullied*, my main goal was to create characters that grow stronger and better over time, despite their bad circumstances. I wanted to show there was light in the midst of darkness, which is one of the themes of this love story.

I'm interested in the bullying trope and the psychology behind it, so that was what set this particular plot in motion. Why are people bullied? What makes people bullies? There are so many reasons, and I did my best to depict the emotions bullied people and their bullies feel. Fear, hopelessness, low self-esteem, and twisted self-image—all these can be possible consequences of the long-time exposure to bullying, but at the same time, these are the same things some bullies feel, which can make them lash out and hurt others.

Sarah may be weak when it comes to standing up for herself, but she has an inner strength that keeps her going no matter what. I hope her character can inspire people to keep going, even when it feels like there is absolutely no light around them.

As for Hayden, we see a different side of him as the story progressed, and we learn about his life with untreated BPD. We see that he is so much more than a heartless, evil person, which just shows that bullies can also be victims. Bullies are victims of their own minds.

This story is about the bullied, bullies, and people who struggle with mental issues. It poses questions about whether Hayden deserves Sarah's forgiveness and whether they should be together or not. Everyone deserves love, care, and understanding, and while Hayden's actions are inexcusable, I believe he deserves redemption.

Acknowledgments

WHEN I WROTE *Bullied* for NaNoWriMo 2016 and started posting it online, I hoped with all my heart that it would find a way to its readers' hearts. I never imagined there would be so many people who would grow to love it and its characters. Now, almost three years later, I'm finally able to make my dream of publishing it come true, and it's all thanks to many people who have been supporting me along the way.

I would like to begin by thanking Milica. Thank you so much for being the best friend a person could wish for. Thank you for listening to me talk about *Bullied*, its characters, and its sequels all the time, and for helping me when I felt unsure about some parts. You know how much I love you, right?

One huge, gigantic, enormous thank you to Amanda. I think luck struck me the moment you decided to message me about my books. I can't thank you enough for all of your help with self-publishing (seriously, thank you for your super patience with my countless questions!), support, and kindness you've showed me. You're an amazing human being.

A. L. O., thank you for being one of *Bullied*'s first readers and for all your supportive comments. My writing journey was much easier with you there.

I also want to thank my editor Bethany Salminen for doing an amazing job with edits. Your suggestions were very helpful. Also, I'm grateful to my beta readers Soumya R. Saral, Estelle Hooper, Selia, Kayleigh Young, K.G., and Manaar A. Mohammed. Your responses helped me to shape *Bullied* into a better story.

Huge thanks to my readers from Wattpad, who have been following my writing journey since 2016. You've been supporting me all this time and helping me make my dreams come true. And thank YOU, my dear reader, for picking up this book. Your support means so much to me.

Last but not least, thank you so much, Rasha, for always being there for me, for your understanding, and for believing in my dream of becoming a published author. You're the light of my life.

About the Author

Vera Hollins is the author of the *Bullied* series, which has amassed over 30 million reads online since 2016. She loves writing emotional, dark, and angsty love stories that deal with heartbreak, mental and social issues, and finding light in darkness.

She's been writing since she was nine, and before she knew it, it became her passion and life. She particularly likes coffee, bunnies, angsty romance, and anti-heroes. When she's not writing, you can find her reading, plotting her next book with as many twists as possible, and playing with her bunny.

Read more at https://www.verahollins.com/.